THE ORDER OF
THE
BELOVED

A NOVEL

THE ORDER OF THE BELOVED

L. D. ANDERSON

iUniverse, Inc.
New York Lincoln Shanghai

THE ORDER OF THE BELOVED

Copyright © 2008 by Larrey D. Anderson, Jr.

All rights reserved. No part of this book may be used or reproduced by any means, graphic, electronic, or mechanical, including photocopying, recording, taping or by any information storage retrieval system without the written permission of the publisher except in the case of brief quotations embodied in critical articles and reviews.

iUniverse books may be ordered through booksellers or by contacting:

iUniverse
2021 Pine Lake Road, Suite 100
Lincoln, NE 68512
www.iuniverse.com
1-800-Authors (1-800-288-4677)

Because of the dynamic nature of the Internet, any Web addresses or links contained in this book may have changed since publication and may no longer be valid.

This is a work of fiction. All of the characters, names, incidents, organizations, and dialogue in this novel are either the products of the author's imagination or are used fictitiously.

ISBN: 978-0-595-43539-5 (pbk)
ISBN: 978-0-595-87866-6 (ebk)

Printed in the United States of America

In memory of my grandparents:
Archie Dean Anderson
Lottie Ivel Johnson
James Patterson Crist
Stella May Thomas

He [Jesus] said, "Whosoever discovers the meaning [*hermeneia*] of these teachings shall not taste of death."

The Secret Teachings of Jesus, [*Nag Hammadi,* Codex II, Tr. 2, p. 32]

>There are no tricks in plain and simple faith.
>*Julius Caesar*
>Shakespeare

Acknowledgments

This book has been years in the making. Many friends have offered help and constructive criticism; some merit special mention. I would like to thank Penelope Parker, Ann Kucera, Sheila McDevitt, Patricia Saras, and Paul Carlson for reading and offering helpful input on the very early drafts of this book. My daughter, Laura Anderson, read and reread the manuscript and caught most of my slips and errors.

Brenda Kluck has guided me through the iUniverse publishing process; she has been an advocate and a friend for this demanding writer. Laura Argiri, my iUniverse copy editor, was spot on with her suggestions. She is a remarkable editor with a nuanced touch. (And she fixed my sloppy Italian.) Sarah Azizi, my editorial evaluator, made several important suggestions that improved the beginning of the book.

My parents, Larrey and Retha Anderson, have supported me in too many ways to mention. I love and respect both of them beyond words.

Finally, I want to express my deepest gratitude to Eileen Ann McDevitt. She believed in me from day one. She urged me to keep writing when I was stuck or depressed. She kept this book readable and accessible. She is my best critic and my best friend.

Peter looked round and saw the disciple whom Jesus loved following.

When he caught sight of him, Peter asked, "Lord, what will happen to him?"

Jesus said, "If it should be my will that he wait until I come, what is it to you?"

That saying of Jesus became current in the brotherhood, and was taken to mean that the disciple would not die.

—John 21:20–23

Note on the Compilation of This Manuscript

On May 30 of this year, Mrs. Sylvia Johnson, my cousin by marriage, knocked on the door of my trailer house. It was late in the afternoon on the sagebrush plateau where I then lived. My trailer was parked at a private campground five miles east of Eden, Idaho, which is a hundred miles from nowhere. It was hot. It was too hot for May. It had rained the night before. The languid air in the cloudless sky was laced with the sweet sweat of spring sage. Roused by the heat, Fluffball, Edward, Alexander, and Cleo—the four feral cats that, last winter, had sequestered themselves in the crawl space beneath my front porch—this day, and under these torrid conditions, commandeered the front porch hammock. They lay in it, precisely placed a paw apart, and panted ... impetuously. I noticed their occupations when I opened my front door.

Sylvia was carrying a box, a cardboard filing box, which had PROPERTY OF THE US GOVERNMENT printed on all four sides. Slung over her shoulder was a black nylon diaper bag. Though I wouldn't know it until a couple of minutes later, she was three months pregnant with her fourth child. The box was heavy; she strained under its weight. She tried to smile, to wipe the drops of sweat glistening on her forehead, and to hand me the box, all at once. She tripped on the step and smacked a shoulder into the doorjamb. I caught Sylvia and the box. The cats disappeared from the hammock; they evaporated like windswept mist under the porch.

There were screams from inside Sylvia's dirty blue Dodge Caravan. I glanced at the vehicle as I righted Sylvia and the box. A mud-spattered Nevada plate hung by a single screw to the front bumper. The FBI had stationed my cousin Nathan in Las Vegas until he … I'll not speculate where he is, *if* he is—because I don't know. The faces of Nathan's three kids were hard to make out through the tinted windows. Their bawling was not.

"I started at four this morning to beat the heat. Nathan wanted you to have what's in here. He said you'd understand what's in here," Sylvia announced in her clean, crisp Utah twang. Three (and a third) children later, she still spoke with the naïve sass of a college cheerleader. She had worked to keep her figure—and had kept it. Her body was as slim and sensuous, as desirable as it had been when she was twenty, when I had met her soon after she and Nathan had started dating, a few weeks before she introduced me to the woman who would become my wife. Sylvia's light cotton dress was drenched with sweat. The green and yellow cloth clung to her muscular belly, pulling the dress up over her knees, exposing the bulky white undergarments worn only by faithful Latter-day Saints, or Mormons. Her thin face was beet-red. Exhaustion had streaked her normally soft brown eyes with red. Fatigue had puffed the sockets black and blue.

I took the box and balanced it on the hammock. "Let's get your kids out of the car."

Sylvia and Nathan's three children scampered around on the front porch, chasing my four cats. I sat on my doorstep and flipped the lid off of the cardboard box. Nathan had packed it with some books, CDs, around half a dozen hand-marked memory sticks, some Dictaphone and other tiny tapes (digital and analogue), and a file of letters and newspaper clips.

Nathan had called me about a week before his wife showed up at my trailer. He had told me a little about a bizarre murder case he had been assigned. He claimed that the murder might involve one of the Three Nephites—one of the three men purported to have been granted eternal life by Jesus Christ in an obscure story in the *Book of Mormon*. He wondered if I might want to write about the investigation.

I responded, honestly, that in the last few months I had received offers on my series of children's books, as well as a nibble on my second novel. My problem was that I had lied to everyone about the status of the manuscripts. I had not finished any of them, and none of the interested parties were willing to give me an advance without a finished product. My agent was threatening to drop me; I was scrambling, as usual, to save myself from my indolence.

I also told Nathan that I was interested. I urged him to keep a good, candid journal, to save and duplicate anything that was relevant to the story, and then to give it all to Sylvia for safekeeping. The box and Sylvia's visit proved to me that Nathan was serious. Nathan is—or was—thorough. All of this is in the record that follows. And that record, or at least the first half of it, was in the box.

* * * *

I came into possession of most of Father Jerome Dougherty's notes, letters and manuscripts a week later. These were in a second cardboard box, which was handed to me by Father Jerome Dougherty on June 5, just outside Taos, New Mexico, under conditions that will be described below.

I was once a graduate student of Father Dougherty's in philosophy at the Catholic University of America in Washington, DC. We had been very close for a time and continued to be good friends until his disappearance. I hope that this relationship, at least partially, explains his trust in me. As of the date of the publication of this book, it is not known if Father Dougherty is alive.

* * * *

Another close friend, whom I will call "Dr. Judy Weintraub," has graciously allowed me to print or reprint herein excerpts from her husband's voluminous writings on the subject of immortality. (In this book, I have identified her husband as "Professor Harold Weintraub" or simply as "Professor Weintraub.") I have also reproduced in this book some of the correspondence between Dr. Judy Weintraub, her husband, and myself.

Under Dr. Judy Weintraub's auspices, I am in the process of editing her husband's unpublished writings on immortality. For those interested, I am at liberty to reveal that Dr. Judy Weintraub will soon publish a series of technical monographs on the biological possibility of immortality in *The New England Journal of Medicine*. However, as has become her predilection, she will use a pseudonym.

* * * *

In addition to the materials provided by Nathan Johnson, Father Dougherty, and the Weintraubs, I have included excerpts from a variety of publicly available documents that might help clarify the "who, how, when, where, and why" that led to the deaths of at least twenty-six people on the morning of June 5 just outside of Taos, New Mexico. All of this material is presented in roughly chronological order. Since some of the events portrayed in this manuscript overlap periods of several days, the reader is urged to pay special attention to the dates of the various documents that make up each section of the book.

I have edited the contributions of Nathan Johnson and Father Dougherty in an effort to make this manuscript as factual and as honest as possible. In particular, I have supplemented their journals with the transcripts I have made from the audiotapes and other recordings contained in the two boxes that have been entrusted to me. As the reader will discover, nearly all of the conversations presented in this book were recorded. In every possible case, I have transcribed and used the *actual* conversations from the recordings rather than the reconstructions of these conversations as they appear in the various notes and journals now in my possession.

One final note: In this book, I have tried to restrain myself from speculating on the meaning of the information in my custody because I feel neither competent nor (this is a vague and haunting feeling) *worthy*. I have used relevant portions of my own journals, conversations, and letters to give this manuscript better cohesion and consistency. I recognize that, in a most unsettling way, I am the weak force that brought this coalition together and then stood and watched from a distance as it was destroyed. It is very important for me to say, at the outset, that I wanted less than that.

Author's May 30 Conversation with Sylvia Johnson

"What do you know about Jerome Dougherty?" Sylvia asked me after she had dropped her black diaper bag on the floor and settled on my couch. At her request, I had already watered her kids. The two girls, Kaylynn, seven, and Sherry, four, had scurried outside, chasing after my cats, in vain. Two-year-old Jeremy had scaled his mother's legs and was sweating when he reached the summit. He fell asleep, shortly thereafter, on her lap. Sylvia lovingly stroked the long, wet strands of blonde hair from his forehead.

"Father Dougherty was my teacher for a while," I answered, somewhat evasively. I sat the box on my little metal table, and then I sat next to her.

"When? Where?" she demanded. There was no love lost between Sylvia and me. I had married her cousin, Brenda, a year after my cousin, Nathan, had married Sylvia. Brenda and I had been divorced for nearly seven years. Sylvia had never forgiven me. I also believe that Sylvia was threatened by my history with her husband. Nathan and I had been close as children, rowdy together as teenagers. I think she thought I was a bad influence.

"When I was in DC, at Catholic U—working on my doctorate," I told her.

"So what's he got to do with Nathan?" she asked. Her brown eyes scanned my tiny trailer. I had crammed it full—with a ragged couch, with piles of books and papers, with stacks of filthy dishes in the sink. She wanted not to look into my eyes but knew that she had no choice. She was afraid that they might harbor the secret of her husband's disappearance; she was terrified that they might not. She got out of her tennis shoes and rubbed each swollen ankle with the other foot. She turned her face to mine.

"A few days ago, or last week anyway, I recommended, to both of them that they get in touch because it seemed like they were working on the same thing," I answered. "I've got one of those blue plastic ice things in the freezer. You want it for your feet?"

"No, thanks. Nathan's been working with this Father Dougherty—I don't know where—I haven't heard much from him. Nathan doesn't even know I'm pregnant. I took the test two days ago. Then yesterday I got this package, and the note said to get all of this stuff to you. There's something wrong. I think he's scared."

"Nathan? Scared? What'd he do—run out of bullets?" I laughed, returning from the freezer with the ice pack wrapped in a dirty dishtowel. "Geez, another kid, huh? You sure you don't want this? For your stomach?"

She ignored me and continued, "Since Nathan went to work for the FBI, no matter where we live, we've always taken out a post office box in a nearby town under false names. We've never told anyone. It's a secret just between us."

"Sounds like him," I replied. I put the ice pack on the floor in front of her and sat back down.

"Nathan said that way," Sylvia continued, ignoring me, "if he ever got in trouble, he could contact me, and no one would know. Sometimes when he goes out of town, I'll check the post office. It always makes me feel better when nothing's there. I never got anything until I checked it yesterday morning. Nathan taped the letter on the inside of the lid of that cardboard box. He shipped it overnight. You can read the letter—it's still in the box, right on top," she said gesturing with her forehead. "There's a note on the back for you."

She reached down, lifted the ice pack, and slid it between Jeremy's neck and her stomach. The boy jerked in his sleep, but the cool moisture made his facial muscles relax. "Is this priest, this Dougherty, someone who would ever hurt my husband?" she asked as I stood up.

"Father Dougherty is a very kind man," I replied.

"Would he betray Nathan—I mean, if there was trouble?"

"No way. Father Dougherty helped me during some very tough times. When Brenda and I were first separated ..."

"When you threw her out," Sylvia interrupted with acerbity. Her eyes flashed angrily, but she expeditiously lowered them: not because she feared me, but because she needed me.

"You want to hear about Dougherty? Or you want to argue about my previous marriage?" I paced the floor between the couch and my computer, which sat next to the box on the little metal table in the center of the room.

"Okay. So he befriended you when you were alone in DC—so what?"

"So we became very close. We've stayed in touch over the years. He's one of the few people who's urged me to keep writing. I love him for that. He's a brilliant scholar; doctorates in philosophy, psychology, and law. He's one of the smartest men I've ever met," I explained. I stopped at the table and thumbed through one of my manuscripts. "Incredible mind. When I was in school, in DC, Father Dougherty told me about some of his research. He shared some … some professional secrets with me. I didn't think much about them at the time, but when Nathan came up with his "Three Nephites" story, it reminded me of Dougherty's "Order of the Beloved." So I tried to call Dougherty. But he was in Italy. So I called Nathan and told him about Father Dougherty, and the two of them eventually got together. I don't know much more than that. I really don't. Maybe the answer's in here."

I grabbed the box and placed it on the floor next to Sylvia. I knelt beside her. We started digging. The first thing that caught my eye was a little black leather-bound book. It was a recent volume of Father Dougherty's journal. A newspaper clipping and a printed e-mail were stuck between the pages of the journal—the pages that covered the first day of April.

Give light to my eyes lest I sleep the sleep of death.

—Psalms 13:3

Excerpt from the Journal of Father Jerome Dougherty

Evening of April 1, home in Silver Springs, Maryland.

I received a most unusual telephone call from Father Domenico Patricelli this morning shortly after five. He was very distraught and frightened. He was calling from Como, though not, I think, from the cloister—I could hear music and women's voices in the background.

"Padre Jerome," he sighed with relief when I answered the telephone. I was still in bed.

"Who's calling?" I was not fully awake or I would have instantly recognized his beautiful voice. The long-distance connection with Italy was quite clear.

"Padre Patricelli."

"It is early here, Father."

"Mi scusi," he spoke hastily. *"Ho qualche difficoltá."* His breathing was rapid, agitated.

"Be calm, Father, and tell me what is troubling you. In English, please." I sat up found a notebook and pen on my nightstand and began to take notes.

"The Order is in danger ... great danger. You must believe me. It is imperative that we leave this place. We should come to the United States. It is critical that you remove the Order to the United States. You can do this for us? Father Jerome? Will you do it?"

Father Patricelli, as ill as he is, is not paranoid. He neither creates nor engenders fear in himself or in others. He is merely self-persuaded that he is immortal, that he has chosen to be immortal. If he claims that his circumstance is ominous, then it probably is.

"Tell me specifically what is troubling you," I commanded.

"Oh, Jerome," he scolded. "How long have I known you, and how long have you doubted every word I have spoken? I can only tell you that we will die if you do not help us, if you do not take us from this place. They know we are here. They know where we are going. They may even know the destination. They know the time is very near. They will kill us."

"Who are *they*?"

"They are the many. They are the few. They are finally working as one. They are the enemies of the eschaton."

"Who? *Exactly* who?" I insisted.

"You have only to open your eyes to see them. 'For righteousness is immortal.'"

"Father Patricelli—every time you come close to revealing yourself to me, you lapse into conundrums or paradoxes or enigmas. Don't you hear it? Can't you hear yourself speak?"

"Of course I hear myself. You are the one who believes that I am insane. How else can I speak to you? If I were to be more specific, I would be committed for suffering from severe paranoid delusions. Evasive speech is a fundamental protection for an immortal."

"If you're immortal … why should … how can you be worried?"

"This is not banter, my friend. They will kill us."

"Tell me how."

"You would never believe me. You must first learn where there is light and peace. You must first give yourself to esperance."

"If you desire my help, you will stop speaking in riddles."

"They will kill us," Father Patricelli whispered. "The rest I will explain to you when I am in America." Almost certainly, he meant exactly what he was saying.

"I am in the middle of orals and preparing for finals. Contact the Vatican—Father Thomas. He is the psychiatrist in charge. He will help you. I'll call him for you," I promised.

"No! Not the Vatican! You are the only one who can help us, not because of what you know, but because of what you do not!" he snapped. In the nearly forty years since we first met, I had never heard Father Patricelli raise his voice. He was doing it now, not from anger but from terror.

"Contact the local police," I suggested.

Father Patricelli laughed with disgust.

"I will make every effort to come. In June, after finals, I will be there," I assured him.

"It will be too late."

"I simply cannot make it before then. Call me if you need help."

"But I have already done that. *L'ho già fatto. L'ho già fatto,*" he muttered as he ended the call.

I have not yet decided what to do.

> Death is the fulfillment and highest task which the individual, as such, undertakes on behalf of the ethical community.
>
> —Hegel, *Phänomenologie des Geistes*

Excerpt from the May 11 Edition of the *Como Gazette* (Translated from the Italian)

Father Domenico Patricelli was brutally murdered in his apartment on Piazza Barbaroux in southern Como. Police detective Rodolfo Eco stated that the housekeeper discovered the body at 8:00 AM Tuesday morning and promptly reported to the police. The detective said that there were no signs of struggle in the small one-bedroom apartment.

The housekeeper, Anna Zappa, told a *Gazette* reporter that someone had bound and gagged the body and that it was horribly maimed. The head was reportedly severely stabbed and beaten. The report also stated that Father Patricelli's personal books and papers had been looted.

Father Patricelli had long served the community as priest for Our Lady of the Rosary and was deeply loved by his parishioners. Neither the names of his survivors nor his date of birth were released by the diocese. The wake will be held Friday evening; the funeral is scheduled for Saturday at noon at Our Lady of the Rosary. A large congregation is anticipated.

"When can my master come to the Castle?" "Never," was the answer. "Very well," said K., and hung up the receiver.

—Kafka, *Das Schloss*

E-mail from His Eminence, Herman Cardinal O'Donnell, to Father Jerome Dougherty (Received May12)

It is with deepest regrets that I inform you that Father Domenico Patricelli of the Order of the Beloved, Como, Italy, has been murdered. As a result of the nature of the crime, there is considerable tension and uncertainty within the community. Your many years as counselor to the members and as a student of the Order make your presence at the cloister crucial at this time. You will be temporarily released from your position at the University, and I request that you continue immediately [sic] to Como. His Eminence, Secretary of State Maurizio Cardinal Capano, has assigned the investigation of the matter to Monsignor Leonardo Greco, and I urge your full cooperation with him. Go safely in the peace of Our Lord and Savior.

Author's May 30 Conversation with Sylvia Johnson, Continued

"But what's any of this got to do with Nathan?" Sylvia demanded after we had read the documents and figured out why Father Dougherty had been sent to Italy.

"I don't know. I mean … not exactly. I've maybe talked to both of them for maybe five minutes on the phone. What's Nathan's note say?" I asked. Sylvia handed me this letter.

My Dearest Alass,
 Sorry this is coming to you this way. Direct communication will be difficult—but just for a while. I have to work hard to drum up sales. My firm is not happy with the competition. Trouble with the boss's boss. It is all very confusing.
 My new partner knows a lot about the product but very little about salesmanship, so things have not been going as well as they might. He is a quick study, and we are learning from each other. We will work in sand.
 I had a great idea last night. It is something that we have talked about for a long time and that we really need to do. Let's go on that second honeymoon we've always dreamed of. No need to tell the neighbors or the boss, just drop the kids off at Archie's and meet me for that trip we've always said we would take. You can meet my new partner and some of his "old" friends that I'm about to meet.
 Please drop off that box of laundry at my cousin's and see if he'd like to come along. Bring Betsy with you and Little B for cousin too.
 See you day after tomorrow, I hope. When you get there ask for One and a Spud and a Tater Tot. Miss you. Give everyone my love. Sorry.
[Typed]
Adolph

"Adolph?" I laughed, having read the letter out loud. "He's losing it. My cousin the nutty Nazi."

"No, stupid. Adolph Dick Tater and Alass Poe Tater, that's how we address each other at our post office box—it's like a secret code."

"My cuz Nathan—King of Lousy Puns: Alas, poor Russet, I baked you well …"

"Actually, they were my idea, Nathan being from Idaho and all."

"No shit. I never would have guessed you …"

"That I, that a woman, could say something clever?"

"I didn't say I thought they were clever," I retorted. "*Dick* Tater's a bit randy. Isn't it?"

"As … enlightened … as you want to believe you are—you really have no respect for … for us, for women," she stammered. Sylvia's eyes glared again—this time with the feminine drollness and the distant sensuality that insinuates that, ultimately, a woman has the upper hand.

"What does the letter mean? What's his firm … the FBI?" I asked as I scanned the letter.

"What else could it mean? He's afraid of them."

"Afraid of the FBI? Nathan *is* the FBI. Maybe he means the government. 'His boss's *boss*.'"

"He's afraid of somebody; I *know* he is," Sylvia said convincingly. She fretfully rubbed one ankle with the opposite foot.

"The other salesman must be Father Dougherty; they seem to be getting along. 'We will work in sand'—what's that?"

"I don't know. Maybe he's going back to Nevada," she guessed. Jeremy wiggled on her lap.

"Uh, 'second honeymoon,'" I said as I continued to examine the letter. "Sounds like he wants to meet you in Hawaii. Isn't that where you went?"

"Our *second* honeymoon. We always talk about Yellowstone Park. Nathan really wants to spend a week at the Old Faithful Lodge with the kids."

"A week in a cabin with your three kids is Nathan's idea of a second honeymoon? Romantic fool," I huffed.

Sylvia's two girls came crashing through the trailer door. They had captured Fluffball, the most nearly tame and the sweetest of my cats. They were tugging on her silky black and white hair, yanking on her legs, and whooping cries of victory over their conquest. Left-wing feline Hegelian that she was, Fluffball was biding her time, waiting for her masters to ease their grip, and plotting her kitty revolution.

"Careful, you two, she's got claws that …" I started to caution them, and the girls, both in faded jeans and grimy T-shirts, fatefully turned their attention to me.

Fluffball struck instantaneously. With a hiss and a scratch, she was on the floor and out the door before either Kaylynn or Sherry could let out a scream. But scream they did—as if the cat had shredded their flesh into spaghetti rather than barely drawn blood from Sherry's wrist. Jeremy awoke, crying.

Being caught with three wailing kids in my small tin-covered trailer was like being trapped in a garbage dumpster with a pack of howling coyotes. "Second honeymoon—in a cabin?" I reiterated over the chorus of shrieks.

"They're hungry. Could you please …" Sylvia began.

"I've got a couple of cans of chicken noodle soup, maybe some crackers," I said, heading to the linoleum floor that formed the 6' x 6' kitchen area. "All the bowls and pans are dirty." I poked at them and shifted them around a bit, but they didn't get any cleaner.

"Kaylynn, take Jeremy and Sherry outside for a few minutes until we get your dinner," Sylvia instructed her eldest daughter after she had washed and then kissed Sherry's wound. Her two younger children grudgingly obeyed their sister.

Sylvia moved next to me. She filled the sink with steaming water, squirted in the soap, sorted the pots and plates, scrubbed them, rinsed them, then thrust the clean but dripping vessels into my hands to dry and put away. Thus did Sylvia femininely forge our interdependence.

I set the letter on the countertop next to the stove and opened the two cans of soup. "Let's say you're right. Nathan wants you to drop the kids off at his folks', go to the Old Faithful Lodge at Yellowstone, meet Dougherty, meet some 'new old friends'—whatever that line means," I said, pointing. "He wants you to give me the laundry …"

"The box full of letters …"

"I guessed that," I said. "He wants me to go with you. But who's 'Betsy and Little B?'"

Sylvia smiled and went back to the couch to get the black diaper bag. She wiped the soapsuds from her hands with a diaper; she pulled a black steel-barreled pistol from the bottom of the bag. "Betsy is my Sig Sauer 228, ten-millimeter. I practice with Nathan at the range all the time. I'm pretty good with it," she said as she slipped the clip out of the handle of the dull black metal semi-automatic pistol. She turned the clip over in her hands and pointed at the bullets. "Hollow points, semi-jacketed. Nathan gave it to me for Christmas. I think it costs a lot." She slid back the action on her gun, making sure the chamber was empty, then she slammed the clip back in and stuck the weapon in the diaper bag. "I shot fourth highest on the course with moving silhouettes."

"Geez. Annie Oakley. And 'Little B'—for me?"

Sylvia wiped her hands on a diaper again, rummaged in the bag's bottom, and withdrew a tiny silver pistol. "Little Betsy. Seven shot, 380 Walther PPK, semi-auto with bellyband. You wear it in the small of the back. You don't even need a sports coat—not that you own one. Both guns are 'clean.' Not registered, not, um ... traceable. Oh, yours has hollow points too," Sylvia said, putting the gun away and returning to the dishes.

"How come you know so much about pistols?"

"Because they're part of my husband's job. Because he loves weapons, and I love him. He carries a Smith and Wesson, Model 1076, stainless steel, semi-automatic, fires ten-millimeter reduced. He's had it ever since he first joined the Bureau. His holds fifteen rounds. We share ammunition."

"Jesus Christ."

"Please don't use that language around me."

"Sorry. The letter said that you should meet him 'tomorrow.' The letter is dated day before yesterday—so the day after tomorrow is today—so you're already late."

"I have cash," Sylvia pleaded, looking hard into my eyes for the first time. "I'll pay for everything. We'll drop my kids off in Burley at his mom's, and we can be in Yellowstone before morning. It says 'day after tomorrow *I hope.*'"

"Ask for 'One and a Spud and a Tater Tot'? What the hell does that mean?" I asked, looking down at the letter, dodging her eyes.

"I don't know. Kaylynn is Spud. Sherry is French Fry. And Jeremy is Tater Tot."

"How old's Kaylynn?"

"Seven."

"And Jeremy?"

"Two."

"Room number one-seven-two," I said.

"See. Nathan needs you. He needs me—so I'm going. But he needs you too. Please ... please. Just read the back."

Hey Cuz,

It's confusing. But it's not a joke. None of it. Plant the kids safely. Stay with Sylvia. Just a few days. Keep Little B close to your fanny. Remember the fahoes. You

owe me. We're family. Besides, it'll make a great book. Everything I've got so far is in this box. We'll discuss my cut later.
[Typed]
Your Cuz

There was a scream from outside the front window. Sherry had grabbed Edward by the tail. Edward was a fanatical Stalinist who resolutely held that the kitty revolution is always in the *hic et nunc*. Sherry had her *petit bourgeoises* hands full. So did I.

[Jesus] turned himself unto the three and said unto them: "What will ye that I should do unto you, when I am gone unto the Father?" And [Jesus] said unto them, "Behold I know your thoughts ... therefore blessed are ye, for ye shall never taste of death but shall live to behold all the doings of the Father."

And now whether they were mortal or immortal, I know not.

—3rd Nephi 28:4–7, 17, *Book of Mormon*

Excerpt from a News Article, dated May 18, in the *Franklin County Bee*, Preston, Idaho

A John Doe was found brutally murdered in one of the rental cabins behind the Beehive Inn yesterday morning. It is believed that he was killed yesterday morning as well. Even though Sheriff Clive Hansen has refused to discuss the matter with managing editor and city reporter Mark Schmalls, the *Franklin County Bee* has learned from sources that the victim was a young adult male, aged approximately thirty-three. It is reported that the victim was brutally stabbed in the face. The victim was probably an Indian, though it was not discerned if he was a Blackfoot or from some other tribe. There was no alcohol discerned in the room.

Samuel Staker, owner of the Beehive, stated, "The room was filthy. I keep a clean place here. There was blood on the floors and on both the mattress and the box springs. One wall definitely needs to be repainted." Mr. Staker refused to speculate further, having been mandated by the local authorities not to. It is believed that the sheriff has no suspects in mind.

The letter that follows (e-mail and fax both received on May 19) was obtained by the author from the office of Edward Thorn, the Solicitor General of the United States, through the Freedom of Information Act

Dear Brother Thorn:

This letter is to confirm the results of your conversation with Elder Kimball of the First Presidency. The Prophet, speaking through the First Presidency, has asked that you, by whatever means possible and through whatever channels available, assign a true and faithful Latter-day Saint to the investigation of a murder in Franklin County, Idaho, that took place on or about May 17. The man chosen should be a member in full standing with the Church and the finest expert in homicide. He should be completely freed from his regular duties in the Federal Bureau of Investigation to complete this inquiry and the apprehension of the person or persons involved in the murder. He will report only to you and must also be able to work closely with local LDS law enforcement authorities that have volunteered to participate in this investigation.

This assignment must be kept secret by the very vows that you hold most sacred. Much is at stake for the Church. Please contact Brother Kimball at the telephone number below when you have found the right Brother for the assignment. Both Senators Thatcher and Young, as well as Secretary Benson and Elder Harris, have been informed and are willing to help you in any way that they are able.

[Signed]
Peter Arrington
Personal Secretary to Grant T. Kimball, Member of the First Presidency of the Church of Jesus Christ of Latter-day Saints

The following is the transcription of two taped telephone conversations between Nathan Johnson (NJ) and Edward Thorn (ET), Solicitor General of the United States; both conversations occurred on the evening of May 20

ET: Elder Johnson, hello. This is Elder Edward Thorn, calling from Washington, DC. How are you this evening?
NJ: Fine, sir.
ET: The light on my desk indicates that you are recording this conversation.
NJ: Yes, sir. I might not be talking to you, sir.
ET: Did you get my e-mail?
NJ: Yes, sir.
ET: Please call me Brother Thorn, Brother Johnson.
NJ: Yes, sir, Brother Thorn.
ET: And did you delete it?
NJ: Yes, sir, Brother Thorn.
ET: Now turn off the recording machine.
NJ: No, sir, Brother Thorn. It might not be you, sir.
NJ: Very well, when you verify that it is me, please delete the recording. [Laughter] Director Lowry told me you were the best Mormon agent he had.
NJ: [Silence]
ET: You don't agree with that assessment?
NJ: In all humility, Brother Thorn, I am the best he's got—period.
ET: Would you mind answering a few questions for me, Brother Johnson?
NJ: I will answer, sir.
ET: Are you a true and faithful Latter-day Saint?

NJ: Sir, I was born and raised a Mormon, and I'm a pretty good one, sir, Brother Thorn.
ET: And are you true and faithful to the covenants you made in the temple with your wife?
NJ: Pretty true and always faithful, sir.
ET: Your bishop told me that you might have an alcohol problem.
NJ: No, sir. No problem with alcohol.
ET: You don't drink alcohol—you keep the Word of Wisdom?
NJ: Sir, Brother Thorn, in my line of work I do whatever I have to do to catch the criminal, to carry out my assignment. Sometimes you have to act like a bad guy to catch one, sir.
ET: Are you comfortable … are you happy with your religion?
NJ: Yes, sir. I love my church.
ET: If you are comfortable with your religion, then why did you refuse to accept the calling in your ward to be a bishop last year?
NJ: Sir, I wanted that job, Brother Thorn. I thought I could have touched the lives of some of the young people in the church. I see what drugs and gambling and prostitution do. I know the down side, sir.
ET: Then why did you refuse?
NJ: I work in homicide. I specialize in serial killings. I have … I don't say this … I tell you this so that you understand. I have killed three people in my career. Two months ago, I shot a man. He had murdered eleven people in twenty-six months. He was working on his twelfth when I showed up. He was a whacker; he beheaded his victims with a machete. I put a ten-millimeter round in the back of his head from eight meters away—just as he was about to chop up a young woman.

I'll tell you something funny, sir, about my job: Last week the young woman's lawyer—the young woman whose life I saved—called my boss. She is trying to sue the agency because a piece of the perp's skull lodged in her eye when I shot him. I shrug it off because it's my job. It is not exactly the kind of role model that I want children to imitate. I'm not the ideal person, right now, to be giving others moral guidance or religious counseling.
ET: And what about your own children?
NJ: That's none—er—that's a tough one, Brother Thorn. You might have been told that I went to medical school at Stanford after graduating from BYU. My last year there, I worked nights in a hospital emergency room. I saw more people stabbed and shot every week than I'll bet you've seen in your entire life. I had a choice to make. Do I spend my life sewing up the victims of other people's hate

and madness—or should I stop ... try to stop ... at least some of it? I dropped out and joined the Bureau. I enjoy what I do—I'm not all that proud of it—but I like it. I'll retire in a few years, finish my residency, be a country doctor, raise my kids and grandkids, and be a bishop, and everybody will call me *Doc* or *Brother Johnson*, Brother Thorn.

ET: I need to return and report. I'll be in touch.

NJ: Whatever. Thanks for calling. And, sir, your recording machine was running too.

[End of first conversation.]

NJ: Johnson residence.

ET: The light on my ...

NJ: I record all my calls, sir. How are you this evening, Brother Thorn? It must be getting late in DC.

ET: Fine. Fine. You are about to be released from your regular duties and ordered to Preston, Idaho, to investigate a murder. Once you leave the Nevada office, you will report only to me, only at this telephone number, and only on a secure line. Your contact in Preston is Sheriff Clive Hansen. Brother Hansen will provide you with all the details of the homicide. He has been instructed to cooperate fully with you.

NJ: Instructed by whom, Brother Thorn?

ET: By the First Presidency, perhaps by the Prophet himself. We have reason to believe that the victim is one of the Three Nephites.

NJ: [After several seconds of silence] Is this a joke, sir—Brother Thorn?

ET: A man has been murdered, a man whom the First Presidency believes is one of the Three Nephites. I have no idea what you will find. But they are taking this very seriously. Brother Wilford Harris, Chief of Staff to the President of the United States, has helped get you assigned to me. I am charged to report directly to the First Presidency. Does that sound like a joke to you?

NJ: No, sir, Brother Thorn.

ET: Can you leave tomorrow morning?"

NJ: Yes, sir, Brother Thorn.

[Remainder of exchange, primarily courteous banter, omitted.]

And there are none that do know the true God save it be the disciples of Jesus who did tarry in the land until the wickedness of the people was so great that the Lord would not suffer them to remain with the people; and whether they be upon the face of the land no man knoweth.

—Mormon 8:10, *Book of Mormon*

Shortly after he spoke with Edward Thorn, Nathan Johnson called me at my home. He recorded our conversation. The date is May 21; time was about 1:00 AM. Here is the transcription

NJ: Hey, Cuz!
ME: Hey, Nate! Where are you?
NJ: Home, in Vegas.
ME: Shoot anybody this month?
NJ: Nope.
ME: Shucks. But don't stop tryin'. Can you get up here and go fishin' at Henry's Lake next weekend? Openin' day. It'll be crazy. Paul and Phil are going.
NJ: Can't do it. I called to see how busy you are.
ME: Buried. I'm finally selling some books.
NJ: Sure—but I might need your help on a case. You might even want to write about it.
ME: Me?
NJ: Yeah. Didn't you do a paper on immortal life, on people wanting to live forever?
ME: In college. My doctoral dissertation sort of dealt with it too.

NJ: I know this is going to sound weird—but I've been assigned a case that deals with the subject.
ME: What—a murder case?
NJ: It's really strange. One of the Three Nephites. You know?"
ME: *Book of Mormon*, I know.
NJ: I'm heading for—I guess I can't tell you that. But they're serious. They think they've got a dead immortal on their hands.
ME: [Laughing] Don't they teach you guys the Law of Non-Contradiction at BYU or Stanford? Did you miss that lesson at Quantico? Mortal or immortal? Dead or alive? Either A or not A, but not A and not not A? 'To be or not to be' isn't the question; it's a law of nature. In my papers, I wrote about why people need to *believe* they can live forever and why most religions promise that. I didn't say it was possible—'cause it isn't.
NJ: I'm not kidding you. The leaders of the Church think that one of the Three Nephites is dead.
ME: Maybe you're not kidding me, but someone's kidding you ... or they're kidding themselves. Nate, every religion—and I mean every one—has at least one myth about some very righteous dude who gets to skip death and hang around until the end of the world. It's exactly the same in every one: you follow all the rules ... you get to live forever. The Jews have half a dozen immortals, the Buddhists have sixteen, the Mormons have three—or is it two? Hell even the Christians have one. Excluding Jesus who, if you believe the Bible, did come back in the flesh after he died. Most Christians don't know this—even though it's in the Bible. It's *John* ... Christ's beloved. He's hangin' around too. So if you meet him, be sure and say "Hi" for me.
NJ: Wow. You're tryin' to be funny *and* educational. But—see what I mean—for once, you actually know what you're talkin' about. Can I at least ask you some questions if I run into problems?
ME: Sure. Hey, Father Dougherty, my old teacher at Catholic U, might be able to help. The Catholics have a kind of mental hospital in Italy where they keep their clergy who claim to be immortal. He helps run it. He knows the psychological type. Let me tell you, they've got some sick assholes over there. People who think they are immortal don't have any rules. They don't need any. I read some of his case studies when I was at C.U. Weird shit. There was this one guy ...
NJ: Sure you don't want to write about it?
ME: Huh? Maybe. Yeah, maybe. Can I make a suggestion?
NJ: Sure.

ME: Keep a good journal. A story kind of journal, not just your regular police report shit. Write down your feelings and stuff. Keep it real. You should do it all the time anyway—someday you can write your own book.
NJ: One writer to a family. 'Economics of scales.' Isn't that what they call it?
ME: No. But nice try. Write it all down. I'll look at it. I'll contact Dougherty. Be careful, though. Sounds like some sort of *National Inquirer* public relations gimmick—like the Catholics and the Shroud of Turin. Don't let them make a fool of you. 'Vision of the weeping Virgin Mary seen floating in toilet bowl.'
NJ: Maybe—but they sure seem serious.
ME: Nate, they're *always* serious. How's the family?

[Remainder of conversation omitted.]

Whoever battles monsters should see to it that in the process he does not become a monster. And when you look long into an abyss, the abyss also looks into you.

—Nietzsche, *Jenseits von Gut und Böse*

Excerpts from the Journal of Nathan Johnson

Salt Lake City, Utah. 10:30 PM May 21.

Barely had a chance to say good-bye to Sylvia. It was a long enough good-bye for me, but not for her.

I called Sheriff Hansen before my flight. He offered to pick me up at the Salt Lake City airport. I told him that I would rather have him maintain the security and the integrity of the body and the crime scene—this he promised to do.

Flew into Salt Lake on United 433. Bumped into Brent Hymas, local bureau gopher, at the airport. He was waiting for someone else. I sent him away, told him I was going fishing; I was dressed in my suit, though. I rented a car, a white Hertz Lincoln with a huge trunk; all my tools, which I carry in a large green duffel bag, fit. Thorn sent a prepaid VISA in my name and two thousand dollars in cash to the Vegas office. I'll spend the night here in SLC.

Preston, Idaho. 2:00 PM, May 22.

Lunch at Whitely's Café (everyone around here is a Whitely, Darrington, Budge, Hansen, Woodruff, or, gulp, Johnson) served by a cute little waitress, Emma *Johnson*, ugh, probably a second or third cousin. I tell myself that's what happens when your great-great gramps was a polygamist who took fifteen wives, and none of his kids' kids ever left town. Emma's eyes were brown and pretty, her hips wide and soft, but both a bit too far apart for my taste. Food was lots and greasy. Canned vegetables, roast beef sandwich on white bread with real potatoes and tons of greasy canned gravy, fountain Pepsi. Emma had dressed for church in a red cotton dress and was very careful not to spill any gravy on it.

Following Miss Johnson's directions, I crossed the street, wandered a few blocks south, and found the sheriff's office in the yellow Oakley stone county building. The sheriff was out catching a rustler. Some poor Mexican got drunk last night, shot a calf, and dragged it home for Sunday dinner. They told me—*they* were his deputy, Bill Budge, his secretary, Sheila, the local part-time prosecutor, Eric Taylor, and the court clerk, Sonja—that he'd be back in two hours. Except for Deputy Budge, who had just come on duty, they had all dressed for church, which, in this valley, means the Mormon Church. The events of the last few days gave them the overtime that, I'm guessing, they rarely saw and really didn't want.

They knew who I was. In half an hour, so did every one else in the town. After attending church service, the waitress, Emma Johnson, swinging her broad but cute fanny like a parasol, marched right over to the sheriff's office. Blushing as red as the maraschino she had dropped in my Pepsi, redder than her dress, she asked me if I were any relation to Sterling Johnson. And what was it like being a G-man? And was I married? But those dim eyes.

Preston, Idaho, late evening, May 22.

I wasn't up to waiting all afternoon for the sheriff to return to town. (I figured that they would have a parade in my honor in an hour our two if, by chance, they discovered that I was related to Sterling Johnson—whoever he is.) So I wrote a little in my journal and then rode out with Deputy Bill Budge to the scene of the cattle rustling. Budge is a young, thin, blond-headed, twenty-two-year-old kid. He has sad, lonely, pale blue eyes. His voice is high-pitched and squeaky, as if hunting for its masculinity. He is very respectful and calls me "Agent Johnson, sir." Back less than one year from his church mission to Guatemala, he has worked as a deputy for six months to earn enough money to attend college next fall. He told me that his Spanish might come in handy today since the suspect in the rustling was a Mexican.

We found the sheriff up a gravel road in one of the many small ravines that run east into the Wasatch Range. The Bear River valley is marked by a series of ranches in southeastern Idaho. They run east and west between fingers of mountains, the Wasatch and the Blue Springs, that stretch north and south and up within the Caribou National Forest. The grass, the newborn calves, and the yellow daisies were kicking through the melting banks of snow in the lush green meadows of the valley. The river was full, not swollen. There have been a number of lean water years in these mountains; but there was enough runoff this spring so that the rainbow trout leapt and rolled in the pure air, declaring today a fish holiday.

The suspect—rather, the guilty party (I can safely call him that since the tiny carcass, crudely skinned and beheaded, was hanging from a heavy chain on the motor hoist in his driveway)—was pleading, in Spanish and very poor, broken English with a young, heavyset cowboy dressed in his best Sunday duds. The sheriff was some fifteen feet away from them, resting his stout frame against his squad car, grinning, waiting for his translator. The rustler lived in a rusted yellow school bus parked on the edge of a rock-littered pasture. On the left of the bus was a canvas lean-to that served to keep his skimpy supply of firewood, an ax, a noisy generator, and the propane tanks dry through the spring rains. Parked on the right was an old primer gray Chevy Silverado pickup.

The cowboy in the suit was the local Mormon bishop. After opening the patrol car door for me, the sheriff shook my hand, introduced himself, and then told me a little about the bishop. The cowboy bishop was also the local rancher who had lost the calf. He was no more than thirty years old. He wore brand-new blue jeans with a blue denim suit jacket, soiled silver and black leather boots with sterling silver toes, a white Stetson hat, and a pressed gray cowboy shirt with shiny pearl buttons and a cowboy-style bolo tie. He was about five-eight and fat for a cowboy; he looked a little too soft for the job. He looked as if he conducted all of his roundups, via cell phone, from the inside of his air-conditioned, four-door, four-wheel drive, blue Subaru.

The short, five-six, one-eighty, crew cut, black bloodshot eyes, scar on right half of upper lip, mid-forties, grease and blood-smeared red flannel shirt, smelling of sweat and tequila (how's that for descriptive, Cuz?), Mexican appeared to be claiming that he had stolen the calf for his sick sister.

While Deputy Budge went with the sheriff to interrogate the suspect, I stood on a rusted wheel rim and peeked through the white lace that hung all along the side windows of the bus. The woman in there didn't look like his sister (his daughter, maybe, she looked about nineteen)—or very sick. She was sitting on the edge of a narrow cot. White lace dangled down the yellow metal wall behind her. White lace skirted the cot's black metal frame. She was dressed in a black negligee that partially hid her slender brown thighs, her tight stomach, and her large bosom with huge—I mean three inches across—dark areolae and pitch-black nipples. Her hair was very long and dark. I could just see the face beneath it. Her teeth were yellow. I watched her fingers, the nails painted dark red, slide back and forth through the lace as she listened intently, over the grinding of the generator, to the voices outside. Her legs were unshaven. In the back of the bus, leaning against the emergency exit, on a metal tray table, sat a portable TV/video player. It was adjacent to a small Franklin wood burner. The television was on, but the volume was down.

Another, wider bed sat in the front of the bus. There were two storage chests, a folded table, and two folded chairs behind the driver's seat. There were cardboard boxes beneath each bed. Beside the larger bed, next to the door, sat a Coleman stove and a Styrofoam ice chest. Behind this bed, the windows were hidden by a large black velour painting of a bighorn sheep crouched on the ledge of a black and silver mountain. Lightning flashed above the ram's head, crashed into and illuminated the peaks to both sides, in front and behind him, as he glared defiantly beyond the flashes into the black heavens. The bolts of lightning formed a rough pentacle that encased the ram's head.

The young woman watched me from the cot, smiling from behind her hair. I could see only the yellow of her teeth and her dark eyes through it. I swallowed and stumbled forward. Then I jerked back as my boots slipped off the lip of the tire rim, and fell on my butt. The sheriff laughed at me. "These ranchers, no matter how much religion they got, git horny," he hollered at me. "You gittin' horny?"

I don't know if the Mexican was only a recent convert to this odd adjunct of the Mormon Church or if he was a Catholic, an atheist, or a member of the plumber's union, but I think he'd have been better off not spouting quite so many Hail Marys or rattling off the names of saints and devils and "de profeet Hosef Smeeth" in his defense. Neither the sheriff nor the cowboy bishop seemed to be able to make much of it. Deputy Budge tried not to giggle, without much success. The sheriff glanced at me apologetically. The cowboy bishop grew increasingly annoyed.

The Mexican asked to speak to the bishop alone. He led the cowboy to the far side of the primer gray pickup, where they gestured and whispered for a few minutes. The Mexican struggled, with the English language and with his body language, to convey the message. He had a tattoo on his right forearm—a knife through a flaming, winged eye. His hands were smudged with black grease, but his fingernails were neatly manicured.

The cowboy soon called the sheriff and the deputy over, and the four of them spoke. Finally, the cowboy bishop stomped and kicked the dirt and said something like, "Well, all right then, if he gits this one. But I'll shoot the sono'bitch next time he comes around my feeders." The Mexican bowed humbly and crossed himself and accepted the settlement.

I left with Sheriff Hansen. Deputy Budge and the bishop followed in their vehicles. I noticed as we left that the deputy ventured anxiously, if furtively, to catch a glimpse of the face peering from behind the black hair and the white fringe that draped the bus windows.

"This is the 'ninety-nine model. If I'd waited a couple years, I'd a got that new computerized turbo-charger they're puttin' in 'em," the sheriff said. He thumped the dashboard of his aging black and white Camaro with callused knuckles. "I've got a brand-new one comin' in this year's budget. This ol' gal's seen a lotta asphalt."

"I'm running my little recording machine here. You don't mind, do you, Sheriff?"

"Mind? I was told by that Thorn fellow, that pushy son of a bitch, that I was not to mind one damn thing that you did."

"Well, since he put me in charge, I can ask you some questions and record the answers. Okay?"

"Okay," he answered dejectedly—as if obeying a younger man was beneath his dignity.

"Then you don't mind if I record our conversation? I've got your permission? It's easier for me to keep track of details."

His nose is bulbous, almost bouncy. He is a heavy man, about sixty years old. I'll bet that he was all muscle when he was young.

"You askin' for permission? You got it. Leave it on," said the sheriff. "You wanna go straight to the cooler or to the Beehive Inn where they found him?"

"Is the crime location secure?"

"Tighter than a heifer's heinie."

"Somebody's on it twenty-four hours a day?"

"I deputized four men, gave two by two twelve-hour shifts, and told them I'd have their *cojones* if so much as a piece of lint got moved."

"Where's the body?"

"The only safe place around."

"Which is?"

"You wanna drink?"

"No. Where's the body?" I asked again.

"At Darrington's," he replied.

"What's Darrington's?"

"Meat locker, freezer, butcher. Where most everybody takes their game and beef."

"Did you freeze the body?" I asked nervously.

"No. We're not idiots. Got him locked in the cooler. You wanna drink 'fore we head over there? Calm you down."

"No—maybe later. Take me to the body first. It will deteriorate, even if it's kept in a cooler. So, what was the deal with the rustler and that cowboy? Looked like the Mexican had something on the guy," I said to the sheriff when we had left the gravel and squealed back on to the pavement, heading north into town on Highway 91.

"You sure you don't wanna drink first?" the sheriff asked me again. He smiled and waved at the passengers in an old maroon station wagon we were passing. The family inside was decked out in their Sunday finest. "What's wrong? You a Mormon?"

"Yes."

"Me too. Thought I saw your garments," he said, and pointed at the outline of my underwear, visible beneath my dress shirt; he tugged under his shirt collar at his garments. "Makes sense for them to send an elder. You don't drink, then?"

"No. Once in a while. Tell me about the cowboy and the rustler."

"I told you that the cowboy is the bishop. Well, he is also a county commissioner, and he's the grandson of a general authority of the Mormon Church, so someday—if he wants to—he'll be Idaho's governor. A few weeks ago, he gits the big idea from his nephew Billy—that'd be my deputy, Billy Budge—he gits the idea that this Indian was one of the Three Nephites. So the two of 'em git all excited and call up Salt Lake City, and they git the Church head honchos all excited 'til the whole bunch of 'em are believin' that they've cornered themselves one of the Three Nephites. They're tryin' to figure out what to do with him when, *oops!* Their goddamn Nephite goes and gets himself murdered. But how do you kill somebody that can't even die? Apparently they hadn't considered that. So now they're up to their assholes in the smelliest bunch of horseshit I ever whiffed.

"Now it seems that Mexican's 'little sister,' well, she's bin making some money on the side by humping a couple of the bishop's ... let's call 'em *acquaintances*. So today, once the bishop found out whose 'big brother' stole his calf, he decides not to press charges. Hell, he didn't even recognize his own brand no more! Some Mormons around here are a little different from regular Church people. Our little corner of Zion's way out here in the boonies. We're a long way from ... everything. Sometimes we gotta ... sometimes we make up our own entertainment. And so long's it don't hurt nobody, the brethren in Utah just kinda let us alone," the sheriff remarked—and then self-consciously laughed.

"What's the rustler's name?"

"Hell, I don't know. Even if I'd wasted my time askin' him, he'd just give me another one next time 'round."

"Illegal alien?"

"Beats me. My farmers need some help gittin' things done around here. They elect me. I don't normally check illegals. I have no concern for illegals unless they break my laws. Pain in the ass border patrol is supposed to take care of that."

"How long have this one and his woman been around?" I asked.

The sheriff scrunched up his nose, best that he could, given the few remaining muscles in it that worked, then haltingly turned his head to me. "Three weeks, coulda bin four. It was not long after the Indian showed up—week or so after. You want that drink?"

"Maybe later, after we see the body. I wanna do the autopsy before we drink. Here." I handed the sheriff his transmitter's microphone. "Get Deputy Budge. Wait ... first get him some assistance. Have him arrest the Mexican and the woman in the bus. Have them picked up and get them mugged, printed, and locked up. I want complete background checks on both of them. Never mind, I'll do that myself. Absolutely no bail until I say so."

"Arrested? What the hell for? They ain't done nothin'," protested the sheriff.

"Rustlin'," I answered. "Cattle rustlin'. And I want to talk to your bishop too."

"Ah, shit, Johnson, you're just gonna make a bigger stink," groaned Sheriff Hansen as we sped along side the windswept meadows beneath the shadows of the snow and pine-covered mountains into Preston, Idaho.

[The following excerpts are taken from the transcription of Nathan Johnson's recorded autopsy notes.]

NJ: Recording. Date is May 22. Time is approximately 7:30 PM. The body has been contained in a walk-in cooler at Frank Darrington's meat locker in Preston, Idaho. In attendance are Sheriff Clive Hansen and myself, Nathan Johnson. I note for the record that Sheriff Hansen has been directed by President Grant Kimball of the L.D.S. Church to personally take the remains of the John Doe to the University of Utah medical center in Salt Lake City after I make my findings. I also note here that the Hispanic male and female I saw earlier today are being held, under my orders, in the Fremont County Jail for grand theft. They have stated that their names are Enrico Avilar and Patty Montaño. That's all ... until tomorrow. Their association, if any, with the deceased is unknown.

I'm working on a butchering table in the rear of a small meat locker under barely adequate light. The body was bagged and has been kept just above freezing since recovery. I have taken a very clean set of prints. Tools on hand are limited to various butcher knifes and hacksaws, though I brought a few scalpels and a portable Makita hand grinder with a carbide blade to use as a craniotome. The sheriff found a pair of tin snips to aid in opening the chest cavity.

General observations of the body: The subject is male, five feet eleven inches tall. Weight one hundred and fifty-four pounds. He is not Caucasian. Subject would appear to be of Native American extraction from the length and straightness of his black hair, from his relatively small amounts of facial hair, prominent cheekbones, and the color and texture of his skin. Age, because of damage to the face, is tough to guess. I would say early to middle thirties.

Subject was wearing a flannel shirt, blue jeans, and white jogging shoes. Underneath these clothes we find ... a full-length, one-piece set of garments. This type of underclothing is peculiar to the Mormon faith. The type worn by the subject, cotton, full body coverage to the wrists and ankles, is not, to my knowledge, manufactured anymore. My grandfather wore garments like these.

Taking pictures of the teeth—there appears to be no dental or gum disease and no visible dental work—the teeth are in outstanding shape. The left jaw is broken at both the ramus and superior maxillary. I suspect the injury might be secondary and might have occurred in the struggle to pierce the eyes and ears. No teeth were dislocated. The inferior maxillary is broken and protruding through the skin at the right front, approximately ten centimeters to the right of the symphysis. This could have been a direct blow, perhaps with a fist, more likely a heavy blunt object. I'll return to the head later. That'll work. Cover it up, Sheriff. Dear God, what a mess. Grab those scissors. Help me cut off his clothes.

There appear to be no wounds to any part of the body—except for the head. There are no bruises on the hands, feet, wrists or ankles. I am not certain why there was no struggle. But the subject didn't seem to fight back; he wasn't bound. It is impossible for me to tell if he was drugged, though there are no puncture marks on the body. Although it is barely visible, there is an old scar on the chest, an inch above and two inches inside of the left nipple, that seems to be a fully healed gunshot entry wound. There is what would appear to be a scar from the companion exit wound on the back beneath the left scapula ...

I'll open the chest cavity first. The organs appear normal, healthy. Lungs are in great shape. Removing the heart. The heart appears to have been injured at some undetermined but distant time. The scar tissue on the right ventricle—possible impact area of a bullet—is abnormal. It is … it shows the same fibrous muscle as the heart around it. It is not ordinary scar tissue, but is almost normal heart tissue. By the shape and size of the entry and exit scars, the damage to the heart should have been much more extensive. This is *very* peculiar. Maybe the university doctors can make something of it.

[Author's note: At this point Nathan individually removed all of the major organs and examined each of them. He drained and scraped the body cavity of blood, placed the organs in a plastic garbage bag, and dropped them inside the chest cavity. His lengthy description of that process is omitted. Except for the scar on the heart, the internal organs appeared healthy and undamaged.]

NJ: Nothing exciting here. Let's get back to the head. Sewing up cavity. Hand me that cord and needle.
[Small talk between Nathan Johnson and Sheriff Hansen, while cavity was sewn up, has been omitted.]
NJ: Cutting through the scalp. Drawing it up over the face. The skull is now exposed.
[Sheriff Hansen is heard in the background just prior to the sound of the buzzing of the saw as it cuts into the skull:]
SH: I've never seen a head cut open before.
NJ: This one's going to be particularly ugly. [The saw continues to whir.] Just like a coconut. Give this a tug here, and *[POP!]* the top of his head just pops off. Shit, what a mess. Wuh—deep breath. Uh … the murder weapon … or weapons … were punched into the left side of the head with such force that the zygoma and the temporal bones next to the ear are cracked on one side, shattered into the brain on the other. Through the front, through the eyes, they cracked the malar bones, fractured that sphenoid bone behind the eye. The brain has been severely lacerated. [Nervous laugh] Hang in there, Sheriff. Looks like gray scrambled eggs, doesn't it? The only portion of the brain fully intact is the parietal lobe, which I will now remove … *Huh? Shit! JESUS CHRIST!*
[Author's Note: There is considerable tumult at this point in the recording. Instruments clang to the floor.]
NJ: Sheriff. Come here.
[The sheriff's response is not recorded.]
NJ: Get over here. How long has this body been in storage?
[The sheriff's answer is unintelligible.]

NJ: And the entire body has been refrigerated?

[Sheriff's answer is still unintelligible.]

NJ: Come here. I want your response on the record. Get over here.

SH: Five, six days, I said. What's the matter? Why'd you jump like that? Scared the livin' shit out of me.

NJ: Touch right here. Here on the scalp. Next to the brain.

SH: You nuts?

NJ: Touch it! What do you feel?

[The sheriff's reply is inaudible.]

NJ: Into the microphone.

SH: Cold. I feel cold, dead skin.

NJ: Cold. Isn't it? Because it's been in the refrigerator for days? Right?

SH: Yeah. Feels like lunchmeat. What *is* your problem?

NJ: Now touch here. This part of the brain. No, right here, the part that's in one piece.

SH: For *chrissakes!* [Then inaudible]

NJ: Sheriff. Get back over here. I need it on record. I need a witness. What did you feel?

SH: It's ... for the love of God! It's still warm!

NJ: Let the record show that I felt it too ... that the body is at about thirty-five degrees Fahrenheit, but that I felt the remainder of the frontal lobe and the parietal lobe, and that they are approximately one hundred degrees or about normal body temperature. It feels as if the intact portions of the brain are still ... alive.

[Remainder of this transcription omitted.]

> The actualization of wisdom is identical with the erection of an absolutely dependable dogmatic edifice on the foundation of extreme skepticism.
>
> —Leo Strauss, *Natural Right and History*

> To every w-consistent recursive class k of formulae there correspond recursive class signs r, such that neither v Gen r nor Neg (v Gen r) belongs to Flg (k) (where v is the free variable of r).
>
> —Kurt Gödel, *Über Formal Unentscheidbare Sätze ...*

On the Author's Relationship to Harold Weintraub

Before I include any material from Professor Harold Weintraub in this book, I should explain a little about the man, his work, and our relationship. Weintraub is in his early seventies. He is a thickset, muscular man, not more than five and a half feet tall. His hair was brown and has grayed with time; but it is still thick and often oily. His peculiar gray eyes flicker aimlessly behind the bulky lenses of his black-rimmed glasses until focused for conversation or for reading. Harold Weintraub was made a full professor of philosophy at Harvard when he was thirty-one. He managed this feat by being a dedicated and estimable student of the finest philosophical minds of his day. He studied at Princeton with Kurt Gödel, at the University of Chicago with Leo Strauss, and finally, just before moving to Harvard, he studied informally with Alexandr Kojève in Paris. As a young man, Weintraub had, for all practical purposes, mastered every major branch of philosophy and picked up seven or eight languages in the process.

His first book, *Analysis as Nihilism,* published when he was thirty, set the tenor for his career. *Analysis as Nihilism* is a trenchant criticism of several modern and post-modern philosophers. It is a scathing attack on the central pillar of modern philosophy—the assumption that human thought is limited and that truth is relative to that limitation. Unlike the ancient philosophers, many of whom held that there was something called truth—absolute truth, Truth with a capital *T*—and that Truth was accessible in one form or another to human beings, modern thinkers almost unanimously preach that all human thought is relative or contingent. Depending upon the school, it is argued that thinking is necessarily limited in many ways: by language, history, social norms, political regimes, economics, psychological necessity, neuron firing patterns, mathematical and metamathematical theories, and—well, numerous others. Weintraub showed, in *Analysis as Nihilism,* that most theories that purportedly prove that thinking is specifically contingent or conditional are riddled with logical inconsistencies and demonstrate nothing at all. He did it without mercy. Weintraub's style might be best characterized as "the slaughterhouse of syllogisms." The ideas of those he criticized entered at one end of his book alive and kicking but left at the other end, shot in the head, gutted, neatly chopped, wrapped, and frozen.

This obdurate honesty—*Analysis as Nihilism* was the first of his books, he got tougher—did not endear him to his colleagues. In a chapter, at times in a few pages, he could blow away a prevailing intellectual dogma as the house of cards that, in reality, it was. Those who had spent their professional lives in the paper domicile construction business resented him. More than that, they feared him. There is little doubt that Weintraub made the intellectual *haute monde* nervous—and little doubt that he paid for it. The professional system of review notoriously ignored his work. After his first few articles, he was not regularly invited to contribute to the more prestigious scholarly anthologies and journals.

The "good old boy" network of the American Philosophical Society—like all professional organizations, I hasten to add—establishes certain unwritten but unbreakable ground rules. If an error is discovered in the work of a colleague, it is permissible to criticize the error as long as polite constraint and proper decorum are observed. The general principle is *After the colloquium and the exchange of papers, will the members of the disputing parties still be able to play a round of golf and enjoy it?* But Weintraub understood philosophy and philosophizing as a far more serious concern than "publish or perish." "If we are mistaken in our thinking," he wrote in a later book, "then we are fraudulent in our existence."

When their efforts to bury him in obscurity failed—Weintraub's intensity put off his colleagues, but it drew the brighter, more aggressive graduate students to him in hordes—the professional philosophers stooped to character assassination. In their responses to his critiques or in their reviews of his books, they referred to him as either "eccentric" (after Gödel), "reactionary" (after Strauss) or as "radical" (after Kojève)—although "fanatic," "zealous," "indiscriminate," and "tasteless" were often thrown in for good measure.

"Reactionary" was the disparagement of choice. Once in the late seventies and twice in the eighties, decade of enlightenment that it was, attempts were made to remove Professor Weintraub from the Harvard faculty because of his "extremist political convictions."

Exactly what are his political convictions? I have known the man for over fifteen years, and I can unequivocally state that his political convictions are boring. He is a middle-of-the-road, slightly liberal, *Time Magazine* editorial kind of a guy; in other words, politically speaking, he is much like those who would destroy him. Not that he takes day-to-day politics—as opposed to political philosophy—that seriously. He once told me, "This election's anarchist is next election's socialist."

To understand him, one must realize that Weintraub never allowed his political views to corrupt his scholarship. While his fellow academicians were striving to justify their commodious and staid political views with half-baked postmodernist or post-structuralist philosophical hunches, Weintraub relentlessly sought a higher goal—the goal of articulating, or of stating precisely why one could not articulate, the *Truth*.

Not all of his repute was opprobrious. He wrote some very popular and humorous articles for the *New Yorker,* the *Jewish Quarterly,* and, more esoterically, for the *Review of Metaphysics.*

He married Judy Weintraub, the theoretical biologist, who is nearly as controversial as her husband. She is the author of *The Symbiotic Origin of the Cell*—perhaps the most controversial book in microbiology this decade—wherein she claims that all cells are masses of evolving microbial life and that all life is inexorably intertwined in the symbiotic relationships of what she has dubbed the "Microcosmos." Instead of Darwinian evolution by competition, she espouses the development of new life forms by symbiotic progression. Because of her work with the British chemist Dr. James Openhäte, she is often mistakenly portrayed as one of the founders of the New Age Gaia movement. Dr. Judy Weintraub, however, is a tough-minded scientist, with a delightful sprinkling of curiosity and puckishness. She has thin ruddy cheeks, fervent hazel eyes, and short brown hair. She is about twenty years younger than her husband. The Weintraubs have two teenage children.

Does it sound as if I am a Weintraub fan? Good. Judy Weintraub is a close friend and the most remarkable woman I have met. Harold Weintraub is the most intelligent human being I have ever known or probably ever will know. But I have only begun my portrayal of the man.

What teacher has the grace—to tell the truth directly to our face?

—Goethe, *Faust*

On the Author's Relationship with Harold Weintraub, Continued

I studied for four years with Weintraub when I was in college at Harvard—though I suppose that "worshipped at his feet" is closer to the truth. I read every word he had ever published, several times. I did not miss a single lecture that he delivered in those four years, either in the college or in the graduate school. I was the first undergraduate student whom he agreed to tutor, one on one, in a special honors program in philosophy and comparative religion.

Crouching at the master's hem, as I was young, impressionable, in desperate need of grounding, I soon wanted more than piquant artifices in logic. Even though Weintraub was very good at razing arguments—he was and still is the best—he was not nearly as adept at building his own theoretical constructs. Perhaps he really felt that philosophy was only the ruthless examination of the ideas of others. Perhaps he was the new Socrates, transmigrated into permanent midlife crisis, fettered by the conventions of academe—rather than by Aesculapius's chicken. Perhaps he was silently searching.

As a student, I required more. I tried to take it. Weintraub had been writing, under an assumed name, a series of articles for the *Review of Metaphysics* entitled "The Myths of Immortality." They were offered as high-level satire of Joseph Campbell, the latest hip New Age scholar. And though his put-down of Campbell was thorough, Weintraub seemed to have left unannounced his verdict on the possibility of immortal life. I write *seemed* because I had never seen him flinch from the *coup de grâce*. Perhaps this was my master's secret teaching. I had found my opening.

Weintraub had agreed to act as chairman of the review committee for my honors thesis in philosophy. He gave me, as he always had, free rein to write whatever I wanted. I was not even required to submit an outline to him. He had scheduled a preexamination discussion of the paper with me, but he ended up in England, going over the proofs of his next book with his publisher, at that time. Weintraub did not see my thesis until a few hours before the oral examination.

My paper was entitled "Eros, Art, and Immortality." In it, I argued that both pro-creation and creation through art were efforts approaching, and reflective of, a state of immortality. I asserted that, unlike manifold religious dogmas that posited the necessity of death before life, eros and art indicated that immortality, if it existed at all, existed in the here and now. (It wasn't a bad paper. A version of it was eventually published in the *New Criterion*.)

Weintraub was late for the oral examination. I sat at the end of a long oak table in a white tile-paneled room on the third floor of the long and narrow Emerson building in Harvard Yard. I waited with two members of the philosophy department, an older man and a young Asian woman who, with Weintraub, composed the committee. I did not know either of them except by name and reputation; I was Weintraub's student.

The woman fidgeted with the black notebook that contained my thesis. I must have looked scared. "This is very good," she finally said, assuring me that everything would be fine.

A tall, wide window was open to my left. The smell of spring, the fragrance of buds popping open on the trees and of sprouting grass, wafted into the room on a warm breeze. I could hear students below me chanting Frisbee conflagration chants. The ferocious and lascivious starlings in the treetops outside madly chirped scattered and shattered love songs between bouts of dive bombings and beak bashings. The old professor lit his pipe and killed the aroma.

The door behind me suddenly opened—I could feel the stale breeze it shoved in from the hall—and instantly slammed. In a tattered tan trench coat, an enraged Weintraub stormed to the front of the table. Like a losing football coach at half time, he smashed down a black notebook. "I have been disgraced and insulted by this student," he began, addressing the committee and ignoring me. It was not my happiest moment. In fact, until a few months ago, it was the darkest hour of my life.

I can tell you, truthfully, that I did not fall apart. I stood my ground and argued with him for an hour—like Custer debating with Sitting Bull. The other committee members stared at me, sometimes with compassion and sometimes with dismay; they stared at him with hate. Neither of them had the courage speak, let alone rescue me.

I got through it—what else can I say? I watched as my four years of work, dedicated to graduating *summa,* were beaten down to *cum laude* by one man's vindictiveness and insecurity. Weintraub had expected me to pick out some poor, dead, mostly forgotten, generally ignored nineteenth-century philosopher and rip him to shreds. He expected me to flex my newly found Weintraubian muscles before his colleagues. Instead, I had written a naïve, impassioned plea for a closer, kinder examination of human creative powers. I had asserted that we can know more than we are told that we may actually know. Perhaps I had come a little too close to the truth. Maybe I was completely wrong. For some reason, way beyond my ability to apprehend, my idea threatened Weintraub—nearly terrified him. When my oral exam was over, I held my tears neatly in check all the way down the hall, out of the building, past the flashing Frisbees and slashing starlings, to Dunster Street. Then, sobbing like a baby, I headed for the nearest bar.

"Somebody's been calling all night for you, Sock," the student working the night desk in the foyer of Mather House hollered after me when I finally found my way home. "Sock" was short for Socrates, which is what my housemates called me. I was smashed by then and wanted to sleep or die—I felt as if either would do. "In my room," I mumbled, thinking that it was my mother or father calling to see how I'd done on my orals.

"I have called to explain," a deep, solid, careful voice said to me.

"Fuck you, Terry, I'm in no mood for your Weintraub impersonation," I slurred, thinking that it was my roommate, who had let me buy him drinks all night, then vanished with his girlfriend.

"Excuse me for calling you at this hour, but I was obviously distressed by today's examination. Please give me a chance to explain." The voice was thick, demanding. It was Weintraub.

"Oh, well, water under the bridge. I'll just have to learn to be happy teaching third grade in Boise."

"I have taken you too far, too fast. I thought that you were ready—but I saw today that you were not."

"Not ready for what? To lick your goddamn boots all my life? That was a great fuckin' paper, and you know it."

"Watch your language with me, young man," he said—though with patience. "Get a grip."

"I know disenfranchisement when it kicks me in the ass," I said angrily, choking back my tears.

"If I had, in truth, renounced my feelings for you, my respect for you, I would simply have patted you on the back today, like my colleagues do to their students, winked at the professor next to me, given you a B plus, and sent you on your merry, mediocre way. I have seen it a hundred times."

"So when you kick the shit out of someone, give him a C, and make him look like a fool, that means you respect him?"

"No! It means you have hope for him! It means that you believe that he might be that one student in a lifetime. It means that you test him by fire."

"Well, your pyrotechnics burned me up."

"Perhaps. I want you to study with me, to do your doctorate with me. I will see to it that you get the Irving Fellowship."

"I don't think so. I've applied to a couple other schools," I said.

"Where? No one can teach you what I can."

"Catholic University, the University of Toronto. There's some guy at Catholic named Dougherty; he writes about immortality."

"I've never heard of him."

"He's damn good."

"I've never heard of him, and you know better than to settle for 'good.'"

"I know better than to take another licking."

"You don't comprehend—do you? If you return and study with me, I will teach you exactly what it is you desire to know. I can answer the questions you posed in your paper. But you must be patient. Don't think that wisdom comes in an instant of grace. Wisdom, if it comes at all, comes only through the most rigorous process of mental discipline that you can imagine. Wisdom is not free."

"I don't know. I worked hard for my *summa*. I don't know. I'll call you. I'm drunk, and I'm sleepy. I don't know."

"Wait. Don't hang up. I want to tell you one thing before you hang up. This you must remember whether you study with me or with anyone else: The servant never instructs the master on the master's gaping holes—the servant gapes at them in wonder. Understand this, and you will greatly lessen your chances of a kicked butt—next time."

"Gosh, that's really insightful. Thanks, Professor, you've made my day." I hung up the phone.

I never studied directly under Weintraub again. I went to Catholic University and finished a PhD under Dougherty. I introduced Father Dougherty to Professor Weintraub, and they became friends. Weintraub asked me to return to Harvard on a number of occasions, but I always avoided a direct response until he offered other means of interacting. Eventually, he invited me to proofread his manuscripts; later, he asked me to index them—a task similar, in his mind, to washing the feet of God. He and I spent two summers together in Paris at the Sorbonne studying Descartes. He wanted me to spend a semester with him in Heidelberg and study Hegel with Dieter Heinrich, but I had just married. We were never teacher and student again. I still correspond, on occasion, with his wife, Judy.

I am not certain that I was ever again a student under anyone after the examination. I was a different person after that afternoon in Harvard Yard. Different by default. I was no longer a *philo sophia,* a lover of wisdom. I became ordinary—in love mostly with myself—I became a writer. One of a billion chroniclers of the *dharna* of life that kneels before this dizzy, decaying, dying world spinning around my front porch. A solemn grazer in the night, when all cows are black—with a burp and a moo and a chew. A knight of necropsy, a prince of prattle, a king of leers, a jester trapped in the labyrinth of folly in the cellar beneath the servants' quarters, deep inside the castle of the squeamish gods. But sometimes I believe, in the darkest corner of my ebon heart, that I am a tale twitcher like none of them has ever even imagined.

"Think carefully, son of Tydeus, and draw back; do not hope to be equal to the god in thinking, since the family of the deathless gods and of mortals who walk this earth is never the same."

Fuck you—Apollo.

De brodiorum Usu, et Honestate Chopinandi

—Rabelais, *Pantagruel*

Author's May 30 Conversation with Sylvia Johnson, Continued

"How long do you think we'll be gone?" I relented after Sylvia and I had fed her children and sent them dashing back into the afternoon heat and their cat confrontations. I had found my old canvas duffel bag and was kicking through the pile of clothes on the floor beside my bed in search of a clean pair of socks.

"Your house is a disgrace. You should have more respect for where you live—for who you are ..." Sylvia began as she straightened the blankets on the bed.

"It's a trailer—not a house. I'm a writer—not a maid. If I had wanted a wife, I'd have remarried. And I'm trying to pack my clothes—not hold a colloquy on my value as a human being or a seminar on housekeeping. I did enough of that with Brenda. That's how people get divorced. How long do you think we'll be gone? Do I need to get someone to feed the cats?" I asked, grabbing the blankets from her and tossing them, with my best pose of defiance, in a corner of the room.

"Get me to Yellowstone. You'll be back tomorrow," she said, changing her tactics and joining me in the sock hunt.

"If they're rolled up, they're probably clean." I smiled at her. "And what if your dear husband has finally flipped it and isn't anywhere near Yellowstone?"

"Then bring me back here, and I'll leave you alone. Here's a pair," Sylvia said, cautiously sniffing at the white cotton socks that she held at arm's length.

"You're sucking me in on this—both of you—sucking me in," I grumbled, holding open the duffel bag.

Sylvia flipped the socks into the bag. "I know," she replied, brown eyes sparkling. "Tell me what Nathan meant in that note to you. What are the fahoes?"

"*Fahoes* is our lazy slang for 'falls holes'—maybe 'false holes'—I don't know. I didn't make it up. There's a place here in Idaho, in the Hagerman valley, about forty miles from where we grew up, sorta by our grandparents' house, where the Snake River runs really deep through a gorge. The river bottom is all old lava flows, jutting rocks, caves and lava cones and tubes, most of it underwater. There is a dam about a mile upstream from the fahoes. Sometimes they close the dam for irrigation, exposing the river bottom. With the river cut off, there are big pools of dark green water that settle in the lava ponds. When the dam was closed, we'd go swimming in these pools, exploring the caves, diving from the cliffs. When the river was running, the rocks would tear you to shreds, so we stayed away. Nate and I kind of discovered the fahoes—you have to walk about half a mile through the sagebrush. We'd take our friends there."

"Girls?"

"Mostly girls," I laughed. We sat, side by side, on my bed. Sylvia scooted away from me to the foot.

"So why do you owe him one from the fahoes? What'd he do?" Sylvia asked me.

"When we were juniors in high school, we went swimming down there. Everybody was pretty drunk …"

"Except for Nathan," she interrupted with disdain.

"Especially Nathan," I retorted. "I was the sober one."

"Baloney. Look at you now. Nathan said you were always getting him in trouble."

"Just like him to blame it on me." I giggled and leaned away from her, against the wall of the trailer, which served as my headboard. "The truth is that Nathan taught me most of my bad habits. You forget he's almost two years older than me, and he's bigger than me. He's always been bigger than me. I was the smart little runt. I skipped first grade. Nathan was my protector and my idol. He was a *crazy* man in high school. I was far more subdued. We spent a lot of time together. I admired him, so I imitated him. Then we went to college. I went to Harvard and kept going downhill. Nathan went to Brigham Young, got religion, and found Jesus—but just because he got religion doesn't mean he never partied. Nathan used to dare me to do stuff that I wouldn't have thought of in my wildest dreams. Except Nathan used to *do it*—not dream it."

Sylvia wiggled uncomfortably on my bed. "He was a virgin when he married me."

"Whatever." I choked back another giggle.

"He's a good Mormon."

"Yeah. He's a good Mormon now, so he says. He used to be *fun.*"

"Tell me about the fahoes. I don't want to hear stories about his drinking."

"That's why you've never heard about the fahoes—it *is* a drinking story. It was a great, hot, sunny summer day. Everyone was drinking beer, swimming, heading off into the bushes with their girlfriends …"

"Everyone but Nathan," she insisted.

"*Especially* Nathan," I laughed. "Hell, he was in the bushes with *my* girlfriend." Sylvia started to get up in disgust, but I reached out, grabbed her arm, pulled her back down next to me, and hurried on with the story. "So, Nathan heard a real loud horn. One of those big powered air-horns. He had never heard it before. Because every time we had been to the fahoes, there was either water covering them—so we couldn't go swimming—or else the rocks were bare, and we could get down to them."

"So why did they blow the horn?"

"Someone from the irrigation company blew the horn to signal that the dam was being opened. Three of us guys were in the lava tubes. I had swum along underwater in a forty-foot-long lava tube to the back of a cave. Maybe the other two guys couldn't hold their breath as long, or, I don't know, I don't think they'd been swimming there before. They were both pretty plastered. We all were. Anyway, those two stopped in what we called the 'first cave'—the first place where you could catch your breath. I never did hear the horn. Nathan heard it; he dove into the trench, found the cave opening, and pulled me out right before the water from the dam hit the opening. He and I were strong enough to swim out of it. The other two … we never saw them. They never even found the bodies. I doubt if they ever came out of the lava tube. God knows how far down the river it ends. Our girlfriends had waited on the bank and watched. After a while, after Nathan and I crawled out, the girls started screaming. There wasn't a goddamn thing we could do. Nathan and I sat on the bank of the river and watched the water rush by us, filling every crack and cranny. We held each other and cried. That's what he means when he says 'fahoes.' Nathan got me out. He saved my life. I'm going to feed my cats."

Alexander, the rotten, and Cleo, the truculent, both tabbies, came racing to me the minute I opened the door with a bowl of leftover chicken noodle soup and soggy crushed crackers. They rubbed against and around my calves in a convincing cat *contredanse*. I poured the soup into a rusty pie plate on the edge of the porch. Sylvia's children ran to us and jumped with glee.

"Nice kitties," one of them said, reaching for Alexander, who was busy lapping up the soup while Cleo slunk out of reach.

Wrong.

I always thought that the term "social anarchist" was a blatant contradiction—a professorial paradox conjured up one stormy night in the damp basement of an empty library by an inept graduate student hopelessly striving for originality—until I found Alexander creeping about my porch one morning. Is it possible to raze all collective norms politely? Can one, in reality, civilly decimate civilization? Kaylynn found out when she tried to tow the long and lean Alexander away from his leftover chicken noodle soup. He rotated cordially in her sweaty hands, hissed graciously, and then gave her a set of claw marks on her forearm that she will carry for the rest of her life. I kicked Alexander, hissing and meowing, into the air and off the porch—not that it hurt him, or taught him anything either. My retaliation inflicted some sort of panicked hysteria into Sylvia's bantam corps. For principles only a child psychologist could relish, now they were terrified of *ME*. All three children joined in an incessant howling fest for the thirty-mile drive from my trailer to Nathan's parents' house in Burley, Idaho.

> Of them Scripture says, "Thy righteousness shall go before thee; the glory of the Lord shall be thy reward" (Isa. lviii. 8). The intellect of these men remains then constantly in the same condition, since the obstacle is removed that at times has intervened between the intellect and the object of its action; it continues forever in that great delight ... We have explained this in our work and others have explained it before us.
>
> —Maimonides, *The Guide for the Perplexed*

Excerpt from a Letter from Harold Weintraub to the Author, Excerpt from the Author's Reply, and Excerpt from an Article by Harold Weintraub. First Letter Dated October, 24, 1995

I spoke with Father Dougherty yesterday. He contacted me first. He stated that he is most concerned about your behavior and about your attitude in your preparations for defending your doctoral dissertation. Dougherty said that your mental state was lethargic, that your approach to your studies was dilatory—at best. He believes that you may not be able to defend your thesis successfully, and he has asked me to speak with you.

I only recognize, but do not address, that my advice may be neither apropos nor appropriate and that you may (knowing you—you will) disregard it out of hand. For the sake of philosophy, it is vital that you finish, and that you do well, in the defense of your thesis. This is not a statement that I would often make. But in your case, it is true. Though I have often questioned your maturity, even denounced your impatience, I have never doubted your aptitude or intellect.

Toughness is requisite in a philosopher. Enough; you will do what you will; only that much is certain.

Elijah, my "immortal" in New York, introduced me to Miriam. She is a dark, beautiful woman who happens to believe that she is the sister *of Moses*. Her understanding of ancient Middle Eastern languages is so extensive that it intimidated me; even Professor Wright's knowledge would be eclipsed. Elijah will not tell me where she lives (she is visiting him in New York); but she would be a splendid subject for study.

I am nearly ready to publish my incipient thoughts on these immortals. I can now proffer, with some certainty, the following rough framework.

A. Immortals take the personae of historically significant individuals within their own religious traditions.

B. The anima is also that of the adopted figure. An immortal will always choose a character with balanced proportions of compassion and self-esteem. (I have personally examined several "splits" that forcefully present themselves as some form of Hegelian world historical personage, for example, a Napoleon; these types are far more assertive and compulsive, but they *do not* believe that they are immortal.)

C. In spite of A and B, immortals realize that they can never convince non-immortals of the reality of their "eternal" being. Thus they are generally introspective and, when communicating, mostly obscure. One might be led to think that this is a method of escaping detection, but those immortals who have trusted me enough to speak openly are astoundingly accurate in historical and linguistic detail.

D. I would estimate that the *average* IQ among the immortals is 170.

E. They frequently meet and have extensive interaction with other immortals. They quietly but relentlessly seek out their own kind.

The last particular is the most startling. And, I deem, it may be the key to preventing the spread of this disease.

Imagine the following scenario (which I consider representative). A young man is raised in a strictly religious setting. His IQ exceeds that of genius, yet the information given to him by his community is closely regulated and extremely context-specific. His parents are highly supportive of his acumen, but only within dogmatic norms. When the youngster reaches puberty, he finds himself torn between erogenic desire and a tight-fitting and, most probably, theosophic mental frame of reference.

It is at this point that the young man would be most vulnerable to an overture from an immortal. The immortals would be constantly seeking a young man (or young woman—though the feminine reproductive cycle, because it grounds the woman's psyche in time, makes a Miriam an even more infrequent event) who fits this description; such a young man would be replacement fodder for them. The young man is approached by the immortal, who is simply an older version of the youth. The immortal introduces himself as, say, Enoch. The young man is curious, youthfully skeptical, confused. The youth, secure only in his intellect, will test the immortal on historical, theological, linguistic, and other subtleties, only to find that the immortal cannot be cornered.

The young man is finally corrupted, but in a fashion that is, within his own moral and intellectual frame of reference, perfectly reasonable. Over time the "immortal" convinces the youth that he too must put on the mantle of righteousness—that, e.g., it is time that Moses returned to prepare his people, that he is the man for that job, that the young man *is* Moses. The young man simply does not know better (other). Becoming Moses is as easy as, for you and me, constructing a syllogism.

Enough of the immortals. Father Dougherty and I have an offer to make you. After you successfully defend your dissertation, we have arranged matters so that you can begin teaching at Boston College. You would be within the realm of the Catholics, something Dougherty finds vital, but you would be in proximity to me. We could, finally, work on the problem of the immortals together.

Judy sends her love ...

[Remainder of letter omitted.]

*   *   *   *

Here are excerpts from my reply, dated November 14, 1995.

Dear Professor Weintraub,

It is difficult for me, in a difficult time, to respond to your letter. I only tell you now so that you will understand that there are things that occur in my life besides ... Fichte. A couple of weeks ago I admitted Brenda, my wife, into the county hospital in Arlington, Virginia; it is about three miles from where we live. She was bleeding internally due to her second tubal pregnancy. Her fears of losing another fetus (she has had three miscarriages) and of becoming sterile were so great that she delayed telling me about the pain for six hours.

By the time I got her to the hospital, she had lost so much blood that no pressure registered. They wheeled her into the emergency room and cut her open, without prep, on the gurney. The doctor told me that he scooped handfuls of blood out of her abdomen, frantically attempting to find and clip the ruptured fallopian tube. Her heart stopped twice on the table. Each time, they robbed death and brought her back. It was the stuff that soap operas are made of.

I sat in the lobby while anticipating the notification, languishing without love, waiting without compassion. I only wanted it to be over, one way or another, so that I could get back to my writing. Her life—or death—was completely incidental. I have become that hard. I have become that which frightens me. So don't speak to me about being tough. If I make it through the defense of the dissertation, fine, if not … I have my writing. I could not be any more distant from myself. She left me two days ago.

As for your initial hypotheses on the immortals, be glad that you have not published them yet. A few words of criticism: 1. Of those immortals whom we have studied, there is absolutely no record of their existence—anywhere. This is a huge mystery. In my opinion, it *must* be solved before we can speculate on any of the other aspects. These people are coming from somewhere. Where is that somewhere? 2a. Generally speaking, they are simple but learned. (An idea that you seem unable to entertain.) 2b. I wonder what relevance IQ has when time may not be considered as a factor in one's life decisions. If I believed I could live a thousand years—if I *really* believed it—I might tackle Mandarin and Ugaritic, etc. Why not? I believe I've got nothing but time. To repeat, their disease makes them simple but learned. 3. Why don't you follow your own advice? I remember when you first taught me that to understand the ancients, I had to take them at their word. You were right. One cannot understand Plato unless one takes him seriously as a writer and thinker of a magnitude that this world sees once in a thousand years. So why not take the immortals at face value—first? Do your refutation rag on them after you understand them. Regarding your "corrupting the young" scenario: did an immortal make such an offer to you when you were a kid? Sure reads like it. Must have scared the bejesus out of you. But why should they intimidate you now?

My advice is to go back to your religious roots. Take seriously your heritage. Take Elijah seriously …

[Remainder of letter omitted.]

* * * *

Excerpts from the article "Elijah Comes to Dinner." Published in *The Jewish Quarterly*, summer 1996, written by Harold Weintraub under the pen name "Rabbi Migosh."

So, upon the advice of a friend, my wife and I invited him to dinner.

Elijah is a small man, hardly five feet tall. His theophoric name means "Yahweh is my God." He appears to be in his mid-seventies, though, by his account, he is three thousand years old—give or take a hundred. His hair is gray. It grows in patches on the back and sides of his head. He currently lives in an apartment in New York. He says that he is semiretired, that there are no permanent pensions for prophets, so he takes on odd jobs as a translator at the U.N.

My wife went to great lengths to cook a completely kosher meal for him, though he ruined it by taking the wrong plate for the meat. He said, sensing my wife's displeasure, that dietary laws were not immutable and that he was hungry and required a larger plate. His appetite was hearty—especially for a man of such meager build. He made a joke about all the empty seats that await him at Passover, observing that, in spite of his appetite, he had only one mouth and only one stomach.

I asked him about his attendance, or lack thereof, at circumcisions. He explained that recent medical data proving that various forms of cancer of the sexual organs are higher in marriages in which the male is uncircumcised justified his earlier complaints that Israel had ignored that covenant. "All the laws of God have a reason. If one lives long enough or thinks deeply enough, one will discover the truth within the law. I attend as many circumcisions as I am able—a random sampling—I am not Saint Nicholas."

My wife wondered about his purpose at present and asked why he had put off death for so long. He replied, "I appear to men from time to time to remind them that the law is transcendent. For example, I remember a Yehoshua ben Levi. He bragged that because he had obeyed all the laws, obeyed them to the letter, that he was representative of the ideal Jew. I came to him, reminded him that the way of the saintly was a higher way, that the *Hasid* also followed the law of the heart, the *devarim ha-musarim la-lev*.

"There is far too much analysis going on in the average rabbinical mind," Elijah continued. "The Pharisaic notion that the common man *(am haaretz)* cannot be a *Hasid* is simply false. Doesn't anyone read Abravanel's *Dialoghi di Amore* anymore? Abravanel was a daring man, a good, though egocentric, friend."

Sensing that it was my turn, I asked if I might address him on a more obscure subject. "I have three questions for you," I said to Elijah. "First, why are you the only prophet who was allowed to return to the Holy Mountain of Revelation? Second, is the mountain called Sinai the same or different from the mountain Horeb? And finally, where, exactly where, is the Mountain of Revelation?"

He smiled at me, as if I were a confused child. Then he said, "I assume that you know the *Heichalot Rabbatie,* the *Sefer Heichalot,* the *Heichalot Zutrati*—so that you understand the *yordei merkavah*?" I nodded that, yes, I was acquainted with the palace literature and that I understood about the path of ascension in the chariot. "Good. The answers are not in them; though, as the son of Maimon noted: 'The secret of the Torah is in the wheels,'" he said with a laugh.

"And the *Sefer Yetzirah*?" he persisted. I nodded again, indicating that I had read the Book of Creation and was familiar with the mystical numbers. "Fine, fine, do not delve there either. And what of the *Sefer Ha-Zohar*?" he asked, his voice deep and serious. I nodded a third time. "Look beyond it," he said.

At this point, I opened my mouth to demur, but he brushed aside any comment I might have made with a wave of his hand. "You know the *olam ha-atzilut*?" he asked me with the conclusiveness of a final question.

"I know of the world of emanation," I answered.

"Where is it?"

"You can't be serious," I protested.

"Where is it? Tell me. Where is the world of emanation? If I am to answer three of your questions, you must answer only one of mine."

"It is ... it is where God lives. It is the point from which God sends His love or grace—His *shefa*—to mankind."

"It is here," Elijah pointed with a finger to his forehead—between his eyes. "And here," he reached over the table and pointed at my forehead. "So, too, by the way, is the answer to your third question. And, as you know, Professor, the answers to the first two questions are deducible, or at least discernible, from the third."

At our urging and, given the amount of wine he had imbibed, in high spirits, Elijah relived his confrontation with Ahab over Naboth's vineyard.

[Remainder of article omitted.]

> I see sitting before me a man already in the angelic state, untouched by the vices of the body, although he is still in human flesh. The man of God said to me, "I have lived ninety years on this island ... I lived fifty years in my native land. The sum of the years of my life until now is one hundred and forty. I have been told, that I must wait here, in the flesh for the Day of Judgment."
>
> —*Navigatio Sancti Brendani Abbatis*

> Triviality is not at issue here, but a simple question of sanity or insanity.
>
> —Aurelius (quoting Epictetus), *To Himself*

Excerpt from the Journal of Father Jerome Dougherty

Evening of May 14, cloister in Como, Italy.

The train from Milano to Como winds through several of the most beautiful valleys I have seen in my travels. There is nothing like this area in the world, unless it is across the Adriatic in Albania, where I have not yet traveled. The Alps, seen from the south, from underneath, have a warm, green belly of luxuriant, rolling pastures dotted with cattle and sheep; then there are the breasts of wilder hills, clothed with a vibrant, shimmering, green deciduous forest and not yet tamed by man. Como hangs as a jeweled pendant between the craggy cliffs. The city is crowned, from above and far behind, by the unforgettable gray-faced glacier that creeps below the white-tipped peaks of the Alps.

Monsignor Leonardo Greco of the Curia Romana and his assistant Davide Palucia, a minor official of the first degree, met me at the train station in Como. Both are assigned to the Secretariat of State. Greco had rented a red Fiat sedan, and Palucia helped load my luggage into the trunk because we could find no porter. Palucia is a dark, thin, not tall, young man who has an aura of callousness. Monsignor Greco is a large, corpulent man of about fifty. Yet his face, his nose, even his chin, are all sharply defined, not rounded, as if his visage has been gradually chiseled by the grisly experiences of his life. He wears a plain black wool suit and looks all too unmistakably like a *commendatore*. His hair is gray. His eyes—no matter—I am now not facing what must be written.

The morgue (we went straight to the morgue since Greco insisted that the body be identified by the Vatican representative of the order) was in an old, thick-walled, two-story, red brick building that sat inconspicuously behind a modern city office complex. Circulation of air in the building was very poor, and we were met at the door by an overpowering smell of antiseptic, embalming fluids, ether, and ... death. We used the back entrance. The narrow hallway was completely lined—floor, walls, and ceiling—with ceramic tile. Originally white, the tile had faded to yellow due to age and countless scrubbings with antiseptic, well up the sides of the walls.

The coroner was—no matter.

[Author's note: Some text is crossed out here; there is also a scribbled marginal note in Latin. I would translate it thus: "God does not play dice—but he does play fools."]

Of all the men I have known, of all the men I have loved, none was kinder, more gentle, as full of grace, and as learned as Father Domenico Patricelli. None more perfect. None closer to God. None more faithful to his parish. Yet Father Patricelli was insane.

His insanity was an enigma, a guileless, innocent—a sweet illness. He accepted, without question, that he would live forever, that his love (the like of which I have never known in man) rendered him immune from death. His was a disturbing, convoluted, nearly transparent sickness. He almost never spoke of his "gift" of eternal life, denying all forms of psychiatric treatment, refusing to cast his most precious pearl before ...

His death was a heinous mockery of his beautiful life. Father Patricelli was found on his kitchen floor still in a white alb—having, Greco speculated, just returned from Mass when he was murdered. This would mean that it was nearly a day before the body was discovered. His hands and feet had been wired together behind his back. The wire was thin, and Father Patricelli had completely severed his right hand in the struggle to free himself. The corpse wheeled before us was emaciated and wrinkled; the legs and the feet were swollen; the head and shoulders were covered by a white towel. I noticed that an old surgical scar across the lower abdomen had turned purple.

"This may be most unpleasant and unusual for you, Father," the coroner, a thick-boned older woman, cautioned me in Italian, without any emotional expression, as she removed the towel.

His head! My God! What atrocities they had committed on his head! They had ripped his eyes from his face. They had driven table knives (taken from Patricelli's kitchen drawer, according to Greco) into his eye sockets and then plunged them into his ears. They had wrenched one knife so savagely into the skull that the knife had broken in two. He had, during the ordeal, bitten his tongue in half. I could not identify the corpse, for there was no face—only shredded muscle and white bone caked with black and crusted blood. "Is it Domenico? Oh my God! Is it really Domenico?" I cried. Monsignor Greco told me that he was sorry but yes, it was, and that identification by fingerprints had already been made. He thanked the coroner, and then he and the young Palucia escorted me from the room. I had to steady myself by gripping Palucia's arm.

As we left the body, I was overwhelmed by a passion I have kept deeply suppressed; I was overcome by a loneliness that is part of the heavy price of celibate existence. I realized that I knew Father Patricelli only by his countenance. I did not, could not, identify the body without the face. With the death of my mother, I no longer know any human being by touch. I distantly remember, from a time before my vows, the familiar and intimate touch and touching of the body of the only woman I have known carnally. I knew that body. I would have recognized … [Author's note: This is not my ellipsis. Father Dougherty left this sentence unfinished.]

Once outside the building, Monsignor Greco had to help me to the car. Palucia followed us. I wept at the hideousness of Domenico's murder. I wondered what kind of horror could destroy such purity. For a moment, I wondered how God could let such wickedness exist …

[Author's note: two pages of text deleted at this point by me.]

Rather than maunder about the goodness of God (which I know in my heart is as real as the morning sun outside this window), I must return to my description of Father Patricelli. He was one of the subjects of an unpublished papal treatise that I wrote nearly forty years ago on the theological and psychological problems presented by the members of the Order of the Beloved. The paper was my first assignment from the Vatican and was the impetus for my first encounter with Father Patricelli.

Though the focus of my mind was narrower, and my spirit was less docile then (and though the science of psychology has advanced a great distance), I would not withdraw any of the conclusions I reached in that study. The description therein of Father Patricelli, even the physical description (for he seemed to me not to have aged one day in the forty years that I knew him—but that is the case with many of those that we love and with whom we grow old), is as accurate as anything I could write from this sorrow. I miss him so …

On the Author's Travels with Sylvia Johnson and Her Children, May 30

Lottie and Archie Johnson's four-bedroom yellow brick rambler in the southwest corner of Burley, Idaho, was dark and deserted. Sylvia shut off the engine and headlights of her Caravan when we were about three houses away and coasted up to the curb right in front. This was silly, given that it was barely twilight and that Burley is an unaffected agricultural town—the neighbors on one side of the Johnsons sat half-asleep on their porches, waiting for a cool breeze from the desert, while those on the other side polished off the potato salad and the olives on the condiment tray from their barbecue.

"Hand me the bag," Sylvia demanded as we coasted in.

"What bag?" I asked, reasonably enough—since there were five or six of them in the minivan.

"Get the guns," she muttered. "You kids will stay right here in the car. Your uncle and I are going to go see if Grandma's home, and then we'll come and get you," she ordered those in the rear.

"The kids are all asleep. I'm not their uncle, and I'm not carrying a gun into that house—or any house."

"You seal the back door. I'll take the front. I'll need to keep an eye on the kids until we've secured the area," Sylvia commanded, having pilfered a term or two from her husband. She reached over the seat and grabbed the black diaper bag.

"What d'you say we knock on the door—like regular people?"

"You don't get this, do you?" she asked as she snatched the tiny Walther PPK 380 from the bag. Her hand and her voice were both shaking. "My husband is in a lot of trouble. Do you know what his job is? He catches killers. He doesn't make them up like you pretend to do. He catches real ones. I don't know who Nathan's after, or who's after him, or why he needs me to come to him. All I know is that my husband is in a lot of trouble. Maybe you're to blame, maybe not. But I think you think you are. I think you feel guilty. Seal the back door." She shoved the pistol at me.

"I'm not sealing. I don't know how to seal, and I don't want to learn. And I never asked Nathan to do anything. *He asked me.*"

"Then why are you here?" she demanded; the pistol remained extended. "Why did you come along?"

I didn't have a very good answer for her. If I had been concerned with my book, I would have stayed in my trailer and gone through Nathan's files. I certainly was not in Burley, Idaho, to experience the nightlife, the unbridled joy of an extended vacation with three kids, or the unmitigated thrill and challenge of keeping sane a pregnant woman who thought her husband was in mortal danger. Sylvia was right. I had come along for one reason: guilt. I accepted the pistol and strapped the four-inch-wide elastic bellyband around my waist. The gun rested uncomfortably but solidly at the base of my spine, beneath my sweatpants and T-shirt. "I'm not shooting anybody unless they shoot me first," I said, with much conviction and little thought.

Sylvia laughed at me and jumped from the minivan. "Cover the back door," she said.

I don't know why Aunt Lottie and Uncle Archie went to the trouble to lock the doors to their home. They kept keys under the doormats to both the front and rear entrances. They had done this for as long as I could remember, and even though plenty of relatives and all the neighbors knew about the keys, I don't think that my aunt and uncle had ever been robbed.

As kids, Nathan and I had loved nothing more than spending the night with each other. In spite of the fact that we lived some forty miles apart, one of us managed to find a ride to Burley or to Twin Falls nearly every weekend. So I knew the sidewalk, the driveway, the garage, the yard, and the house by heart. I did a little detective work on my own as I trotted around to the back door. Glancing in the side window of the garage, I saw that Archie's old powerboat and older Ford Bronco were gone. I'd have bet my small bank account that he and Aunt Lottie were fishing, probably at Redfish Lake in the Sawtooth Mountains—it would be cool there. In case I was wrong, I listened for a moment at the back door. Dead silence. I lifted the mat, picked up the key, and let myself in.

> They were advised to conclude with their brother-enemies a temporary truce, during which the titans should be induced to help them churn the Milky Ocean of immortal life for its butter—*Amrita, (a* = not, *mrita* = mortal) "the nectar of deathlessness."
>
> —Joseph Campbell, *The Hero with a Thousand Faces*

Excerpts from the article, "The Myths of Immortality," in *The Search for the Everlasting: Collected Essays of Harold Weintraub*, Oxford University Press, 1998, pp. 122–3. (The essay was originally published in the *Review of Metaphysics*, winter 1989, under the pen name "Doctor Rushdit." Footnotes have been omitted.)

Shall we assume that immortality is achievable? If it is not, there is no point in discussing the matter. Our next question must be "What is immortality?" I have shown that for the Brahman, the Taoist, the Buddhist, the Jew, and the Christian, immortality is an *aufhebung,* a mystical union, an absorption of the particular and finite into (and here all differ in specifics) some greater or more permanent form of being. More specifically, the myth of Osiris and the forty-two judges; the cult of Mithra, judge of the dead; the resurrection and final judgment of the dead by Jesus Christ; the Messianic prophecies that covenant to raise the righteous from the dust—all of these (and many more) make one fatal supposition: *To live eternally, one must die.* This is rather like maintaining that to satiate hunger, one must starve, or to keep warm at night, one should sleep in a freezer. If immortality is *immortalitas,* then the myths of life after death, but only through death (myths that, whatever else they might accomplish, teach the absolute inevitability of death), might well hinder, obscure, even prevent the achievement of the state of immortality ...

There is a plant, *Xeranthemum annuum,* a white flower so pure in fragrance and flawless in structure that it is called the *immortelle*—the everlasting flower. How does this flower achieve its particular brand of immortality? Very simple. It survives in its perfection. It *is*—hence it cannot not be. Here is an immortal not subject to the myths of man. Here is an eternal-in-itself because it is not indoctrinated from birth that it must obtain otherness to become real, that it must die to live. Immortality is its nature. Its nature is to be black at the root, with a white flower sweet as honeyed milk. If one were to offer a consistent and viable theory of immortality, one might begin with the man who first discovered "goldenrod in sylvan dale." Though I must counsel that it is difficult for mortals to unearth *Moly*—by which name its black root is sometimes known. (To avoid being again adjudged "an intellectual anarchist," I faithfully conducted a set of controlled experiments in my own plot last spring with twelve *immortelle* plants, for I have a friend who shares the root. Unfortunately I will not be able to report my findings until next year because a late spring frost killed all the bulbs. I stand determined to make a second effort, the Tishbite, who calls himself the Gileadite, willing.)

Elijah said to Elisha, "Tell me what I can do for you, before I am taken from you."

Elisha said, "Let me inherit a double share of your spirit."

"You have asked a hard thing," said Elijah.

—2nd Kings 2:9–10

Letter, dated May 16, from Harold Weintraub to Father Jerome Dougherty, marked "received" by Dougherty on May 25

Dear Jerome,

Excruciating news (though I suppose, from one perspective, *sub specie aeternitatis,* it is quite humorous and that Spinoza would find all of this uproarious), my friend, the one who called himself Elijah, is dead. Our student knows of him and met him once, I believe, on a trip to New York. Elijah and I had exchanged letters for twenty years. I flew him to Cambridge for dinner on occasion.

My wife was utterly taken with him—was nearly persuaded by him! She could speak, very technically, on her symbiosis theories, and he would follow her with precision and apparent ease. To test him, she would press him on some point of belief in unification, as the Gaia types are wont to do; he would smile condescendingly and tell her that science still had a long road in front of it and then tersely present a devastating and technically correct criticism of the unification theory. Astounding!

He was most interesting company for me as well. He really thought himself to be Elijah. He once confided in me, privately, that he knew Moses and that he had helped edit the Pentateuch!

He said that the two of them (Moses, understand, is dallying about as well) had taken a particular liking to a young carpenter named Jesus. He claimed the young fellow (scarcely thirty) cherished being called the Son of Man and insisted upon it. He told me that Jesus had been crucified but had risen from the grave, not to heaven, but to this earth, and that He was still alive. Making Him … the … what? The What Not! The Ultimate Eschatologist! Liberated Libido Libretto! The meaningless become the Meaning Thus: no more zealots for David Strauss; but such a sordid and tainted echelon are His vicars, who have been lying for millennia through their collective teeth.

I have well over a hundred pages of notes from interviews with Elijah and had planned, someday, to do a book—although I'm not certain how I would have approached it. I have always found it most difficult to write coherently on the subject of immortality—witness the previous paragraph! Imagine, on the other hand, the *elegantiae psychologicae* of pulling it off. There is eternity waiting in such a work. *Amour-vanite* forever. In any event, it is now malapropos.

I gave a paper at Columbia last Tuesday, and because I had not heard from the old kook for several months, I looked him up. I took a taxi across town to his squalid lodgings on Sixty-second Street. The door to his apartment, which was on the top floor, was unlocked. I let myself in and found the body in the bedroom. Elijah had been tied to the bed. The policeman or detective who came later told me he had been dead for almost a week. (New York smells so wretched these days that no one had noticed.) The head had been mangled in the most loathsome fashion. He kept cats, and they had been eating at his face and then drinking out of the toilet. Their round little footprints were all over the place. Dry, black blood. I cursed the cats and threw a book at them. Though, in retrospect, they had probably kept the rats away. His eyes and ears were gone, somehow gouged out by his murderer and then eaten, I suppose, by the cats; though I admit that the head was so ghastly that I did not inspect it in detail.

The odor, as you can imagine, was dreadful. I had not smelled death since the Korean War. It is a smell that never changes. It fades, as do all sense impressions, but the property, the moment, the essence (bad pun) of the sensation never departs. I think I shall write a book called *The Eternal Return of the Stench*—"*Umsonst, dass all mein Ekel schreit: Fluch, Fluch dem Schlunde der Ewigkeit!*"

I had always wanted to have you and that student of ours interview the man. Elijah told me that he knew all about your Order of the Beloved and, what was it? Three Mormonites or the like. He was endlessly entertaining, unfathomably insane. Do you think that those suffering from the disease could have somehow networked? I have been looking into the possibility. The three of us might work together on a book about these immortals. That would shake some foundations! We could spend our twilight years in the peace and quiet of the asylum of our choice.

Please let me know how the members of your Order are doing. I would like to visit Patricelli again. I am curious to hear his reaction to Elijah's death. Had it not been insulting to you, I would long ago have urged that we introduce these two remarkable men to each other.

If you hear from our student, tell him to write or to drop by. Perhaps I am getting old, but I miss him.

I would like to get together soon, at your convenience, to talk. We should all three get together.
[Signed]
Harold

On the Author's Travels with Sylvia Johnson and Her Children, May 30, Continued

The house was empty and dark. I could feel its darkness. I could smell its emptiness. Not the musty, dusty, deserted-for-months odor that houses get; it was the "Where the hell is everybody?" trail of scents that remains in a house whose occupants are just not there. I could smell that the last meal cooked was bacon and eggs. I could tell that someone had taken a shower just before they left, probably Uncle Archie because I vaguely perceived Old Spice. I pictured plump Lottie, my favorite aunt, who is redheaded—thanks to her hairdresser. I see her sitting in the Bronco, honking the horn, exhorting Archie to get off the toilet. Uncle Archie always headed for the pot just as the rest of his family climbed into the car. It drove them nuts. "If the rest of you'd take care of your business 'fore we started, it'd make one less road stop," he would say.

I turned on the light in the kitchen and trotted by the family room and hallway to the front door. "All cleared and sealed at your bidding, ma'am," I said, and saluted Sylvia through the screen door. "None dead. Two missing and probably fishing." I saluted again.

Sylvia turned and stomped back to her minivan in disgust. "You want to help me with these kids?" she asked from the curb while the next-door neighbor dumped the ashes from his grill in the gutter and then washed them down the drain with a garden hose.

"Only if I can call you 'ma'am' ... ma'am."

Once the kids were inside and spread out on the purple velour sofa in the living room, Sylvia went to work. I do not know how much investigative acumen a woman can absorb from a detective husband—by what type of diffusion I cannot guess—but Sylvia had somewhere and somehow gleaned a few trade secrets. Either that, or she was innately nosy. She prowled from room to room. She opened closets and cupboards, the clothes hamper, the refrigerator, and the wastebaskets. She played back the answering machine for clues.

Not that their destination wasn't conspicuous. I have already mentioned that Uncle Archie's boat was gone; so were his waders, his creel, his tackle box and poles, Lottie's boots and tennis shoes, their light jackets, sleeping bags, and tent. The biggest surprise was that either Lottie or Archie had left the insect repellent behind. It was sitting on the kitchen table.

"A clue! A clue! I know this means something," I said, clutching the bottle of repellent with one hand and grabbing behind my back for the pistol with the other. "Something gruesome ... something—unspeakable!"

"It certainly does." Sylvia smiled cruelly at me. "You and I are on our way to Yellowstone Park, and we now have no place to leave my children. Help me take them potty and then load them back in the car."

> Heaven is as much down as up, and as much up as down; as much behind as before, and as much before as behind and as much to one side as to any other. In fact, whoever has a true desire to be in heaven is in heaven spiritually at that very time. The high road there, which is the shortest road there, is run in terms of desires and not of paces of feet.
>
> —*The Cloud of Unknowing*

Excerpt from the Journal of Father Jerome Dougherty

May 24, in transit, Rome to Washington, DC.

I have kept a detailed recital of my few days in Como in this journal. Missing from this record, however, are my reflections on the death of a dear friend and on the five present members of the Order of the Beloved and on their dilemma. I must keep that in mind for this entry.

As noted, Monsignor Greco and his assistant, Palucia, accompanied me yesterday morning to the train that I took from Como to Rome. I have little respect for either of the men. Greco seemed far more concerned about sampling the regional cuisine and maximizing the use of his expense account than he did in solving the murder. He has spent most of the last week eating his way through every menu at every café in the city. His dilatory attitude affected the local police, who refused to make the case a priority when the Curia Romana's own representative displayed such disregard. This type of indolent behavior in the bureaucracy is something I have noted before: It is deemed worthy and appropriate to mimic the behavior of one's superior, especially if that superior's behavior is lackadaisical.

Greco's assistant, Davide Palucia, seems far more sinister in intent to me. (It just occurred to me that Palucia, in Italian, might be spelled "Paluzzia" or even

"Paluzzi.") He is, as I may have already written, a thin young man, deeply tanned, with dark hair and eyes. He dresses snappily in long trousers with high waists and baggy legs and silk shirts worn without a jacket or tie. His hair is long. Sometimes he even pulls it into a ponytail. His Italian is abrupt and often disrespectful; his English is limited to the coarse and vulgar, as if he learned the language in a movie theater or watching those horrid music videos. His family is old Italian. It is well known that the Palucia family is a powerful segment of the Mafia on the southeastern coast of the country. Still, I am no expert in the politics of the Church in Italy, and I certainly believe that the blessings of eternal life through our Savior and his holy Church should not be denied to any person …

While Greco ate, Palucia spent most of his time in what was, I am certain, a fruitless effort at interrogating the members of the Order. This caused them much unnecessary distress and seemed to me to be pointless, from the perspective of finding the murderer—unless Palucia suspects one of the members—a notion I find inconceivable …

Over the years, the names and faces in the Order of the Beloved have changed and yet have stayed the same. Most of its members come and go as they please. They are usually free to take assignments in other areas and often do so. For example, Father Richard Holden, who joined the Order in 1978, spent three arduous years secretly rebuilding the Church in Vietnam, in the early 80s, at the behest of Cardinal Benerdetta from the Philippines.

Father Holden became the unofficial spokesperson for the Order after the death of Patricelli. Richard Holden is a distinguished English gentleman of average build and height, with striking silver hair and prominent gray eyes. He lacks the breadth of acumen of Patricelli; but Holden is always marvelously composed and surprisingly well acquainted with numerous languages and cultures and with people. It is rumored in the cloister and elsewhere that he has occasional, but always clandestine, contact with His Holiness. Certainly, if not for his disease, Father Holden would be a significant and highly visible power within the Church.

Like Father Patricelli, Father Holden is extremely reluctant to speak about his immortality. For Richard, it is almost a matter of civility; he avoids the issue as a well-mannered gentleman with wealth would refrain from flaunting his riches before the indigent.

Thus, it was easy to understand my astonishment last week when Father Holden rapidly approached me on the oak-lined street that runs before the entrance to the cloister and the adjoining monastery. He had come directly from hearing confession. He was still in his black biretta and a white robe that flapped and folded behind him and thus replicated the intensity of his stride.

"Father Jerome, you have arrived safely," he said.

"I came as soon as I learned of Domenico's death," I answered. I had only minutes before seen Father Patricelli's corpse at the morgue. The hideousness of the injuries was very fresh in my mind.

"It is very good that you have come here. But you seem distraught. Your face is quite pale," he said. "I gather that you have been to view the body?"

"Yes."

"You should have come to the cloister first. I was notified by the maid and was the first—the only—member of the Order to see him. I apologize that you were put through this as well."

I could tell that he was anxious about speaking frankly with me. He did not do so, however, until Greco and Palucia had unloaded my luggage and left for their hotel.

"I assume that Patricelli spoke with you about our need to go to the States?" Holden stopped before me in the cloister portico, arms folded; we stood nose to nose, so to speak, for at six feet, he is just about my height.

"Yes," I answered.

"You did not act upon his solicitation?"

"I told him that it would take some time."

"And, I am certain that Domenico told you that we had precious little of that commodity. *Lo porti in camera da letto*," Father Holden said. A young boy, not more than ten, in worn black cotton pants and faded green cotton shirt, picked up my bags.

"He told me that the matter was urgent."

"And now, Father, I will tell you as well. In fact—and mark these words, for like Domenico, I will ask you only once—wait … no … now I must make an even more specific request. I need you not only to take the Order to the United States, I also need you to arrange ground transportation for the entire Order from Washington, DC, to the Southwest of the United States, to a place which I will describe in more detail once we are in America. And, as long as it is kept secret, I think you will find that His Holiness will give his approval.

"If there is anything you need during your stay here, please let me know. Shall we have dinner before you depart?" he asked as he escorted me, arm in arm, to a guest room in the monastery. I told him that we should. "Ah! Here is Father Dobo coming from the library. He also wishes to advise you of our exigency." Father Holden bade me good day.

Father Dobo, head bowed, face skulked beneath his black robe, shuffled down the hallway toward me.

The frail and emaciated Father Dobo, from Uganda, never shows emotion. He has always been subdued and studious. Yet there is such mystery beneath his coal-black skin and behind his amber eyes; even his mouth and his pearl-white teeth (which he seldom shows with a smile) and pink tongue, seem recondite. Father Dobo's self-chosen calling has been the compilation as well as the translation of sundry African dialects into English and Latin. He has been at the project—I was about to write "forever"—longer than the fifteen years that I have known him.

Several summers ago I invited Father Dobo out to dinner in Como. He went grudgingly. We ate on the patio of a small café. It was a placid evening in the hushed and soft purple shadow of the southern Alps. He was averse to speaking about himself but did converse, with poised concentration, about his African languages project. One thought of his was most provocative, and I shall never forget it: "If we can save the languages," he told me across a candlelit table, "then we can preserve the souls of those declining cultures."

"What do you mean?" I asked him.

"When you have lived a long time," he replied, opening up to me for the first and only instance, "you discover that language is the mirror of the soul. Yes. Presently I am codifying the Fula, the Wolof, and some related dialects. And here I find the soul of a people as well as the soul of the man. The immortals understand this. We love languages because we love the human soul."

The light, which flickered from the candle, glinted off his jasper within jasmine tiger-eyes but was absorbed by the darkness of the skin that surrounded them. "The eyes too," he laughed, for I am afraid that I was staring at his. "Yes. The eyes are the mirrors of the soul. Plato knew this, and so did my Shakespeare. And their knowing became their immortality. It is so. But the eyes belong only to the individual, not to the community. The eyes learn to lie. Easily. It is so.

"Words, however, are always true. Yes. A falsehood spoken or written, a lie with words, is true, of course, only within its context. Yet it is always true because it has meaning. Yes. We know the lie is false. This is knowledge. It is so. So we search for a thousand years and some more. We search for the truth. I tell you this: words are the only mirror of the truth for man."

That was then. A few days ago, however, in the hallway in front of my room, Father Dobo was a man who wished not to be seen. He hugged me and kissed my cheek, as he always did in greeting, then whispered in my ear, "Please, Father Jerome, for the sake of our Order. Yes. Our Order. Yes. It is so. For the love of God, take us to America. Yes, to America. Now I must return to the work of my translation." That was all he said to me. He walked away, in his black robe, through the splashes of sun on the hallway's wooden floor …

I should mention the only female member of the Order who remains at Como. Maria Sanchez was one the early members of the Order of the Beloved. Sister Mary was SF1 in our original study. She had worked, off and on, in the Vatican, but was permanently "assigned" to Como in, I believe, 1969. In her youth she was, and I can witness to the fact (for when I first met her she was still in her teens), a voluptuous young woman, a real dark-eyed beauty.

She responded more to the treatments than did the others. On one of my visits to Como in the 1970s, Sister Maria even recited for me the story of her birth, in 1952, in Barcelona, if memory serves. She has suffered frequent relapses and has come and gone many times from the small sisters' wing of the cloister. There were rumors, about twenty-five years ago, that Sister Maria had returned to her family in Spain because of a pregnancy. She was, however, back at the cloister in less than a year, again filled with the belief that she was immortal. I dare say that she has aged far less gracefully than the other members …

Only two other members of the Order of the Beloved currently live at the monastery in Como. Jose Quindilar, another Spaniard (or perhaps Portuguese), is new to the Order, and I know very little about him. He is probably forty-five and is the prototypical Latin male: tall, dark, handsome, and reserved. Father Quindilar joined the Order about three years ago, just as I was finishing a textbook on jurisprudence. He was in Rome the last time I visited Como, and I have not been able to spend much time with him. I understand that he was an accountant with the Curia Romana before he became ill. It is said that he is a mathematical genius and is working on some proof of the existence of God. This was only reported to me.

Father Brad Hugo, the sole American, is also a founding member of the Order. I first knew him as S3, or perhaps it was S4. Hugo is a world-class historian and is the current editor and author of much of a nearly completed twenty-volume history of the Church commissioned by Pope Pius XII in 1948, shortly before he established the Order of the Beloved.

Hugo is a short man. He is as unkempt now as he was nearly forty years ago when we met. Unlike the others, he has gained thirty or forty pounds. His hair, like many of the other members' hair—like my own—has turned silver with the years; it is a reminder to me, whenever I begin to doubt, that he is not what he believes he is. There is a capricious glint in his blue eyes and an impish grin on his chubby face. He is the in-house comic and the favorite of the other members, though he is most demure around anyone from the outside. Father Brad's only comment to me, and it came with a wink as he passed me in the courtyard, was, "New Mexico in the summer! Surely, Father, we are on our way to heaven—or hell."

> It is also not to be omitted that some wicked women perverted by the devil, seduced by illusions and phantasms of demons, believe and profess themselves, in the hours of night, to ride upon certain beasts with Diana, the goddess of pagans ... and to obey her commands ... to be summoned to her service on certain nights.
>
> —Burchard, Bishop of Worms, quoting from *Canon Episcopi*

Excerpts from the Journal of Nathan Johnson

Preston, Idaho. Late evening, May 22.

    Finished my examination of the body—it scared the hell out of me—and congratulated myself for the hundredth time on not practicing medicine for a living. I really do not regret not finishing my residency. I left with Sheriff Hansen, just after nine, to get a drink. It is against the law to drink in Franklin County on a Sunday. The bars are closed. (I take it back. There are no bars. There is only *one* bar. There is *the* bar—the Getaway Bar and Grill—and it was closed.) The state liquor store was shut down. The grocery store can't sell wine or beer on Sunday, but it was closed anyway.

    That's what the law says. What the law *is*—that's another matter. The law in Franklin County is Sheriff Hansen. And the sheriff, with several of his Mormon buddies, enjoys a stiff shot or two after Sunday services. So on Sundays, at about nine in the evening, it's tough to find a parking space up and down the alley between the back of Jenk's Grocery Store and the back of the Getaway Bar and Grill because the Franklin County elders have reconvened. Two knocks and a furtive glimpse from behind the peephole of the rear door of the Getaway and you're in, assuming you have the right face. The cowboy bishop was there. His name is Heath Kimball. He was amiable and talkative. Took me aside for a moment and said, "Damn glad they sent you." Also there were the county prosecutor, the service station manager, the local radio station owner (who made a weak effort to get more facts on the murder), the manager of the grocery store, Millard Lee (owner of the Getaway), and some others, mostly old cowboys. There was no cigarette smoke in the bar. These were Mormons. There were no women in the bar; only men in the church are ordained to the priesthood.

The sacrament began with the community of saints partaking of Jack Daniels and Coke or Coors beer and mixed nuts. Then each member shared with the congregation some ribald event or rowdy joke he had seen or heard the previous week. The service concluded, around eleven, with the singing of a traditional hymn, "Show Me the Way to Go Home." With many shushes and staggers and whispers, many of the whispers being invocations to the Almighty that their wives were safely asleep, the parishioners stumbled off to their cars. These Mormons are different.

The church, my church, in Las Vegas, in Los Angeles—anywhere the church is culturally insignificant—is a harbor for its members from the corruption and vicissitudes of the world. The strict moral doctrines, vows of fidelity, and prohibitions against alcohol, tobacco, and drugs are comforting and compelling standards of behavior. Mormons flock to the church for safety and refuge. But in a small Mormon town like Preston, Idaho, where the church *is* the society, every rule, every dogma, every standard, is another brick in a cultural cell. Every vow is a covenant made under duress. It is strange, but in life, freedom is often distance from the proximate, no matter what the proximate might be. To be sociable, I nursed a few Cokes with Jack Daniels for about two hours.

By the way (did I mention this?), no one said anything of value about the death of the Native American tonight, even though it was the main topic of conversation. The response I'm getting from the locals is that the John Doe was just another itinerant, an Indian who wandered off one of the local reservations. Millard Lee, the bar owner, speculated that the Indian had probably slept with the chief's wife and that the tribe had tracked him down and killed him—"Indian style." Millard Lee doesn't know much about either Native American culture or homicide.

About half an hour ago, around eleven-thirty, the sheriff and I drove by the county building to check on the Mexican cattle rustler and the girl. Because I had the sheriff post his personnel at both Darrington's meat locker and at the Beehive Inn (the site of the homicide), Deputy Budge was on duty alone. He had bought a six-pack of Mountain Dew. He said he could make it until shift change at six in the morning.

Budge smiled, lifted his tired blue eyes to mine, and told me that the prisoners had complained vehemently about their arrest but had quieted down some after their dinner. I went to examine the prisoners for myself. They are being held in cells at opposite ends of the building. Both of them refused to speak to me. On my way back to the front office, I secured my own copies of both subjects' fingerprints. As I came back into the office section, I overheard Budge's thin voice lecturing the sheriff. He told Sheriff Hansen, with squeaky but stalwart zeal, that the sheriff should be a better example, that he should never have taken me to the Getaway, that the Getaway was a shameful and sinful place for a good Mormon to be.

The sheriff replied that Budge would understand better in a few years. "It's not an easy job. You'll find out. It closes in on you. Life closes in on you," the sheriff said, half apologetically, to his deputy. "I think this Johnson's okay. I think he understands us."

"But that's not the point, Sheriff. That's not the point."

"All right, Billy, then what's the point?" sighed the sheriff.

"The point is that what you and Millard, the whole bunch of you, what you're doing is wrong," Budge said in a pleading whine.

"Don't go and start preachin' to me," ordered the sheriff, but without any authority in his voice.

"I'm not preaching," Budge said, firming his tone. "Forget that we're even Mormons. You're the sheriff and, like it or not, it's against the law to serve liquor on Sunday in this county."

"I've heard that one too. But I'm tellin' you that the points all git blurry after a while. The older you git, the blurrier they're gonna git for you too. The point is that when you git older, you git tired of all the damn points. We're only havin' some fun. We're only killin' time," he answered.

I picked this moment to enter the room.

"Sir, Agent Johnson, sir, do you mind if I offer an opinion?" Budge looked up from the front desk and from his can of Mountain Dew and smiled.

"What is it, Deputy Budge?"

"The man we arrested today," he began, nodding at the hallway and toward the back cell, "he's not a Mexican."

"Why do you say that?" I asked him.

"I lived in Guatemala for two years, sir, on my mission. I've heard all kinds of Spanish and all kinds of accents. His isn't Mexican. He pretends to be lazy in his speech. But he misses a lot of … you know, sir … localisms or whatever they're called."

"His accent sounded strange to me too," I answered, smiling back. "What do you think it is?"

"Well, Agent Johnson, sir, it's not English or not even American, North or South. It sounds more European to me, sir. Kind of Spanish. Maybe Eyetalian or Portuguese."

I started for the front door. "Good man you've got here, Sheriff," I said, glancing over my shoulder at both of them. "Extremely observant and perceptive. I heard it too. That's why I thought we should hold them until we find out who they really are."

Budge beamed.

Tonight I am staying in the front section of the Beehive Inn. It is a long, linear cinderblock motel that runs parallel with the highway. Truckers don't have to turn off Highway 91 to enter; they swerve in front of the room of their choice, plop down their twenty bucks, and hop into bed.

There are some small "rustic" log cabins behind the motel. They preceded the cinderblock section of the motel in time and now precede it in cost, sixty bucks a week. The murder took place in one of those. I just took a sec and examined the area. The two young deputies are awake and listening to rock and roll on the radio. They have parked the squad car in front of the cabin where the murder occurred. There is no rear entrance, and there are no rear windows. The front door and side windows are locked. The building is secure. It is much too dark to inspect the scene of the crime, and I'm tired. So that's it for tonight.

Preston, Idaho. 5:45 AM, May 23.

There was a mint on my pillow when I got to my room. The bedding was folded back. I thought, for a sec, that both things were strange. But then I remembered that Mr. Staker, the owner of the motel, was really excited to have a real FBI agent as a guest. I was so tired that I decided to eat the mint rather than brush my teeth. I tried to write on my computer but fell asleep after describing the cabin. I think it was the truckers zipping by on Highway 91 that kept me half-awake. Maybe it was the mint. It didn't settle with the whiskey, and it made me dizzy. Later, about three this morning, I thought I heard a door slam, a car door, right in front of my room. I heard voices, male and female, though I think I just as well could have been dreaming it all. I tried to sit up, but I was very dizzy. There was a noise in the back of the motel, a scraping at the window. I think I fell asleep. And then I had this dream.

I saw the face of the woman I had only glanced at in the cattle rustler's bus, though her face was obscured by the dark. She was in my motel room, still in her black negligee. She sat straddling me on the bed. She brushed the long, black hair from her face. She was crying. There were tears streaming from her deep, round, black eyes and down her dark cheeks. The mascara ran with them. Her eyes looked as if they were bleeding through the darkness. She was breathing heavily. Her thick, round tongue was pushing against her upper lip with each breath. Her chest was heaving from sorrow and from passion. Her nipples were black, huge, hot to the touch of my finger. With her hands, which I could not see but could feel, she was tugging wildly at my pants even as she ripped her underwear away. She took off my pants. I could feel them sliding down below my waist with each tug and jerk. The knee-length one-piece underwear I had on, my garments, hindered her efforts to get at my groin.

My head was spinning. Like I was in high school. Like I was drunk. But I'd had only a couple of whiskeys. I thought that I had been drugged.

She whined, bit her tongue, and cried harder. Running her hands up and down my body, traversing the underwear, she searched for entry. She found none. She tugged from the neck, trying to pull them off from the top. I grabbed her wrists to stop her. She hissed at me almost like a cat. She ripped her hands free and grabbed the back of my neck. There was no strength in my arms to resist her, even if I had wanted to. And I don't know if I wanted to. She lifted to her ankles with the balls of her feet. She fell forward on her knees, thrusting her vagina into my face. She forced my mouth to her, digging with her fingernails into my neck.

I tasted blood there—not blood, but something like blood—the flavor warm and tingling, the tang earthy and sodden.

"They will not have me," I think she said as she rocked back to her feet. I think I helped her pull down my garments. My mouth and tongue fumbled to hold the nipple. The burning nipple.

"I followed you down; to this, to the Nigredo, to the black sun, the Nigredo—you understand?—I will follow you," she said, shoving my underwear to my knees. "You come to me, and I follow you to the white stone. Hear, Hagith. Witness, Pipi. Asmodeus, my head is bare. Mother Lilith, I am Naamah," she said. She grabbed my penis and slid it into her. "Hear, Hagith. Witness, Pipi. Asmodeus, my head is bare. Mother Lilith, I am Naamah," she chanted again, again, then again. Once, twice, lunging, sucking at her nipples; dizzy, whirling, a third, a fourth shoving, twisting, thrusting. Such incredible warmth and softness. I did come to her.

I don't remember any more. I jerked awake from the dream a little while ago. I am still a little dizzy and still sweating. I had set up my computer by my bed to write last night. It was such a bizarre dream. While it remains fresh, I am writing this. It is almost six. I set the alarm for six. I need to get up and get going.

> [Jesus said,] "I will speak the truth: Anyone who fears death will not be saved. For the Kingdom of Death [*mou*] is reserved for those who allow themselves to die."
>
> —*Epistula Iocobi Apocrypha, Nag Hammadi,* Codex I, Tr. 2, p.6

Author's Note on a Telephone Conversation between the Author and Father Jerome Dougherty, Late Evening, May 25

I had tried to contact Father Dougherty on May 22, the day after I had spoken with my cousin about his new assignment, and interest him in Nathan's dead Nephite. (My May 21 conversation with Nathan was transcribed above.) Sheila McClusky, Dougherty's secretary—we are pals, first rule of a clever graduate student: make friends with your advisor's secretary—told me that Dougherty was in Italy and that someone had died. It took me ten minutes of "How's the kids?" and "Is your dad's arthritis improving?" but I finally learned from Sheila that Domenico Patricelli had been murdered and that Father Jerome was trying to get Vatican approval to relocate the Order of the Beloved temporarily to the United States.

Father Dougherty returned my call on May 25 in the middle of the night. He had just returned from Italy. He was apprehensive yet firmly positive. It must have been difficult for him, given that he had recently lost an old friend. I was sitting on my front step under the porch light when the telephone rang. I had given up editing a chapter and was teasing the cats by dragging a catnip-filled cloth mouse on a string across the porch.

"I realize it is late, but you're up and writing as usual, I hope," he said in response to my "Hello." He voice sounded, as it usually did, ambiguous, melancholy, and playful.

"Father Dougherty, great to finally hear from you. I talked to Sheila a few times. I've been worried about you. I've been trying to get hold of you."

"Don't you have my cell phone number?"

"Yeah, but you know me. Couldn't find it. And I hated to ask Sheila."

"*You* can ask. Write this down. 202-555-5452."

"Got it. Sheila told me about Father Patricelli. How you holdin' up?"

"I will survive it. I went online and found a review of your latest children's book. It was most complimentary. I will buy a copy tomorrow."

"Thanks. You'll double my sales."

"It will come. You are very bright and dedicated to your work. You will achieve everything that you are striving for," he promised me.

"I've been working at it for so long, I've forgotten whatever it was that I wanted to achieve. Anyway, I called to find out how you are doing," I said.

"I will be fine. What are you working on now?" he asked.

"Just some rewriting. Are you avoiding talking about Patricelli—or do you really want to hear more about me and my quest to relentlessly hunt down split infinitives?"

"It was very difficult for me." His voice was choked by sorrow.

"I'm sure it was terrible. I know that you were close to him. Talk to me. Tell me how he died," I nudged, as gently as I knew how to nudge.

"It is very difficult."

"It's me. Come on."

"He was killed by the hands of utter deviants, loathsome monsters. Poor Domenico loved nothing more than to serve his parish, to read, to listen to his Chopin. They took them away, feral, soulless beasts."

"Took what away, Father?" I asked him.

"His kind voice, his reading, his listening, his eyes. His eyes!" he wept. "They cut out his eyes! They stabbed his ears! My God! They stabbed his eyes!"

"Jes …" I started to curse but caught myself. "I'm so sorry, Father. Do they have a suspect?"

"No. No one. He was a sweet, guileless man," Father Dougherty whimpered, his voice quivering with childlike pain.

"I wish that I'd known him. Your stories about him always fascinated me."

"Oh," Dougherty laughed through his tears, "he was more than fascinating. He was … pure. I loved him so much."

"I know."

We spoke of Father Patricelli for five or six minutes, and then, when it felt appropriate, I asked, "What about the other members of the Order? Sheila told me that they might be coming with you … to the University?"

"Yes! In a few days. They expressed a desire to go to the West, to the southwestern part of the United States." His words came with sudden vigor and elation. "I think I've used up every ounce of influence I might have had with the Vatican!"

"The whole Order's coming?" I asked in amazement.

"Only five remain. I would ask you to come and help me get them settled, but you are so busy writing," he teased.

"Yeah, yeah. Rub it in. Coming to America? Why?"

The playfulness was instantly gone; his voice began to fade, "Father Patricelli warned me that every member of the Order was in danger. I should have listened … I could have saved … He was my friend … I am responsible for …"

"Bullshit. Don't you go there. I won't let you go there. That's nonsense, and you know it. I remember a time, when my marriage was finished and I felt that I had failed, failed at the most fundamental of human relationships," I began. There were tears in my eyes; but I tried to hide the sadness in my voice. "I remember that I told you that I had murdered love. You remember what you did?"

"I am too old for emotional misdirection," he sighed.

"Consider it Platonic recollection. Remember what you did?"

"Probably counseled you to be strong, to pray, and to have faith in God and in tomorrow," he answered.

"More, way more than that, Father. You called bullshit on me. You told me that one person could not fully control what by nature belonged to two. You said that one can only govern one's own destiny, and no one could accomplish that without God's grace. You called bullshit on me. Don't you remember?"

"Yes. You were so distraught. So lost."

"Yeah, well, has the truth changed? God's on vacation—is He? Life and death—it's all on your shoulders now?"

"No. No … but he tried to tell me."

"That's my point. So did I. So have a thousand others tried to tell you. You're a brilliant, loving, insightful man. People love you and seek you out for your advice and understanding. But that's all that you can give them. All you can give them is your help and advice. You can't give them happiness. You sure as hell can't give them life. I can't believe that *I'm* telling this to *you!*" I laughed through my tears.

"No. No," he sobbed. We were both crying.

"Father Patricelli's death was not your fault, Father."

"No. No."

"Say it, you old church mouse."

"No. No."

"Say, 'Not my fault.'"

"Not my fault." He sighed again. He blew his nose. "It's not my fault."

"Damn right, it's not. Now, listen to me, I've got someone you need to speak with right away. He might be able to help catch Patricelli's murderer. He might even be able to help you protect the others. I'll have him reach you tomorrow, or as soon as he can. His name is Nathan Johnson. He's an FBI agent. He knows a little about immortals."

"How might he help? What does he know?" asked Father Dougherty.

"I'm not exactly sure. He's working on a case similar to Patricelli's, sort of, I think. I do know that you can trust him, and I know that he's good at his job. Hell, he's my cousin. From what I hear, he's the best agent in his field. My blood in his veins, you see."

Father laughed then said, "I greatly anticipate his call. The Monsignor assigned from the Vatican was not … not competent … not assertive. Oh, by the way, I received a letter from Harold. Did you know his friend Elijah?"

"Elijah who?"

"Just Elijah. He lived in New York."

"Oh, Elijah the fruitcake. I met him. Once, I think. He didn't like me. Would hardly talk to me," I said.

"He is dead. Professor Weintraub found the body."

"The letter said that?"

"Yes. I've got it right here in front of me."

[Author's note: At my request, Father Dougherty read to me the letter dated May 16 from Professor Harold Weintraub, which was reproduced above.]

"Sounds as if Patricelli was murdered the same way," I said.

"My thought precisely. If the deaths are related, we may be able to help in the apprehension of the murderers," Dougherty replied.

"I'll get my cousin tonight. I'll call him right now."

"It is getting late," he said.

"I'll call him right now, and then he can call you," I said.

"I mean that I am tired, and that it is two hours later here."

"Sorry. I'll call him now and have him call you first thing in the morning. How's that?"

"That's fine. I'll be in my office at the law school. Don't worry about me. Call your cousin and then get back to your work."

"Father ... I love you."

"And I love you, my son. Work hard at your writing."

"I will. Get some sleep," I said, and then I heard his receiver click.

As soon as I got off of the telephone with Father Dougherty, I called Nathan Johnson's home. It was very late in the evening on May 25. Our conversations were recorded, and the transcriptions of those conversations follow. Participants were Sylvia Johnson (SJ), Nathan Johnson (NJ), and myself (ME).

SJ: Johnson residence ... hello?
ME: Hi. Sylvia? How ya doin'?
SJ: Hi, Sweetie! ... Oh, hello. It's you. I didn't ... for a sec, you sounded like Nathan."
ME: Sorry. He's not in, huh?
SJ: He's supposed to be home tonight. He called this morning from Salt Lake. He was really upset.
ME: Angry?
SJ: Really angry and scared.
ME: Nathan scared?
SJ: I think so. I've never heard him so upset.
ME: He tell you why?
SJ: No. But he called about two hours ago and seemed better. He's in a hurry to get home. He needs to talk to you. He said your line was busy.
ME: I need to talk to him too.
SJ: Wait. [Silence] He's here. He's just pulled up. He's here. [Whispered:] He's here. [Aloud:] I'll have him call you—in a few minutes. He's here.
ME: How long's he been gone?
SJ: What? Oh ... three, four days ... I don't know.
ME: Three days? The poor bastard.

SJ: What? He's here.
ME: Good-bye, Sylvia.
SJ: What? [Sound of door slamming]
ME: Good-bye, Sylvia.
SJ: Wha … *Oh!*

[End of first conversation.]

Twenty minutes later, Nathan called me.

NJ: Hey, Cuz!
ME: Hey, Lucky.
NJ: What? Oh, yeah. [Laughs] Get married, get lucky. Stay married, stay lucky.
ME: Asshole.
NJ: I need to talk to you.
ME: Me too. Are you okay? Sylvia said you were pissed.
NJ: I settled down on the flight home.
ME: What did you want to tell me?
NJ: You go first.
ME: You're not gonna believe this.
NJ: I never believe anything you say.
ME: Real funny. Remember, last time we talked, I told you I had a friend who might be interested in helping you?
NJ: Vaguely. A priest at C.U.?
ME: I tried to call him, but he was in Italy. I couldn't get him until tonight, a couple of hours ago.
NJ: That's when I tried to call you from Salt Lake.
ME: Sylvia told me. His name is Father Jerome Dougherty. D-O-U-G-H-E-R T-Y. Got it?
NJ: Yes. Your old prof?
ME: Yeah. You can get him at the law school at Catholic University in the morning. Two-zero-two-three-one-nine-five-one-four-zero. Got it?
NJ: Two-zero-two-three-one-nine-five-one-four-zero.
ME: Okay. He is in charge of, sort of like the monitor of, an Order within the Catholic Church. It's called the Order of the Beloved. And there are only, now, I think he said, five people in it. They're all loop-the-loops. They think they're immortal.

NJ: So he's familiar with the psychology, behavioral patterns, acquaintance types—things like that?
ME: Yeah. Knows more about it than anyone. Except Professor Weintraub.
NJ: Who?
ME: Professor Harold Weintraub at Harvard.
NJ: Oh, yeah. Way back when, you sent me a bunch of his stuff to read. Real temperamental, real smart?
ME: That's him.
NJ: He's up on this immortal stuff too?
ME: More than that. He's also found a dead one.
NJ: What?
ME: They both have.
NJ: Both have what?
ME: Found dead immortals.
NJ: And I thought I was the one losing it.
ME: Shut up and listen. One of the members of Dougherty's Order of the Beloved was murdered in Italy. That's why he was over there.
NJ: Who? Over where?
ME: [Slowly] Father Jerome Dougherty went to Italy because Father Domenico Patricelli, a member of the Order of the Beloved, a man who claimed to be immortal, has been murdered.
NJ: Got that one.
ME: Then, when Weintraub was in New York City, he found the body of an old guy who called himself Elijah.
NJ: Who?
ME: Elijah—as in flaming chariots Elijah—as in disappearing in the clouds Elijah.
NJ: Oh.
ME: Weintraub actually discovered the body.
NJ: Of Elijah?
ME: Yes.
NJ: Dead Elijah?
ME: Exactly.
NJ: In New York City.
ME: Now you're tracking. You oughta be a detective.
NJ: Yeah, well, you keep some pretty strange company.
ME: Eat shit. The weirdest, and I mean weirdest …
NJ: It gets weirder?

88 THE ORDER OF THE BELOVED

ME: You're not funny. This is important. Don't interrupt.
NJ: Sorry.
ME: The strangest part is that each of them was killed exactly the same way.
NJ: [Silence]
ME: Don't you want to know how?
NJ: [Silence]
ME: Hey. You still there?
NJ: Yeah. Still here. Tell me.
ME: They were stabbed. In the ears and in the eyes.
NJ: [Silence]
ME: You with me?
NJ: [Rapidly] We can't talk anymore. Not on this line. Maybe we're okay tonight. Maybe not.
ME: Wait a second. Slow down. You said you had something to tell me.
NJ: [Rapidly] Later. I'll be in touch. Tomorrow at noon. Fith. Got it?
ME: No.
NJ: *Fire in the Hole.* F-I-T-H. Tomorrow at noon. You got it?
ME: Yeah. I'll be there.
NJ: Remember the fahoes?
ME: Sure.
NJ: [Rapidly, voice quivering] I'm going in first this time.

On the Author's Travels with Sylvia Johnson and Her Children, May 30–31, Continued

I drove all night. I usually write then, so I was up for it. Sylvia fell asleep against my shoulder a few miles outside Burley and slept until after Sugar City, Idaho. I would be lying if I said I didn't find comfort, as well as enticement, in the smell of her hair and in the warmth of her face against my neck. The kids slept most of the way too.

    We pulled into West Yellowstone between three and four in the morning on May 31. After a pit stop at a Circle K, I parked the blue minivan in an empty grocery store lot, stuffed my duffel bag between my head and the driver's side window, and tried to sleep. The kids, however, were wide awake and, having spent the better part of two days cramped in the vehicle, were aching to get up and go. Sylvia strapped Jeremy into his stroller, grabbed the black diaper bag, and marched him and the girls up and down the street beneath the flashing signs of the silent curio shops and motels. I slept fitfully. The night sky grayed with the rising of the sun.

    "Breakfast time," Sylvia called as she opened the passenger door and the kids climbed and clamored into the back of the minivan. I awoke with a start. The purple horizon to the east was streaked with pink and gold. The cool mountain air was heavy with the scent of pine. "There's a place two blocks down that opens in half an hour," Sylvia told me. She leaned across the seat and ruffled my long hair.

    The five of us stood at the front door of Randy Hutchins's Big-Little Western Café in downtown West Yellowstone, Montana. We huddled and whined and shivered in the mountain morning chill until Randy Hutchins himself opened ten minutes early and let us in. We were the first customers served and the first ones finished. Sylvia's checked anxiety had given way to unshakable dread. Her feet tapped, almost uncontrollably, beneath the table, and she was constantly pushing her palms against her thighs. She stuffed bites of syrup-drenched pancakes and greasy fried eggs down Jeremy's throat like a mother robin trying to rid herself of a beak full of worm. Jeremy did not get a chance to either stew or chew. His mother's stern and frantic brown eyes let him know that this morning he would swallow, not complain.

Not that I feared for their safety, at least not yet, but to make things easier for them, I offered to go on to the lodge alone. I told Sylvia that she should rent a nice motel room and sit around the pool and let the kids romp, and that I would call her from Old Faithful Lodge.

"He wants us both," she said. There was turbulence in her eyes; there were tears. There was a vehemence that, in itself, said "No!" to my offer.

Nathan loved to drive through the national parks in southern Utah and through the Grand Canyon. The Johnson family minivan had an America the Beautiful pass that gave the vehicle year-round entry into any national park. Nathan was so proud of his America the Beautiful pass that he had taped it into the corner of the windshield of the Caravan. At the western entrance to Yellowstone Park, a tired young Hispanic woman, in a Smoky the Bear hat and a Ranger Rick suit, spotted the pass, yawned, and waved us through the gate and down the straight and narrow road that leads east into the Rocky Mountains and the queen of National Parks.

The morning sun had just traversed the horizon when we entered Yellowstone. It was swiftly flooding the forest with light. I noticed that, unlike the rays that shimmer and glitter through the dancing leaves of deciduous trees, sunshine through stolid pine needles is slit into countless, yet distinct and fixed, beams that saturate and illuminate with precision. A pine forest is permeated by a majestic, mechanistic light that is quite distinct from the luxuriously diffuse illumination within deciduous woodlands.

After the long walk and early breakfast, the kids settled back into their car seats and, noses to their respective windows, psyched themselves up for spotting a bear. They sang and pointed and shouted out the names of the animals and then counted them. I started to understand why Nathan so loved the trips with his family.

Sylvia refused to let me slow down so that the kids could get a good look at the elk, moose, and buffalo that lined the banks of the Madison. The game animals stared anywhere except at the gawking tourists. We hurried on by the bored big game, the trumpeter swans drifting down the river, the steam-soaked skies above the Fountain Paint Pots, and the geyser basins. Neither the children nor I were pleased.

Old Faithful, a sprawling and haphazardly homely little settlement, was crammed with the camera-toting devotees who had flocked like Moslems to Mecca to catch a glimpse of *THE* geyser. The parking lots were packed. A huge crowd had gathered at the site. The kids yelped in anticipation.

"Old Faithful! Yessiree, Old Faithful. The most famous geyser in the world," I jabbered—sounding much too much like a doting father.

None of it mattered to Sylvia: the crowds, the geyser, or me making a fool of myself. Sylvia's anxiety had reached an eruption potential way beyond the geothermal. I stopped the vehicle, as instructed, in the loading zone in front of the Old Faithful Lodge.

"Wait right here," she ordered. She grabbed the black diaper bag, which held her ten-millimeter Sig Sauer, shoved open the minivan's passenger door, and sprinted into the lodge. Her sweaty cotton dress stuck to her body.

The kids and I scanned the horizon through the van's tinted windows, looking beyond the crowd of tourists and into the white vapor tumbling up from the ground for a glimpse of Old Faithful. "I think it goes off every hour," I told them.

Jeremy stared with us for a minute or so and then began to cry for his mother. He smelled of fresh urine and baby powder.

"I gotta go potty," Sherry whined, as soon as she had caught the scent.

"Me too," Kaylynn moaned, stabbing at her crouch with the palm of a hand.

"Oh, God! Okay. Okay! Hold on. Your mom's coming right back," I answered.

Sherry shrieked and bobbed up and down in the seat; she was clawing at her crotch too. "I gots tahgo now!"

"Okay, all right! Take off your seat belts. Everybody get ready to go inside to the bathroom," I said, shutting off the engine. The kids' whines subsided to sniffles. The girls' crouches, however, were now clenched.

At that moment, Sylvia came flying through the doors of the lodge, eyes blank with fear, tears streaming down her cheeks. She clutched a small piece of paper in her hand. I instinctively reached for the tiny pistol I had stuffed into the cubbyhole the night before, but I checked myself and turned again to the children. "Here comes your mother. Get ready, and I'll take you to the bathroom," I said, in an effort to distract them. But they had already seen her. They sensed their mother's panic. All three of them started to cry.

E-mail from Father Jerome Dougherty to Professor Harold Weintraub, sent 2:09 AM, May 26

Dear Harold,

It is late, and I am very, very tired. However, I just read your letter, and I am afraid that I have disturbing news that I must also share with you. Father Patricelli is dead, murdered in much the same fashion as your Elijah. I have just returned from his funeral in Como. Domenico was such a rare human being. A man of pure love and pure intent. His death has staggered me.

I called our student (There—now you have me doing it. Why do you call him that? "My student." "Our student." Why do you refuse to use his name?) this evening with the news. He comforted me. He told me that his cousin, Nathan Johnson, an FBI agent, might be of help in solving the murders. I am expecting a call from this Agent Johnson sometime tomorrow.

I am planning on bringing the members of the Order of the Beloved to the United States. Before leaving Italy, I spoke at length with them, and most implored that they be allowed to come to America. Peculiarly, most of them also expressed a desire to travel to the southwestern U.S.—specifically, to a place called Four Corners. While I could not arrange for their immediate transfer, I have received permission to bring them to DC. But after reflecting upon your letter, I am no longer certain that such a move is in their best interest. I will speak with the FBI agent tomorrow, and I would also like to have your advice on this most serious matter.

On the brighter side, you should obtain "our student's" new book. I have not read it yet, but the online review that my secretary gave me said that he writes in such a manner that "only the children he addresses understand his esoterically adolescent underpinnings." Sounds like his work ... Yes?

I am very tired and morose. But I anxiously look forward to hearing from you soon on this matter of moving the Order of the Beloved.
Your faithful friend,
Jerome

> There is a whole psychology in all of this, though. Perhaps it is simply that I am a coward.
>
> —Dostoevsky, *Notes from the Underground*

On the Author's Relationship with Candice Ballard. Followed by the Transcript of the May 26 Telephone Conversation between Nathan Johnson (NJ) and the Author (ME)

My thoughts and feelings have little to do with this book; but I must digress here with a personal explanation which should not, however, be construed as an admission. I believe, though I am not certain, that my relationship to one Candice Ballard and the actions I later took as a result of that relationship, as I walked into Twin Falls High School on May 26, may have had something to do with delaying and possibly altering the events that I have heretofore and will hereinafter describe. (If the preceding sentences read as if they were written by a lawyer, it is because they were. I have had my legal counsel review this manuscript, and he insisted that I reconstruct and reword certain passages of the book "for my own protection." By the way, her real name isn't Candice Ballard.)

FITH. *Fith* means *Fire in the Hole*. It was a very inside, very adolescent, and very vulgar joke that Nathan and I shared in high school. At noon every Friday, each of us would wait by the pay telephones in our respective high schools for the other to call. If either one of us had picked up what we believed, or often only imagined, to be a hot date for the weekend, we would call the other person on the telephone and say "Fire in the Hole!"

What Nathan meant when he said "Fith" to me last May 25 was that I should await his call at the pay telephones in the south hallway at Twin Falls High

School the ensuing day at noon. It was a coded command that only I would understand.

* * * *

Until a few weeks before Nathan's call, the hallways and classrooms of the old, sprawling, single-story, orange brick building had been my last place of refuge, the last bastion of my youth. I was a pretty regular substitute teacher there at my old high school. Substitute teaching was good income, usually fun, and it left me free to write most of the time. I had been published, twice, which, along with my long hair and sloppy attire, made me a bit of an artistic celebrity among the students. Most writers have fragile egos. Barely published writers have very fragile egos. I was known as the "writer dude." I am not ashamed to say that I needed to hear that, that I loved it.

I think it's fair to say that the kids were fond of me as well. In March, the senior class had voted overwhelmingly to invite me to be their graduation speaker. I had received their letter of invitation on a beautiful spring day, the same day that my agent had called and told me she had sold my second novel. It was probably the happiest moment of my life—which, I am well aware, does not say much for the happier moments of my life.

Two weeks later (in the last week in March), I received a call from the superintendent representing the Twin Falls School Board. He regretted to inform me that a terrible mistake had been made and that Idaho's United States senator, Sam Stevens, not I, would be addressing the graduating students. "I'm sorry, but ..." The superintendent finished up and said good-bye. I looked out of the window of my little tin trailer. It was raining outside. The senior class president called a few minutes later. He was outraged, of course; all the seniors were. A demonstration was being organized in the hallway in front of the principal's office. He hung up. My agent called. Where the hell was my completed manuscript? This was the last straw. She hung up. The class president called again; his classmates were getting bored and deserting the cause. Support for the protest had withered with the dwindling rain. He hung up; he had some motivating to do.

My agent called again. "How could you do this to me? How could you put me in such a position with the publisher? I'm sorry, but ..." It stopped raining.

The class president rang again. "Hey, dude, I'm sorry but ..." I took my phone off the hook, walked outside, sat on the porch on my sorry butt, and called my cats.

Adding insult to multiple injuries, I knew a thing or two about the good Senator Stevens. While a student in DC, I had worked part-time on the staff of one of Idaho's congressmen. Rumors about the senator were rampant. He was said to be sleeping with anyone who would have him. I was told that his wife had been seen, on a number of occasions, storming into his office, screaming the names of young women or men. (Apparently he wasn't picky.) But all of that was secondhand information, and most of it was a few years old.

Last January, however, Candice Ballard, a high school classmate, came pounding on my trailer door late one evening. Candice is a stunning woman: tall, with long, thin legs, full breasts, sad green eyes, and long red hair. She was the prettiest girl in our class. She was active in the Republican Party and had met the senator once or twice. She stood at my door, recently divorced, heavily perfumed, and crying. I opened it. It was snowing outside. A couple of my cats were peeking over the edge of the porch. They were lured either by the smell of her perfume or by the plaintive tone of her whimpers. I was attracted by both.

I sat on my couch and patted the dusty cushion. Candice sat next to me, leaned her head on my shoulder, and cried. She had been my first love a long time ago, when we were sophomores in high school. We had made love so awkwardly, so madly, and so selfishly—then. We had been young.

Anyway, Candice poured her heart out to me. She told me about her hysterectomy, about her husband's infidelity, about her divorce, and about Senator Stevens. She had seen the senator earlier that day. When I asked her, she did not deny having flirted with him the week before at a fundraising dinner, giving him her telephone number, or inviting him to call next time he was in town.

He had not called her. He had shown up, instead, on her doorstep at ten o'clock in the morning, a wicked smile on his fat, wrinkled face. Or so she told me. She had gotten out of bed to answer the door and was still in her white cotton nightshirt. Looking beyond the senator's lusting eyes, she saw a black Lincoln Town Car parked at the curb. A staff member was peeking over the top of his newspaper, sneaking a glimpse of the senator's "new friend."

Senator Stevens marched right inside, out of the cold. He pushed his way past her and quickly inspected her home. When he came back, she was standing, dumbfounded, at the front door. He grabbed her hand and pulled her down the hall in the direction of her bedroom.

"Wait a second, Sam," she said, yanking free, stopping in the hallway in front of her bedroom.

"Come on ... Candice," he said, remembering her name. He threw his jacket on the floor, undid his tie, and started to unbutton his shirt.

"Come on what?" she snapped.

"You know," he nodded at her bed through the doorway. "Come on."

"You've got to be kidding."

"Look, Candice, I'd love to talk but ... look," he said with frustration as he picked up the jacket and reached inside for his pocket calendar. "Look at my schedule for today," he persisted, thumbing nervously through the pages. "I speak at Rotary in less than an hour. TV interview at two. Then the newspaper. My plane leaves at three thirty. I only have twenty minutes. Let's get started today. I'll be back in the state next weekend." By the time he had finished his agenda, the calendar was tucked away, and the good senator was, once again, working at his shirt buttons.

"You son of a bitch," she screamed. She threw him out.

Stevens had ducked his head and trotted out to the idling car, buttoning his shirt and reknotting his tie on the way.

After she told me her story, she made love to me on my dusty green couch. It was our first time together since high school. It was still awkward, mad, and selfish.

Two more facts about Candice and, my attorney tells me, I can return to my conversation with Nathan. Candice Ballard works as the swing shift manager at a Simson's Grocery Outlet—that is, she used to be thus employed. We see each other now and again, whenever I am able to return to Idaho—or sometimes when she comes here to visit me.

* * * *

It was just before noon, on May 26, when I walked up the cement stairs and through the glass doors of my old school to take Nathan's telephone call. I hadn't returned to the high school since the barrage of telephone calls from the superintendent, the class president, and my agent. I could never teach there again; I could never face the students again. My high school days, even my feigned ones, were over for good. It hurt to walk back into the building. I wasn't good enough to address the students who wanted me, but Senator Stevens was. Yet I was sleeping with a woman whom the senator could never have—a fact from which I stole some consolation. The deepest, most daunting feeling was both vague and terrifying: somehow I knew that I was about to receive a telephone call from my cousin that would radically change both of our lives.

ME: Hello.

NJ: Fith.
ME: Fire in the hole!
NJ: Hey, Cuz!
ME: Hey. Where are you?
NJ: Airport. Chicago. I bought a bunch of disposable cell phones, and I'm making my calls.
ME: Where you going?
NJ: DC.
ME: Did you talk to Dougherty yet?
NJ: He's next.
ME: Tell me what's going on.
NJ: There's not much I should tell you … yet.
ME: What the hell does that mean?
NJ: It means that, for now, what you don't know can't hurt you—maybe.
ME: You really are a jerk. Why … why can't you tell me?
NJ: An example. I have two sets of fingerprints from people I think are involved in a murder. And I have the prints from the victim. I had all of them checked yesterday. I ran them through Ident …
ME: What's Ident?
NJ: Ident is our system. Identification Bureau. I ran them through Ident and no hit …
ME: What's 'no hit' mean?
NJ: No hit—no luck, nothing in the system. So I had a friend of mine in Ident double check, then I had him run them through Interpol. Guess what?
ME: I'm in no mood to guess. [An aside remark to a student passing in the hall:] Sorry, I'm gonna be talking for a while.
NJ: Still nothing on the victim. But the suspects' prints are blocked.
ME: Blocked?
NJ: They're identified, but all information is classified. They're being protected.
ME: How do you know?"
NJ: Just a feeling. I'll check it out when I get to DC—take a friend or two out to lunch—I'll find out. But it's getting scary. Want to jump in with me?
ME: Nope.
NJ: That's what I figured.
ME: I'm busy writing.
NJ: Sure. Tell me about this Dougherty. Tell me everything you think I should even possibly know about him.

ME: We've talked about him before. Father Dougherty teaches philosophy and law, sometimes theology, at Catholic U. He's very kind …
NJ: What about his Order of the Beloved?
ME: He only spoke to me about them a few times. It's secret Catholic stuff. It was right after Brenda and I separated, right after Dougherty's mother died. He opened up to me. There are a few people in the Catholic Church, priests and nuns, who believe that they are immortal. A long time ago, Dougherty did a study of the Order. I think it was controversial within the Church. Some parts wanted to lock the members of the Order up. Father Dougherty talked the Pope into leaving them alone—into letting them preach or teach or do whatever it is that they do.
NJ: What else?
ME: Not much more. Like I said, it's secret Catholic stuff.
NJ: My butt's on the line here, and you're no Catholic."
ME: I know. Really not much more. I think he half believes that they are telling the truth—at least some of them. He spoke to me a number of times about Father Patricelli, whom he loved very much.
NJ: The guy who was murdered in Italy?
ME: Yes.
NJ: Why you? Why does this Dougherty confide in you?
ME: He was my teacher.
NJ: Come on, he's taught hundreds of students.
ME: We were close.
NJ: How close? What? Tell me.
ME: Look, I gave him my word.
NJ: Damn it, Cuz! I could die because of your word.
ME: He told me that he had once tried to love Patricelli but had been spurned.
NJ: So this Dougherty's gay?
ME: He's not gay. Before he became a priest, he loved a woman.
NJ: So now that he's a priest—he's into men?
ME: He's celibate, and he's lonely. That's not something you'd know a whole *fucking* lot about.
NJ: Okay, ease up. I'm sorry.
ME: He told me he was in love with me.
NJ: Who's in love with you?
ME: Dougherty.
NJ: Come on
ME: He did. He told me.

NJ: When?
ME: Same time he told me about the Order.
NJ: So what'd he do?
ME: What do you mean, 'What'd he do?'
NJ: Did he ... you know.
ME: He told me that he loved me, and then he tried to kiss me.
NJ: You mean kiss you like a brother?
ME: I mean kiss me. You're the fucking med student. What's the Latin? *Osculum* or *suavium?*
NJ: Not Latin. It's *French* kiss.
ME: Yeah. Well, I kissed him on the cheek.
NJ: *Basium?*
ME: [Laughing] *Basium.*
NJ: [Laughing] The messes you get yourself into.
ME: Hey, Cuz, it's not my ass that's in a sling.
NJ: Yeah. So you think he still loves you?
ME: I know he does.
NJ: He tell you or something?
ME: Or something. It's not erotic. It's love.
NJ: Hey, that was my line. 'That cousin of mine only wants you for your body; but I ... I really respect ...'
ME: *Fuck you.*
NJ: Whoa! Take a chill pill. Calm down and tell me what kind of contacts you have in DC for me.
ME: Let me think ... not much. I know a few people on the Hill, but they love to shoot their mouths off. I've got an old girlfriend who works for the secretary of agriculture. Actually, Father Dougherty's about it. Oh, I know a couple more professors ... but they'd be no help. Why? What's wrong?
NJ: I don't know yet. I'll call you back in six or seven days. Exactly the same time.
ME: Are you keeping a detailed journal?
NJ: I was doing great—until a couple days ago. It's closing in on me. I haven't got time.
ME: Find it. On the plane, at nights, in the taxi. This could be big stuff you're working on. I want careful records.
NJ: I'll try harder.
ME: Can you wire yourself?
NJ: What?
ME: Can you wire yourself for recording?

NJ: Yeah, a couple of different ways.

ME: If things start moving too fast, just try and record everything. Get as much detail as you can for the book. If not for you, then do it for me.

NJ: I am. I do. I'm recording this.

ME: Figures. You wearin' a wire?

NJ: I've got digital and analog. Right now, I'm wearin' my beauty. It's a Nagra, Swiss-made. Analog. It fits in the side of my boot, wires up my legs to a belly belt. Stereo, high fidelity, real clean, either three- or six-hour tapes. It's got a slick little accessory for phone taps. You can't play it back without a separate amplification system, but it will ...

ME: Okay, all right already, you can wire yourself.

NJ: Think hard about DC. Maybe I'm paranoid, but I don't think that the good guys are on my side. I'm scared. Really scared.

ME: All right. I've got an idea. If he's in the state. Maybe.

NJ: Anything. You know ... it could mean my life. [Voice faltering] I gotta get off. I gotta get off and call Dougherty. What's he look like anyway?

ME: About your height, thin, not muscular, just skinny. Almost eighty—but he really doesn't look it. He's got gray hair, plenty of it. His eyes are blue, I think. His nose is aquiline. His face is long, narrow, fairly handsome. Except for his blue eyes, he looks about like you will in forty or fifty years.

NJ: Okay. Thanks. Cuz?

ME: Yeah?

NJ: Remember the fahoes.

ME: I will. I do.

NJ: It's dark and cold.

ME: I know. I remember.

Immediately after he spoke with me, Nathan (NJ) called Father Jerome Dougherty (JD) in Washington, DC. Nathan also taped this conversation. The date is May 26

NJ: Father Dougherty, it's a pleasure to be able to speak with you. Please thank your secretary again for tracking you down.
JD: I will. I told her to summon me immediately if you called.
NJ: My cousin has told me a lot about you.
JD: He is prone to exaggeration, which is odd behavior for someone that intelligent ... unless they are terribly insecure. However, I know that he loves and respects you a great deal—and that is very high praise—for he *never* exaggerates his love or respect.
NJ: [Laughing] Sounds like you know him pretty well. He's been my best friend and worst enemy—feels like forever.
JD: He was the best and the worst student I have ever had. [Both laugh.]
NJ: Sounds like you know him *really* well. Look, Father Dougherty, I'm in Chicago, headed for DC. My plane's about to leave. I wanted to see you tonight, but I have some catching up to do. Can you meet me first thing in the morning and talk to me about the death of your friend?
JD: Yes. I am anxious to speak with you about that and about other matters. Where shall we meet?
NJ: You name it. Somewhere busy. Public.
JD: There is a McDonald's near the campus. I am not certain which direction you will come from. It is on Capitol, a few blocks south of Michigan.
NJ: I can find it.
JD: If not, call my office. We can have breakfast. Is McDonald's suitable?
NJ: [Laughing] McDonald's is perfect. Eight in the morning?

JD: Eight, yes. Do you take your Egg McMuffin with or without sausage?
NJ: With—two of them. See you at eight. Oh, Father Dougherty ...
JD: Yes.
NJ: I'll explain more tomorrow, but, for now, don't tell anyone, I mean *anyone*, about the murder or the circumstances around it.
JD: [Hesitates] I will meet you at eight in the morning.
NJ: Your life could be in jeopardy.
JD: I understand. I will meet you at eight. Good day.

Excerpts from the Journal of Nathan Johnson

En route Chicago to DC. Afternoon, May 26.

I've just spoken with my cousin and then with Father Dougherty (both tape N3). Cuz is right. I must keep a much better record. This is not easy for me. I'll go back to the 23rd and reconstruct from there.

I was dead asleep when someone started banging on the motel room door at the Beehive Inn. That would have been the morning of the twenty-third, at about 6:30 AM, after the dream about that woman. (I write much more self-consciously when I know that you will read it, Cuz.)

I jumped up, dressed only in my garments, my Smith and Wesson hidden behind my thigh. One of the sheriff's deputies was pounding on my door. I think his name was Lyle. He was young, younger than us, and pudgy. He and another deputy had been keeping an eye on the cabin behind the motel. His face was ashen. His hands were shaking. He had drawn his gun and was waving it in my face.

I was not fully awake, and I was scared. I disarmed him. I took him to the ground—hard—my 10mm up his nose. "Sheriff needs you right away," he said, nonplussed, his eyelids clamped tight, his body spread-eagled on the ground.

"Don't ever take your weapon in hand unless you intend to use it," I lectured him as I yanked on the shoulder of his jacket and jerked him to his feet.

"Somebody shot Billy Budge," he sputtered as he leaned to the ground for his revolver.

"Dear God! The deputy? The kid? Dead?"

"Yeah. And those Mexicans are gone, both of them."

"I'll be out in two minutes. You watch that cabin for me—gun in hand. Nobody gets in until I get back."

"Yes, sir."

I was at the sheriff's office in five minutes. A crowd had already gathered. Numerous people had pressed their way into the county building. Others stood outside—eyes focused on the front office window that had been shattered in the night by an assassin's bullet. A woman, no doubt Budge's mother, burst out of the building and through the crowd, screaming, "My Billy, my Billy." A thin man with gray hair and blue coveralls ran after her, trying to console her through his tears.

I ran up the stairs and, before I went in, made a half-hearted effort to clear the area around the window of onlookers. Whatever clues the grass might have held had been tromped beneath the feet of the curious townspeople. Inside the building, things were just as chaotic. The front door—double doors, glass—had been smashed in, probably right after the round was fired. Any evidence telling us exactly how the building was entered had also been destroyed by the trampling throng. Billy Budge must have been related to half of Preston, Idaho. There was wailing and gnashing of teeth aplenty. The sheriff was in the middle of the crowd, bent over the body—crying.

"Everybody out!" I screamed at the top of my voice. The red eyes of the mourners stared hard at me, an outsider.

"You heard him," rumbled the sheriff's voice as he stood.

"They're out front on the grass by the window too," I gently told him.

"Now git the hell off that grass!" he screamed. "Now git the hell out of here!"

The crowd dispersed, except for a couple of weeping old women in housecoats, who sat down on the curb and hugged each other in the early morning light. "Oh, Lord, sweet Jesus!" the sheriff wept when we stood alone with the body. "He was such a good boy. Such a fine boy. Always tellin' me how to be better. Such a good boy."

The night desk faced away from the front window in the direction of the hallway, where the cells were built. Budge had been shot once, in the back of the head, through the window behind him. He had been shot with a fairly large-caliber weapon at fairly close range. I found gunpowder on some glass shards. There is nothing as repulsive as an exit wound through the face. Brain matter, facial bones, blood, and skull fragments had been blown across the front of the desk. I found one eyeball about six feet away under a chair. The murderer had used a hollow point. There were minute metal slivers embedded in some of the chunks of skull. Billy's face had slammed into the desk, and the body had rolled left onto the floor. I estimated time of death between midnight and two o'clock. He had finished half of his second Mountain Dew.

"Prints, Sheriff—we need someone to dust and to conduct forensics," I told him.

"That'll be the state police."

"Get them here quickly."

"I've already called 'em. And I called Salt Lake too."

"You what?" I fired the question at him.

"I called Grant and told him …"

"Grant who? You don't call people in the middle of a murder investigation."

"Grant Kimball. President Kimball to you. He's my brother-in-law. My wife's brother. Why the hell do you think they sent you here in the first place?" he asked as he covered the body of his deputy with a wool blanket from an empty cell. "Because I asked him to. 'Cause Billy and Bishop convinced me that that dead Indian could've been a Nephite. It's all horseshit, and look what it got me. All horseshit, and now Billy's dead. You git your fancy FBI guns and recorders and cameras and git the hell out of my county."

"Sheriff … Billy was probably killed by a professional—probably more than one. They freed the prisoners you arrested. That bishop who was out there yesterday; Heath was his name—Heath Kimball; Heath might know something …"

Sheriff Hansen stiffened his back, rubbed bloodshot eyes, took out his handkerchief, and blew his bulbous nose. He was a couple of inches taller than me, around six feet three, and at least fifty pounds heavier. "That bishop you're talkin' about is Grant Kimball's grandson. Billy Budge here was his great-grandson, his oldest great-grandson. I don't want no more Nephite stories gittin' my people killed. You can go now. Go do what you got to do today, but President Kimball wants to see you tomorrow at his office in Salt Lake. Now git!" He shoved a piece of paper at me. It was a fax from Brother Thorn, sent at 8:10 AM Washington time, ordering me to report personally to President Kimball at church headquarters on May 24.

I left the building, confused and angry. But I still had one day, and I still had a job to do, so I hurried back to the Beehive Inn. The fat little deputy named Lyle was still there. Apparently he feared my 10mm more than he feared the sheriff. I told him to keep the cabin secure while I took a shower.

I went into the bathroom of my motel room and undressed. It was then that I smelled it—her—on my penis, in my pubic hair. I rubbed myself and sniffed my fingers. Then I felt my neck for the scratch marks from her fingernails. It had not been a dream. My guess would be that I had been drugged, probably with the mint, as quick and short-lived as the drug had been—maybe flunitrazepam. I consider myself fortunate—it could have been LSD—it could have been strychnine. They probably have video or photographs of some kind. Sylvia will understand—when I find the guts to tell her. I wonder how they will use it to try to stop me?

After the shower, as hot as I could stand it, I dressed quickly in my standard clothes, black cowboy boots, and navy blue wool suit. Lyle was killing time in the squad car, eating powdered-sugar doughnuts and drinking Pepsi; his friend had deserted him and trotted to the police station. I told Lyle he could take half an hour off; he left in a hurry.

I then walked to the white house at the front end of the property to get the key from the owner, Samuel Staker. Mr. Staker was very cooperative and told me how he had heard odd crunching noises coming from the cabin upon returning from the grocery store with bacon for breakfast. He had knocked on the door. Then he had shouted for the occupant to let him in. By the time he had gone to his house and had come back with a key and his shotgun, the noises had stopped. Staker had opened the door and found the body of the victim on the floor. He told me that the victim's head, or what was left of it, had been propped against the wall next to the bed. His hands and feet were spread apart across the floor. "Like one of them snow angels we made flopping around when we was kids," Staker said as he unlocked the door for me.

The cabin was unadorned: one room with a bed, a sink, a toilet, and a primitive corner shower stall, two sides of which consisted of white plastic curtains hung from hooks screwed into the ceiling. The upper part of the bed and the lone pillow were soaked with blood. The pillow had been ripped by a sharp object that had penetrated the mattress and box springs at least eight inches deep. The blankets had been ruffled but had remained on the bed. It looked as if he'd been sleeping, or waiting, in the bed. He had been fully clothed at the time of death. After the first assault, he had been hauled out of the bed, and the job had been finished on the floor, probably because the "give" of the mattress did not allow sufficient penetration into the skull. Though, as noted by Staker, the victim's arms had instinctively flailed, it did not appear that he had struggled. (I thought of the mint and of the woman who had been in my room last night. I felt fortunate.)

The blood trailed off the bed and down the wall, where it puddled on the pine plank floor. The blood had dried black and hard. The gray chunks of dry, curly brain matter on the floor confirmed my theory that the cruelest blows had been delivered there.

"I'm gonna have to repaint that west wall," Staker complained.

Other than the bed, the only furniture in the room was a narrow, old pine dresser. The top drawer had been ripped out; the contents rummaged; some of the clothing had been thrown to the floor. Staker must have knocked on the door at about the time that the assailants had begun their search of the room. (I am assuming that there was more than one perpetrator. It is hard to imagine the victim's injuries being caused by a sole assailant.) My heart jumped at the sight of the untouched drawers. It was the first real mistake that the murderers had made.

Being careful not to disturb areas for printing, I first went through the clothing on the floor. It was socks and underwear—two more pairs of full-length Mormon garments. They were old, yellowed with age, like clothes one sees on display in a museum. The second drawer contained two Sears flannel shirts, identical to the one he had been wearing when killed. There was a pair of faded jeans in the third drawer, pockets empty.

The bottom drawer held the prize. Inside I found a very tattered, though neatly folded, brown wool sports coat and two worn blue paperback copies of the *Book of Mormon*. One was in English, and the other was in Vietnamese. I thumbed through the pages of the books. Identical passages had been marked in each copy. Could the victim have been using the English as a study guide for learning Vietnamese?

In the sports coat, I located his wallet. There was no type of identification, no credit cards or driver's license. I found $107.00 in cash in various denominations, the largest of which was a crumpled fifty-dollar bill. Tucked inside the wallet liner, with the fifty-dollar bill, was a bus ticket to Farmington, New Mexico, and an ancient photograph. The ticket was for a bus that left Logan, Utah on June 1 and arrived in Farmington thirty hours later. The photograph had been hot-sealed in plastic and was wrapped in cellophane, yet the portrait was so old that the face was barely recognizable. I took the wallet, its contents, and the two books with me. I am examining the photograph now, on the airplane, while I wait for my meal. It is the face of a very old Native American, a thin face with long, white hair and sad but playful eyes. If I am not mistaken, it is the picture of a woman.

Staker agreed to keep the cabin locked and not to let anyone in until the state police got there to dust. I left a note with him, instructing the troopers to take some blood samples for DNA, to search for fibers, and to perform a few other tests—like IDing, P.G.M., the hair in the shower for genetic markers, amido block, and luminol tests in case there is other blood. I doubt that much will come from any of it.

I drove by the county building on the way out of town. The sheriff was in the back hallway, talking to the two state troopers who were dusting down the place.

"Whoever murdered Billy took the fingerprints we made of the Mexicans," he said, only glancing my way.

"I have copies. I'll get a set to you," I assured him.

Any lingering hope that I had for convincing the sheriff to cooperate with me was shattered with his reply: "How the hell did you get those? I want you to turn them over to me."

"I always back up my prints. I said I'd get you a copy."

The senior trooper, Lieutenant Porter, seized his opportunity to take a cheap shot at me.

"We should have been called in first on this." His remark was directed to the sheriff. The state boys always love the chance to put down the bureau.

"You're right. I'm sorry," replied the sheriff.

"Since you gentlemen have everything under control, I think I'll be heading out," I told them, knowing that a successful investigation requires teamwork and mutual respect. Those things are more important than any other factor, and I would have neither of them here. As I walked out of the building, I passed the hunchbacked, bald janitor. His white coveralls were smeared with the blood of Billy Budge, especially at the knees, where he had knelt to mop up the floor. With every pass of his rag, the probability of finding any hard evidence plummeted.

No one had informed the janitor that I was no longer in charge. He stopped sweeping up the glass from the window, reached into his coverall pocket, and produced a sizable chunk of the bullet that had shattered Budge's head. "I found this on the desk, sir. Is it important?"

I thanked him, took the sliver, and said, "No." However, I think the piece may be large enough to display lands and grooves sufficient for rifling ID. And I'll have DC do an elemental analysis.

Huge wet snowflakes slapped against the car window as I drove south on Highway 91 toward Utah. The storm was sporadic; the air was cool, not cold; and the flakes melted upon contact. They evaporated before the wipers on the rental Lincoln could get a swipe at them.

I turned east up the gravel road that led to the site where the old bus was parked—where I had first seen the two suspects. They were ahead of me again. The school bus and the pickup truck had been set ablaze. The propane tanks on the left side of the bus had exploded during the fire, ripping a large section out of the rear of the bus and scattering much of the firewood that had been so neatly piled under the tarpaulin.

Stopping the car a hundred feet away from the bus, I popped open the trunk and grabbed the fire extinguisher from my duffel bag. Except for the area around the firewood, the flames had died down and posed no real threat. I kicked the bus door open. The tank explosion had broken most of the windows, so the inside of the bus was relatively free of smoke. The boxes in the front of the bus, under the larger bed, were black and smoldering. That was good news. I powdered them with the extinguisher, then dragged and kicked their contents out the door and into the pasture and the falling snow.

Upon first glance, I saw only charred and smoking clothes scattered upon the rocky ground. It was chilly outside, so I walked back to the Lincoln and put on my trench coat and cotton gloves. In a large pile of woman's clothing, I found a book and a small pamphlet. The book was a paperback copy of *Gray's Anatomy*. The cover was burned off, and many of the pages had been singed. The pamphlet, which was in pretty good shape, was some type of bulletin from a church or a religious order. The religion was probably New Age rather than Christian because the pages described a "harmonic convergence" that was soon to take place. As near as I could tell, there was either confusion or competition as to the time and place of the convergence. This pamphlet argues for a date of June 2 in Boynton Canyon in Arizona. But it also refers disparagingly to June 4 and the Valley of the Gods in southern Utah. I must find out what this is about.

I have since had the time to examine the anatomy book. It is almost new, free of inscriptions and marginal notes. I have found one page in the book that has been marked. It is page 657, a page that illustrates a transverse vertical section of the brain from the front. The words *corpus callosum* have been underlined and circled. The portion of the picture depicting that central section of the brain, which divides the left from the right hemispheres and probably is the vehicle for communication between the two, has been crossed out. Above these markings, on the same page, is a bizarre set of letters set out in a square. Unless it is written in a language that I am ignorant of, the letters seem to say nothing. The square looks like this:

C	A	S	E	D
A	Z	0	T	E
B	0	R	0	S
E	T	0	S	A
D	E	B	A	C

That is about everything of importance that happened on the twenty-third—three days ago. The stewardess has announced that we are on final approach to Dulles. I must shut down my computer. Tonight I will catch up with this journal and write about what happened yesterday in Salt Lake.

> Life is the medium in which self-consciousness experiences and seeks itself. Life constitutes the first truth of self-consciousness and appears as its other.
>
> —Hyppolite, *Genèse et Structure de la Phénoménologie*

> We have still not come, face-to-face, have not yet come under sway of what intrinsically desires to be thought about in an essential sense. Presumably the reason is that we human beings do not yet sufficiently reach out and turn toward what desires to be thought.
>
> —Heidegger, *Was Heisst Denken?*

Excerpts from the article "What is Immortality?" published by Harold Weintraub in the fall 2000 edition of *The Review of Metaphysics*. Pages 198–217. Notes omitted

Taking the idea of immortality seriously entails calling into question the entire history of philosophy as well as theology. Plato, Aquinas, Descartes, Locke, and Kant argued, each in his own way, not for immortality but for the existence of an *undying soul*. Kant is, once again, the historical fulcrum for both the preservation and the negation of this concept. He ingeniously obfuscates, if not obliterates, in the *Kritik der reinen Vernunft*, what he will later offer as postulate in both the *Kritik der praktischen Vernunft* and the *Kritik der Urteilskraft*, namely that the immortality of the soul is one of the three postulates of pure practical reason, a postulate that is a "theoretical proposition not demonstrable as such, but is an unpartitionable corollary of an *a priori* and unconditionally valid moral law."

On the other hand, Hume, Hegel, Nietzsche, Marx, Wittgenstein, and Russell were less skilled in transcendental huckstering and denied outright that man has a soul and, being soulless, is necessarily mortal. The arguments on either side of the question of immortality are only true (or false) if immortality is (asserts) the existence of an eternal soul.

Would that immortality were so convoluted. Would that these moderns had shown that all human existence ends in what Socrates called "an eternal and dreamless sleep." They did not. Logically, as I shall demonstrate in a future article in detail, they cannot.

Using Bertrand Russell as an example, let me offer a nontechnical sample of how my demonstration shall proceed. Russell was the most simplistic-minded of his ilk, stating that "we know that the brain is not immortal." Why? Because, Russell tells us, "All evidence goes to show that what we regard as our mental life is bound up with ... organized bodily energy." Here is a semantic tableau that Charles Sanders Peirce would have been proud of! Why should "mental life" be the common bound variable? Perhaps "bodily energy" is, to create my own good, old-fashioned dyadic rheme, the A in "Every A is an R of some B" (A—(—R—B)); where A is "bodily energy;" B is "mental life;" and R is "instance." To his credit, Russell recognized that his argument had far more bark than bite. He concluded this crucial paragraph with the remark that "the argument is only one of probability." Indeed ...

Even the atheistic *proponents* of immortality (J. M. E. McTaggart and, more recently, C. J. Ducasse come to mind) miss the point. Ducasse claims, in effect, that immortality is proven because some reliable observers allege to have seen ghosts!

Consider for an instant that immortality is a purer idea that has absolutely nothing to do with the concept of a "soul." Postulate that immortality is specifically what it means—not what theologians and philosophers would have us believe—that whoever first asserted that "men are mortal" was simply wrong, that immortality is the mere absence of death.

> For there are tokens with which we two are alone acquainted, and which are hidden from all others.
>
> —Homer, *The Odyssey*

> And a white stone is given to each of those who come into the celestial kingdom, whereon is a new name written, which no man knoweth save he that receiveth it. The new name is the key word.
>
> —*Doctrine and Covenants* 131:11

On the Author's Travels with Sylvia Johnson and Her Children, May 31, Continued

Sylvia's hands shook epileptically. I jumped from the minivan and grabbed her shoulders. "Come on, Sylvia, get hold of yourself. You're scaring the shit out of your kids."

"Don't you dare curse like that in front of my children!" she threatened, her mind grappling for a focal point other than the note in her hand.

"Look," I said firmly, squeezing her shoulders tighter, "you stay with the car. I'm taking the kids to the restroom. Give me a diaper for Jeremy. Stay in the car. We'll talk about it as soon as I take care of the kids."

By the time that I returned, herding the kids in front of me, each child munching on a candy bar, Sylvia had composed herself a little. "We have to hurry," she exclaimed, through the open window from the driver's seat, as I packed her children back into the vehicle and strapped the two smaller kids into their little safety seats.

I walked to the driver's side door. "We'll hurry with *me* driving." I snatched the keys from the ignition.

Old Faithful huffed and puffed behind me. The trees, the cars, and the people blocked our view of the base of the geyser; but the steam tumbled and grumbled up into a cloudless sky. "There it is! There it is, kids! Old Faithful!" I shouted, sounding much too much like a dad, jumping up and down in the parking lot, flailing my arms in the general direction of the white vapors like an idiot.

The distant breaths of steam, puff after puff obscured by the treetops, merely evaporating into the blue, were not the children's idea of raw, undulating excitement. "I wanna see a buffalo!" Kaylynn objected, and turned her head away from one of the world's most renowned natural phenomena. Sherry and Jeremy imitated her reprobate example. "We wanna see a buffalo," Sherry bellowed, scrutinizing the vinyl armrest. Jeremy, who had not yet quite mastered sentence formation, but who was already adept at attenuate articulation, shouted, "Bufflo! Bufflo!" He rocked back and forth in his car seat, giggling. Sylvia reinforced this miscreant behavior. She laughed at me too. "Get in here," she said. She scooted into the passenger's set and leaned over to open the driver's door for me.

"Tell me about the note," I asked after I had turned north on the road that would take us back to West Yellowstone.

Her sad, tired, and perplexed brown eyes analyzed the bit of paper over and over. "In a few minutes. Let's stop someplace and let the children run around and look at the animals."

"Is he okay?" I whispered.

"Let's stop in a minute and talk." She nodded toward her children in the rear of the minivan. I nodded back. We followed the Fire Hole River back to the Madison and then headed west toward the park exit.

After driving several miles, I found a turnout on the south side of the road, a few hundred feet from the river. There were some buffalo wandering around by the riverbank. There were elk lying in the grass on the far side of the crystal waters. The only tourists in the game-viewing area with us were a German family in a rented motor home. They were just finishing their late morning snack. I spoke to them in their tongue for a minute while their teenage kids packed the rig. By the time that Sylvia had walked the kids to the grass and then gone back to the van for her black diaper bag, the Germans had pulled away.

"What does the note say?" I asked Sylvia when we had settled at the sole picnic table.

"Here, I'll let you read it," she said. First she tore off the upper left-hand and the bottom right-hand corners; tore them into tiny pieces, and put them in the garbage can a few feet from the picnic table. Then she gave me the paper. She had torn off both the appellation and the signature. The message was dated May 30 and was written on Old Faithful Lodge notepaper in a feminine hand, not in Nathan's.

"I am sorry that I have been unable to reach you by telephone. I will not be able to make it to Yellowstone just yet. I am very busy back East. So I called and left this note with the clerk. I have reserved the room for this week. It is paid for. Catch you in a few days. Tell cousin F. I. T. H. around noon the 31st or the 1st. Check with Dad. I'd love to talk with you then too. See you in a few.

"P.S. Do me a favor. Have Mendy go next door and change the message on the answering machine. Tell her to say that we'll be vacationing at Yellowstone for a week. Have her include the room number at the lodge. Big hugs to the kids.

My love forever,"

As I stated, she had torn off the names. She wept as I read the message. She opened up the diaper bag and blew her nose on a diaper.

"What's so bad about this? He wants to meet you here. He's running late. If everything weren't cool, he'd certainly not be leaving your room number on the answering machine. Remember, he said in his last letter that he would meet you here with some of his new friends. He got held up. He's calling us today or tomorrow. You'll be in his ever-lovin' arms in a couple of days," I teased, hoping to cheer her up.

"It's not what he said; it's ... it's what he called me," she sobbed.

"Oh, my God! Not ... not 'fat and ugly?'"

"Don't be a turd." She smiled weakly.

"Well, what then?"

"I can't tell you."

"Huh?"

"I can't tell you."

"You can't tell me what?"

"I can't tell you what he called me."

"Why?"

"Because it's a secret."

"What?"

"He called me the name that only the two of us know."

"What kind of name?"

"My 'new name.'"

"What's your 'new name?' I don't mean what is it—I mean tell me what 'new name' means," I said, striving to end the confusion.

"If you'd ever go to church, you'd know."

"But I *never* go to church, except funerals, *so tell me about the goddamn name!*" I lost my patience and shouted, though not at the top of my lungs.

"There, that's just why I'm not telling you," she bawled. "Taking the Lord's name in vain. Your language is terrible. Whenever ... whenever Nathan's around you—he starts to swear."

"Okay, okay. I'm sorry." I took the diaper that she was wringing, reached across the picnic table, and wiped her tears with it. "I promise. Honest. I promise I'll watch my language around you and the kids if you'll tell me what this means. You forget that I'm just trying to help here. I'd rather be back in my ..."

"It's the new names given when we were married in the temple," she interrupted me. "All good Mormons get one. Just the husband and wife know the names, and they are never supposed to speak the name, never write it, never tell anyone, except in one place."

"Where's that?"

Sylvia burst into tears again. "He could have called me 'Sylvia' or 'Alass' or 'Mrs. Tater.' No one would know."

"Where? Where do you speak the new name?"

"After ... after we die. That's how we know each other in heaven."

"Holy shit."

"You promised," she cried.

Excerpts from the Journal of Nathan Johnson

Washington, DC. Late in the evening. May 26.

I will finish catching up on my journal tonight. However, I need to say, before I forget, that I've started to set things in motion to protect my family. Just in case.

This section will be mostly about my meeting with Grant Kimball the day before yesterday, on May 24. I arrived in Salt Lake City about 9:00 PM on May 23. After checking into my hotel, I flopped down on the bed and fell asleep. I awoke late, about 8:45 AM the next morning, and hustled to take a shower and shave.

To refresh your memory, Cuz, Grant Kimball is one of the leaders, called a "general authority," of the Mormon (LDS) Church. He is a member of the Council of the Twelve (which means he is one of the twelve apostles of the church). The Prophet of the Church usually picks three of the apostles to be members of what is called the "First Presidency." The First Presidency is like the executive board of directors of the Church. Kimball is also a member of the First Presidency. I had never met a general authority of the Church (maybe once when I was a kid), so I was nervous and a little confused about how to contact Kimball and what to say when we met.

I dialed the number for the headquarters of The Church of Jesus Christ of Latter-day Saints in the Salt Lake City telephone directory. After a couple of transfers, I had Kimball's secretary, a man named Peter Arrington. Arrington was expecting my call and was very kind. His voice was soothing; mine may have been shaking a little. He asked if I could meet with President Kimball in the Church headquarters at two thirty. I said that would be fine.

After breakfast, I spent the morning and early afternoon shopping for presents for Sylvia and the kids....

[List of presents, and their descriptions, is omitted.]

Traffic was light, and I quickly found a parking space on a side street by the high-rise office building, the tallest building in Salt Lake, which houses the Church headquarters. The sun was shining brightly on a warm spring day, and the white, nearly translucent, alabaster exterior of the building gleamed in the sun like ... like some celestial palace. Security in the tower's warm mahogany foyer would appear to the casual observer to be light. There is a large oval reception counter in the entry. The receptionist behind it is a demure old man in a dark blue suit. I spotted some cleverly hidden cameras, inside and out, and some one-way mirrors. My guess would be that there is an array of surveillance equipment on the second floor, southeast corner, which would make the Langley crew go "Ah!" Nobody gets into that building without scrutiny.

After signing in at the counter, I was escorted to a keyed elevator. The receptionist set the panel for the fifteenth floor.

Peter Arrington, President Kimball's personal secretary, met me at the elevator. President Kimball's office complex was at the end of the hall behind double, brass-handled, mahogany doors; President Kimball met us just inside the doorway.

"Brother Johnson!" he said warmly as he took my arm and led me through the waiting room and into his office.

President Kimball is a short man, around five feet and four inches. He is rotund and waddles a little when he walks. His face is round and smooth (except for deep wrinkles around his eyes), his hair white and thin. He has bright hazel eyes and a warm, radiant smile. Put a red suit, white beard, and big black boots on the man, and he would make a nearly perfect (a little too short) Santa Claus. From what I have read about him, President Kimball fought his way out of Preston, Idaho, and into big-league corporate America. He is considered by many to be one of the great financial geniuses of the century, and some say his stature in the business world led to his appointment as an apostle and to the First Presidency. He is supposed to be the man who controls the purse strings of the church—a purse holding billions and billions of dollars.

His voice was as warm and reassuring as his smile. We entered his conservatively furnished office. He told me he had occupied the same massive old oak desk for fifty-three years. He looked out across the city into the wan haze that so often covers the Wasatch Mountains and said, "I know that the last few days have been surely difficult for you. Please understand that they have also been painful for me. For I am, I think you can appreciate it, I am this." He waved his right hand toward the dozens of framed pictures on his desk, bureau, and lamp tables. "Seven children, twenty-three grandchildren, and thirty-eight ... thirty-seven," he caught himself but choked on the emotion, "great-grand kids. I know all of their names and all of their birthdays, not bad for a seventy-nine-year-old."

"Remarkable, President Kimball," I answered.

"William was a special young man," he stated, and reached across his desk for Billy Budge's picture. It was encased in a black plastic frame. In the picture, Billy was dressed in a suit and tie, hair short, well-scrubbed, looking very much the Mormon missionary he had been not so long ago.

"I am sure ..."

"No. I mean *special*. William had a special calling from the Lord. After he came home from his mission in Central America, he sat there." President Kimball pointed at a worn leather arm chair in front of his desk. "Right there. The Prophet and I put my hands upon his head and gave him a blessing. He was called by Jesus Christ to render the gospel to Franklin County and to help the people there get back on the straight and narrow path of the Lord. He has some relatives who do not live the gospel as they should. They have broken so many hearts by their unrighteousness. He was sent to set an example for them, to love them, to bring them back to the Lord." President Kimball sat behind his desk and motioned for me to sit in the same chair in which he had blessed Billy. "Tell me what you know about those who killed him," he ordered me, replacing the picture of Billy and then rearranging those around it.

"I have only conjectures."

"Then please speculate."

"Sir ... President Kimball, I could give you a few rough guesses; but in my profession, I have found that if I guess early and guess wrong, I start believing my own mistakes and end up spending a lot of time on dead-end trails. Your input might help me eventually give you the answer you want. Would you mind if I asked you a few questions first?"

"No, of course not."

"What made you think that the Native American was one of the Three Nephites?"

"That was William's idea. He called me, very excited, I think it was six or seven weeks ago. The day before he called, he had seen a Lamanite, as I prefer to call our Native American brethren, walking along the highway and had stopped to give him a ride—and to see if, well, to observe him—he was a deputy. William was extremely impressed by this person, by his demeanor, his knowledge, his humility. Apparently, the Lamanite spoke Spanish plus many other languages and was well-versed in the scriptures. William dropped him off at that ... at the Beehive Motel. The Lamanite told William that his name was Helaman."

"Helaman? Like in the *Book of Mormon?*" I asked him.

"I was amazed too. Though since I became an apostle, I have heard many stories. Imagine my delight, my joy in the Lord, when my anointed met one our Lord's own anointed! And in the place where the need for teaching and examples was so urgent!"

"So you think that this Helaman was one of the Three Nephites?"

President Kimball leaned back in his chair and plucked at his thin upper lip with stubby fingers. "I am a practical man, a businessman most of my life, a result-oriented man. I believe that the Lord works with us when the cause is righteous. We must act, positively and courageously, and the Lord will give us the strength and the means to see us through our trials. True religion is acting through faith, doing the work of the Lord in righteousness."

"What more do you know about the victim, about Helaman?" I asked him.

"Nothing more. Heath, my grandson, William's uncle, called me about the matter. We brought my brother-in-law, Sheriff Hansen, into our confidence. They agreed to watch Helaman for me. William called me the day they found Helaman's body. He was extremely upset."

"What did Billy say about the homicide?" I continued.

"Nothing much. I asked him for details, but he was vague. Evidently the murder was brutal. I think he was protecting me from the heinousness of it."

"What did Billy believe about Helaman?"

"He said that he believed that the Lamanite was who he claimed to be. William was young—trusting. That is one of the reasons I invited you here today. I want to know more about this Helaman. I want you to find out for me."

This was, of course, exactly what I wanted to hear. I sat forward in my chair and looked intently at President Kimball. "I am afraid that Sheriff Hansen is being less than cooperative."

"Clive? This is bigger than Clive. Never mind Clive," President Kimball said, shaking his head. "The murder of this Lamanite brother could have grave consequences for the Church."

"How so, sir?"

He studied me before he answered. "I am going to tell you about some very delicate matters. I thought yesterday about how much to tell you, but I believe that you should know as much as I do. I want you to find whoever killed my William." He stopped there, checked his emotions, and awaited my reply.

"As best as I can, I will keep confidential everything that you tell me."

"That was an honest response. To begin, as you probably know, the Prophet is not well. He is still recuperating from surgery and he is a *very* old man. So the day-to-day business of the Church is conducted by the First Presidency. Each of the three of us takes a particular area of Church business to supervise. My expertise and calling is in finance. It keeps me busy. I do not have too much to do with the spiritual side of things. When William first called me about Helaman, I presented the matter to the other members of the First Presidency. We agreed to have William try to stay in contact with Helaman and to report to me.

"There are stories," he continued, "of contacts between the Three Nephites and the leaders of the Church. Not a lot of stories—but neither are they rare. Some of them, I am sure, are apocryphal ... and there are always the lunatics. But this Helaman was acting very much the part. So we were interested.

"Upon his death, however, things started to change. There was deep disagreement between us," he sighed, and turned to gaze out of the window at the smog-shrouded Wasatch Mountains.

"Why, sir?"

"Because the prophecy states that ... here, I'll read it." He opened the copy of the *Book of Mormon* on his desk and read aloud, "Ye shall never endure the pains of death ... but when I [meaning Jesus] come in my glory ye shall be changed in the twinkling of an eye from mortality to immortality.' My brethren in the Presidency argued that Helaman could not possibly be one of the Three Nephites since his death would render this prophecy false. If the Church legitimized rumors about this Lamanite with an investigation into his death, it might cause a scandal, it might call into question the validity of the *Book of Mormon*; it might panic faithful Church members."

"Even if Helaman was not one of the Three Nephites, I have reason to believe that he thought he was. I also believe," I told President Kimball, "that those who killed him thought he was too."

"That's exactly my conclusion. It is why I insisted, a few days ago, that you be brought quietly in to investigate. All of that changed yesterday. With the death of William, we might well lose control and attract unwanted publicity. My brethren are skeptical and may rethink the authorization we granted you. They are concerned about the image of the Church. That is why I called you here today. When there is a disagreement in the First Presidency, and they are rare, the Quorum of the Twelve decides the issue. I cannot win a vote before the Twelve. If my brethren force the issue, they will take you off the case."

"So I don't have much time?"

"I'm afraid not," he said, and he suddenly stood up, acting as if every second was precious, now that I understood his position. "Do you ... do you have your weapon with you?"

"No, sir. I left all my gear in the car."

"I will see you out."

We spoke mostly about my family as we rode down in the elevator and walked outside the church headquarters to my rental car. He intently watched as I opened the trunk and took out the brushed aluminum case that held my 10mm.

"Let me see the gun," he ordered. The sidewalk on the side of the office building was pretty much empty, but there were cars moving in the street.

"Out here? In the daytime?"

"Just open it a little. Tell me what kind of gun it is."

"Smith and Wesson, Model 1076, ten-millimeter," I responded. He huddled next to me to block the view of the people driving beside us. I opened the case and gave him a peek at my stainless steel sweetheart.

"Is it a powerful gun?"

I picked it up and handed it to him. "Very."

He gently hefted the gun up and down in his hands, like balancing and bouncing a baby. "Okay. Thank you. Put it away," he whispered, and he handed it back.

I slipped the pistol into my shoulder harness and closed the lid of the trunk.

"You may only have a few days, perhaps less than that," President Kimball said, motioning for me to enter my car. I did as he ordered. As soon as I climbed in, he leaned against the door, so I rolled down my window. He is so short that we were looking almost eye-to-eye—without him bending over.

"I will stall for time with the Brethren," he continued. He reached in his suit coat pocket for a thickly stuffed envelope. "This is twenty thousand dollars. It is my own money."

"I can't take this," I said, and offered the envelope back.

He shoved the envelope at me. His eyes blurred with tears. "You *will* take it. The money will let you travel freely. There is a telephone number in the envelope. I want you to report directly to me. There is one more thing I must tell you before you leave."

"Yes, President Kimball." I set the money on the front seat.

"You must understand that I say this not as an apostle, or as a general authority. Do you ... do you understand?" He fought it; but he started to weep.

"Yes, sir."

Before he continued, he took a deep breath and got some control. "I tell you this ... I say this one man to another." A tear rolled down his cheek. He jerked up his sleeve to wipe it away.

"Yes, sir."

"I … I … I say this as a great-grandfather, as a man who has lost an immeasurable treasure." He reached through the window opening of the car and squeezed my arm.

"Sir?"

"When you find the murderer of my William, I want you to … I want you to kill the bastard. Kill him. Do you understand?" he pleaded.

There have been a few other occasions, when interviewing family members of a murder victim, that I have been asked to kill someone for revenge. I usually divert the suggestion or ignore it. But this time, looking into his sad and innocently probing hazel eyes, feeling the firm yet trembling old fingers on my arm, knowing that this was an apostle of the Lord, I could not deny his request. I patted the weapon hidden under my jacket with one hand and gripped his wrinkled fingers with the other.

"Thank you," he said, and leaned into the car and kissed my cheek. President Kimball turned, head bowed, chest heaving as he sobbed, and walked up the sidewalk, to the white, shining tower; he walked with the hobbled steps of a very old man.

Socrates: "Just because we have started to speak of [the new role of] women we must not be afraid of all the jokes—of whatever kind—the jokesters might make if such changes took place ... in a woman's bearing of arms."

—Plato, *The Republic*

On the Author's Travels with Sylvia Johnson and Her Children, May 31, Continued

There was a scream. It was a whopper. It came from beyond the gravel parking area, beyond the picnic table, way on the other side of the garbage can, almost from the river. Kaylynn let it out.

While we were discussing Nathan's note and her new name, neither Sylvia nor I had kept watch on the children, who were roaming around somewhere in the meadow that hugged the bank of the Madison River. More than likely, Sherry and Jeremy had tagged along behind Kaylynn as she traipsed around the grassland, determined to get a good, close look at a real, live buffalo. Kaylynn had led them to within twenty yards of the water. She had also taken them within a hundred feet of an enormous bull, one that I had noticed earlier when he was pawing at a stump, digging for new shoots of grass.

It is difficult to find fault with a child in such a situation. The mid-morning air was fresh, pristine in its chlorophyllose cleanliness. The sun beamed brightly, happily, as it reviewed the parade of fluffy white clouds that sauntered before it. The river's waters sparkled in the sun's rays as they danced and bubbled around the moss-sheathed boulders in their bed. The verdant meadow, grass whipping in the breeze, each blade fain for resurgent life, spread out from the river to the edge of the forest on one side and to the perimeter of the gravel parking lot on the other. On both sides of the river, the buffalo and the elk chomped the new-grown grass with slow, rolling jaws. To a child, the animals appeared as tranquil as their surroundings. Kaylynn and her rank had stationed themselves for a much closer view of the buffalo.

The huge bull was disheveled and ornery. He was wearing the worse half of a winter coat that was no longer functional. His dark brown mane was—mangy. The thick hair on his hump and rump was falling out in fitful clumps. His legs looked as if they had been trimmed, here and there, by a drunken barber. It had been a long winter. He was hot and hungry and wanted to be left alone to feed and to shed.

He must have snorted and pawed the ground just before Kaylynn screamed, because when I looked out over Sylvia's shoulder and across the meadow, I saw the bull slowly shake and raise his wide, dark head, paw again, and then charge.

"Oh, shit," I mumbled. I had jumped up from the picnic table and was racing into the meadow before Sylvia had time to turn completely around. The kids were at least a hundred feet in front of me and less than that from the bison. Sherry hauled her baby brother a step or two, but then dropped him and scampered toward safety. Kaylynn, still screaming for help, tripped as she stooped to pick up Jeremy and then toppled over him. The buffalo was advancing so swiftly that he had closed to within sixty feet of the children in the mere seconds that it took for Kaylynn to reach for her brother and fall down. His hooves pounded the earth like syncopated thunderclaps. He snorted once; the air burst out of his nostrils in a high-pressured grunt. I waved my arms and shouted as I ran, hoping to distract the charging beast, nearly certain that I would fail. He was less than fifty feet from Kaylynn and Jeremy, his hulk of a head bent, his horns pointed, bearing down on them. He would not turn aside.

Instantaneously, or so very near an instant that I could not tell which happened first, there was a buzz and swoosh of air just beside my right ear. There was a massive BOOM from behind me, and then a large portion of the bison's forehead exploded and cascaded over the mammoth body in a spray of red blood and white bone in front of me. In less than a second, before I could grasp the previous moment, the event repeated itself—another buzz and swoosh, another BOOM, another chunk of buffalo splattered into the air.

The bull's front legs shuddered beneath his surging bulk. Swoosh, BOOM, thud. In the dirt—a miss. Swoosh, BOOM, thwack. In the ribs. Swoosh, BOOM, crunch. This one, I think, hit him in the leg. The bison's right front leg collapsed with a dry snap and sent his body spinning down and to his right. Half of his head missing, legs still churning, the buffalo crashed into the grass and sprawled, kicking the air, some five feet to the right and a good twenty feet beyond the children.

It took me five or six seconds to reach Kaylynn and Jeremy. Sherry, her tears coming as briskly as her cries, dashed by me and headed for her mother. Not until I knelt beside Kaylynn, who had already enfolded her terrified brother in her arms, did I glance back at Sylvia. Towing Sherry with one hand and aiming her smoking pistol at the dead buffalo with the other, Sylvia trotted through the tall grass, her cotton dress and hair flapping in the wind. The bison's muscles jerked irregularly; air hissed from what remained of its nose.

"Are they okay?" Sylvia shouted after she had traversed some twenty feet of the meadow.

"Yes," I hollered back.

"Both of them?"

"Not a scratch."

Sylvia turned abruptly and briskly jogged to the parking area, dragging the limp-kneed Sherry behind her like a rag doll. When Sylvia reached the graveled edge, she knelt and began probing in the pebbles. "Bring the children. Let's get out of here. Now," she screamed at me, then immediately returned to her search.

"Come on, kids, we gotta go," I said, lifting Jeremy up by his arm.

"Mommy killed that stupid, mean buffalo," Kaylynn whispered maliciously.

"We have to get out of here now!" Sylvia shouted.

"Mommy shot that stupid buffalo right in the face." Kaylynn spoke again to her crying brother and to her fears.

I don't know why I was thinking so slowly; but only after Kaylynn had said it twice did it dawn on me that Sylvia had killed a bison smack in the middle of Yellowstone Park. I grabbed Kaylynn with my free arm and ran, as best as I could, across the meadow toward the minivan.

"Sylvia, Sylvia!" I hollered as I hauled the kids away from the twitching carcass. "Sylvia! Hey!" I yelled as I lurched through the grass, packing her two whining kids. Though I was only fifty feet from her, Sylvia ignored me and recommenced her gravel scan. For the first time I noticed the sound of the river churning behind me. The noise irritated me because it competed with my shouts. The water gurgled and burped like the warm blood that spurted from the dead bison's wounds. "*Sylvia!* You shot a fucking buffalo!"

> Is it not recognized that ours is a cabalistic art? By this I mean that it is passed on orally and is full of secrets. But you, poor deluded fellow, are you so simple as to believe that we would clearly and openly teach the greatest and most important of all secrets, with the result that you would take our words literally?
>
> —Artephius

Excerpts from the Journal of Nathan Johnson

DC. May 27.

Back to writing—more difficult things. I don't know where to start. I think I'll write down my feelings and try to explain where they come from. I am frightened. For the first time in my life, I mean in my career, I feel as if I might die. I've dealt with death many times. First in med school. Now in the Bureau. I've always known that it was the other guy who was going to die. Now—I don't know how to describe it. It feels as if I'm being hunted. It feels like the good guys are after me, and I don't have any reason why.

I try not to think about it; but I can't shake it. My mind wanders repeatedly to the Fahoes. I almost died there. I almost died pulling my cousin out of a lava tube. I don't know if this is an apology or repentance, but I need to write down the story.

To tell the truth, I was bopping his girlfriend behind a crop of sagebrush while he and Harvey and Luey were exploring the lava caves in the riverbed. Not that he hadn't done some of my girlfriends before. We were competitive in everything—everything. Our seductions were acts of playful vengeance. If there is such a thing.

Right during my orgasm, the siren on the top of the dam screamed. At first I thought—not really thought, I just reacted—that it was the voice of God or the

Devil and that I was caught in the act. I was surrounded by this grim, high-pitched wailing—like a banshee screaming at death's door. I had just come and felt that draining of spirit, that death wish, or whatever Freud called it, that men feel. [Author's Note: Nathan was referring here to the sublimation of the libido by the ego in mastering sexual tension. "The ejection of sexual substances in the sexual act corresponds in a certain degree with the separation of soma and germ-plasma." Freud, *Ego and the Id*.] I jerked out of her, my cousin's girlfriend, and shrank before the blue heaven above me.

The siren continued its pulsating cry. I knew that something was very wrong. I was sweating. I had been sweating already, but now I felt it. I pulled up my swim trunks—my penis still half erect, the rubber was still on—and dove into the cold, dark green water.

The mouth of the cave was underwater. It was coal black—as black as the rocks around it. I had been in the cave a hundred times. I did not need to feel my way. I popped up inside it and spotted our two friends, Harvey and Luey. They were sitting on the ledge, with their feet dangling in the water, drinking beer and playing with my waterproof flashlight.

"Where is he?" I asked them of my cousin.

"Said he was going up the tube," one of them replied, shining the light some thirty feet away at the far end of the cave.

"Get out. The siren's gone off."

"What siren?"

"Listen!" I yelled.

We listened. Except for the splashing of their feet, the cave was silent as death.

"The siren's gone off. You can hear it outside. I'll go get him. You guys get out of here."

"Soon as we finish our beer," one of them said. They laughed.

"Get the fuck out of here, now!" I shouted.

I swam to the end of the cave. The opening to the tube was just a fissure in the rock about three feet below the water's surface. Harvey and Luey were laughing and shooting at me with the flashlight's beam. I held my breath, dove under, and felt along the slimy rock edge for the crack. The flashlight beam disappeared. The water around me turned black. I guessed that they were swimming out.

I found the fissure, but it was pitch black inside. My cousin was either a long way in or he had turned off his flashlight. Everything around me was dark. Absolutely pitch black. Every bone in my body told me to turn back. My love for him—and my guilt—pushed me on. I slipped through the crack and swam into the cold darkness of the lava tube.

I swam on my back and felt the jagged rock above me. The first part of the tube was about thirty-five feet long. It opened up into a small alcove, which was above the water line, and which then narrowed and went farther in—all of the distance underwater. I had already decided that if my cousin was not in the alcove, I was turning back.

"Who's there?" his voice came from the darkness as I surfaced.

"It's me," I replied.

"This fuckin' flashlight's trashed. I'm all turned around and can't find the way out of here," he said laughing—but his teeth were chattering, and I could tell that he was really happy to hear my voice. "This is the sixth hole I've been in since it burned out. I don't know where the fuck I am. Got your flashlight?"

"No. This is the second cave back. We gotta get out of here. The siren's gone off."

"Jesus. Hey, Nate, come on, don't bullshit me."

"It's gone off. I have my hand on the crack. Find my arm. Grab on. Follow me. Hurry."

"I'm cold. I've been in this goddamn water for half an hour. My leg's cramped."

"Grab my arm. We gotta get out of here now." I tried to stay calm.

The water splashed in the darkness. I could feel the cold, wrinkled skin of his hand when he caught my arm. I could feel the warmth of his breath against my ear. "Thanks, Cuz," he whispered. I pulled him out.

By the time we reached the opening to the first cave the first water released from the dam hit us and nearly shoved us back in. We clawed our way up the rocks and onto the bank. Harvey and Luey were never found. That's the story. I don't think I've ever told anyone all of it before.

*　　　*　　　*　　　*

Mike Freely met me at Reagan International Airport last night. [Author's note: This would have been the evening of May 26.] I served on a mission for my church with his son, Curtis, so I have known his family for years. Mike and I have been friends for a long time. He is a ballistics expert who works in our DC office. I guess *ballistics theoretician* is a more accurate description. He doesn't do much fieldwork; his specialty is improving ballistic identification techniques. He is a skinny man with gray hair. Because he is old and skinny, his skin hangs loosely on his bones. He dresses in old, nearly ragged, black wool suits and looks very professorial. I had called him during my layover in Chicago and asked him to meet me at the airport because I wanted to get a quick fix on the bullet fragment from Billy Budge's head wound and to have him do some research for me.

"Holy cow, Johnson!" Mike said with a knowing smile. He had been waiting for me just outside the gate. He has sparkly blue eyes. His short gray hair is usually tussled—like a mad professor's.

"Holy cow what?" I asked.

"You found a dead Nephite?"

"I ... Who told you?" I asked. By his face, I could tell that he knew.

"Small world, Nathan. Word's spreading like wildfire. We heard some strange rumors a couple of days ago when they pulled you out of Vegas. When President Kimball's great-grandson was murdered ... well, I have relatives in Soda Springs, and Preston's just down the road."

"Yeah. Okay. We have a dead John Doe, probably Native American, and a dead deputy," I said reaching into my suit pocket for the plastic bag that held the bullet. "Here's part of the slug from the deputy. Can you make it?"

"Let's go in here," he said. Freely led me into a men's room just outside of the secure area.

"Stay here," he ordered after he scanned the restroom to make certain that we were alone. He shut himself inside a toilet stall. He opened his briefcase and set it on the floor. He bent over and retrieved a black cylindrical eyepiece from it and, I assume, because I could only see up to his shins, examined the bullet fragment. "Can I take it to the lab?" he asked from behind the gray metal door.

"Sure."

"Thanks," he said as he placed the eyepiece and plastic bag into the briefcase.

"Ninety percent," Mike said with his usual smile as he stepped from the stall and checked the room again.

"Ninety percent what?"

"Ninety percent sure it's a Glock. Probably a Model 19. Semi-automatic nine millimeter. You know—plastic stock. Interpol uses 'em. Model 19 is the short barrel—model 17's the long barrel. Don't ask me why they got the numbers backwards. Have you fired one?"

"Yeah."

"I've fired thousands of rounds through them. Rarely jam. Heck of a weapon."

"Interpol?" I asked.

"Yeah. Something like their standard issue. I can probably tell you where this bullet came from when I do the metallurgy tests tonight. I might even be able to get you within a few hundred, give or take, of the weapon's serial number."

"Thanks, Mike."

"Think nothin' of it. Can you talk about the Nephite investigation?"

"No."

"Okay. Just curious. I'll drive you to your hotel. Did you know that Curtis and Jamie are pregnant?"

"Hey, that's great," I told him. "You're finally going to be a grandpa?"

"Yeah. About time. My wife is so excited that she's fit to be tied."

Mike was kind enough not to push the Nephite issue, and we talked about his family as we drove through the night across DC until we pulled up to the Holiday Inn, adjacent to the campus of Catholic University.

"Nathan," Freely began as I reached for the door handle, "word in the office is that the case is untouchable. It's not official, but I think that the spooks are involved somehow. Maybe, after looking at this slug, Interpol's in on it too. We might be ordered—you know—hands-off, so I'm going back to the lab and process this for you tonight." He patted his brief case, which sat on the seat between us.

"Why would the CIA kill an Indian and a kid?"

"I didn't say they did. I don't think they would. I heard that they were covering for some other agency. Keeping things iced. My guess would be that you stepped right in the middle of it. A couple of friends of mine are spooks. One of them got really nervous when I joked about the dead Nephite at the gym yesterday. It's mostly conjecture on my part, except for the hands-off by the Bureau. Lowry's secretary—she knows I know you—told me that the director's going to bring you in. I'd expect it—if I were you."

"Thanks, Mike. I guess I'll just wait and see what happens."

"'Bout all you can do. I'll run the tests. Remember, you have a lot of friends in the Bureau. Lots of people here respect you, think you're a heck of an agent. One way or another, we'll be there."

"Thanks a lot, Mike. Oh. Couple more favors. I submitted some prints to Ident a couple of days ago. They came back 'no hit.' But when I ran them through Interpol, they were blocked."

"You want someone to get a positive ID on them?"

"Can you do it?"

"No, but I have a friend in Ident who owes me—owes me a huge favor. If he's home, I'll get his butt over there tonight. If it's in the system, he can pull it."

"Great," I answered. "Have him run these too." I handed Mike a copy of the Indian's fingerprints.

"Geronimo Doe's?" Freely guessed as he opened his briefcase and stuffed them inside.

I nodded. "And see what you can make of this." I had written out the letters from the strange square I had found in the *Gray's Anatomy*. I also had written down the chant that the woman used when she had raped me.

"Occult stuff?" he asked.

"I don't know. Maybe. Thanks, Mike. Really. Thanks a million." I grabbed my bag and suitcase from his back seat and went into the motel.

* * * *

Freely knocked on my motel room door at six fifteen this morning. [Author's note: The date is now May 27.] He looked awfully tired. His face was chalky, but he was smiling. His hair was still messy. He had swapped his dilapidated business suit for wrinkled gray sweats and running shoes. "Got a lot to tell you," he said as he stepped into the room and closed the door.

"Why didn't you just call?" I asked him, rubbing the sleep from my eyes. I sat up, looked around, grabbed a digital Dictaphone, and flipped it on.

"Taps. I was right about the Glock. The probable serial number of the gun makes it very likely that it was among an Interpol batch purchase. The bullet was made in Italy, probably Interpol issue. Sure smells like Euro-cops to me."

"That's pretty scary."

"Yeah. Worse yet, my friend in Ident came up with some really bad news. The prints that were blocked are from two convicted criminals." Mike removed a pen and a legal pad from his brief case. He scanned the top page of the yellow pad. "The woman's name is, well, you can read it."

He handed me the pad then stood beside me next to the bed and pointed down at his notes with his pen. "She's twenty-six years old, give or take, and has a list of aliases that takes up half a sheet," Freely continued. "She's Spanish—that much is clear. She's been arrested several times, once in Spain, twice in Italy and Portugal, for dealing drugs. There were charges for animal cruelty and paraphernalia that were dropped. Occult stuff."

"The guy's name is Enrique Avigno. Assault, robbery, drug trafficking. He beat the murder rap. He's forty-two. Spanish. He was last arrested in Rome on a narcotics charge."

"What's any of this got to do with Interpol?" I asked Mike.

He dragged a small table, which had been stuffed in a corner behind the AC unit, nearer the bed and pushed two chairs up next to it. "Sit down and turn the page," he ordered me. "The question, the first question, is not Interpol—the gun that killed the deputy didn't belong to either of the Spaniards—the first question is how did two convicted foreign drug dealers come waltzing into the United States?"

"You know?"

"We guessed. By two this morning, there were six of us tracking all this stuff down. I had guys from—well, better you not know who—let's say that the Elders of Zion, from in and out of the Bureau, pitched in. We called in a bunch of chits last night. A bunch."

"I can see that," I said, thumbing through the notepad as I got up from the bed and moved to the table. "Why?"

"You know why. We never expose our own. The consensus is that you're in danger. We're not gonna let anybody else get one of ours—not if we can stop it."

"You think it's that bad?"

"Don't you?"

"How'd they get in the country?" I asked, still flipping through the pages of the yellow legal pad.

Mike took the pad back from me. "State Department cleared a path for these two that you could drive a tank through. It was so clean that it must have come from way up. Way up. Their passports were issued by the Vatican, and their visas were cleared through the State Department."

"Vatican?"

"Yeah. The Pope's got his own government. His state department—or whatever they call it—issued the passports. Then they contacted our State Department to secure the visas to get them in. It happened quickly. Look at this. All the paperwork was done in less than three days. All of it. That's why we think it was coming from up top," Freely said, tapping the notes with his pen as he spoke.

"Weird. But what's any of this have to do with Interpol?"

Mike flipped through a couple of pages of the notepad and then said, "That's a lot harder to figure out. We didn't find much. But if you'll look at their rap sheets, look at the time served, nature of the crimes, repeat offenses, and all the rest of it, you'll see that during the last four years, these two spent less than eight weeks in jail, *eight weeks total,* for eleven separate convictions in three different countries. Indicates to me that they're working for Interpol, maybe SIS or Spanish security, freelance, part-time—could be informants. Some people go to jail on purpose. Anyway, that's what their record says to me. It's just a guess; but when you throw in the State Department's shenanigans and the hard ballistics evidence ... I think it's a pretty good one."

"What about those letters in the square and those names in the chant that I gave you?"

"Here." He turned the pad's pages again. "Weird stuff. I had two guys in the library all night long on it. Ted Stanfield was one of them. You've worked with him on a couple of cult killings. Short, fat, red hair? Remember? He sure remembered you. He's the Bureau's specialist on the occult."

"Ted? Sure. Smart guy."

"He told me to tell you to hang tough. Anyway, it's black magic. Three of the names in this chant are Jewish, from Jewish occult lore. Lilith and Naamah are female vampires," he said, consulting his notes. "Probably Lilith was originally an Assyrian demoness named *Lilitu*. In legend, Lilith was Adam's first wife. God blew it because he made her out of mud and scum and the like, so he made Eve later out of Adam's rib. Lilith gave birth to Adam's first kid, who was Asmodeus. Asmodeus was the father of all the demons. Ted said Lilith has hairy legs and long, black, messed-up hair; she likes the night. Her son Asmodeus is the devil who killed Sarah's seven husbands. The story's in the *Book of Tobit*. Get this—in a book of magic, Ted called it a *grimoire,* named the *Lemegeton*. It says that 'Asmodeus must always be invoked bareheaded.' Seems he's the devil of lust. Uh, Ted didn't find out much about Naamah.

"Let's see," Mike went on, "*Pipi* is the Greek word for Jehovah—backwards, it says here. Magicians use it to summon power. Ted said they also had a heck of a time finding anything reliable on *Hagith*. It is, professedly, another word for Venus. It is used to describe an 'olympic spirit'—whatever that is. Ted said to see a book called the *Arbatel of Magic*. He also said that in the *Fourth Book of Occult Philosophy,* by Agrippa, that the spirits of Venus reveal themselves as young woman, sometimes naked, who lure magicians.

"I think you had one other term." Freely forged through his notes. "Oh, yup. Here it is: *Nigredo*. This one has a history. It's a word used in alchemy. It's the first stage, or the first matter, in the creation of the Philosopher's Stone."

"What's that?"

"Well," Freely said, thumbing back through the pages, "it says here that Nicholas Melchior, a sixteenth-century astrologer and alchemist to the King of Hungary, compared the Nigredo to the Crucifixion of Christ. Here's the quote, 'Then will appear in the bottom of the vessel the mighty Ethiopian, burned, calcined, bleached, altogether dead and lifeless. He asks to be buried, to be sprinkled with his own moisture, and slowly calcined till he shall arise in glowing form from the fierce fire … Behold a wondrous restoration or renewal of the Ethiopian!'"

"No. I mean, what's the Philosopher's Stone?" I clarified.

"Oh," Freely answered, flipping the other way. "That's a magic rock. Alchemists are supposed to be able to make them. Ted said that the stone did two things. One, it turns base metals into gold. The quote he found is from J. B. van Helmont, a seventeenth-century chemist. The book is *De Vita Eterna*. 'I have seen and handled more than once the Stone of the Philosophers: in colour it was like powder of saffron but heavy and shining, even as powdered glass. There was given to me on a certain occasion the fourth part of a grain, or the six-hundredth of an ounce. Having wrapped it in paper, I made a projection therewith upon eight ounces of quicksilver, heated in a crucible, and promptly all the quicksilver, having made a little noise, was congealed into a yellow mass. This being melted in a strong fire, I found eight ounces minus eleven grains of most pure gold.' Wow! We gotta get hold of some of this stuff!"

"Yeah. Right. And the other use of the stone?"

"Ted tried to explain it to me. The *process* of making the stone, the process itself, leads to some sort of change in the body of the alchemist. Here's a quote from an Egyptian guy, Zosimos of Panopolis. Great name, huh? Lived around 300 AD. 'I have accomplished the action of descending the fifteen steps towards the darkness, and the action of ascending the steps toward the light. The sacrifice renews me, rejecting the dense nature of the body. Thus consecrated by necessity, I become spirit.' I guess this parallels the process of making the stone. So your Nigredo would be at the bottom of the stairs. Um, another quote, here, somewhere. Here it is, from a book called *Hermetic Triumph*: 'The philosopher's stone grants long life and freedom from disease to the one who possesses it.' Here's another. It's from a Gnostic prayer written about the same time that Zosimos wrote his. 'Saved by thy light, we rejoice that thou hast shown thyself to us whole, we rejoice that thou hast made us gods while still in our bodies through the vision of thee.' Ted said—I wrote it here, somewhere, here—'The mysteries of Mithras and of Isis taught essentially the same thing—that one could live forever without dying.' Ted said that in some traditions, the stone isn't really a stone. This quote, from *The Book of Seven Chapters* by Hermes Trismegistos (don't laugh, how would you pronounce it?) says, 'The work [of making the stone] is with you, amongst you; in that it is to be found within you and is enduring; you will always have it present, wherever you are ...' Ted told me the Orientals have similar legends—but he didn't go into it. The basic point is that, if you can make the Philosopher's Stone, you can make yourself immortal."

"What about the letters in the square?"

"Yeah. It's called an Abramelin square. Ted found the one you gave us in a book by MacGregor Mathers. Evidently he translated a book called *The Sacred*

Magic of Abramelin the Mage. It's in there too. Mathers was from England or Scotland. Died in 1918. Ted didn't say where Abramelin was from. Abramelin said that this square (I guess there are a bunch of them, but this particular square is a real nasty one), this one is used to curse or kill people. There's a list here of what the words in it mean. CASED means *an overflowing of unrestrained lust.* AZOTE means *enduring.* BOROS—*devouring.* You can read the rest of them yourself."

"So they tried to use this to kill the Indian?"

"Did they?" he asked me.

"I think so."

"I haven't got a clue. That's your piece of the puzzle," Mike smiled.

I blushed, feeling young and naïve. "Yeah. I know. I'm working on it," I replied.

"Not for long. Rumor is you're gonna get pulled today or tomorrow, as soon as the director gets back in town. Maybe it's better to just let go."

"Why don't you call President Kimball and tell him that?" I demanded of Freely.

Mike smiled at me. "You know something, Nathan, that's exactly why we worked our butts off for you last night."

"Why?"

"Because we knew that you wouldn't—that you couldn't let go."

"What about the prints of the John Doe?" I asked him.

"You're not gonna believe it."

"Try me."

"Someone named Helaman Little Brook, someone with prints just like your dead Indian's, was arrested once during a protest in Alabama for disorderly conduct."

"So?"

"So he was arrested in Selma, Alabama, in July of 1963. His recorded age at the time was thirty-three."

"Come on."

"Hey, that's what we found."

"Criminy."

"Yeah," laughed Mike.

> You would stay where you are, keep house along with me, and let me make you immortal, no matter how anxious you may be to see this wife of yours.
>
> —Homer, *The Odyssey*

> Death is the real inspiring genius or *Musagetes* of philosophy.
>
> —Schopenhauer, *Die Welt als Wille und Vorstellung*

Excerpt from an E-mail from Dr. Judy Weintraub to the Author, Followed by the Author's Description of a Conversation with Dr. Judy Weintraub, Both May 26

So, I apologize for burdening you with what follows. I did try to call you this morning but sent this e-mail when I could not reach you by telephone.

Harold is gone. He has set off to rescue a woman friend of his, a woman named Miriam, from assassins—or some such nonsense. It is all very complex, so I will tell you everything and then ask you for your help. In spite of the distance between the two of you, Harold greatly respects you and will be open to your advice in a manner different from mine.

We had a mutual friend, a brilliant eccentric man, named only Elijah. I believe that you met him. He worked for the UN as a translator. Harold met Miriam through Elijah. She is a dark-skinned woman, small yet buxom, about forty years of age. She has been here once for dinner. Like Elijah, she believes that she is immortal. Harold is fascinated by the woman. I would be less than truthful if I did not tell you that I am distrustful of her, of her claims, and of her intentions.

A few days ago while in New York for a lecture, Harold found Elijah's body. He had been murdered in his apartment. Apparently the assault was quite vicious. Harold came home visibly shaken by the experience. However, I anticipated that he would soon recover and throw himself back into his work. Unfortunately, it was not that simple.

A sequence of events, also involving the question of immortality, happened at nearly the same time. First, a graduate student of mine finally produced the data from a computer analysis of mortality rates that he had been constructing for nearly two years. His experiment is quite complex and is of particular interest to Harold. Let me give you some background before I tell you of his findings.

Several years ago, Dr. William M. Schaffer conducted a series of studies on the epidemiology of certain childhood diseases. Constructing a mathematical model with strange attractors (using Lyapunov exponents that he had computed) Schaffer was able to produce Poincaré mappings of the probabilities of recurrence of chicken pox and measles in certain populations. Schaffer was able to write a program that determined what appears on the surface to transpire on a nearly random basis: namely, the fluctuations of these communicable diseases. He accurately predicted what course or pattern nature followed in the case of these diseases. Roughly speaking, that was Schaffer's program.

When a student of mine approached me with the idea of applying the same sort of analysis to mortality rates in humans, I was intrigued. I shared the proposal with Harold. He became extremely excited about the idea and insisted that he be allowed to oversee my student's project—to insure its accuracy. It was not without enormous exertion that we persuaded the administration to allow Harold to participate in the experiment, an experiment that has nothing to do with his areas of expertise. (Though I must tell you that his grasp of the mathematics involved is far superior to that of anyone else involved in the project, including my own.)

It took nearly two years to set up the database, criteria, exponents, and maps. Keep in mind that this was a test of the mathematical theory that combines fractal geometry and the new science of chaos. We already knew what the mortality rates were. There is a huge amount of data on this subject. What we wondered was whether we could create a program that could accurately predict at what age specific populations die of natural causes, using biological descriptions of the human organism—and nothing else.

In February, my student first ran the program, using the age of two hundred years as the upper limit. Remarkably, his program predicted the mortality rate for the target populations with a margin of error that was less than one-thousandth of a percentage point. This was an astonishing accomplishment.

Harold was more excited than ever and directed my student to change the age limit to ten thousand years and then, if possible, to an infinite number of years. Five days ago, my student finished reprogramming as instructed. I don't know if you have ever seen a Poincaré map. They are beautifully abstract, almost crystalline, structures. The maps generated by the program with the upper age limits of ten thousand and infinity showed a number of, well, incomprehensible results: There were "spikes" at the years one thousand and four thousand. These spikes indicated that approximately one out of every one billion persons would live to be a thousand years old, and two in five billion would live to be four thousand years old. Using the same process (though the result at infinity was much more problematic), the program suggested that of an infinite number of persons, one, only one, would live an infinite number of years.

My husband was ecstatic. "My God!" he exclaimed as he scrutinized the findings. "Perhaps Elijah was telling us the truth!"

Miriam called him yesterday. I cannot say that he hid anything from me. He told me that she had telephoned him at his office and had asked him to come to New York. She believes that she is in grave danger and asked Harold to help her get to somewhere in the Southwest, I think in Arizona, within the next few days. As I said, Harold discussed her call with me and expressed an urgent need to help the woman.

I strenuously objected, not because of the woman—not just because of the woman. I have deeper concerns. Harold has been very lethargic of late. About two weeks ago I noticed jaundice (*icterus*, I believe, is the medical term) in the conjuctiva of his eyes. I urged him to see his physician. He was diagnosed last week with cancer of the pancreas. This can be a deadly disease, and if he is to live, Harold requires prompt and radical medical treatment. Even given that such treatment takes place—being a scientist, I understand that his odds are not good—not good at all.

Instead of submitting himself to the treatment, Harold chose to run to the aid of a woman who is living a delusion. We discussed his decision—as I said, there was nothing concealed between us—with plaintive voices and words of resignation. Harold believes that his chances of survival are greater if he can learn what he calls "the secret of the immortals" than by submitting himself to any medical treatment. He asserted that he would have made this same choice had he not been ill. He laughed sadly and said that he had waited a long time for the opportunity to "taste the flat peach." I do not have the foggiest notion what he meant.

I am a research scientist, not a philosopher. Cancer is not an abstraction. Cancer is not a concept. My husband will die if he does not receive proper medical attention soon. That is more certain than any truth ever spoken by any sage.

Harold left this morning. He promised to call every day. What shall I tell him? What would you say to him? What would you have me say to him for you? If not for his sake, then for mine, please tell me what to do.

*   *   *   *

I called Judy as soon as I read her e-mail. She was at her office on campus; I was in my trailer in Idaho. Judy is a strong, astute, forcefully opinionated woman; that is why I was shocked and concerned when, upon hearing my voice, she started to cry. "He called," she sobbed.

"It's okay. Everything's going to be all right," I assured her.

"He's not coming back."

"He'll be back."

"No. He said that they are *driving* to Arizona. Renting a car and *driving!* Can you imagine the gall of the woman? He's dying, and she refuses to fly in an airplane. My God! Such arrogance. Such foolishness. Can you please talk to him?"

"Listen, Judy, you know how it is between us. If I talk to him, he'll just try and pull me in. You know he will. He believes in what he's doing. He's always half-believed in this immortality stuff. He's been on the edge for a long time. Sounds like he's over it now. He's going for it. There's nothing I can do to stop him ... maybe nothing you can do."

"For God's sake, I just can't let my husband wander off and die—die like some animal."

"Why don't you go with him?"

She hesitated, then asked, "What?"

"Go with him."

"Harold and *Miriam* and I?" she said with disdain.

"And others. Father Dougherty called me. His Order of the Beloved, his bunch of immortals, is coming to the US. Sounds like they're headed for the same place that Miriam wants to go. Tell that to your husband. Tell him you think that you should meet Father Dougherty at Catholic University. Tell him you'll go with him and the others to Arizona. I think he'll do it."

"What about this Miriam? What if she disagrees?"

"You're the wife. It's a compromise. Ask him for it."

"All right. When he calls tomorrow, I will ask him," she said. Then, after a hesitation: "Would you consider coming with us?"

"I've got a lot of work to do right now," I replied—rather curtly.

"Are you still so bitter?"

"Judy, you of all people should know that I'm headed in a different direction. I'm not a student anymore. I'm not a philosopher ... or a scientist."

"He's dying."

"I know. It will be a great loss to the world. But that's got nothing to do with me. *My life is mine.*"

The tension was palpable by this point. We spoke briefly of her children and my work and then said good-bye.

Excerpts from the Journal of Father Jerome Dougherty

Afternoon of May 27, office at the Law School, Washington, DC.
Nathan's cousin is smaller in stature than Nathan, who is over six feet tall and appears to be both swift and powerful. Also, his eyes are more penetrating but generally less observant than Agent Johnson's.

    I first met Agent Johnson this morning at the McDonald's near campus and was struck by the similarity between the two men. Both have intelligent brown eyes and curly brown hair. Both are thin yet broad-shouldered, with a muscular, catlike strength and quickness about them but, as noted, Agent Johnson's frame is larger.

    There were few people in the restaurant. I was in my collar, and Agent Johnson noticed me immediately upon his entrance. He examined me carefully, yet not without a playfulness in his eyes. It almost seemed as if I were the object of some type of casual amusement. This was unsettling, even chafing at first, but Nathan (as he insisted I call him) was so composed and amiable that we were soon on cordial ground. He ordered a rather large breakfast. I had coffee. We sat at a corner table, near a window that looked out at the busy intersection.

    We spoke—actually I spoke, almost exclusively, after he told me that he believed that the members of the Order were in great danger, about the Order and about Father Patricelli's murder. Nathan listened intently—not with an ear for nuance, for the purpose of argument, like his cousin—but with a mind tuned strictly to detail. The questions he asked were atypical and traumatic because of their narrow focus. He wanted to know the oddest, most minute particulars about Patricelli and his death, as well as specific information about the other members of the Order and their history. For example, he questioned me at some length about the wounds to the head and face of Father. This was, of course, a most trying subject for me to discuss, because of my ignorance and because of my grief and fears.

Only after answering several inquiries did it occur to me that he was not interrogating me out of curiosity or out of the desire to learn, as his cousin undoubtedly would in such a situation. Rather, he was gathering the information that he needed to solve a specific crime ...

There were two instances when Nathan either allowed himself or could not prevent himself from reacting emotionally to my answers. The first instance was in response to his question, "Are the members of the Order mentally ill?" I told him yes but that in a few cases, some members had, through their vows and because of their special devotion to Christ and His holy Catholic Church, reached a level of perfection that allowed them special insight into the mysteries of God. I tried to explain how such insight could easily be mistaken for mental illness and that I, at one time, had considered it such. I expeditiously qualified this hypothesis by stating that I did not believe that the members were immortal, in the sense of transcending death. Rather, I said that these special people had a particular kind of beatific vision that allowed them to understand the nature of eternal life.

Nathan was agitated by my answer, possibly because it presented a threat to his faith in his Mormon Church. He asked me if a righteous person outside the Catholic faith could obtain such insight. I told him that, except for Professor Weintraub's Elijah (and I doubted his claim to immortality) I had never heard of anyone outside the Catholic Church attaining such perfection. However, instead of arguing the point with me, Nathan chewed his Sausage McMuffin and drank his orange juice while inspecting an elderly black man in work coveralls who had seated himself two tables away from us. Johnson has a habit of examining and/or being suspicious of nearly every person who enters a room—unlike his cousin who, unless he finds someone of passing interest, ignores people completely.

The second time Nathan became upset, excited really, was when I told him about the request of some of the members of the Order to be taken to the Four Corners territory in the Southwest portion of the United States. He became both vexed and enthusiastic at my comment and asked me if they had mentioned any specific time frame. I told him that one of them had mentioned something about the first of June. This point especially seemed to perturb and arouse him.

"Will security be provided for them?" Nathan asked me.

"I was under the impression that such was your responsibility," I replied.

"No—I mean I don't think so. I'm investigating a murder. That's my assignment."

"I understand. But if the Order is being pursued by those same murderers, then surely the best way to apprehend them is to stay with us."

"I may or may not be able to do that. You need to …"

"Why do you hesitate?" I asked, for he seemed puzzled in a hopeless manner.

He got up, moved around the small table, and sat next to me.

"It's hard to explain, and I don't know how much to tell you. To begin with, I kind of fell into this investigation. It was a special assignment. But the people who got me the assignment have lost interest—or lost the ability to keep me on the job. I could be dismissed as early as today," Nathan whispered nervously.

"Why? Can you tell me why?"

"I'm not sure. Politics. I know that's a dumb answer."

"But you said that I need protection for the members of the Order."

"You do."

"Then surely the authorities will help me."

"Look, Father, there's not a lot I can tell you. But I have some information that leads me to believe that these deaths are being sanctioned, or at least ignored, by parts of the government. There is some evidence that Interpol might be involved."

"Really?"

"Maybe the Vatican, too."

"I cannot believe that."

"Well … let's go someplace where we can talk, you know, openly," Nathan requested.

Before we spoke of the subject again, I escorted Agent Johnson out of the restaurant and onto the campus, where we sat on an isolated bench beneath a huge oak tree. The day was lovely, though the air was quite humid.

"I know, almost for certain, that the Vatican's equivalent of our secretary of state's office has been involved in procuring passports and visas for the only suspects I have in the murder of a man who claimed to be immortal—a man probably afflicted with the same illness as the members of your Order," Nathan continued.

"That is a string of very weak inferences."

"Maybe. But he was killed exactly the same way your Patricelli and that Elijah person were killed."

"Are you certain?" I asked him.

"I autopsied the body," he replied. His speech was quite colloquial—even more so than his cousin's.

"I see. Your victim was a Mormon?"

"Yeah. Seems so."

"An immortal?"

"They're called the Three Nephites. There was speculation …"

"Three Nephites—that is what they are called?"

"It's from the *Book of Mormon*. There's speculation …"

"And your church—you are a Mormon?"

"Yes."

"Your church gave you an assignment to investigate the murder and has now withdrawn it?"

"Something like that."

"Why?"

"Internal politics. It was pretty controversial to begin with. Then it got complicated …"

"And you expect your superiors in the FBI to remove you as well?"

"I think so."

"Why?"

"I've been trying to tell you. The government wants this thing kept real quiet. They—I mean the State Department, I think—may try to ice it. If they do, your Order is in big trouble. That's why I can tell you for sure, there is almost no doubt, that the members of your Order need to be protected."

"Would you do it? If given the chance … could I count on you to keep my people safe?"

"Unless I'm specifically ordered not to, I'm gonna catch the killers. That's my job and I'm damn—'scuze me—darn good at it, Father. These people are dangerous. They're scum. They murdered a young man—a very kind and loving boy—they blew his brains out, Father. I'm gonna catch them. Could be that the best way for me to do my job is to help you do yours."

"I agree. Perhaps I can help you. Then we could help each other."

"How?"

"We will see. I have a class in twenty minutes. I must return to my office for notes. I will make some calls for you. The members of the Order start arriving here over the next few days. They have refused to fly on the same airplane, and so the members will be trickling in during the week. They too, you see, believe that they are threatened. Will you, if you are allowed, go with me to the airport to meet the first arrival?"

"That'd be great. Do you have some files on them that I can study?"

"I'll leave some things with my secretary. You may pick them up at the law school this afternoon. My cell phone number is 202-555-5452. Let's stay in touch."

"Got it. Thanks. Thank you, Father. One more thing. Do you know much about the occult?"

"Yes, unfortunately. Why do you ask?"

"There might be some, some, you know, some satanic stuff involved. We can talk about it tomorrow."

"Then I will need detailed information as well," I told him.

"I understand, Father. I really hope that we can work together on this. I think we can get the job done."

"God willing we certainly can." And with that I bade him good day.

> Whoever subjects himself to duty, as such, necessarily subjects himself to duty forever.
>
> —Fichte, *Das System der Sittenlehre*

Excerpts from the Journal of Nathan Johnson

DC, May 27

Just when I thought my life was in the dumpster, Mike Freely came over early this morning. The Elders of Israel had been up all night covering my rear end. I know ten times more about what I'm up against than I did yesterday—I wrote enough about that earlier.

Then breakfast this morning with Father Jerome Dougherty. That conversation is on tape, so I'll skip the details and give my impressions of Dougherty instead, since I think we might be spending a lot of time together. He is a thin, lanky, gray-haired man. He is at least seventy, but his face is still a little freckled, and his eyes are still so very ... needy. I smiled today when I first met him. I thought about his sexual advances to my cousin. I thought about how awkward it must have been for both of them. My smile was a little defensive as well. I don't know much about that kind of thing; I am not into sexual nuance, especially between men. He seemed taken aback a bit with me at first. Maybe he thought I was making fun of him. I wasn't—it was just all so bizarre. His blue-gray eyes are innocent, kind, and loving; but behind that, or mixed in with it, is the need of a sexual desire that has gone unanswered for—for God knows how long. Such need and such longing! Anyway, it's clear that I am not very good at such descriptions, so I'll move on to the next important matter.

Someone from Director Lowry's office called me on my cell phone just before noon. I was to be in his office by one. I figured that I was about to be pulled from the investigation, so I took my time driving my Hertz down to FBI headquarters on Constitution Avenue—hoping that Dougherty could pull off a miracle. There was some construction on Capitol Street; there was a pro-life march gearing up; traffic was a jumble; I had my excuse for being late. After making clearance, taking the slow service elevator, and walking the long way around the top floor and down the marble tile to the entrance of his office it was almost two thirty. I felt pretty down. I kept seeing Billy Budge's grin, kept hearing his squeaky voice. I kept feeling the warmth of the Indian's brain tissue on the tip of my finger.

[Author's note: Johnson's journal entry for May 27 ends at this point. The following is the entire conversation, taped by Johnson, between Nathan Johnson (NJ) and Herman Lowry (HL), Director of the Federal Bureau of Investigation.]

HL: Johnson?
NJ: Yes, sir.
HL: Sit down. You're late.
NJ: Sorry, sir. I ran into a demonstration.
HL: What?
NJ: Protesters blocked traffic.
HL: Oh. It's just as well. I didn't have to embarrass myself, and we won't have to do this twice. The woman you saved is suing us.
NJ: The Oracle Murders? I've been served.
HL: That was very good work. That was a bizarre case, wasn't it?
NJ: Yes, sir.
HL: Goddamn bone fragments in her eyes. [Laughing] You've been served?
NJ: Yes, sir.
HL: Blew the bastard's head off, huh?
NJ: A sizable chunk, sir. Ten-millimeter at about twenty-five feet.
HL: [Laughing] Jesus. Johnson, Johnson, Johnson. Do you have any idea what kind of hornets' nest you've stirred up?
NJ: Sir, I'm certain that the bone fragments were an irritation, but he was about to whack her head off. I was told that the operation went perfectly, that they saved the eye, and that she lost very little of her vision.
HL: Not her. Hell, I commended you for that one. Greedy lawyers are not your problem.
NJ: The murders in Idaho?
HL: More than that.
NJ: I don't know about anything more.
HL: You've put my nuts in a vise, mister.

NJ: I don't understand, sir.
HL: There's a football game going on here, and it feels like I'm the pigskin.
NJ: I'm still confused, sir.
HL: Confused? What don't you understand? What's so confusing? There's a tug of war going on, and I'm the goddamn rope!
NJ: I ... I'm ... I ... Who's tugging, sir?
HL: You really don't know—do you?
NJ: Sorry, sir.
HL: This morning I got a call from Ed Thorn. You know Ed Thorn?
NJ: Yes, sir. He's the Solicitor General.
HL: A week or so ago, he called begging me to do him a favor. He wanted me to assign a Mormon agent to the murder of some Indi … some Native American in Idaho. I said I didn't know, that I didn't make those decisions, that the request did not follow protocol. Within twenty minutes, both of Utah's senators had called me, the Secretary of Agriculture called me, the President's Chief of Staff called me, every goddamn Mormon in DC called me, asking me to put a Mormon agent on this case and to have him report to Thorn rather than through ordinary channels. Did you know that?
NJ: Kind of.
HL: They said that it was imperative for their church. So I told someone on staff to find them a Mormon.
NJ: Yes, sir.
HL: They found you.
NJ: Yes, sir.
HL: Two days ago, Thorn calls me again—I'm on vacation, and I don't like to be called when I'm on vacation—he calls me again to tell me that he's changed his mind. He tells me that there was a big mistake and that I should take the agent off of the case. And even if I don't, he says that he doesn't want the agent reporting to him anymore.
NJ: I had heard a rumor somewhat to that effect.
HL: I made a call of my own to find that, in addition to a dead Native American, we now have a law enforcement homicide on our hands.
NJ: Yes, sir, I can tell you about that.
HL: I already know about it.
NJ: Sorry, sir.
HL: So … did I tell you about Thorn's call this morning?
NJ: No, sir.

HL: So, Thorn called this morning and insisted that you be disassociated from the case. He claimed that it could cause great embarrassment to the Mormon Church. He asked if I needed to speak with all the Mormon brass again. I don't like that kind of power play bullshit. Do you?
NJ: No, sir.
HL: Me either. It didn't matter, though—I told him that I had already decided to take you off the case …
NJ: But, sir …
HL: Just keep a lid on it 'til I'm finished.
NJ: Yes, sir.
HL: So, I told Hollings, my executive assistant, to bring you in today, to debrief you, and to send you back to … where are you stationed?
NJ: Las Vegas.
HL: Back to Vegas. But about an hour ago, I got a call from Cardinal Murphy. You know who he is?
NJ: No, sir.
HL: Of course not. You're a Mormon.
NJ: Yes, sir.
HL: Cardinal Murphy … he's the … hell, I don't know exactly what he is either. He's something like the head of the Catholic Church on the East Coast. He's a … he's a goddamn cardinal. That's what he is. Now, the cardinal called an hour ago, and he wants a favor from me. Guess what it is.
NJ: I can't guess, sir.
HL: Oh, sure you can—or you wouldn't have wasted half my day dragging your slow and sorry ass across the District.
NJ: Okay, sir. I guess that he wants me on the case.
HL: By God, that's it, Johnson! But *why* does he want you on the case?
NJ: There was a similar murder within a Catholic order.
HL: He didn't tell me that. You just happen to stumble on to it?
NJ: Sir. I do my homework. My job is to catch the bad guys.
HL: Your job is to follow orders.
NJ: Of course, sir.
HL: So I'm caught here in a squeeze—aren't I, Johnson?
NJ: Yes, sir. Now I understand, sir.
HL: The Mormons want me to look one way; the Catholics want me to look the other. What do you think I ought to do?
NJ: Sir, I think you …
HL: Do you know what church I go to, Johnson?

NJ: Sir?

HL: The Catholic Church, Johnson. Saint John's Prep, Notre Dame, then Georgetown Law. Saint Michael's every Sunday.

NJ: I remember, sir.

HL: But that doesn't really concern us here—does it, Johnson?

NJ: Not if you say it doesn't, sir.

HL: I say that. I want you to do the right thing, Johnson. I want you to do your job. I want you to get out there and catch the bad guys, Johnson. But, Johnson …

NJ: Yes, sir.

HL: Low-key. Very low-key. This time you report directly to me. That'll be all.

NJ: Thank you, sir.

Letter from Judy Weintraub to the Author, Dated May 28

I did it! Harold called yesterday, and I asked him if I could go with him. There was silence on the line, and for a moment, I thought that I would be shunned. My heart beat faster than it has in years. When he answered me, his voice was trembling, and perhaps he was crying. I have never known Harold to cry. He said that he loved me. He said *yes*!

I feel like a little girl skipping school to rendezvous with my boyfriend! I have never been anything but responsible, professional, matriarchal, analytical. Yet last night I called the head of my department and told him that I was leaving for an undetermined period. He asked me if I had gone mad. I told him that I was in love. (It occurs to me that I forgot to tell him with whom. The rumors will fly around campus today!) I kissed the children good-bye (Benjamin, the youngest, is eighteen—he is vaguely aware of my existence) and took a taxi to the airport.

Harold met me at La Guardia. There were two people with him, the woman Miriam, about whom I have written, and a Chinese gentleman who calls himself Hsi Ssu T'i. Mr. T'i *(T'i* is pronounced like *tie* in *bow tie)* is a singular person, and when I have time, I will tell you some about him. Harold kissed me warmly (I cannot remember him kissing me in public for twenty years) and thanked me for coming. It made me tingle inside. I told him that it was your idea, and he smiled sadly. He wants me to invite you again to join us. So I ask you to please reconsider. He also said that Father Dougherty was expecting us in Washington tomorrow.

Harold had rented a car, and we were on our way as soon as we retrieved my luggage from the carousel. We drove to Atlantic City and were going to spend the night there, but could not find any rooms. This first night of our adventure is being spent in a small beach town, just south of Atlantic City. I have much to tell you—Harold insists that I keep you fully informed—but I do not have the time at this moment. My conscience is bothering me; I feel that I must send proper letters of explanation to appropriate friends, colleagues, family, and students. We will stay in touch.

Harold's skin is quite jaundiced, and he is eating poorly. I pray that this adventure of ours comes to a resolution soon. Very, very soon.

Warmest regards,
[Signed]
Judy

SECOND WOMAN: Suppose the police try to drag you away. Then what will you do?

PRAXAGORA: I will put my hands on my hips.

—Aristophanes, *The Ecclesiazusae*

On the Author's Travels with Sylvia Johnson and Her Children, May 31, Continued

Sylvia gathered up the empty casings from the gravel. Her gun—still smoking, I swear it—lay next to her knee.

"I said, 'You shot a buffalo,'" I reiterated, trying to stay calm.

"I know why you're a writer," she answered without looking up. Her voice shook, but her slender fingers, which sifted through the gravel, were steady. "You're just so ... so *damn* observant. Nothing gets by *you*. Does it? I mean I just killed a buffalo, didn't I? And you just spotted that right away. You are just so amazingly perceptive. Now please put the kids in the car seats and buckle them up so that we can get out of here."

I loaded the kids in a hurry. They ululated like a tent full of Pentecostals with the gift.

Sylvia snatched up the last of the spent cartridges. The pistol had kicked it into the grass, but she found it. She opened the black diaper bag on the run and stuck the weapon inside. "Let me drive," she demanded, trotting around to the left-hand window. I had already taken my place behind the wheel and had started the engine.

"No way. You're a basket case. I mean, I'm a little spooked, but you're way worse than I am."

She glared at me. Her eyes were different. The panic was gone. She had replaced it with adamant resolution—the blank glare of a puppy tugging on a rag doll. "Scoot over," she growled. I scooted.

Sylvia drove without speaking, at least to me. Her hands gripped the steering wheel harder and harder until her knuckles were white. Her sweat-drenched hair clung to a cheek and to her forehead. She muttered to herself now and then, but I could not make it out.

The kids dropped off as if a canister of ether had leaked into the minivan. Sleep is, ostensibly, how kids defend against psychological trauma; within two minutes they were as still as the black boles that flicked by the window. I bent my knees against the dashboard, gazed at the pine trees, and smiled—I had gotten Sylvia to swear.

*   *   *   *

"Oh, shit!" I swore, looking down the tunnel of evergreens that lined the road at the West Yellowstone exit.

"I see it. I see it," Sylvia shot back.

The rangers were stopping all traffic leaving the park. The locals were helping them. There were two police cars parked next to the park entrance ticket booth—red and blue strobes flashing.

"Guess they don't like tourists blowing away their buffalos," I said.

"Just shut up while I figure this out."

"Oh, no. You're not going to figure anything out. We're gonna stop and apologize and explain the whole thing. Right now it's just a big fine you'll have to pay. We try to sneak past 'em, and we're in big trouble. I'm not going to jail for evading arrest."

"Nathan's going to contact us today or tomorrow. We have to be in Twin Falls for his call. How will you explain *that* to the police? If we stop, we'll be arrested, and we may not get out of here for days. I'm not telling them anything," declared Sylvia.

"Come on. You gonna outrun 'em? Or you gonna outshoot 'em?"

"In my purse—get it—inside zipper."

"Get what?" I asked as I fumbled with her purse.

"There." She glanced down from the wheel. "It's one of Nate's bureau IDs. You look enough like him. If they check the car for weapons, tell them that you're with the FBI."

"No way, no *fuckin'* way. I could be arrested for impersonating a federal agent."

"Then just forget it. I knew we couldn't count on you. You just tell them whatever you want," Sylvia said, not looking at me. She stopped the Dodge minivan at the back of the line of cars and campers at the roadblock. "I'll go talk to them first." Black diaper bag in hand, she jumped out of the minivan before I could stop her.

"Fuck it," I muttered under my breath. I shoved Nathan's ID into my pocket and tagged along.

There were three rangers and two cops inspecting all vehicles leaving the park. Sylvia marched right up to the ranger who appeared to be in charge. I trotted after her, sizing up our situation and listening to Sylvia's line.

"What is the delay, sir?" she asked him.

The ranger was a hefty man with dull brown eyes and a graying mustache. In his green uniform, he looked like an enormous, unripened tomato. "Get back in your car, ma'am. Wait your turn," he replied.

"Our turn for what? We're in a hurry," she responded.

"Everybody's in a hurry..." he slowly began. I was within his periphery and within hailing distance by this time. He bobbed his head in my direction and with the chronic languor of an inveterate bureaucrat, said, "Mister, take your wife and get back to your car."

"What seems to be the problem?" I asked him.

He took a deep, labored breath, his inhalation a lusty calisthenic, and said, "It's *our* problem, so get back in your car."

"Nathan Johnson, special agent, FBI, perhaps I can assist. Honey, did you put my ID in the cubbyhole? Never mind. Here it is." I reached into my front pocket, grabbed the ID, and flashed Nathan's picture in front of the ranger's dreary eyes. "What is your name, sir?"

"Steve Meyers," he said, without shaking my hand. He examined my long hair with incredulity.

"It's me, it's me," I showed him the ID again. "I've been undercover for almost three months. Cocaine ... Colombians. What can I do to help out, Ranger Meyers?"

"It's nothing we can't handle. Some idiot shot a buffalo up on the Madison about half an hour ago. We're checking cars, trying to spot suspects."

"I see. Is the animal ... dead?" I asked, furling my brow in an impression of Rathbone's Holmes.

"Blew its head off with a high-powered rifle. I think everything's under control. Just get back in your car. They'll do a perfunctory search, and you'll be on your way."

"Darling, my mother," Sylvia said, tugging at my wrist. I turned to her. Her brown eyes danced with mischief. She was getting off on the ploy—eager to collaborate with me. She continued, directing her next remark to the head ranger, "My mother is quite ill. She lives outside of Pittsburgh. I have to get to the airport in Idaho Falls in less than three hours."

"I'm sorry to hear that, Mrs. Johnson, but, as I'm sure that your husband understands, if I let one car go through the roadblock, most of the people in that whole line of cars are going to march over here and demand that they not be inspected," he said.

"How do you know that the weapon used was a rifle?" I asked Meyers.

"What?"

"What makes you conclude that the animal was killed with a rifle?"

"Honey, please, let's hurry," Sylvia interjected. My question made her nervous. She wrenched my arm. Her apprehensiveness added a touch of integrity to our deception.

"I'm sorry, sweetheart; but you know it's my job. These gentlemen need a little supervision. A little professionalism, and we can nab this creep. Wake the kids up. We'll put them over there in the booth. You've got someone who can watch them for a while, don't you, Ranger Meyers? They're hungry and will need some lunch pretty soon. You take the car to the airport, sweetheart; I'll rent a car later and follow with the kids. Now we should not rule out the use of a handgun. The search should definitely not be limited to a rifle," I said, shifting from Sylvia to Meyers to Sylvia and back again.

"The kids are asleep. They'll be screaming bloody murder," she complained bitterly. She was mad at me for going too far—but it played well.

"We really have everything under control," Ranger Meyers quickly assured me.

"Are you certain? Take that elderly gentleman, next in line there, driving the tan Winnebago. Very jumpy. Look at his eyes. Look at the way he's gauging the officers at the car in front of him. Now I'd say that we have, maybe not probable cause, but certainly we have a reasonable suspicion that he may be the culprit. I think it is incumbent upon us to do more than take a casual glance at his motor home."

"Really, Agent Johnson, it's all under control." Meyers choked on his breath, as if he had just swallowed a cupcake whole.

"We'll have to conduct a few strip searches. You can hide a handgun anywhere," I said, with a toss of my head. Then, with a flick of the wrist, I produced the tiny pistol hidden under the tail of my T-shirt. "Tricky procedure, strip searches, I mean constitutionally," I said, slipping the pistol back under the bellyband. "I'll need separate rooms. Each must be totally enclosed—we don't want anyone peeking in on us—one for men and one for women …"

"*Strip searches?*" the ranger wheezed.

"You got a problem with that?" I demanded.

"Honey, please!" Sylvia whined on cue.

"Exactly when does your plane leave?" Ranger Meyers asked Sylvia with sudden kindness and creeping panic.

"Two forty five," Sylvia answered with a succorable sigh that almost made me laugh. She was good.

I was having fun. "I'll need a female assistant to help probe the women …" I started to outline my approach to the investigation but was rudely interrupted.

"Agent Johnson, thank you for your advice. But we can handle this. If you leave right now and drive 70, you will barely make that flight," Meyers said, glancing at his watch. "You take your wife and go. I'll wave you right around this roadblock, then call the Idaho state police and notify them to let you by any speed traps," he huffed. He put one flabby arm around my shoulder and the other about Sylvia's waist and escorted us toward the minivan.

"I don't know …" I began to object.

"Please, honey, for my mother …"

"How big are your detention facilities? We may end up holding a few," I said as I pulled away from him.

Ranger Meyers turned with me, setting Sylvia free, and spoke softly in my ear. "Never mind us. We'll handle it. I know mothers-in-law. I would hate to be in your shoes if anything happens to her, and your wife is stuck in some airport waiting for the next flight. The Idaho Falls airport is not exactly O'Hare. If you miss your flight, it could be a whole day before you get out. I appreciate your suggestions, but let us take care of it. You're on vacation, and you have your family to consider." He shook my hand, then locked his arm in mine.

I pretended to think about his offer as I scanned the line of vehicles and their impatient drivers. "Okay, we'll go. Forget the call to the state police. When it comes to driving, I'm just a citizen like anybody else. We follow the posted speed limit, make it or not."

"I respect that," he answered sincerely.

"And we'll take our turn in line."

"No. No, I insist that you go on through," he nervously urged.

We walked together to Sylvia's car—arm in arm—brother bureaucrats. Sylvia already had the motor running.

"Thank you! From the bottom of my heart, I thank you," Sylvia said to Ranger Meyers, her eyes tear-filled. She was *perfect*.

"No problem, Mrs. Johnson," smiled Ranger Meyers. He stepped back from the minivan, ducked his head to see inside to salute me, and then waved us around the roadblock.

Excerpts from the Journal of Nathan Johnson

DC, May 29

After I called Father Dougherty and thanked him for helping me keep my assignment—he denied having anything to do with it, but his childish, gigglng voice gave him away—I went to the Library of Congress to try to figure out what the pamphlet that I found in the old school bus means. I'm really not the library type; God only knows how I made it through med school. I still have nightmares about sitting down for an exam totally unprepared; but the pamphlet was the last real question mark, so I buckled down at a terminal, did some research, and made a few phone calls. It wasn't as bad as I thought. Thank God for the Internet!

Anyway, what I found out is hilarious. I won't know how it all fits together, or if it matters at all, until I can speak with the members of the Order, who begin arriving soon.

Here's what I have so far. In August of 1987, there was something called a "harmonic convergence" that took place around Sedona, Arizona, a little town south of Flagstaff in the Coconino National Forest. A New Age guru named Edward Stuphen claimed to have found "multitudinal vortices of varying potencies" in this area. A vortex, Stuphen wrote, is a "positive or negative power spot where a great concentration of energy is emitted from the earth." According to Stuphen, other vortices can be found in the Bermuda Triangle and at Stonehenge. 1987 was a particularly good year for vortices. About three thousand people gathered in the desert near Sedona at Boynton Canyon to participate in the harmonic convergence that took place. Now, a harmonic convergence is some type of "energy alignment between the vortices and the planets and the universe and the human beings present at the vortices, who direct their own energy towards effecting peace, love, and enlightenment through the balancing of their chakras." I didn't make this up. By the way, those who witnessed and reported the convergence said that nothing eventful happened—except that many of the participants who stood around in the desert on that hot August day in 1987 had "inexplicable feelings of extreme heat in their hands and feet and in the sixth chakra."

The 1987 harmonic convergence was such a success that another has been scheduled for, depending on which school one wants to believe, June 2 or June 4 of this year. It seems that since the last harmonic convergence, there has been a rift among the faithful. A group called "Sedona Watch" is still soliciting for Sedona on June 2, but a woman who calls herself "Plutonion" (I believe that both she and Stuphen are Californians) has proclaimed that the true convergence will take place in the Valley of the Gods in southern Utah on the fourth.

The humorous part, as I see it, was the notification and then the renotification of the dates for the competing convergences. Sedona Watch, which receives some of its funding from the Sedona Chamber of Commerce, originally settled on another August date for their convergence. Plutonion—who, according to the Sedona Watch newsletter, had purloined that organization's mailing list—sent out invitations and registration forms for her June 4 date, arguing that the weather was much more pleasant at that time of year.

I'm not being quite fair to Plutonion. She also offered "technical" reasons for the new time and location. Her arguments—they seem more like ramblings to me, but admittedly I am not an initiate—revolve around Navajo religious beliefs, the science of "telluric energies" (Stuphen refers to these as well), and something called *feng shui* that, I think, is an oriental type of astrology. Plutonion said that Sedona Watch had badly miscalculated the earth's *ch'i* and thus had gotten both the wrong time and place for the next convergence.

In a brilliant countermove, Sedona Watch sent out their invitations and registration forms three weeks later. A free issue of their monthly newsletter, "World Vortices," was included with their invitations. Sedona Watch admitted, after studying Plutonion's "calculations," that they had predicted the wrong date but that their "vortices' sites" were absolutely correct. Sedona Watch based their reanalysis on Yavapai Indian legends, on telluric energies, on the *feng shui*, on hydrologic cycles which they contrasted with the human circulatory system, on Rupert Sheidrake's morphic fields, *and* on an oracle of Nostradamus that reads:

> *La verge en main mise au milieu de Branches,*
> *De l'Onde il mouille et le limbe, et le pied:*
> *Un peur et voix fremissent par les manches,*
> *Splendeur divine, Le Divin pres s'assied.*

Sedona Watch had its empirical juggernaut rolling. The correct date was proven by the "best scientific methods available" to be June 2 at Sedona; those who registered early received a twenty-dollar discount.

Plutonion responded in her bimonthly newsletter, which is entitled "The Mysteries Unveiled," with an "incontrovertible proof that the *Ni"alnii'gi* of which the Navajo speak is in the Valley of the Gods." Her evidence, not as convincing as that found in "World Vortices"—because her source "of necessity remained anonymous"—was simply, *"Lapis niger, vilis et fœtens, et dicitur origo mundi, et oritur sicut germinantia."* However, Plutonion did offer a "twenty-five-dollar discount on all preregistrations and a free memento, a piece of the genuine Omphalos, hand-carved from the original."

The thoroughly convinced or totally confused can attend either or both convergences.

It will be interesting to find out to which one we are headed ... if either.

Heaven and earth last forever. The reason that heaven and earth last forever is that they do not live for themselves. Hence, they last forever. Therefore the true person leaves self behind and thus is found in front, is not guarded and thus is preserved, is self-free and thus is able to find fulfillment.

—TAO (The Sacred Way)

The Buddha said, "You should all know that all living beings are continually born and continually die simply because they do not know the everlasting true mind, the bright substance of the pure nature. Instead they engage in false thinking. It has been so since time without beginning. Their thoughts are not true and so the wheel keeps turning."

—Shurangama Sutra

Excerpts from the Unpublished Writings of Professor Harold Weintraub

[Author's note: Professor Weintraub does not keep a journal per se, though he has kept copious notes of incidents that he thinks he might use in a book or article. His unpublished notes include well over a thousand pages of reflections on the subject of immortality and of interviews with persons claiming to be immortal. The author is in the process of editing these manuscripts.

In fairness to Professor Weintraub, the reader should bear in mind that these are only notes, transcribed quickly and without aid of references, and were not intended for publication. I have tried to provide the citations or actual quotations to the sources Weintraub mentions. The ensuing sketch of Hsi Ssu T'i was probably written en route to Washington, DC, on May 28 or May 29 of this year.]

I have no reason, unless it be psychological, to explain my inability to grasp the simplicity of the concept of immortality ...

Perhaps it is due to the influence of Professor Strauss. I have spent much of my life in the examination of his doctrines of hermetic writing and the esoteric nature of truth, traversing that "longer way" onto which Strauss guided his students. Wisdom, the gold center beneath the silver filigree-work; Truth as the quest in itself, Truth as the In-Itself—these were the paths I followed.

The notion that Truth is elusive because exclusive was reinforced in me by Gödel, who placed "truth," as a mathematical proof, just out of reach by demonstrating that any proof, within Peano arithmetic, is either incomplete or unable to establish its own consistency. Yet I understood, I *knew*, in the sense that I fully grasped these theories; I *shared*, with the few, in knowing the limits of the knowable. This reinforced my sense of exclusivity. Are we who demarcate the realm of knowing inside or outside the boundary we draw? This is not an isolated instance—take as another example the Löwenheim-Skolem theorems—think of the psychological import of understanding, of *knowing* that an axiom set, *any axiom set,* cannot uniquely specify any system of mathematical objects. Axiomatics does not do what we intended it to do—and we can prove it!

Perhaps it was because of Alexandr Kojève who, in his own peculiar fashion, thought himself to be God. Kojève articulated, as forcefully as any human being ever has, the concept and consequences of the realization of wisdom.

Paradoxically challenging this aristocratic purview of the exclusivity of knowledge is the notion of the possibility of the achievement *in this life* of immortality through mystical vision. This point has been reinforced in my recent conversations with a man who calls himself Hsi Ssu T'i. This man could easily turn Descartes' assertion of the superiority of intellectual elitism on its head.

... Hsi Ssu T'i claims to be a *Lo-han,* one of sixteen Buddhist saints who attained enlightenment and immortality. He has, according to Buddhist tradition and according to himself, lived for nearly three thousand years. His life has been spent in doing acts of kindness for his fellow man, including saving the baby Jesus from drowning when the infant was hidden in a vessel in a stream to conceal him from the troops of Herod.

Though by no means loquacious, T'i is the most talkative of the immortals I have interviewed. Unfortunately, I am not fully acquainted with Eastern religions, their metaphysics or epistemologies, and much of his technical conversation escapes me. His arguments are fresh and new; some are even exhilarating; though I have the uncomfortable feeling that they have been present in me—though just beyond my grasp—for ... a long time. He is a short, solid man with coal-black eyes and hair. He wears a black suit and thick glasses and looks—I do not intend this to be demeaning, for the man is a genius—like Charlie Chan.

To begin, T'i has no love for religion. Had I understood him better, I might have picked up some crushing criticisms of various oriental sects. Essentially, the argument is that religions are necessarily the enemies of the immortals. Religions—any religion—all religions—sense the transcendental, literally transhistorical, nature of the immortals and attempt to integrate immortality as idea into a social, theological, and mystical structure of worship. T'i claims that the existence of immortals is the ground of religion—an argument that has overtones of both Platonic irony and of the dialectico-speculative logic of Hegel. Religion is the search for eternal life. Religion knows eternal life through the immortals that religions venerate and emulate. But because religion cannot make good on its offer to the masses of eternity in the here and now, religion posits immortality in an afterlife or in a soul perfected in a series of lives.

"In religion, Nirvana is never now," T'i told me. During our drive from New York to Washington, he gave us lengthy examples from secret *Shingon* and Taoist rituals as well as portrayals of perversions of sexual yogas in the Tantras of Shaktism—all of which supported his assertions.

Immortals are the foundation of, but also a danger to, religion. "Immortality comes from within," T'i said, pointing to his forehead (a gesture I now find most disturbing). "No one can give it. No one can take it. No one can teach it." He went on to explain that religions can only imitate the internal process achieved by the few, a statement that reminded me of Alfarabi's *Principles of Beings*.

[Author's note: The reference is most likely to the following: "For religion is but the impressions of these images imprinted in the soul ... Most men accept such principles as are accepted and followed, in the form of images, not of cognitions. Now the ones who follow after happiness as they cognize it and accept the principles as they cognize them are the wise men. And the ones in whose souls these things are found in the form of images ... are the believers."]

These few are thus an actualized threat to religion, for only they have the fruit that religion proffers but cannot provide.

"Knowledge of our existence by the many would be the end of religion, and the priestly class is fully aware of this," T'i said. "The many would never be satisfied with the vapid promise of salvation tomorrow; they would demand it today. And while it is true that no one—most certainly not an immortal—could provide it for them, nevertheless they would demand it as their birthright."

What religion offers instead is a thousand corruptions of the Truth. T'i's list of deceptions was long, and, I am certain that I detected this, bitter. He began by citing the Taoist alchemical writings of Ko Hung and Wei Poyang, who promised ("Whether implicitly or explicitly is no matter," said T'i) an elixir of immortality made from liquid gold and cinnabar, yet delivered only frustration, poison, sickness, and death.

Worse still, T'i reported, that *nei tan* [internal alchemy] was further perverted and applied to sexual practices in trials to reverse the aging process. "None of this," he said, quite emphatically for an immortal, "has anything whatsoever to do with eternal life."

As it becomes clear that there is no magical prescription for achieving immortality, alchemists become esotericists. They take their formulae and chants and meditations underground, where they can maintain credibility from behind a veil of secrecy. Immortality is real, they claim, but is available only to the elect with their "Secret Instructions for Ascent to Perfection." [Author's note: A reference to the *Teng-chen yin-chueh* by T'ao Hung-ching. Outwardly, T'i, a Buddhist, was, apparently, not fond of Taoism and its offshoots.] "Thus arise the perversions of *Shingon,* Tantric Buddhism, and the *I Kuan Tao.*"

Esotericism is not, T'i asserts, an endeavor to conceal that knowledge that might be dangerous to those who are incapable of using it correctly; *rather it is a pitiful attempt on the part of the deluded to cloak their ignorance and failure in mysticism and obscurity.* Professor Strauss would be livid. Yet T'i's idea is a powerful one.

[Author's note: Emphasis is Weintraub's. In *Persecution and the Art of Writing,* Leo Strauss wrote, "Suppression of independent thought has occurred fairly frequently in the past. It is reasonable to assume that earlier ages produced proportionately as many men capable of independent thought as we find today, and that at least some of these men combined understanding with caution. Thus, one may wonder whether some of the greatest writers of the past have not adapted their literary technique to the requirements of persecution, by presenting their views on all the then crucial questions exclusively between the lines."]

"Shall I tell you, at this very moment, shall I tell you what the true esoteric teaching is? Shall I reveal to you the secret of the immortals?" T'i queried my wife and me, squinting and smiling at each of us. Miriam, who sat in the front of the vehicle with Judy, laughed softly. (Judy, though driving, was immersed in our conversation.)

My wife and I responded emphatically in the affirmative.

"The esoteric teaching is this: There is no esoteric teaching." He paused briefly—chuckled at the diligence of our attention. "At least not for immortals. How is it that I would explain this to you in your own culture's symbols? I am but the wheel of the chariot." (Miriam found this statement to be particularly amusing. "Only a man would utter such egotistical nonsense," she laughed.) "Even so, woman," T'i chided her, "you know as well as I. Thus it is; thus it must always be. Those who profess knowledge of any secret of immortality lie, for there is no secret. Though very few traverse it, the path to immortality is open to all. Such is the secret that is none." Those were his words.

Immortality is a pragmatic concept, according to T'i. [A partial sentence that begins "This is another uncommon, yet fruitful, idea ..." is crossed out.] But I am tired, and my stomach is always troublesome. I want only peaceful sleep. I will write more of T'i later. Though now I do recall that Cicero spoke somewhere of the pragmatic genesis of the concept in his *Republic*—perhaps it was Virgil ...

[Author's note: The entry ends here. The citation from Cicero is: *"Haec, quæ de animæ immortalitate dicerentur caelogue, non somniantium philosophorum esse commenta nec fabulas incredibiles, quas Epicurei derident, sed prudentium coniecturas."* I am unable to locate the reference to Virgil.]

E-mail from Dr. Judy Weintraub to the Author, Sent May 30

In any event, his fever has broken, and the vomiting has subsided, and he is far better this evening that he has been for a week. Harold contends that he is up for this trek. I have vowed to see it through with him.

Excepting his size, your cousin looks remarkably like you. Yesterday, in fact, when we first met at Catholic University, Harold called out to him, using your name. Agent Johnson blushed. I apologized to him and told him that Harold was feverish. Johnson said that he took it as a compliment—he jocularly but firmly requested that we call him Nathan from then on.

Be that as it may, your cousin is very different from you. I noticed it almost immediately. The way that he constantly examines those with whom he has contact—he is very cautious and very aware. Like my own silly Socrates, your head is always in the clouds, but Nathan is a well-grounded human being.

He has rented six rooms in a hotel near the campus. The rooms are all in one end of the building on the top story—that is, the fourth floor. We have three rooms on each side of the hall. The middle room of each set of three has passage doors to the rooms immediately adjacent. Agent Johnson has nailed these passage doors open. He literally took a hammer and nailed them open. I have no idea what type of agreement he made with the hotel management!

He has assigned my husband and me one of these central rooms. He and Father Dougherty occupy the other—directly across the hallway from ours. Our guests—our "immortals"—are, or soon will be, in the four adjacent rooms. Nathan will give each of us ("issue to each member," as he puts it) a key to the appropriate central room. The hallway access from the other four rooms will remain locked. Thus Father Dougherty, Nathan, Harold, and I are charged with the coming and going of the "immortals" who must exit our respective rooms to reach the hallway. Nathan is quite adamant that his procedures are to be obeyed.

Having now spent some time with these people, I am glad of it. Nathan says that during our coming travels, whenever possible, our lodgings will be arranged in this fashion.

As you well know, Harold has been interested in his "immortals" for a number of years. His friend Elijah was a guest in our home on a few occasions. I too was interested in the quaint gentleman, though I look at the nature of these "immortals" from a perspective very different from that of my husband. Neurology is closely related to my field of specialty microbiology. The laws of the two are practically interchangeable, for both sciences deal primarily with the theoretical nature of the cell. Though there is no extant literature on the mental disease these people suffer, I am in the process of formulating an initial theory—which I have, over the last few years, been running by some neurologist and psychiatrist friends of mine.

At the risk of boring you, I'll set out some specifics. The neurons, or nerve cells in the brain, never actually touch each other when interacting. Each of their electrical firings triggers a chemical release. The chemicals are called neurotransmitters. These chemicals jump the space, the synapse, from the axon of one neuron to the dendrite of those nearby. Put very simply, there are two different types of chemicals released, one that is an exciter and causes nearby neurons to fire, the other is an inhibitor. In epileptics, for example, the exciter is unleashed in explosive waves that start in the center of the brain and cause millions of multiple neuron misfirings within it.

There has been very little study done on the amount, frequency and location of neurotransmitter reactions in the brains of geniuses. However, there is some sketchy evidence that exciter neurotransmitters are emitted in inappreciably elevated amounts in the frontal lobes of such persons. Practically speaking, the cognitive portion of the mind of a genius operates on a minutely higher metabolic level than that of a normal person. Brain size or shape has little or nothing to do with genius. Genius is, from the physiological perspective, a more often repeated pattern of thinking due to elevated chemical activity in the reasoning part of the brain than that in the normal human mind. Think of it as memorization, or patterning, or complex structuring by biochemical necessity.

I have spent nearly three days in close contact with two "immortals." I will probably have the pleasure of several more such days with several more. Two points strike me as initially critical: First, they clearly have sagacity far superior to the common lot of humanity. They are, without doubt, geniuses. Second, excepting brief spurts of incredible and often confused states of mental energy, they are quite lethargic. Their brains seem to shut down automatically after what might be called the "exacerbation."

Unlike the "healthy" genius, who must often resort to chemicals like alcohol or barbiturates to inhibit the mental process, I wonder if the brain of an "immortal" naturally ameliorates the effect of the exciter neurotransmitter by counterreleasing, say, GABA, an inhibitor chemical in the brain—like a reverse form of epilepsy. All of this is pure speculation on my part, but it is a place to start valid scientific research, as opposed to my husband's mystical and philosophic meanderings.

After Harold and I had settled in our meager hotel room, and before Nathan and the others left to pick up the first arrivals from Italy, your cousin came and asked to speak to us in private. As I told you, Harold has been ill. He was just falling asleep when Nathan dropped by, so Nathan and I went down to the lobby. I drank some stale coffee and, as if to prove that he was your flesh and blood, Nathan drank two cans of Pepsi. We sat in the lobby on an orange couch and spoke over the racket spewing from the ragged speaker of a blurry old television set.

I learned that Nathan has attempted to enjoin you to come with us. As we spoke further, we discovered that it was you who had brought Father Dougherty, Nathan, Harold, and me together. I said that I was not in the least surprised and that such would be in keeping with your mystique. We both laughed.

I told him that I had been writing to you. He urged me to keep it up and told me that you are considering a book on our little adventure. I agreed to try to keep an accurate account of our travels.

Late in our conversation, after he had finished his soft drinks and had scrutinized me (such attention, by the way, would have been most disconcerting had it not been for the fact that his soft brown eyes remind me so much of yours), Nathan asked me if I would wear a miniature machine to record some of the conversations that I might have alone with some of the members of our group. He said that our traveling companions might interact differently with a woman. I have since spoken with Harold about Nathan's proposal, and I have decided to wear the device when it seems appropriate.

Later today the four of us, Father Dougherty, Harold, Nathan, and I, mutually decided to extend yet another invitation for you to meet with us here. We were all agreed that you know as much about these people as any of us, including, I think, even Harold. Certainly if a book is what you have in mind, the firsthand experience will be invaluable. In addition, your presence would be, as always, entertaining and enlightening. I'll ask you again, on their behalf as well as mine, to reconsider.

Harold is, thank God, feeling much better this evening. I believe that I have already written of that. So I will end for now, but I promise to write more tomorrow.

With love,
[Typed]
Judy

> That which is eternally moving is immortal.
>
> —Plato, *Phaedrus*

Excerpts from the Journals of Nathan Johnson and Father Dougherty

DC, May 30

Quick note for you, Cuz, because most of what happened yesterday and today is on tape. I met my first "immortals" last night; two of them, Miriam and an Asian man they call Mr. Tie [Hsi Ssu T'i]. They drove from New York to DC with Professor Weintraub and his wife, Judy. The immortals say almost nothing, at least not to me, and when they do speak, they make no sense whatsoever. The Weintraubs are nice enough, but he seems quite sick. I left it alone. His wife is watching him like a hawk, and I have enough on my mind. I've rented hotel rooms for everyone. I'm trying to keep a handle on location and movement. [Author's note: Nathan's description of the arrangement of the hotel rooms is omitted. Judy Weintraub described it in the e-mail reproduced above.]

This morning I drove with Dougherty, Miriam, and Tie to Dulles to pick up two more of them—Father Dobo, a black man, and a Sister Maria. I had requisitioned and received an armored transport van. It has a bored-out 440 Dodge engine. Runs like a bat out of hell. But it only gets five or six miles to the gallon.

The van is wired internally so I can digitally record all the conversations as we travel. These could provide some interesting material for you. There will probably be a lot of empty space on the disks and a lot of background noise, but you'll just have to sit through it if you want to hear what we're talking about, which isn't much so far. There's also a police radio in it—though it's hard for me to imagine to whom I'll be talking.

I say again that these are the most evasive people I have ever met. The intent behind their speech does not seem criminal or threatening; on the other hand, they don't appear to be frightened or concerned or to understand fully the severity of their own situation. They seem stuck somewhere between playfulness and boredom.

My first impression of them is that they are all quite sophisticated but crazy as loons. I'm not looking forward to trucking them clear across the United States. I can't let myself forget that none of them are above suspicion.

I have a new method for ordering the recordings. Disks made in the van will be marked with a V and begin at V1. As of yesterday, tapes from my body wire start with B1. Recorded telephone conversations (as of yesterday) T1. All others, like my Dictaphone, will start at M1. (M for miscellaneous.) Conversations for May 29 and 30 are on V1-V3 and B1-2. Everything before that I have already shipped, including (at his insistence) some of Father Dougherty's documents.

* * * *

Father Dougherty, late afternoon of May 30, home.

"Home," I write, describing my current location. I have little affinity for the notion. Strangely enough, it is only recently that I have given thought to it—while awaiting the arrival of the members of the Order of the Beloved, arranging my affairs, packing my clothes again.

After all of these years, I never miss leaving this place of abode. Certainly I miss my students. I have, of course, many friends here. I have my parish on the weekends. There are many people here who depend upon me, many who love me. Yet none of it has ever equated to home. Nothing ever has. *Nothing*.

Even as a child, I always had a wanderlust, a feeling—more an instinct—that I was not in the right place, that I was not in my place. My parents were kind to me, decent to each other, but the love there was perfunctory. I was an only child. Like Abraham and Sarah, Zachary and Elizabeth, my parents were married for over ten years before my arrival. I was the answer to their prayers. But there was disappointment in the promise. They realized that they had grown old as they tarried for a child—that they had spent their lives hoping—not living.

They gave me back to God, to the priesthood. Sometimes I resent them for that. Sometimes I think that they resented God.

There was a very pleasant surprise yesterday. Harold and Judy Weintraub are here. They arrived in a rental car, accompanied by two of Harold's New York immortals. One is Miriam, a strikingly beautiful woman of whom Harold has spoken often, the other is a Mr. Hiss Sue Tie [Hsi Ssu T'i], an Asian man—a Buddhist monk, I believe he professes to be—though he dresses like a meretricious Japanese businessman.

Harold is in very good spirits but very poor health. Judy is perceptibly distraught over the matter of his health, although there has been no time to discuss it with her.

Nathan has arranged rooms for all of the members of the Order at the Holiday Inn near the University. He has dictated that the Weintraubs and I also take rooms there until we are ready to travel. He has apportioned the rooms in a most unusual manner.

[Author's note: Dougherty's description of the hotel arrangements is also omitted.]

The first two members of the Order arrived this morning. Sister Maria Sanchez and Father Dobo flew to Dulles on Air Italia. Seemingly the other members of the Order will be arriving either separately or in groups of two. Father Holden told me last week, when we spoke by telephone, that it would be a simple matter to eliminate the entire Order if all of them flew in the same airplane.

Yesterday I told Nathan that Father Holden had requested that the Order be taken to the West by automobile. Nathan somehow managed to secure a van that, he told me, is used by the FBI for the transportation of essential witnesses. Evidently the vehicle, which looks to me like an ordinary white delivery van, has bulletproof windows and walls. There are three bench seats and two folding seats in the rear that are separated from the two front seats by a metal panel that, according to Nathan, is also bulletproof. There is a sliding door in the panel so that those in the driver's cab will be able to speak to the passengers in the rear. Nathan assures me that the vehicle will transport at least ten people comfortably and quickly and that the van will take all of us wherever it is that we may be going.

Nathan drove the van to the airport to pick up Father Dobo and Sister Maria. Miriam, Mr. Tie, and I accompanied him. The Weintraubs remained at the hotel to rest. It is difficult to describe our reunion at the airport or to accurately relate the conversation that took place after it, on our way to the hotel—difficult because the interactions between these people are usually so unique and subtle.

I hugged both Father Dobo and Sister Maria and welcomed them warmly. However, the exchange of greetings among the four "immortals" could only be classified as nonchalant. There was little physical contact between them. They nodded heads and exchanged glances. It was as if their knowledge of each other was considerable but secondhand.

Least cordial was the reception of Sister Maria by Miriam. I would call it less than polite. Both women are exceptionally beautiful; though Miriam appears to be at least twenty years younger than Sister Maria. Miriam was dressed in a blue wool business suit with a jacket and skirt, Sister Maria in a black frock. It was Miriam, rather than Sister Maria, who was aloof. Miriam looked harshly at Sister Maria and said only, "You are Sanchez."

I am making far too much of very little. Even before we arrived at Dulles, Miriam stated that her sleep had been troubled the last two nights. Sister Maria has a cold and has said little to anyone since her arrival. She lay on the backseat of the van on the trip from the airport to the hotel. She has complained to me of earache, and I will have her see my physician tomorrow.

I would say that Father Dobo was happy to see both Miriam and Mr. Tie. Ostensibly, he and the Buddhist have traveled together from time to time. So this was a genuine reunion for them.

"Do you remember, Hiss, when last we traveled here?" Father Dobo asked the monk on our way to the hotel. They sat on the front bench, nearest Nathan, who was driving, and looked through the door to the cab and out of the windshield. Miriam and I sat behind them. Nathan said nothing on the return trip, but the door between us was open, and I am certain that he could hear the conversation.

Tie, who is a diminutive man with pronounced Asiatic features, replied, "Tell, me. No, I recall. It has been seventy years."

"Seventy-three years next October. There were many more farms. The roads were unpaved, and most of our travel was by rail," Father Dobo said, motioning at the traffic on the freeway that circles the District of Columbia.

"Yes. Has it been so long?" asked Mr. Tie. "I remember that the trees were so beautiful."

"Seventy-three years, and I have not been in this country since," Father Dobo said to Tie. Turning to me, he continued, "This country is not as wonderful as many Americans believe—as you are taught. It is so. The America I knew was populated by the most vulgar ... when I was last here, I was treated inhumanely."

"Ah, the train! Of course, I remember now. We were not allowed in the passenger cars!" Tie laughed.

"A person of 'color' traveled in the ... my recollection is that they were denoted 'box cars.'"

"Or with the animals being transported for slaughter!" Tie laughed harder still.

"Yes. It was so in America. Though I found it considerably less amusing," Father Dobo responded, not with bitterness but rather with, as they say in school, *taedium vitae*. He turned to me again. "Does this help you to understand? When you have asked us, as you have on many occasions, why there are so few of us—how can I explain to you—the reason? The world has not been a place for us to be, to grow. Especially in this 'blessed' America. In this land that is the example for all others. Yes, it is so."

"But, Father, most societies have been, at their core … they have been racist," I argued.

"To a degree, all societies," Mr. Tie said—in my support, I believe.

"But most societies recognize and value genius and self-initiative. Indeed, they reward it of necessity. The people of these United States pride themselves on self-achievement, on self-worth, but only for one race, only for one creed—not for all," replied Father Dobo.

Miriam smiled at me as if it were me, rather than Father Dobo, who needed succor. "But that is changing," she said.

"Perhaps," answered Father Dobo without emotion.

"We have grown much as a people since your last visit," I promised Father Dobo. However, I admit that I was greatly confused by the nature of the conversation that took place around me and yet seemed directed to me.

"Yes. And everywhere," added Tie.

"Perhaps it may be," Dobo replied. "But in the past, these same societies left us to ourselves. Now they hunt us down like animals."

"But the FBI man is here for us," argued Miriam, again as if to hearten me.

Mr. Tie nodded at me with a smile and then turned and spoke through the open panel to Nathan. "Yes. My thanks to Father Dougherty and to you, Agent Johnson." Then the Buddhist monk said to Father Dobo, "I did not expect so much. Did you?"

"I do not know," replied Father Dobo. "I did not know what to expect. And I do not. Though I am certain that we shall soon enough know if … it is so."

Father Dobo smiled at me. His yellow eyes, deep in his gaunt black face, looked so very, very weary. Yet nothing in them betrayed hope—or sadness. My mind tells me that this inscrutability is only symptomatic of the illness. My heart tells me that it is so much more.

> It follows that every class is a class of classes, and hence that everything is a class of classes.
>
> —W. V. O. Quine, *Set Theory and Its Logic*

> Therefore, if Man is Concept and if Concept is Time (that is, man is an essentially temporal being), Man is essentially mortal; and he is Concept, that is, absolute Knowledge or Wisdom incarnate, only if he knows this. Logos becomes flesh, becomes Man, only on the condition of being willing and able to die.
>
> —Kojève, *Introduction à la Lecture de Hegel*

Excerpts from Harold Weintraub's *Analysis as Nihilism*, Oxford University Press, 1979, pp. 374–376. Footnotes omitted

Life, as I have shown, contrary to Hubert and Bernays, falls outside any virtual class, even beyond what Quine calls the "identity of indiscernibles." Indeed, when we speak of life, from the perspective of human consciousness, that is when I speak of my life or you of yours, we speak of a *life lived.* We speak of a process of which we are in the midst. We speak of a whole that is becoming—a whole that is necessarily both less than (because incomplete) and greater than (because the "speaking of" is within the context of the "living through") the sum of its parts. Life is neither quantifiable nor predicable. Life is lived.

We live the life that we see. That is what I mean when I say "lived life." This seeing is conceptual; our human living is often a series of conscious acts. At this level, life itself is conceptual and, thus, quantifiable—albeit in only rough approximation. Thus the concept of life *from the perspective of the lived life* is quasi-analyzable since the lived life is, as we discussed in Section 5 above, post-intuitive, which is to say that we have a conscious continuum of *this life* as *our life*. More precisely, the "lived life" is a translogical series of concepts regarding the original concept "life" and, as Aristotle might say, we "somehow" know this. This is another way of showing that the lived life is a process. Note that neither our concept of life nor the parallel process we identify as the "lived life" can ever be a *specific* set or class because each is infinitely definable.

We have reached the end of our topic for this chapter. But before we proceed to a last look at Gödel's consistency-proof for the generalized continuum hypothesis, I want to mention an anomaly one encounters when venturing to examine the reflexive formulation of the concept of life from the perspective of set theory. We saw earlier (Section 12) the problems involved in offering a formal analysis of a concept of "life" which was noncontradictory *and* tautological. We found that there will always be consistent analyses of "conscious existence" *outside* any given formal theory and that we can prove such analyses are true from axioms *within* that theory. We proved that the concept "life" is essentially one of a process that must be translogically described not as "the concept of life" but as a "lived life" in order to maintain (even limited) analytical access to the original idea.

But what of the concept of the concept of life? Clearly, such a reflexive construction is intelligible and meaningful in ordinary speech. I see that there is such a concept of the concept. I present it to you as meaningful. But how do we *know* a concept of a concept? Then, more specifically, what is the concept of the concept of *life?* Let me suggest, and I can only suggest it at this point without taking us far afield from the issues at hand, that this knowing is inherently intuitional. Seeing that there is a concept of the concept of life (or of any concept) is a "now-knowing." I write (or read, or hear) the words, and they instantaneously "make sense" to me outside all procedures of analysis. In necessarily imprecise language, in conceptualizing a concept, I see myself looking at my own seeing, I listen for myself hearing my voice—the first as in a mirror, the second as to a self-recording. Or, again, we conceive this now-knowing as a knowledge of the whole *prior to* knowing in the theoretical or analytical sense.

I intend to discuss from whence this "now-knowing" arises on another occasion. Until then, I offer the following speculation—understanding full well that it is only speculation. Like the concept of life, the concept of the concept of life seems imbued with ontological significance. Since we have proved that we can assert that any fully explicated "concept of life" falls within the (translogical) domain of the "lived life," then the concept of the concept of life might well take place within the "now-knowing" of the lived life or, to put it less obliquely, within the intuitive instant that is the realm of "living the lived life." What would it be like to live within the pure moment of this eternal, because timeless, now-knowing? I suggest that herein may reside the solution to the mystery of human existence, of being, even of immortality.

On the Author's Travels with Sylvia Johnson and Her Children, May 31–June 1, Continued

Things were different between Sylvia and me from the moment that we drove past the guard station and out of Yellowstone Park. The tension between us had changed markedly. Our mutual resentment had not disappeared or even abated. Neither of us will ever be the founder of the other's fan club. But our anxieties were deeper, thicker, more nuanced—merged. She had killed, and I had lied to cover for her. We had done more than break the law. We had shared sin.

Sylvia laughed—morbid laughter, with an icy, splintered edge—as she drove much too rapidly through downtown West Yellowstone. Her laughter awoke the children. It frightened them.

"Whahut'so funny, Mommy?" Sherry yawned with fear.

"The-the bu-buffalo wa-was mean." Kaylynn, the eldest, half understood the disturbed laughter and sobbed the words in a valiant effort to reassure her mother. Then she broke down, crying.

Jeremy awoke bawling.

"For chrissake, slow down!" I ordered Sylvia in a snappy whisper. I turned to quell the children. "Hey, kids—anybody hungry? Come on, don't cry. There's nothing to be scared of. I'm hungry. Anybody else hungry?"

"Mommy, are you hungry?" asked Kaylynn.

"Mommy, we's hungry," said Sherry.

"Hunry," snuffled Jeremy.

"Yeah, Mommy, we's hunry," I teased.

"It's okay. I'm all right. We'll stop. That was ... you were hilarious! You had ... you had that ranger ... buffaloed," Sylvia chuckled, staring hard at the road, gaining control of her emotions, slowing down the blue minivan, melting the edge of her laughter.

"I'm so hungry, I could eat a buffalo!" I bellowed. Sylvia laughed louder, but more warmly. Kaylynn and I joined her, then Sherry; then, finally, a confused Jeremy.

"Bufflo! Bufflo!" snorted Jeremy, pawing for some laughs of his own. He got them. We hooted.

Sylvia stopped in front of Randy Hutchins's Big-Little Western Café. "Not a single word about what happened to the mean buffalo," Sylvia admonished. The kids and I solemnly nodded our heads in abjection. We all piled out for lunch. I swear to God—once inside and seated, we all ordered buffalo burgers from Randy Hutchins himself.

*   *   *   *

I had never made a conscious decision not to have children. However, with each miscarriage and with each tubal pregnancy in my marriage, I had grown more and more attached to my writing, less and less attached to my wife. I'm not proud of it; but somewhere along that path of pain, I lost all hope of ever becoming a father. I did not know it, at least I had never consciously realized it, but my books had become my children. As our goofy, giggly, silly, slobbery lunch in Randy Hutchins's Big-Little Western Café came to an end, I understood that the only family I would ever have was my work.

"You got quiet all of a sudden. Is everything okay?" Sylvia asked me as we loaded her kids back into the minivan.

I rubbed my eyes with the palms of my hands. "Sure."

*   *   *   *

We spent the night in Idaho Falls. I slept in the van. Sylvia rented a motel room for the kids and her.

At about eleven the next morning, we stopped in Burley—at Aunt Lottie's and Uncle Archie's house—on our way to Twin Falls, on our way to await Nathan's next telephone call. My aunt and uncle had returned from fishing. The Bronco was parked in the driveway. The boat was back in the garage. Uncle Archie was waiting for us at his front door. He stepped onto the porch, waved at the approaching vehicle, then turned and yelled something into the house. A moment later, before Sylvia had even pulled curbside, Aunt Lottie emerged in her bathrobe and bounced out to the minivan, wet red hair flapping out from under a towel. She had spent her entire adult life in an unending battle against gaining weight. No matter how hard she tried, she remained a plentiful 180 pounds or so. Her puffed face was distraught. Her usually cheerful eyes were unquiet.

"Let's get the children and hurry right in," Lottie said as she attempted, in vain, to smile.

I glanced at Sylvia to gauge her reaction to her harried mother-in-law. Sylvia tightened the muscles of her thin face, squeezing out a bit more courage. It was a tough squeeze. The flesh beneath her left eye twitched at the exertion. She rubbed an ankle with her foot, rubbed her thighs with her hands, and then reached behind the driver's seat for her black diaper bag. "Come on, kids. In to see Grandma and Grandpa," she said through gritted teeth.

When Adam transgressed my statutes, then was decreed that now is done. Then were the entrances of this world made narrow, full of sorrow and travail: they are but few and evil, full of perils, and very painful. For the entrances of the elder world were wide and sure, and brought immortal fruit.

—II Esdras 7:11–13

If one holds, with Hegel, that history can be completed in and by itself, and that "absolute knowledge" (= wisdom or discursive truth) results from the "comprehension" or "explanation" of history as integral (or integrated in and by this very knowledge) by a coherent discourse (Logos) which is "circular" or "uni-total" in the sense that it exhausts all the possibilities (assumed to be finite) of "rational" thought (that is, thought which is not in itself contradictory)—if one grants all this, I say, one can equate history and eternity.

—Kojève, *Tyranny and Wisdom*

Excerpts from the Journal of Father Jerome Dougherty

Evening, the Holiday Inn near the University, Washington, DC, May the thirty-first.

Father Hugo arrived today. He is such a delight. Holden and Quindilar arrive tomorrow, and our party will be complete. Before I recount this day's activities, I note that moments ago, Nathan came into the room. I have no idea where he has been this afternoon, but something is troubling him deeply. He will not discuss it with me. He is in the shower right now. I only know that he has told me to tell the others to be ready to leave in the morning as soon as we pick up Fathers Holden and Quindilar. Apparently we will not spend another night here.

Two health notes. My physician examined Sister Maria this morning. He prescribed some antibiotics for her ear infection, which, he told us, is not serious. Professor Weintraub is feeling much better and was all about today, asking questions of everyone, receiving answers from no one.

As I mentioned, Father Hugo's plane landed this morning. Harold wanted to go with Nathan to the airport to receive him. Nathan objected at first, stating his wish that the Weintraubs remain in the hotel with the others. Harold was adamant. But because Nathan has declared that everyone shall stay together or in groups supervised by the Weintraubs, Nathan, and myself, six of us (Nathan, Harold, Father Dobo, Miriam, Mr. Tie, and I) went in the white van to greet Father Hugo. Judy Weintraub stayed at the hotel to look after Sister Maria.

The topic of conversation on our trip to the airport was led by Professor Weintraub, who tried to elicit from our companions our exact destination. Interestingly, in this discussion, it was Mr. Tie who acted as the spokesperson for the group.

"So, who will tell me where we are going?" Harold asked when all were seated and the van was traveling southwest toward Reagan Airport. Nathan drove the van, leaving the sliding door, from the front to the rear of the van, open. The other five mentioned above, including Harold and myself, rode in the back. Today was a lovely spring day with few clouds and very little humidity.

"Yes, someone speak to us of our destination. I am interested in this topic myself," said Father Dobo.

"Come now, Father, surely you know where we are going and why we are going there," Harold said to Father Dobo.

"I may know why. I have not the faintest idea of where," he replied.

"Let us begin with intention then," Harold said to him.

Father Dobo pursed his thick lips and laced his thin fingers, "I said only that I may."

"Well, then?" asked Weintraub.

"I will know with more certainty when I am told where," answered Father Dobo. He shrugged his shoulders to indicate that he could proffer no more.

"Surely one of you can inform us of our destination," the professor stated.

"It'd be real helpful to me too," Nathan added over his shoulder through the door to the rear of the van.

"I don't believe that any one of us has been informed of that detail," responded Mr. Tie.

"How can that be, Mr. Tie? Are you telling me that all of you have been given only a general location?" asked Weintraub.

"Yes. Excellent. Only a bearing. We only know that we are to begin. We are decided upon that."

"Begin what?" Weintraub asked.

"It is difficult to explain until we know more," Tie replied.

"Know more from whom?" Weintraub questioned Tie.

"I will not know from whom until I am told the destination," Tie answered.

"Who will tell you?"

"I do not know. It may even be that I will be the one who decides. Or Father Dobo or Miriam or any of the others," Tie answered with a hint of exasperation.

"Don't push so hard, Harold," Miriam interrupted at this point. "It will be easy to understand as it unfolds. That is what we have learned to do. If you really desire to know us, then watch as events unfold. We only know that we are uncertain. We are uncertain for a reason."

"Is it pushy, and I put the question again, to ask 'What is that reason?'"

"The reason is that we do not yet know," answered Tie.

Father Dobo then said, "At this time, that is as clear a response as can be provided by any of us. It is confusing, but it is so."

"Perhaps a little clearer. Life is process. You said that somewhere in your writings, Professor—did you not?" Tie inquired.

Harold thought carefully before answering. "Yes, as part of an argument about the limits of analytical reasoning. Yes, I have offered the argument, but it was only an argument."

"Precisely. In your occupation, you argue for a living," responded Mr. Tie. "But life is not an argument."

"I, too, am at a loss," I added.

Miriam looked at me with kindness. "I can assure you, Father, that we are just as bewildered. The difference between us is that we know and accept our ignorance. We stand ready to act upon it. You must trust that we are all working for the same goal. You must have a little faith and patience with us—with yourself."

"That may be. But I am still confused," I admitted.

"What is that goal?' the professor asked her.

"I do not know," she replied.

"It can be stated this way, and then we should say no more about it. The goal is to teach the unteachable. That is our destination," said Mr. Tie. Father Dobo nodded in agreement. Miriam only smiled.

*   *   *   *

"Ah, Father Jerome! Miriam! What? Here is Hiss! By God, a worthy reception from my homeland!" exclaimed Father Brad as he pushed his way through the turnstile at the airport portico.

"Welcome. Father Brad Hugo, this is Professor Harold Weintraub, and this is Agent Nathan Johnson of the FBI."

"FBI? Intriguing," Father Hugo responded. He glanced at Father Dobo, who tipped his head ever so slightly to encourage him. "A pleasure, Agent Johnson." Hugo extended his hand. "And, you, Professor Weintraub. What an honor! You are a man I have wanted to meet. It is absolutely remarkable that anyone ... did you know ... you are this close," Father Hugo said, and he held his hands before his chest, palms facing one another, a foot apart. "Soon we shall have you this close." Father Brad held a plump forefinger and plumper thumb up to one eye and stared at Harold through the opening. "It is so—right, Father Dobo?"

"Is it possible, please, for him to be accompanied back to the airplane?" Father Dobo asked Nathan.

"I don't think so," Nathan laughed. "We're at a half-hour meter, so let's get moving. Do you have luggage?"

"All in here," Father Hugo replied, lifting his thick briefcase with one hand and a small canvas duffel bag with the other. "Purse and script only. Oh, yes, and a present for Father Jerome," he said with a waggish smile. Like all immortals, he travels with the barest of necessities.

At that moment, I noticed that something about Father Hugo's appearance had changed. Though I could not tell why, he appeared much younger.

"Here, I'll have no more need for this," Father Hugo said. He reached into the pocket of his jacket, pulled out a small half-empty bottle, and handed it to me.

It was a bottle of hair dye. Now I understood why he looked younger. His hair was the same ruddy brown that it had been when we first met some forty years ago. He looked not a day over thirty-five. I read the label on the bottle. The color of the dye was gray.

*   *   *   *

"Father Brad," I asked Father Hugo when we were all in the van and returning to our hotel, "how is your work on the Church history progressing?"

"Finished. Ah, me, finished," he answered.

"Wonderful! What a magnificent achievement!" I told him. "A twenty-volume history of the Church," I said to Professor Weintraub.

"Prolific, indeed," Weintraub agreed. "Though I would not have hypothesized that an immortal would deign to preserve himself in such fugacious fashion."

Father Brad grinned his broad, puckish grin. "This close to the truth, Professor," he said, holding up his hands, a foot apart, again.

"One would think that immortality would preclude such an enterprise. As Hegel said, we mortals endeavor to live beyond death through our work." Harold pushed the issue.

"Jesus does not write. Nor does Socrates …" Father Brad began his response.

"Are you implying that Socrates is still alive?" Professor Weintraub demanded.

"In fact, they both are. Their deaths and resurrections are the two greatest mysteries in history—and, speaking of history—Moses is also alive and living in …" Father Brad looked to Mr. Tie for the answer.

"Stettler, Alberta," Tie said.

"Somewhere in Canada," continued Father Brad. "Moses, as everyone except Wellhausen knows, authored the Pentateuch. Like myself, and like Father Dobo, he did this, he wrote, not to preserve himself, his ego, or his ideas—whatever those may mean—he did it to preserve history."

"Then immortals are free to write about history for the sake of the preservation of history—or of the truth?" asked Harold.

"Ah! A trick question! But, to begin an answer, for a beginning is all I have, I would not say that we are *free* to do it. I would say, wouldn't you, Father Dobo, that it is a requirement?"

Father Dobo was riding on the rear seat of the van between Miriam and myself. "Earnestly, it is so," he answered over the bench in front of us.

"Requirement is culling," Miriam said. "Don't let this man mislead you, Harold. We don't have to write anything. It is a decision each of us makes on our own. I do not write. Others don't—most others. There is something unnatural, deathlike—decaying—about it. Father Dobo is an etymologist, not an historian. Father Hugo is a prankster. Every word from his mouth skirts the truth."

"Every word skirts the truth," Mr. Tie said in Father Brad's defense. "Which makes Miriam, like the rest of us, an etiologist."

"You don't write," Miriam challenged Mr. Tie.

"Because I am so often occupied defending those who do," Mr. Tie smiled.

"It is so," added Father Dobo with a *giggle*. I was stunned. I have never heard Father Dobo laugh—let alone *giggle*.

"We all are etiologists, but the intention does matter," Miriam answered on her own behalf, as well as the professor's, with a blush and a smile. Her eyes, dark and mysterious, flashed with amusement. Indeed, at this moment, albeit for only a moment, all of the immortals were as enlivened as I had ever seen them.

"Why, then, to rephrase my earlier question, are you required to write only on history and, I gather, on related subjects? Is it to preserve the truth?" asked Professor Weintraub, who also seemed delighted by the conversation.

Father Hugo tugged at his eyebrows for a moment and then, in a voice suddenly weary, said, "No. No. We write with a motivation that has escaped the many. We write so that history may end."

> In the beginning of the world there was no such thing as death. Everybody continued to live until there were so many people that the earth had no room for any more. The chiefs held a council to determine what to do. One man rose and said he thought it would be a good plan to have the people die and be gone for a little while and then return. As soon as the man sat down, Coyote jumped up and said he thought people ought to die forever.
>
> —Caddo Indian Legend

Conversation between Nathan Johnson (NJ) and FBI Director Herman Lowry (HL). Probable date is June 1

[Author's note: As of this date (June 1) entries in the journal of Nathan Johnson, whether written or recorded, become sparse and not very coherent. Accordingly, there will be few references to the same for the remainder of this manuscript, with one exception that will be noted several sections below.

Nathan did, until the end, force himself to record as many conversations as possible. These recordings are consistently and legibly marked; and I have used, and will continue to use them, in the reconstruction of the conversations that occur throughout this book. (The last few recordings I received were not labeled. The reason they were unmarked will become clear later in the manuscript.) What follows is a conversation between Nathan and the director of the FBI sometime, I would postulate, during the day of June 1.]

HL: [Apparently to someone else:] Yes, next Friday. [Then to Johnson:] Go ahead, sit down. Sorry to keep you waiting.
NJ: Sir.

HL: I'm going to tell it to you straight.

NJ: Sir.

HL: The Bureau's no longer involved in the Idaho police officer's murder case—or in anything that deals with these so-called immortals.

NJ: But, sir …

HL: Hear me out, Agent Johnson.

NJ: Sir.

HL: Seems like the Mormons are not the only ones with cold feet on this immortal matter. I got a call yesterday from the Vatican's ambassador here in DC. He told me that the official position of the Church was to leave the matter alone—hands off. He told me, quite emphatically, that the Church wanted me to leave it alone. I told him about the same thing that I told you—there had been a murder of a law enforcement officer and what was almost certainly interstate flight, and that it was the Bureau's duty to investigate, and that we *would* do our duty. And that was the end of the conversation.

NJ: Thank you, sir.

HL: Obviously, I'm not finished.

NJ: I know. I think I've half-guessed what's coming. I mean, thanks for trying.

HL: I've done a hell of a lot more than try. This morning I got a call from Harris, the president's chief of staff. He's a Mormon—did you know that?

NJ: Yes, sir, I did.

HL: He told me, no, not *told* me, he *ordered* me to back off the case. Looks like the Catholics and the Mormons are acting in concert on this one. Doesn't it?

NJ: Yes, sir, it does. Wow.

HL: Yeah, 'wow.' First time they've ever agreed on anything, I imagine. I want to show you something, something I'm really proud of.

NJ: Sir.

HL: When I was first appointed as director, *U.S. NEWS* ran an article about me, about my life, and about my goals as head of the Bureau. [Sound of drawer opening and papers crinkling, as Lowry probably withdraws a copy of the article just mentioned.] It says, 'Lowry is a tough, independent, outspoken but fair-minded leader, the best appointment this president has made.'

NJ: I know many people in the Bureau feel that way.

HL: Thank you. Whether or not it's true, it fairly well sums up the kind of man I strive to be.

NJ: Sir.

HL: So I asked Harris if this order came directly from the president. He said, 'Consider it so.' I asked him if the president had been informed of the legal consequences of interfering with an ongoing investigation by the Bureau. He said that the matter was the concern of the attorney general, not of the director of the Bureau. I felt like asking him if he were attempting to make the President another Nixon—but I didn't. I told him that I would proceed as directed under the law. He told me to consider it a national emergency and then ordered me to stay close to the telephone.

NJ: I'm sorry, sir.

HL: About what?

NJ: I don't know. About … this predicament.

HL: Bullshit. You didn't blow that boy's brains out back in Idaho.

NJ: No, sir.

HL: That's all the detail you need. Officially, the Bureau's out of it—as of about three hours ago.

NJ: But, sir …

HL: I said 'officially.' I made two promises to myself when I came on board as Director. The first was that I would never violate my own standards of right and wrong. The second was that I would obey the law to the very letter. I figured that if I did the first, I would be able to sleep nights, and if I followed the law, I would best serve the interests of my country in spite of what my personal feelings might be on an issue. Now I'm caught right between doing what I know is right or obeying the law. Last time you were in this office, the choice was easy. But this time, I tell you, I don't know what to say.

NJ: There's nothing I can do …

HL: But there is. That's what I'm getting at. Last time the decision was mine. This time the decision is yours—and it's not going to be easy.

NJ: I don't understand.

HL: There's a lot that I don't understand either. What is clear to me is that my government has decided that it wants nothing to do with either solving the murder of that deputy sheriff or in protecting that Catholic Order of … What's it called?

NJ: The Order of the Beloved.

HL: Right, the Order of the Beloved, as it travels in this country. Since we have reason to believe that the Order is in imminent danger, we can infer that our government must somehow be involved in the acts taken against the Order. Just as clear is that the two churches involved in forcing the government to its position are not in full agreement within their own hierarchies about these issues. They, too, could be involved in the commissions.

NJ: I've wondered—feared that, too.

HL: I've been given no concrete reason for not proceeding with the investigation. I have only been ordered to desist. I intend to do that. What I will not do, however, is directly order you to desist. I think I know your feelings on this matter. I think that they are about the same as mine.
NJ: Nearly, sir.
HL: If I am in a moral dilemma, then you must be too.
NJ: That's correct.
HL: If you proceed with your investigation—do you know the risks?
NJ: Yes, sir. With respect, I can genuinely say that I want to finish the job, sir.
HL: I thought so. There will be no support, no direct, visible assistance from the Bureau. You cannot come to me and ask for logistical, tactical, financial, or even political support. It won't be there. On the other hand, no one in this Bureau is going to lift a finger to stop you. You've got my word on that.
NJ: Thank you, sir.
HL: You should make efforts to protect your family.
NJ: Sir?
HL: Whoever is after these people didn't think twice about killing a young deputy. I doubt that they would feel much different about anyone else who might stand in their way. They know who you are. They will try to stop you. Your family will be vulnerable.
NJ: I know. I've taken steps in that direction.
HL: Good. You've got a lot of friends in the Bureau, and what we do on our own time is our own business. And I know some of us feel we've got some unfinished business.
NJ: Thank you. I mean it. Sir—what about the van? Can I keep the van?
HL: What van?
NJ: The white trans—
HL: What van? I don't know of any van.
NJ: Thank you.
HL: Get out of here.
NJ: Yes, sir.
HL: Oh, Johnson.
NJ: Yes, sir?
HL: I still want you to catch the bad guys.
NJ: Yes, sir.

On the Author's Travels with Sylvia Johnson and Her Children, June 1, Continued

"Something's wrong ..." Aunt Lottie began, as soon as she and Sylvia and I had herded the children into the living room of her house.

"Oh, it's no big deal," Uncle Archie interrupted with a frown to his wife. The frown slid easily into a grin for his grandchildren. "Kaylynn, there's some sandwiches in the fridge. You go get 'em. Sherry, sit Jeremy up at the kitchen table. Sylvia, you stay in here and sit on the couch."

"Come on, Sherry and Jeremy," Kaylynn said, taking the baby by the hand. As an eldest child must, Kaylynn was learning adult responsibilities far too quickly.

Archie Johnson is a wiry man with tough, leathery hands marred by age, scarred by use. He never worries much, or never shows it; he always works hard and talks a lot. Shortly after my divorce, he had called to give me some advice about life. The gist of it was that if I worked hard enough, I would never have time to feel the pain inside me—or notice it in the lives going on around me.

"Now, there was no reason for you to frighten the children like that," he scolded his wife.

"Well, I'm sorry. But there's trouble, and I want to know what you're going to do about it," demanded Aunt Lottie.

"You don't know that there's trouble," my uncle retorted. He and his wife had taken their places in identical reclining chairs, gray velour La-Z-Boys. The purple sofa was against the opposite wall. An oval, heavily lacquered pine coffee table split the middle of the room. The antiquated color console TV, covered with framed family photos, was against the far wall, near the kitchen entrance.

"I talked to him—you didn't. Don't you ever tell me what I do or do not know," Lottie fired back. She unwrapped the towel from her head and vigorously fluffed her hair with it. The smell of peroxide and cheap hair rinse drifted our way. Water droplets splattered on Archie and the coffee table. He growled.

"For cryin' out loud, will you two knock it off and tell us what Nathan said?" I interjected from the squeaky sofa.

"He said ..." Archie began, but his wife butted in.

"You didn't talk to him! I did!"

"Fine, then you tell them," Uncle Archie huffed. "Just don't exaggerate it this time."

"I never do such a thing!"

"You're always exaggerating, and you know it."

"There you go again. There he goes," Lottie said, as she faced Sylvia and me across the coffee table. "*I exaggerate every time, he says.* Now who would you say's the exaggerator?"

"Aunt Lottie, please ..." I tried to stop them long enough to pose a question.

"If Katie were here, she'd tell you who's the family fabricationist," Uncle Archie said to Sylvia and me.

"'Cause she's your little girl. She's your favorite, and she always sticks up for you," argued Lottie.

"See! See! Now *that's* an exaggeration. You forget to mention that Katie's your girl too; she sides with you twice as much as me. She has to because you need it, 'cause you're always exaggerating," Archie rambled, in a red heat that did little to firm his position.

"Tell me about Nathan, Lottie. Tell me now," Sylvia demanded—though the stern look was directed at her father-in-law.

"Nathan called yesterday just after lunch, about one o'clock ..." Lottie began.

"It was two-fifteen," Archie intruded—though he was nearly out of breath from his last tirade.

"It was right after lunch," Lottie snapped.

Uncle Archie sat straight up in his recliner and with outstretched palms pleaded with Sylvia and me, "I looked right down at my watch—this watch." He turned his wrist and presented it to us. "Two fifteen."

"Okay, he called at *two fifteen.*" Lottie looked at Archie with rancor. "Nathan said that I shouldn't ask any questions, but that Archie and I should go to the cabin for a few weeks until he called. He said that we should leave tomorrow."

"And not to tell anyone," added Archie.

"Well, now you just told *them* that he said not to tell anybody—didn't you?" Lottie spat the words.

"Criminy, woman, you'd already just told them 'fore I did! Now there! There's 'zactly what I'm talking about. He told us not to tell anybody we's headed to the cabin. He didn't tell us not to tell nobody not to tell anybody. So she blames me for tellin' you when she just told you anyway—'cause she'd already told you what he told her she couldn't tell. Besides, I'm sure he didn't mean that we couldn't tell our own family," Archie grumbled.

"Maybe he did," Sylvia quickly responded. "From now on, you'd both better behave as if that's exactly what he meant."

"Never mind. I can't win." Archie threw up his hands and settled his thin frame deep into the gray recliner.

"He said that if I saw you, I was to tell you to keep the kids with you," Lottie softly said to Sylvia.

"Is that it?" Sylvia asked.

"No." Aunt Lottie tipped her head and looked at me with the protective, motherly menace I had not seen since high school. "He told me to tell *you* 'fith' at noon today or tomorrow." She said "fith" with disgust.

I laughed at Lottie. She remembered too. "It's got nothing to do with girls. It's just how I'll know where he's gonna call next," I reassured her.

"Better not," she threatened me.

"Honest."

"See. See. No real trouble," Archie said triumphantly. He got up from his chair and left to tickle his grandkids.

"No trouble at all," I agreed.

"Better hurry it up, though. It's already quarter after 'leven," Archie called from the kitchen.

Sylvia and Lottie said nothing.

Our good-byes were rushed. All the kids went potty. I ushered the two girls outside while Sylvia slipped a fresh diaper on Jeremy. Archie accompanied us out to the road and gave each of his grandchildren his big, sweaty, warm Old Spice hug. Aunt Lottie cut up some apples, wrapped them in cellophane, and raced them to the blue minivan, blowing kisses as she ran.

As I pulled away, I looked in the rearview mirror. I thought I saw something that I had never seen before. I thought I saw Uncle Archie crying. I did not say anything about it to Sylvia, who was busy trying to get fussy Jeremy to sleep.

We waited by the pay telephones in the foyer of Twin Falls High School until nearly four in the afternoon of June 1. Nathan did not call. We went back to Burley to spend the night with Nathan's parents—but they had already left for their cabin. I lifted Archie's front doormat and picked up the house key. There was nothing we could do but wait for tomorrow and for the telephone call that would change all of our lives ... forever.

They watched a Samaritan as he carried a lamb on his way to Judea.

[Jesus] asked of his disciples, "Why is he carrying the lamb on his way?"

They said to him, "So that he might kill it and then eat it."

He [Jesus] answered them, "He will not eat it while it is still living, but wait until after it has been slaughtered and is become a carcass."

They replied, "That is the only way that it can occur."

He [Jesus] answered them saying, "The same is true of you. Find a place of refuge for yourselves, so that you will not become a carcass and will not be eaten."

—*The Secret Teachings of Jesus, Nag Hammadi,* Codex II, Tr. 2, p. 43

Excerpts from a Letter from Dr. Judy Weintraub, Followed by Excerpts from the Journal of Father Jerome Dougherty, Both Dated June 2

[Author's note: As has been my practice thus far in this manuscript (a practice that becomes more routine—and more complex—at this point, as the various members begin their travels together), when a single event has been related by two or more people, I will do one of two things: Either 1) I will choose, edit, and then present one account—the account that best preserves the flow of the narrative and, to the best of my comprehension, the truth; or, 2) I will, for the sake of accuracy and cohesiveness, merge the chronicles. In all circumstances, I will attempt to keep the reader apprised of the author or authors of each account—even if portions are taken from different sources. (Keep in mind that for the dialogue, I have used the transcripts of the actual recorded conversations whenever such recordings exist.) I believe this method will allow the reader a more objective view of the increasingly bizarre events that follow. Perhaps it will allow the reader to determine the meaning of these events—an achievement, I readily admit, I have not attained.]

So his health is holding. I am most grateful for that.

This morning's events were absolutely terrifying. I have had to labor at the task before me, at documenting the day's events accurately, for I have never been party to such brutish behavior, to such seaminess. I have determined that I will simply relate the events chronologically and without commentary—without much commentary. Though I must say at the outset of this letter that I am angry and distressed and ready to leave this insanity right now. *At this very moment!* I would certainly do just that if it were not for my husband. Harold is quite entertained by it all.

To begin, Nathan has become a severe taskmaster. Last night he went from room to room, ordering all the members of our party to be packed and ready to leave the hotel, for good, this morning. He was not rude, but he was short-tempered. If I did not know better, I would say that he was frightened.

I find his behavior both heartening and disturbing. It is reassuring to think that someone is in control of our situation—especially after dealing with the flightiness of our "companions"—but it is most unsettling to hypothesize why such dominant authority is necessary.

The last two immortals, I will call them that from now on to distinguish them from the remainder of our party, arrived this morning from Italy. They are two more Catholic priests. The youngest, a handsome, middle-aged Italian, is Father Quindilar; the other is Father Richard Holden, an Englishman, a somewhat prudish man with airs of nobility.

Only Father Dougherty and Agent Johnson went inside the terminal at Dulles to greet the two men. The rest of us were ordered to remain in the van that Agent Johnson had parked directly in front of the terminal in a *No Standing* zone. Before the two entered through the automatic doors, Nathan spoke to a thin, young, black policeman patrolling the sidewalk. The young officer held his shoulders straight and proud; I would speculate that he had once served in the military. He was wearing a pistol on one hip and a truncheon on the other.

While Father Dougherty waited at the entrance, Agent Johnson displayed his badge to the policeman. The two exchanged whispers for nearly a minute. When the conversation was over, Nathan and the policeman shook hands. Nathan and Father Jerome then entered the building.

Not long after Nathan and Jerome left my view, a man in a trench coat, with a plump face, swollen red eyes, and very thin brown hair knocked on the passenger window of the van. I happened to be seated there and, as I had just turned to speak with the others in the rear of the van, was quite startled by his interruption. His face was not entirely unfriendly; it was, I should say, most businesslike—somewhat anxious, a little confused. I could be wrong, but he seemed uncertain of his calling. In any event, he held an identification card next to the window. "U.S. Immigration," he shouted through the glass as he rudely knocked on it—for, as noted, I was sitting directly beside the window, and I could easily discern his identification.

"I can see who you are," I said rather curtly.

"Open the door," he coarsely demanded.

Nathan had given us very specific instructions not to allow anyone access to the van, and so I told the immigration official, through the closed window, that I was unable to grant his request. "I can see who you are, but I will not open the door." These were my exact words.

He pounded harder still. "US Immigration," he shouted again. He stopped and studied a piece of paper he pulled from his blue suit jacket, which was covered by the trenchcoat. "There is a Father Ugwalla Dobo in this vehicle. He has entered this country illegally. Open the door."

"Nonsense," Father Dobo said from behind me. "All of my papers are in perfect order."

"That is not true. And I will not do it," I replied to the immigration official.

"Judy, don't open the door. I will come forward and speak to the man," Harold said from somewhere in the rear of the van.

My next thought was to call out to the young policeman with whom Nathan had spoken. Looking up and down the sidewalk for him, I noticed that the policeman had disappeared. As I waited for Harold, I verbally refused, yet again, to oblige the immigration official. At that moment, Nathan burst through the terminal doors with the young policeman close behind. Nathan's head swerved quickly left and right, as if to size up his situation, as he raced across the broad sidewalk to the van. He tucked his right hand inside the left breast of his sports coat. He motioned, with a nod of his head, up the sidewalk. The young policeman, though he looked very nervous, nodded back. The policeman unbuckled the strap on his holster that kept his gun in place and started to walk slowly to the area that Nathan had indicated.

"Keep that door locked!" Nathan shouted at me as he dashed to the van. He stopped very close to the gentleman in the trench coat. They stood nose-to-nose. "FBI," Nathan told him.

"I know who you are. I'm Kevin Douglas, with Immigration, we worked—"

"I remember. Have your man behind me replace his weapon."

"Can't do it," Douglas said.

"These people are in protective custody and in transit under my supervision. So tell your man to back off," Nathan again ordered Douglas—whose face had turned quite ashen in color. I believed at that time, though I could not see it clearly, that Agent Johnson held a metal object to the immigration official's stomach; this may have upset Mr. Douglas.

"FBI's out of it. Just turn 'em all over, and there'll be no trouble. I don't want any shit from ..." Douglas started to say, but I am afraid that Nathan smacked him in the ribs with whatever it was that he held in his hand. As I said, all I could see at the time was that the object in his hand was of silver-colored metal.

Nathan must have jabbed him roughly, for Mr. Douglas lost his breath. Please pardon the succeeding expression, but I am trying to relate these events accurately. I think the immigration official, that is, Mr. Douglas, called Nathan a "cocksucker." This was not a prudent thing to say, for it angered Nathan. He punched the official even harder in the stomach. Mr. Douglas fell to his knees. Now I could tell that Nathan held a pistol. It was a large, shiny pistol, silver or steel or aluminum. It looked very modern and sleek—nothing at all like the six-shooters I see when Harold watches his favorite Western movies—and nothing like the little pistol I keep in my nightstand for protection.

Out of the front window of the van I noticed, much to my horror, that another man, in a similar trench coat and sunglasses, had emerged from a luggage terminal and had drawn a weapon and was pointing it at Nathan's back. Thank God that the young policeman had maneuvered behind the man who had the gun aimed at Nathan. The policeman drew his pistol, held it to the head of the man in the sunglasses, and then disarmed him.

Agent Johnson brusquely lifted Mr. Douglas back to his feet. Holding tightly to the lapels of his trench coat, Nathan slammed his face against the side of the van. "Never pull a gun, or give the order to pull a gun, on a federal agent," he snarled at Mr. Douglas. He shoved Mr. Douglas into the side of the van with such force that the vehicle rocked back and forth. I had to hold on to the armrests. Nathan then removed a small pistol from a holster inside Mr. Douglas's jacket. All of this happened right next to my window. It was most brutish and disgusting, but I admit, also very thrilling.

At that moment, Father Dougherty exited the terminal, accompanied by Fathers Quindilar and Holden. Nathan kept the gun to the immigration man's stomach and said, "Somebody unlock the side door. Father Jerome, Fathers, please hurry to the van."

"I'll get the door," my husband shouted over my head to Nathan, for, as I mentioned earlier, Harold had come forward through the van to be at my side. Harold sounded very excited as well. (I think he was enjoying the confrontation.) The three priests were soon inside the van, and the door was safely locked.

Nathan asked the policeman to bring the fellow in the sunglasses to him. The policeman complied with the request. Nathan frisked the man in the sunglasses but found nothing. Nathan thanked the young police officer and handed him Mr. Douglas's weapon. Nathan kept Mr. Douglas at gunpoint and pushed him along until they had walked around the front of the van to the driver's door. I reached across the cab and unlocked the door for Nathan. He released Mr. Douglas as he climbed into the van and shut the door. Nathan drove slowly from the loading area. I do not believe that we were followed.

We are finally on our way. Things will surely get better.

* * * *

That is how all four of us made it into the van. It is clear to me now, and my knowledge of his family had led me to surmise earlier, that Nathan efficiently channels his fear into anger.

He was quite upset when he stepped into the van. "Goddamn game's over! This goddamn game's over!" Nathan shouted as he slammed his fists again and again against the steering wheel of the van. As he drove away from Dulles with the full compliment of the Order of the Beloved, as well as Miriam, Mr. Tie, the Weintraubs, and myself, he asked what I considered to be indelicate questions, using language that was exceptionally pointed and profane—even for him. It was an obdurate display. Yet he drove conscientiously—south, I believe, taking a side road from the airport and carefully checking the rearview mirror for any vehicles that might have been following us. I would infer from these two actions, namely his outburst of anger in tandem with his cool assessment of our situation, that Nathan was firming up his position as the commander-in-chief of our little party.

Although it may have been a necessary exercise for his ego, if he had seen the confused and quailing faces in the rear of the van (with the exceptions of the Weintraubs and, possibly, myself) he would probably have burst into laughter rather than thrown his fit of rage. These good people are as meek as lambs. The immortals—Judy, Harold, and I have agreed to refer to them as such in both conversation and writing—are the least competitive, least emulative, humans I have ever known. They shirk responsibility as if it were a contagious disease.

I am convinced that his outburst had a more profound and underlying intention. Nathan is a subtle and, in an almost paradoxically unrefined fashion, an inscrutable man. What Professor Weintraub could not extract from the immortals by inquiry, Nathan would attempt to secure through intimidation. Several minutes after his fervid display with the steering column, Nathan stopped the van on the shoulder of the road. We had gone through Manassas, Virginia, on Highway 28 but then turned directly south on a country road—234, I believe the sign said. The day had turned dour and drizzly. A thick gray fog floated just above the tops of the trees that lined both sides of the road. The air was dead and dank. The back of the van, encased in sheet metal, was cold and humid—like a crypt. It was shortly after one o'clock. I, for one, had skipped breakfast and was now missing lunch. Though this was certainly not a propitious moment to discuss our repast or lack of same.

"I want to know now, not tomorrow, not next Easter, I want to know *right now* where the fuck we're going," Nathan shouted through the doorway into the rear of the van. I could not see much of Judy, who was in front in the seat beside Nathan. I assume that she huddled against the door. I know that the rest of us had cowered back into our seats.

"Agent Johnson, I can attest to you that nothing has changed..." Father Hugo began.

"Don't give me that shit, Hugo. It's not just me; it's not just the Bureau anymore. When I drove away from the airport, after I decked that Immigration guy, things changed—lines were drawn. My family's been hauled into this. My wife and kids could be in trouble. And if you think this little outing of yours means half a shit next to my family, then you really are all nuts. I don't want any more evasion. I don't want any more cute answers. As far as I'm concerned, you can all get out of this van right now and try walking to wherever the fuck it is that you don't know you're going."

"So, this is Agent Johnson," Father Holden spoke for the first time. He had scooted the others aside and situated himself on the bench directly behind Nathan. "Excellent. You managed the miscreants at the terminal like a true professional. Father Dougherty told me that you were the best—but I had no idea … We are most fortunate to have you as our protector."

"Which one are you?" Nathan glared back through the doorway, first at all of us; then his eyes settled on Father Holden.

"I am Father Richard Holden."

"First, Father Holden, don't patronize me. I'm really pissed right now. I need answers, not flattery. Second, I'm not that great. I wasn't that great at Dulles. I just dumped a shitload of troubles on that young cop—probably fucked up his whole career. He's back there trying to explain why he pulled his weapon on a federal agent who was, in all likelihood, holding a valid warrant. He could go to jail for it. That doesn't make me a hero. It was actually pretty chickenshit. Tell me, do you consider someone like that cop a necessary sacrifice for your holy Order of the Beloved? Do you people really believe I should have done that to him? Do you think he *owes* you something? I don't."

"I had not even considered it … We were running … You told us to hurry … that there was trouble … Things happened so quickly …" Father Holden stumbled for an answer—something that Father Holden is never wont to do.

"Yeah, shall we drive on back and explain it to that young cop? To Kevin Douglas and the boys in Immigration? I'll bet Kevin's in a great mood right now. I'm finished with this whole business unless I start hearing some answers that make some sense, unless I get some reasons to go on—some real good reasons why I ought not just throw you people out and let you walk. Tell me what we're supposed to do," Nathan demanded unequivocally. "And tell me why I ought to do it. I'm going to pull into a service station up here and make a few calls. You decide—who wants to go first? You've got about thirty minutes."

Conversation, June 2, about noon, Mountain Daylight Savings Time, between Nathan Johnson (NJ), Sylvia Johnson (SJ) and the author (ME)

ME: Hello?

NJ: Fith.

ME: Fire in the hole!

NJ: Yeah, sure. Is my wife there?

ME: Good day to you too, Agent Johnson!

NJ: Goddamn it! Don't say *Agent Johnson!* Let me talk to Sylvia.

ME: Christ! Better eat your Wheaties, Cuz. Here she is.

SJ: Nathan?

NJ: Hey, honey. How are the kids?

SJ: Nathan! For heaven's sake! Tell me what's wrong.

NJ: Everything's going to be fine.

SJ: [Crying] Everything is not fine!

NJ: Honey. Okay. Honey? Listen. Now just listen. I'm sorry about sending you to Yellowstone, about scaring you. I thought you might be in danger. I needed to send you someplace I knew you'd be safe. I couldn't take a chance. Sorry about the note—I needed to warn you so that you would understand that it was very serious ...

SJ: [Crying] Nathan ... are you ...

NJ: I'm okay. Honey, come on. Stop it.

SJ: [Still crying] Nathan ... I can't ... Nathan ... I just can't.

NJ: Come on, honey. You can. I know you can. Everything's going to be fine. Please. I love you. I won't let anything happen to you. There, now. Come on. Come on, now. There, now. Get a pen and paper. Get ready. I'm going to tell you a whole bunch of things to do. Can you write it all down? [Sylvia is still sobbing.] Sylvia? Sylvia, I need you. Sylvia, honey, listen very carefully to what I'm going to tell you. Write it all down and then repeat it back to me.

SJ: Nathan, first you tell me what's wrong.

NJ: You trust me?

SJ: Tell me first.

NJ: Honest, honey, I haven't got time right now. Obviously a lot is wrong. But we can handle it. Just do everything I tell you. I swear that I won't let anything happen to you or the kids. But you must do exactly what I say. Can you do it? Are you ready? Come on, kiddo. Are you tired?

SJ: No.

NJ: Good. Leave as soon as I finish. If my cousin goes with you—that'd be great. If he doesn't, you'll have to make the drive without stopping. It could be about twelve hours. Can you do it?

SJ: I can do it.

NJ: Ready to write?

SJ: Wait a sec. Okay. Ready. Tell me where.

NJ: That's my girl. South on 93 to Nevada through Jackpot, then straight through Wells. Take 93 all the way to Ely. Okay?

SJ: Easy. Ninety-three to Ely. Then what?

NJ: I'm not sure what will happen, but I want you to park right in front of the sheriff's office. It's in the county building. Just park there and stay in the car. Wait in the car until six o'clock tonight. If anyone comes to the car—anyone except Sheriff Duffy—I mean if anyone tries to get in—go immediately inside the building. Use your gun. Don't shoot anybody, just fend them off if you can, but get yourself and get the kids inside the sheriff's office.

SJ: Why don't we just go inside and wait?

NJ: My way. Stay in the car. Okay?

SJ: Okay.

NJ: My way. Exactly.

SJ: All right.

NJ: Sheriff Dewey Duffy owes me a favor. He knows that you're gonna be parked outside. So he'll try to keep an eye on you. But he might be under a lot of pressure.

SJ: From who?

NJ: Honey!

SJ: All right.

NJ: If you have to go inside the station, then I've asked the sheriff to get you to Las Vegas. You are to take the children and go straight to my office in Las Vegas.

You go no place else, no matter what anyone tells you to do. Even the sheriff. Get to my office. If you have to use your weapon. If you have to kill. Do you understand?

SJ: Nathan …

NJ: Sylvia! Do you understand?

SJ: Yes. Go to Ely, wait in the car 'till six by the sheriff's … but what if nobody comes?

NJ: Listen very carefully. If nobody comes, then that's good. At six o'clock, Sheriff Duffy's going to come outside. You can't miss him. He's a short, fat, little guy, but strong as an ox. He's bald-headed, but I doubt if you'll see it 'cause he never takes his hat off. He smokes all the time. Now, don't do anything he tells you. Do you understand that?

SJ: Yes. Don't do anything he says. Why?

NJ: Because I am going to give him false instructions—just in case. If he asks you to come inside, you tell him—are you getting this?

SJ: [Hesitates] Yes.

NJ: You'll have to memorize it.

SJ: I know.

NJ: If he asks you to come inside, you tell him that I told you that I was going to call you at a telephone booth at eight o'clock and that you have to go. Then immediately drive away. Understand?

SJ: You don't know if you can trust this man?

NJ: You just write down the notes. Understand, honey?

SJ: Just drive away if he asks me to come inside.

NJ: No! First tell him that you are expecting a call from me at a pay telephone booth at eight o'clock.

SJ: Sorry. Okay.

NJ: If he doesn't ask you inside, then he is going to tell you where to go. He will say that I told him, and it will be true. I will give him directions for you. But remember you are not to do anything he tells you to do.

SJ: Then where are we supposed to go?

NJ: I'll tell you that in a minute. You must remember exactly what he tells you. Okay? You're gonna talk to me afterwards, and I need to know, so remember exactly what he says—but don't do anything he says.

SJ: I will. I mean, I will and I won't.

NJ: Are you writing this down?

SJ: Sort of.

ME: I'm taking notes.

SJ: He's had his ear to the phone.
NJ: Put him on. Hey, Cuz. Sorry I was …
ME: An asshole? You can't help it.
NJ: You gonna go with them?
ME: I don't know that I've got a choice. I'm already a fugitive. Your wife shot a buffalo.
NJ: What?
ME: Sylvia shot a buffalo. It was chasin' your kids through Yellowstone Park. She blew its fuckin' head off with that cannon she carries in her diaper bag.
NJ: [Laughing] You're not lying, are you?
ME: *Blooey! Kapow!* Right between the eyes. We can go to jail for that—right? I mean, can you—pull strings or …
SJ: [Yanking the telephone away] Sweetie, it was almost about to trample them. Nathan, I swear I …
NJ: It's okay. Put him back on.
ME: Ranger Rick didn't think it was so swell.
NJ: They stopped you?
ME: They had a roadblock. Sylvia gave me your G-man ID. It was just like sneakin' past the bouncer at Stoney's Saloon—remember? 'Shit, yeah, I'm twenty-one! And Nate's my uncle!'
NJ: [Laughing] You get my wife and kids to me and—I swear to God, you'll never go to jail. And I'm gonna give you the story of the decade—maybe the century. But I do need a favor from you. Sylvia, let us talk alone for a second.
ME: Just another little favor, huh?
NJ: I know; I owe you. Remember when I asked you if you had any strings you could pull in DC?
ME: Yeah.
NJ: Well?
ME: Yeah. Something.
NJ: I need it.
ME: Are you sure? I mean, I've got something. But it cost someone close to me a lot—a ton of pain. If I use it, it's going to cost a lot more. It's big stuff, dynamite—but it's vile.
NJ: I'm sorry. But I need it—whatever it is. I need time. Two days. I think Secretary of State Herbert Granfield is behind this. Probably Harris, the president's chief of staff, as well. Can you give me two days?
ME: Herbert Granfield? He's the guy we've got to persuade?
NJ: Yeah. Maybe Harris too.

ME: That's good. Maybe. I think it's good. Yeah, maybe I can. Two days? That's all you need? What happens if I can't?
NJ: Two days, and I can wash my hands of it—walk away clean. But if I don't get the time, I'm dead. Me and about ten other people.
ME: Senator Stevens and Secretary of State Granfield are good friends—right?
NJ: I don't know. I suppose.
ME: College pals. Not college, law school. They attended the University of Chicago Law School—same class.
NJ: I didn't know that.
ME: They play golf together every week.
NJ: I didn't know that either.
ME: It'll take me an hour—and I've got to do it before we can leave town.
NJ: You can do it from Twin Falls?
ME: Yeah. Right here. Two days, huh? I think what I have is worth two days. But that's it; that's all I'm gonna push for.
NJ: That's enough.
ME: I'll do it right now. Here, Sylvia wants back on.
NJ: Jesus, thanks. Okay. Do it. Thanks. Jesus, that's a real load off me. Do it fast and get on the road. Thanks, Cuz—for everything. Give me back to Sylvia.
SJ: Sweetie, don't swear like that.
NJ: I'm sorry, honey. How many rounds did it take?
SJ: Five. Four hits, I think. And it was running.
NJ: Wow. How many yards?
SJ: Forty, maybe only thirty-fi—
ME: [Yanking the telephone away] For chrissake—we gotta get going. What do we do after we talk to Sheriff Duffy?
NJ: Sorry. Okay. You tell ... you tell the sheriff that you're supposed to get a call from me from at Lund. Just tell him at Lund. Then you go to the shortcut south off of 93 onto Highway 318. You know the place I'm talking about? Did you get that, honey?
SJ: The way we usually go back to Vegas?
NJ: Right. That little truck stop just north of Lund at the bottom of the mountains. Where we get lunch for the kids. Oh, and, from now on, pay for everything with cash. *Everything.* They can track you if you use a credit card.
SJ: I know. I know. I have been. I took a thousand dollars out of savings before we left home. I thought you'd be okay with ...
NJ: [Laughing] You're perfect.
ME: She's paranoid.

NJ: [Still laughing] Get to the truck stop north of Lund.
SJ: But the sheriff ...
NJ: Either he'll let you go, or he'll follow you.
SJ: Okay. Then what?
NJ: Then I'll call you. At the pay phone. At the truck stop just off 93 on 318 South. Should be around eight o'clock your time.
SJ: Then what?
NJ: I'm not sure, exactly, maybe there'll ... [Sound of a car horn] ... Shit! [Rapidly] Someone's headed to the van! Call you at Lund tonight.

In the present situation, however, this problem of consistency is perfectly amenable to treatment. As we can immediately recognize, it reduces to the question of seeing that '1≠1' cannot be obtained as an end formula from our axioms by the rules of force, hence that '1≠1' is not a provable formula. And this is a task that fundamentally lies within the province of intuition.

—Hilbert, *On the Infinite*

We feel that even when all possible scientific questions have been answered, the problems of life remain totally untouched. Of course there are then no questions left and this itself is the answer. The solution of the problem of life is seen in the disappearance of the problem.

—Wittgenstein, *Tractatus Logico-Philosophicus*

Excerpts from an Unpublished Article by Professor Harold Weintraub, "On Gödel, on Cantor, and on Continuum: A Peek at Immortality?" started in 2002. [Notes omitted, though some citations are explained by this author.]

Hence, the questions never directly considered by the logicians are these: What does the non-demonstrability of the consistency of mathematics say about the nature of human consciousness? Related, but deeper still, from where, precisely, does the "knowledge" of the incompleteness of any formal system emerge? And how is the knowledge interrelated, not just with consistency (as an idea), but also with human consciousness, with human existence, which is to say, with the process of life itself?

We will let Quine, because he would offer the strongest objections to the speculations that ensue, set the stage for us, "But Gödel showed, as a consequence of his incompletability theorem, that the one thing the set theory cannot (if it is consistent) prove about the class of its own theorems is that it is consistent ..." Consistency can be proven, but it must be done so outside the (first) given set of axioms—"you can continue as before with a new axiom affirming the consistency of all that." Then Quine demurely adds, "We see the familiar pattern of transfinite recursion setting in." Indeed we do.

[Author's note: The quotes are from Quine's *Set Theory and Its Logic.*]

The question is: Why do we find transfinite recursion setting in? Certainly it cannot be because, as Quine elsewhere states, "Mathematics is true by convention."

[Author's note: This statement is from an early paper by Quine entitled, "Truth by Convention."]

For the sake of argument, let us suggest that "set theory" is another phrase, say a foreign phrase, for human existence. Human existence then can be shown to be always incomplete. How? Because human existence is inherently inconsistent. The human being must look outside himself for proof of his own consistency and is thus unable to complete himself. Where is that consistency to be found? In and through other also inconsistent and, hence, also incomplete human beings.

A short story will lay the foundation for our speculations: We have placed ads in all the popular magazines and on several television shows, offering a large reward for the first person who can prove that he or she is both complete and consistent.

Our takers are legion. We have several thousand people who have come to the designated quadrant to pick up their reward for being both consistent and complete. What it means to be a complete person is to be capable of and willing to answer correctly any question put to that person. For example, we should expect that a complete person would be able to tell us that two plus two is four. What it means to be a consistent person is that only one answer per question can be given. If, for example, we ask, "What is two plus two?" a respondent is not allowed to answer, "Five—er—three, no, no, I mean four." In other words, to be consistent is to be noncontradictory.

Because it is our contest and our money, there is one elementary statement that we will give, followed by a simple question about that statement that we will put to each entrant. The first person to give the correct answer to this question will win the grand prize of a million dollars. We hand each entrant a slip of paper. The paper reads as follows.

STATEMENT A: A complete person will never say that STATEMENT A is true.
QUESTION: Is STATEMENT A: true?
ANSWER:_____

If our contestant is striving to be a complete person, then he or she might think that the answer to the question is "No." If the contestant answers "No," then he asserts that STATEMENT A is false. What he means is that a complete person would say that STATEMENT A is true—for to assert that it is false that a complete person will never say something is to assert that a complete person would, in fact, say that very thing. Our contestant who answered "No," did not understand what he meant until sometime later, on the drive home, when it occurred to him why he so quickly failed in the contest. In striving to be a complete person, our contestant was inconsistent.

What happens if our second contestant answers "Yes"—if he tells us that STATEMENT A is true? Well, this contestant has denied his own completeness from the outset, for he has admitted that a complete person would never say such a thing as STATEMENT A, while saying it. Our second contestant is a consistent human being; unfortunately, being incomplete, he also leaves without the prize.

Consider a third possibility. One of our first contestants, having discovered the nature of his error on his way home, returns to our contest the next day with his elderly mother. He waits patiently in line with her as we dismiss the hundreds before him who answer either "Yes" or "No" to our simple question.

His mother comes to her turn. We show her the paper, but she stares blankly into space.

"I'll answer that," says yesterday's contestant.

"Sorry," we say to the gentleman, pointing to the fine print in our rules. "One entry per person."

"Ah, but I am not here to speak for myself," he tells us. "I am here to answer for my mother." (The members of our rules committee are suddenly nervous, and its members are flipping furiously through the manual.) "She is, as you can see, an invalid who does not see clearly and whose hand is no longer steady. I have been given power of attorney for her and am allowed to answer any question that you might ask on her behalf."

"But ... but," we start to object. It is too late.

The new contestant's son has already penned her answer: "My mother will never say that STATEMENT A is true."

On the Author's Relationship with Candice Ballard, Continued

It was during Nathan's telephone call at Twin Falls High School on May 26 (four days before Sylvia showed up at my trailer) that the idea of pressuring Senator Sam Stevens occurred to me. ("Pressuring" is my attorney's choice of word.) Nathan had asked if I had any leverage in Washington, DC. I had told him no. There is no need to go into further details of our discussion—for the transcript of that conversation has been reproduced several sections above.

After Nathan and I had spoken, I drove to McDonald's, went in, and ordered a hamburger, fries, and a Coke. I sat down at a corner booth and watched the high school boys spend their lunch hour hitting on the girls. Their sexual innuendo was more stilted, less lewd, than I remembered. I didn't know if that was a result of a growing respect for females—or fear of an epidemic.

One of the students recognized me. "Hey, it's the writer dude," he said. Three or four of his friends turned and waved at me. I smiled back. "Hey, man, we want you to know that the administration really fucked you over, man." His friends nodded. I shrugged my shoulders in thanks. I could feel my face heating up, turning red. I tried to eat but was nauseous.

I trashed the food through a hinged flap stamped THANK YOU and drove to the Simson's grocery store, where Candice worked. She was busy at a checkout counter. I told her that I really needed to talk and asked if she could come over later.

She said, "Sure."

Candice stopped by my trailer after her shift, which ended at midnight. I got up to let her in. She threw her long brown coat across the chair at my table, where I had just been writing. She wore a long-sleeved white blouse, a red skirt, and a green work apron. There was a red name tag pinned, slightly tilted, near the neck of the apron; the tag read, in big white letters: I'M CANDICE. HOW MAY I HELP YOU SHOP SIMSON'S? She had pinned her hair into a bun for work.

As soon as she had dropped her coat, she excused herself to the bathroom. I backed up my work and shut off the computer. I waited for her on my old couch. When she came out, her hair was down. She had shed the uniform and slid into blue jeans and a black sweatshirt. She shook back her long red hair and sat close to me on the couch, her long leg touching mine.

"You want something to drink? Or I can fix you some soup?" I studied her green eyes, wondering if they could read my mind, wishing for it, wanting to make asking her easy. What I saw was that her eyes were tired and longing.

"This isn't about us. Is it?" she complained. Her reproach caught me by surprise. I shivered at the thought that maybe she was telepathic, that she knew my fear, my helplessness, my rancor, and my shame.

"No. It's not about us. I need ... You know, I've been thinking all day about how to talk to you. I've got to tell you first ... you've got to understand that what I *need* from you is not what I *want* from you. This is so hard because it's never been that way between us," I began.

It was her turn to look into my eyes—she *was* trying to read my mind. "You want my advice about another woman. Goddamn you—that's such a lousy thing to do to me right now." She scooted down the couch.

"No, no. I'd never do that to you. But ... oh, Christ ... what I do need is much worse than that."

"Finally comin' out of the closet?" She scooted farther away—but her words came with a smile.

"Let's have a drink," I said, and we both laughed.

A couple of shots of Cuervo, and I tried again, "I feel like a caitiff—coming to you for this—for help."

"You're gonna have to cut the Harvard crap—especially if we're gonna drink tequila—just tell me what you need," she said, wiping the salt and lemon pulp from her lips.

* * * *

Her lips. I don't think that I've written about her lips. They are thick, fleshy, and pink; her lips are the essence of the sexual ambiguity of the labia, the plural of *labium,* bred by a Latin noun, baseborn from the verb *lambere*—to lick or to lap up.

In high school, when the other guys would talk about Candice (I have mentioned that she was often the center of our palaver), they would speak about her tits. While my classmates could only conjecture, I would fantasize about my next date with Candice and about her warm, soft, caressing, curious, adulating lips. Because my body, not theirs, would be the object of her desire, her exploration, her supplication, every portion subject to pilgrimage. When her lips finally encountered, enfolded, and enveloped me, it was then that I offered my first veneration. For at that moment I did cry out, "Oh, God!"

* * * *

"One more drink, and we'll talk," I vowed. I poured more tequila.

"You want me to do something?" She slurred the words a little.

"I told you. I *need* you to do something. It's not even for me. It's kind of for Nathan."

"Nathan? Nathan—your cousin? He's such a prick. In high school, he was always after me—because I was in love with you. He was always trying to get in my pants."

"Yeah, but that was a long time ago," I responded out of the swirling tequila maelstrom. The words swirled around the space between us. You can only float so far from it, I told myself. I locked my throat into its 'speaking carefully and clearly while under the influence' mode and said, "Nathan's a great guy now. He married Sylvia Lancaster. You know, Brenda's cousin …"

"Stuck-up Mormon bitches. I told you that too. You know I told you that you shouldn't have married Brenda. I told you she'd try to change you—and she did. Didn't she? She tried to change you," Candice demanded, sliding back my way. She poured the next round. We drank it.

"Yes, you're right. She tried to change me. But that's not what we're talking about. Nathan's got three kids. He's all right. It's not really for him, anyway. I'm working on a project with him—not really with him. He just knows about it. What I want—I mean what I need is …"

"Hold it. You stop right there. We always talk about what you *want*—what you *need* for your writing. This is about your books, isn't it? You want me to do something for a book—something horrible … or, I don't know, unmoral or illegal. Nothin' to do with me at all. That's it. Isn't it? You selfish son of a bitch."

Things had gotten a little out of hand. I scooted close and put my arm around her. The scoot—maybe it was that last shot of tequila—restarted my head swirling. Her hair was in my face. Any other time, that would have made me as horny as a bull in April. Now it made me want to throw up.

"I'm gonna tell you the truth. I've never said this before—to anyone. You're the only woman who's ever really listened to me when I told her that ... that that's the way a writer works. That's the way I am. I have to be selfish, not for me, not for me. Look at me. Look at poor, pitiful, broke all the time, livin' alone, fucked-up me—not for me—for my books, I mean. Yeah, I am selfish. All I care about is my stupid goddamn work! *I stand convicted!*"

The words were twirling around, with my mind in a tumbling, lockstep, swelling, swerving polka. The drunken part of me (which was most of me) thought that I had just made one helluva speech. The rest of me didn't. *You don't have the goddamn guts to ask her,* I swore at myself. Then I started to cry—before she did—which, coming as it did in the middle of a drunken colloquy, embarrassed the hell out of me. I cried because she did not understand why I was crying—or I cried because she did. It was embarrassing either way.

Candice snuggled against my neck. "You've said it before—to me. I still believe in you. And I never tried to change you. I would have married you in a second. I still would if you'd ever ask me."

"I'm gonna ask you to do something. I know this sounds like one of my high school come-ons—but somebody might die if I don't ... if you don't do what I ask."

"Somebody like Nathan?"

"Yeah, I think he's in a shitload of trouble. He asked me to help him, and I said I would try. The only way I could think was ... I need a video of you and ... you and that senator you told me about."

"You ... *you fucking rotten bastard!*" She slapped my face.

"Never mind."

"You want me to screw Senator Stevens? You wanna tape it yourself? Maybe you'll want to hop in at the end? You're so alike that you two would probably get off together."

"Stop it. Just stop it. I said, 'Never mind.' It's not my problem if somebody wastes Nathan—he's just my fuckin' cousin."

She raised her hand to strike me again, but instead broke down in tears. "I hate you. I hate your guts. In high school—did you know that nobody—I mean *nobody* ever touched me except you? Nathan was always after me. Kelly, you remember Kelly Mecham? He was twice as cute as you. He wanted me so bad. He used to call me on the telephone. He was beating off. I could tell. I could have had anybody, but I saved myself for you—while you were screwing every bitch in the school. I hate you. I hate you," she sobbed, hugging her arms to her breast.

"Never fuckin' mind. It's okay. Just drop it. I'll drive you home. You're drunker than I am."

"I hate you because I love you."

"Shut up. I'll drive you home."

"I hate you because you know I'd do anything for you. And I hate you because you're asking me to do this."

"And how, just exactly how, how do you think I feel about myself having to ask? *How do you think I fuckin' feel?*"

"It's how *you* feel. It's what *you* need. You'd do anything in this world for your books. Wouldn't you?"

"I told you somebody's going to kill my cousin. Whether you believe it or not—he means a lot to me." My stomach had joined my head in the dance, except my stomach had decided to reel.

"He's got something you want, or he wouldn't even be asking you. And then you wouldn't be asking me."

"Goddamn you. I hate it when you're smarter than I am. Put your coat on. I'm driving you home."

"Fuck you. Give us another drink. Then tell me what you *need* me to do. The senator's already called me. He'll be in town day after tomorrow. Lucky you. Lucky, fucky you. Tell me."

I did.

It is said, "If one child obtains the Way, nine generations will leap over birth and death."

—Tripitaka Master Hsuan Hua, *Reflections of Water and Mirror Reflections*

Excerpts from a Letter from Dr. Judy Weintraub to the Author. Dated June 2. Continued

From there we drove south to a little town called Independent Hill. Nathan parked the van to the side of a convenience store. He allowed us to go inside, to use the restroom, and to buy lunch. The selection of foods in the store was scant, and little of the food was healthful. I was torn between wanting Harold to eat but not wanting to feed him any of the food from that store. Harold was not hungry, so the dilemma resolved itself—though unsatisfactorily.

We were told to get back to the van and to lock the doors while Nathan used the telephone on the front corner of the store. Nathan was at the telephone for at least twenty minutes. He poked his head around the corner, now and then, to check on us. I could see him through the two square windows on the back doors of the van. He would smile at me and then wave. In spite of his temper, he is a wonderful young man.

While Nathan was making his calls, there was discussion among the immortals on what their answer to Nathan should be. Harold had moved to the passenger seat in the cab to rest better—though I believe that he was listening closely to their conversations. I sat in the back with Father Dougherty and the immortals. I am convinced that they genuinely do not yet know, or have not yet determined, our precise destination. However, I also believe that there are more of them, perhaps several more, who are making the same trek that we are. I am led to this presumption because of a conversation that took place at this time between the members of our party. I have no idea how to spell many of the names they mentioned. I shall try to remember them correctly and spell them phonetically.

[Author's note: The conversation was picked up by the transport van's digital recorder.]

"Before we tell Agent Johnson anything, we must first determine if the movement is one of the whole," said Father Dobo.

"I agree. Are the people coming from the West?" Father Holden asked Mr. Tie.

"All. Yes. Jabala and LowLynn have been in the orient. Key was already in the United States. I think she is making transportation for them. The last time I heard, however, YoungTwo had gone to South Africa. I have had no contact with any of the Africans, so I am uncertain if he is still there. Father Dobo, have you heard?"

"Not for weeks. Kayklu and Gunta were coming. Moses had left Canada to be with them. Kayklu told me that Jesus was still there. I presume, and only presume, that nothing has changed. Except, perhaps, that Moses has wandered off. I did not know that YoungTwo was in Africa," replied Father Dobo.

"Moses *always* wanders off. On that alone in this long life, one can depend," said Father Hugo. The others laughed.

"Jesus is no longer in South Africa. I spoke briefly with him two days ago. He was in California with Key," said Mr. Tie. "He told me that YoungTwo was following. Socrates is already somewhere on the West Coast, at least that is what they think."

"Africa was the last obstacle, so Jesus always says," added Father Hugo. "He left there? Hmm. Well. It must mean that it's going to be his big day soon."

"You are just like him. You both want it to come all at once," laughed Miriam.

"It appears—does it not?—that we may have our way," Father Hugo answered her.

"We will see," Miriam sighed, as if she wanted to believe Father Hugo—but was afraid. Maybe she had heard it all before. "Moses will be there. I've talked to him. He's coming alone. Before he was murdered, Elijah told me that he had spoken with Fernando and Gustav. Evidently Renardo had been the second to be murdered. They were leaving Brazil—that was a month ago."

"I had not heard about Renardo. My God! It happened before or after Patricelli's murder?" asked Father Holden.

"A few days after. I think it was two days after," answered Miriam.

"Yes, three or four days," Father Quindilar affirmed. He sat on the front bench with Sister Maria and Father Dougherty. All three had turned to face the others in the back of the van.

"How many ... have dead so far?" asked Sister Maria—whose English is rather poor.

"With Renardo, it makes four. Patricelli, Renardo, Helaman, and Elijah. If John is still alive," said Father Holden.

"I have heard from John. Someone tried to kill him. It was several weeks ago. They set him on fire—rather, they set his dwelling on fire, and he was in it. He is healing. He is already in the Southwest with Lemual and Sariah," Miriam said. "Sariah is negotiating for us in one area, Lemual in another. John is giving direction."

"As I said, Jesus was waiting with Key for the others," repeated Mr. Tie. "They will be coming from the West Coast. She said they would drive."

"So?" asked Sister Maria. "What do we tell to Agent Johnson?"

No one said anything for a moment. Then Father Dobo said, though I do not think it was in direct response to Sister Maria, "We have determined that the movement is of the whole. I consider that significant. Perhaps, it may be so, perhaps even the significance suggested by Father Hugo."

"We will not know until it is upon us. Even then ..."

"But what do we tell to Agent Johnson?" Sister Maria repeated, interrupting Father Holden.

"Let's wait and see precisely what he wants," answered Father Holden.

Excerpts from the Journal of Father Jerome Dougherty. Dated June 2

That would mean there are at least twenty immortals, including the seven traveling with us.

Harold, who I thought had been napping in the passenger seat in the front of the van, ended their discussion. I later learned that Nathan had asked him to survey the area in front of the van while Nathan was making his telephone calls. "There are men in camouflage uniforms skulking about in the forest. They appear to be quite interested in this vehicle," Professor Weintraub proclaimed through the doorway to those of us in the rear. "I think I shall honk the horn and alert Agent Johnson."

I scurried into the driver's seat as the professor reached over to honk the horn. I had been sitting on the bench just behind the cab. I had been instructed beforehand by Nathan that if anything unusual should happen, I should promptly start the van and pick him up—unless he had been killed, in which instance I was to drive away and proceed toward our destination.

But Nathan reached the driver's door at about the same time that I sat in the seat. I unlocked the door for him and moved over as he quickly took my place.

The forest the professor had spoken of was to the south of us, to the right side of the service station. Nathan had parked the van so that it faced the trees. The foliage therein grew right to the edge of the parking lot. A dense mist covered the trees and the undergrowth, for, as I mentioned above, the day was damp and gloomy. There was some movement within the trees, though I had seen nothing that resembled a man.

Nathan started the engine. Rather than back up and drive away, he ascertained that all the doors were locked. Then he assiduously examined the foliage to the left and in front of us. "Quantico's training grounds are right through those trees," Nathan said to me. "Could be ..." he began, but stopped because someone had stood up from behind a clump of bushes and was striding in our direction.

The man was dressed in green and gray camouflage fatigues and carried a very short rifle with a long clip. He had blackened his face, but I could see that he was smiling because of the angle of exposure of his teeth and gums. Four more men stepped forward. They were dressed alike but armed with different weapons.

"I'll be damned," laughed Nathan. "It's my team."

"Three, four, five. As in ... basketball?" asked Father Hugo over Nathan's shoulder—for all the immortals had crowded to the front of the van.

"No, as in SWAT," Nathan replied.

"Special Weapons and Tactics," explained Harold for the benefit of the immortals, who were gawking like children on a first trip to the zoo.

"Yeah," responded Nathan. He rolled down the driver's side window as the first man who had stood approached the van.

"Graylett, you son of a bitch, what are you doing out here?"

"Looking for our lost leader. Someone told us he got abducted by a van full of crazy assho—" Mr. Graylett decided not to finish his sentence when he noticed how attentively attuned we all were to the conversation. "Sorry. So these are the immortals?" he asked instead as he slung his weapon over his shoulder. He made peculiar motions, nimbly pointing at several places behind him.

Nathan introduced all of us. Then he said, "This is Franky Graylett, leader of the SWAT team I'm on."

Graylett is a tall and muscular man. His eyes are blue, and his chin is square. His face was covered with what looked like charcoal. Graylett told us that he was happy to meet us, then said, "Nathan here's the real team leader. I'm only in charge when he's down, missing, or absent."

I noticed that, after Mr. Graylett gave his hand signals, the other four men in fatigues had positioned themselves in places around the store and in the trees. This action appeared, at least to me, to be protective in intent. Nathan stepped outside the van and spoke with Mr. Graylett in private. I do not know the content of their conversation.

[Author's note: The conversation was recorded on Johnson's body wire. Frank Graylett is FG.]

NJ: What the hell are you doing here?
FG: Well, the van's got a nice little locator beacon ... actually, I think it's stuck *inside* the transmission—slow somebody down if they tried to get rid of it. So Central can track you.

NJ: Yeah, I know. I asked for it. I came down by Quantico and called Hepworth because I figured he'd have the latest scoop. I've been taking care of my family. I figured that if he needed to get something to me, a courier would only be a few minutes from here. But I sure as hell didn't expect you guys to show up. Hepworth just told me to hold. I told him I would, for twenty minutes. Just called my wife, trying to get things arranged, then you show up. How'd you guys get down here?

FG: It's weird. We got orders from the director himself to get our butts on the road. Flew in last night from Vegas, on our own dime. We were in his office a couple hours ago. Had a nice little off-the-record chat. Then you had the skirmish at the airport and started heading this way; so he sent us down here to have a talk with you.

NJ: So what'd he tell you?

FG: Strange stuff is happening. Lowry said that the State Department had granted visas to several very nasty people—had let them into the country and promised them protection while they were here.

NJ: What do you mean, nasty?

FG: Terrorist types. Khalifah and his pal Mohammed—Mohammed whatever his name is—you know, the two al-Qaeda that are suspected of shooting the ambassador in Lebanon. Those and one or two more of their pals.

NJ: The State Department let them in? Christ. What the hell is going on?

FG: Yeah. That's what everybody wants to know. That guy you think killed the Indian in Idaho—Avilon, was it?

NJ: Avilar, I think, if you mean the Spaniard.

FG: Yeah. Avilar met with Khalifah in Syria about six months ago. But that's the only al-Qaeda connection we've got.

NJ: Shit. One's plenty.

FG: Oh, there's more good news. I hear that Lowry was ordered to hold up the search for Mezzano and Bottare.

NJ: The Mafia hit men?

FG: Yeah. The Attorney General is gonna cut some kind of deal with them.

NJ: Deal? What kind of deal? Jesus Christ, they've killed half a dozen people between 'em.

FG: Yeah, well, the director guessed that maybe they were supposed to kill a few more. Including ... [Author's note: I assume that Graylett motioned at the van at this point.]

NJ: But these are good people. Strange as hell, but good. What is going on, Franky?

FG: I haven't got a clue. Lowry wants you to tell me so that I can tell him.
NJ: Let's see what we can get out of them. Don't expect much.

[Author's note: Father Dougherty described this interrogation in his journal (supplemented, as usual, by Johnson's tapes).]

Nathan soon came back to the van with Mr. Graylett. "Mr. Graylett tells me that there are some people trying to hunt you down and kill you. He indicated to me that the State Department has granted them visas. Can any one of you tell me why? Does anybody have an answer for Mr. Graylett?" Nathan asked, speaking to all of us.

The immortals looked at each other with bewilderment. Father Hugo finally said, "It appears that we may not be welcome in America or in any other realm or glebe."

Professor Weintraub spoke. "Let me present some conjectures, and we shall see if our friends here find some kernel of truth in my offering."

Mr. Tie answered for the immortals, "Professor, lift this veil from our eyes—if you are able."

On the Author's Travels with Sylvia Johnson and Her Children, June 2, Continued

After speaking with Nathan on the telephone, we hurried back to my trailer. I grabbed the box of tapes and documents that Sylvia had brought to me and threw them in the back of Sylvia's blue minivan. I also picked up two copies of a DVD I had made a couple of days earlier. Sylvia and the children waited in the Dodge Caravan.

I caught sight of my neighbor, so I hollered over the barbed wire fence to him. My neighbor was called J. P. He had been farming for seventy-five of his eighty-five years—so he always told it—with two years off for the war. I asked him to keep an eye on my cats while I was gone.

He stopped clearing out the feeder end of a corrugate tube with his shovel. He tugged on the tops of his black rubber, knee-high irrigation boots. Then he leaned his left elbow on the shovel handle while he lit up a cigarette. He took a couple of long drags and then hollered back, "There's water in them goddamn ditches, and the pasture's clear full of goddamn mice. So just 'zactly what do you want me to do for your cats? Wipe 'em after they shit?"

"Thanks, J. P. That'd be swell. Just swell. Show 'em that special love and concern you're always showin' me," I yelled—because J. P. didn't hear so well.

"How's that? What's swellin'? What's the concern?"

"Tender care, give 'em tender care, J. P." I really belted it this time.

"How long you gonna be gone?" he hollered back.

"I don't know—couple of days."

"Long enough for me to get rid of the carcasses?"

"Real funny, J. P., real funny."

"You get gone. I'll keep an eye on 'em."

"Thanks, pal. When I get back, I'll have you over, and we'll split a bottle of whiskey."

"Any women comin'?" J. P. asked. His wife had died nearly a decade ago. Some nights, when he'd get lonely and couldn't sleep, he would see my light on and walk across the pasture and climb the fence that separated his house from my trailer and lightly tap on my door. I'd let him in, and we'd have a couple of drinks. He would tell me stories about his wife—try to persuade me to write a book about her.

He brought more than worn-out love stories. He knew how poor I was and often brought over vegetables from his garden. When he butchered a steer, one in the fall, one in the spring, we both had all the meat we could eat for weeks. I always bought the (usually) cheap whiskey.

"How many women can you handle these days?" I yelled across the fence to the old man.

"Three—if they're older than sixty. Don't bring any *real* young 'uns—or they might damn well kill me."

"I'll see what I can round up. Whiskey for sure. Thanks, J. P."

* * * *

Sylvia, the kids, and I went straight from my trailer to the Twin Falls regional office of Senator Sam Stevens. He had seven such offices to serve his constituents all across the state. This particular office complex was on the first floor of a two-story federal building, just across the street from the local television station and straight across the hall from the Internal Revenue Service.

It was after one o'clock when we got there. The Twin Falls office's secretary and field representative had just parked and were climbing out of the secretary's little orange Honda. I had Sylvia and her children wait in the minivan while I accompanied the senator's local staff into the building.

The secretary, a buxom brunette named Karen O'Keller, looked as if she were in her early twenties. She wore a blue print dress with a low-cut, white, ruffled collar, a red jacket, and white shoes. Her face was badly pockmarked, and her brown eyes had the uncanny ability to direct my attention away from her face to her torso or legs. I do not say this to indicate that I never scrutinize a woman's body. However, as a writer, my initial focus is usually, habitually, on the eyes. She managed this adjustment by keeping her head slightly lowered and barely tilted so that her eyes and her chin, a pointed chin, guided an observer's eyes away from her scarred face. Fresh out of college, enthralled by the power of politics, she was, knowingly or not, currently or not, fornication fodder for the good senator.

The senator's field representative had been a classmate of mine in high school. His name was Mitchell Miller. He always insisted on *Mitchell.* In his youth, he had been lean and hungry for power—his ego swollen by hormones for hegemony. Now he was fat and boring—bloated by Burger King.

Mitchell caught partisan psittacosis in high school when he ran for class vice-president and then for student body president—unsuccessfully both times. He enrolled at Boise State University so that he could be an unpaid intern for the state legislature that meets in the capital city during the winter months. He ran for the student council at Boise State and lost. After graduation, he worked as a part-time salaried staffer for Idaho's secretary of state.

At age twenty-five, Mitchell ran for public office, this time for the Idaho state legislature, and lost again—badly. He tried it again two years later and lost still worse. He eventually went on staff for Senator Stevens and has been sitting behind the same desk in the Twin Falls office as the senator's field representative for nearly four years. I think that in his heart, Mitchell felt that someday he'd be sitting behind the senator's desk in DC. He was the only person that I knew who believed that or even considered it a remote possibility.

"Hey, Mitchell!" I called out to him. Evidently, he and his secretary had just gotten back from lunch. She unlocked the door to the office and removed the OUT TOO LUNCH FROM ELEVEN UNTIL ONE *(sic)* sign from the window.

They recognized me and tried to smile in welcome. I had, on a few occasions, used the auspices and the equipment of the senator's local office to retrieve information from the Library of Congress.

"Working on a new book?" Mitchell asked. Not waiting for me, he followed Karen through the door.

"Nope. I need to speak to the senator today," I told him as I trailed them both into a small, wood-paneled reception room.

"Is it important?" he asked.

"Really important," I responded.

Mitchell grinned at Karen as if I were a third-class shithead for entertaining the notion that I might speak to the senator. She raised her eyes and grinned back.

"Well, you know that we run these things through channels. Come on back to my office and let's figure out which staff person can best help you with your problem. By the way, I ran into Brenda when the wife and I were shopping down in Salt Lake. She looks great. I guess she's remarried. I met him too. I think she's found herself a real nice guy. He's a widower, five little kids. Funny how life works out," Mitchell said, shaking his head as he led me into the back room.

It was another small, wood-paneled office with a large oak desk and tall black leather chair taking up most of the space. Two flags were poled as sentries behind the desk; Old Glory stood in one corner and the Great Seal of the State of Idaho in the other.

"I need to speak directly to the senator. And I'm in a hurry," I said to Mitchell. He sat in his leather chair—or, rather, in the General Services Administration's chair. I stood and leaned, arms extended, both palms firmly pushing against the front edge of the desk.

"First tell me about your problem," Mitchell repeated.

"I haven't got a problem. The *senator* has a problem, and I need to speak to him about it—right away."

"Wahell ..." Mitchell tugged at the word *well* with his beefy tongue. "The senator has his staff to help with his problems as well as with our constituents' concerns. You tell me what you think is wrong, and then I'll be sure and get the message to him."

"Mitchell. Listen. For your own good, don't jerk me around on this. Stop all this bureaucratic bullshit. Just get the senator on the telephone and let me talk to him—right now, in private—or I will not only tell you the senator's problem, but when I've finished, and you've busted your ass to get him on the telephone, I'll mention to the senator that I tried and tried to talk to him first but that you just wouldn't let me get through. I'll tell him that you insisted that I relay the information through you."

Mitchell made an effort to stiffen his upper lip; it quivered instead. "Our office procedure is straightforward. You must tell me first. Period. Unless you want to put it in writing and send it certified mail. Even then, it's likely that staff will open it in DC and respond. If we did it any other way, I can assure you that every day there'd be all kinds of kooks demanding to speak directly with the senator."

"Look, Mitch, trust me on this one. We went to school together. I'm just trying to save your ass. It doesn't matter to me if I tell you first or him. So I'm asking you one more time, please get the senator on the telephone."

"Can't do. Or he would kick me in the butt." Mitchell blushed. He was a good Mormon, not a person practiced in profanity.

"Okay," I told Mitchell as I removed a DVD from my pocket. "Know what this is?"

"Sure. It's a CD ... or it's a digital movie thing."

"This is a copy, Mitchell. It is one of several copies. There's some footage of your boss on this 'digital movie thing' doing some stuff he ought not be doing. Stuff he could go to jail for."

"That's a lie," he shot at me.

I had lost my patience with Mitchell, who (as you have probably guessed from my portrayal) has never been a personal favorite of mine. "Wanna see the DVD, do you, Mitch? Yeah. Let's take a look. Then you can tell the senator how you screened a video of him raping a woman. Tell him you did it just to make sure it was important enough so that I could talk to him about it."

Mitchell lost his breath. For a second, I thought he was going to have a seizure. He clutched at the arms of the leather chair and took several deep breaths. "Look, Mitch, you asked for it," I told him when the blue in his cheeks had reverted to red. He started to pant, and then he wheezed and finally coughed in an effort to speak. I couldn't make out whatever it was that he was trying to say.

"Call your boss right now," I continued after Mitchell failed to emit any coherent sounds, "and ask him if he wants to talk to me about the other night—that would be May 28th. Ask him if he wants to talk to me—or if he wants me to walk this disk across the street to the television station. Tell him if the police are called, that the copy I've sent to DC will be delivered to a national network. Tell him he's the fucking criminal … tell him … never mind, don't tell him anything—just get him on the phone; I'll tell him. You've got five minutes, Mitchell. Either you get your boss on the telephone, or I take a walk across the street, and they can stick his bare ass on TV."

* * * *

"I know who you are," Senator Stevens's voice came quite clearly and most threateningly through the receiver. Mitchell had left me alone in the back office—to speak privately.

"My name's not the secret either of us is concerned about keeping," I replied. "The publicity would probably generate sales of my books. I'll bet I can get fifty thousand from the *Inquirer.*"

"What could you possibly have …"

"Senator, I have a DVD of you and Candice Ballard."

"There's never been anything between …"

"Well, then I'll just let some of my friends across the street at KMVT make that judgment."

"This is entrapment. Goddamn you, this is blackmail!"

"It's neither. Her house. You're uninvited. We can just play the disk for the media and let the chips fall where they may," I answered.

"Cocksucker. How much do you want?"

"I don't want any money. Like I tried to tell Mitchell, I'm just a loyal Republican trying to help out his senator."

"What do you want?"

"Listen carefully. Call your buddy, Mr. Secretary Granfield, as soon as I hang up. You get him to back off from the Order of the Beloved. You get him to leave them alone for two days. That's all I want. Two days ... make it three ... three days, that's seventy-two hours, of safety for the Order of the Beloved. He'll understand. I'll call you at your DC office in exactly two hours. Repeat what I just told you and then give me a direct telephone number."

"Tell Herb Granfield to lay off the ... order of the lovers ..."

"The Order of the Beloved. Get it right."

"The Order of the Beloved for three days. My number is 202-999-8890. What happens if I get him to do it for you?"

"Three days from now—or when this is all over—you get the original video and the copies."

"What happens if he won't do it?" asked the senator.

"It's an election year. And, by God, all us Republicans got to stick together if we're gonna get them no-good, stinkin', immoral, big-spendin', commie, pinko, faggot Democrats out of office. Right, Senator? He'll do it. If he won't—then I suggest you call the president and get him to do it. You got two hours to get me my three days." I hung up.

And last, but not least, the possibility is by no means excluded that the originators of some of the superstitious practices or beliefs, and hence perhaps authors of some of the superstitious codes, were themselves philosophers addressing the multitude.

—Strauss, *The Law of Reason in the Kuzari*

Excerpts from a Letter from Dr. Judy Weintraub to the Author. Dated June 2. Conclusion

Harold mentioned that he might be able to explain why the State Department would allow the members of the Order to be hunted by killers.

Mr. Graylett spoke into a tiny headset. He gave instructions to the members of his team to remain in place, protecting us. Their presence lent our party the first real sense of security that we have felt as a group.

Before Harold started his explanation, Nathan invited Mr. Graylett to join us in the van. When all of us had squeezed together on the benches, there were twelve people huddled in the van, including Mr. Graylett.

Harold began, "I doubt that I would ever write what I am about to tell you. Even though I think it may well be true—or as close to the truth as a philosopher can come. I will tell you today because I think it may explain why we are here … and why we are in trouble.

"Human consciousness has been changing, evolving, if you will, since—well, since the first instance of self-awareness. Whether it originally occurred in Adam or in some half-ape in Tanzania, I do not know—but it has been changing ever since.

"Now, philosophers are salient because they have taken it upon themselves to document and sometimes to affect—or at least to attempt to affect—the development of this process called human consciousness. There were philosophers long before there were psychologists, a fact that Nietzsche saw and deplored. Nevertheless, we were the pioneers, and we are the historians of human consciousness and human self-consciousness.

"Without going into hours of a banal lecture on the history of philosophy, let me summarize it for you, Mr. Graylett. There are two basic views on this evolution or process of human consciousness. One is that it is happening to us in spite of ourselves. This is, essentially, the Platonic school, which holds that the Truth is both eternal and apart from us and that we participate in the truth only to the extent that we accurately mirror it. Thus, we have become better to each other, more tolerant, less violent, because we have become better images of the form or idea of human perfection.

"The second theory is essentially Hegelian. It is that we make ourselves. It is that human consciousness has developed by its own internal engine—that we control our own destiny. Truth is what we make it."

"A brief, pleasant, and fair summary," Father Holden stated.

"Thank you," my husband replied.

"Though one should add that precisely the same schism exists in Eastern thought," noted Mr. Tie.

"In all branches of thought," said Father Dobo.

"Even in mathematics," added Father Quindilar.

"Correct. All correct. Thank you. Now to the point," Harold continued. "Regardless of the position one adopts, it is very clear that human consciousness is rapidly changing. We are on the verge, it seems to me, of outgrowing our need for violence, for instruments of mass destruction, for racial and sexual barriers. Tremendous changes are taking place at breathtaking speed ..."

"To this, we immortals can attest," Father Holden interrupted. "We have seen more change in the last twenty years than in the prior thousand years. I do not mean technological change, which is also patently true. I mean in basic human relations. The death of totalitarianism, the emancipation of women, the growing equality of the races—it is a miracle."

"So far it sounds like History 101," objected Mr. Graylett.

"But it is not. Far from it." Harold spoke, his voice quivering with excitement. "For you see, Mr. Graylett, societies, technologies, governments, and religions have had very little to do with this development. Christianity has taught brotherly love for two thousand years. The notion of equality goes back even further, to Plato's *Republic,* or to ... never mind the details. These ideas have been around since the beginning of human consciousness—yet they are just now coming to fruition—and coming very fast."

"The professor is correct." Father Dobo entered the discussion at this point. "But what I do not understand is *our* relationship to that change. We immortals are merely a few. We are not the leaders of any movement. We shall all admit to being spectators. It is so. Occasional participants, perhaps. But we have not effected the change you speak of in a fundamental or constitutive manner."

"That is precisely the point," exclaimed Harold. "You are not the cause. *You are the effect.* You are the result, the end product, the Platonic Idea or the Hegelian Man at the end of history. Take your pick. You are what we are supposed to become."

"Soon?" pleaded Father Hugo. We all laughed.

"Stop it, Brad,' said Miriam. "The professor is saying that this must be the reason for our coming together. Is that correct?"

"I believe it to be true," Harold replied. "Why do you think that you are being called together?"

"I don't think that any of us know. I'm not even certain that one can describe it as 'being called.' When we speak about it among ourselves, we only wonder," answered Miriam.

"May I add something?" asked Father Holden. "We are drawn to it—at least I am. I have lived over one thousand years. Never settled. Never certain of why I was chosen—if 'chosen' is the word. Now, with this talk of meeting together, of finding our place, it is as if I am finally going home."

"It is so," Father Dobo nodded.

"I do not mean to be presumptuous, and this may be out of place, but I too have had a sense of home that I have never had before," said Father Dougherty. At which point Father Holden, who was sitting next to Dougherty, hugged him and whispered something in his ear.

"Still don't see what that has to do with the state department," said Graylett.

"Let's begin with the transparent examples," Harold urged. "Take Agent Johnson's Mormon Church as our first example. They believe that they have three Mormonites…"

"Three Nephites," Nathan corrected.

"Now two," Father Hugo clarified from the back bench.

"In any event, the response of the church—and it is a young church—to the death of one of its symbols of immortality was stupefaction, confusion, and concern. Is that correct?" asked Harold.

"That's about it," Nathan admitted.

"But when the issue became more complex, the church pulled away, having determined that its public image, self-preservation, and sustained growth were more significant than solving the riddle of a dead Native American. True?"

"Only partly. Some of the authorities wanted to resolve the matter," Nathan said defensively.

"Good. Exactly. There was tension within the organization. There was ambiguity and irresolution. In the end, the church opted to ignore, or more accurately, to encapsulate the issue," Harold stated.

"Yes," Nathan admitted.

"Now, our second example: the Catholic Church," Harold advanced his argument.

"Yes?" Father Dougherty said, prepared to respond.

Harold changed seats with Mr. Tie so that he could face his friend, Jerome. "Your church is older, more sophisticated, more diploid."

"It is a complex structure," Father Dougherty agreed.

"Aware enough, mature enough, to have discovered, located, then brought together and cared for its immortals," Harold asserted.

"Yes, I suppose we did that," affirmed Father Dougherty.

"Why?" asked Harold.

"Why did we bring them together?" asked Father Dougherty, seeking clarification of Harold's question.

"Yes."

"I have thought about that. I will be honest and tell you that my thoughts trouble me. First, it was to study them. We did this but discovered little. Then I think it was to 'treat them.' Then, when that failed, to observe and protect them. But, frankly, I think that there is a part of the Church that wants them under scrutiny and now, possibly, wants them dead. There is a darker side to the Church—one which is most abominable."

"It is not surprising that such tension and ambiguity exist in this organization as well," Harold replied. "The Catholic Church is much older and far more sophisticated than the Mormon Church. I would hypothesize that distinct lines have been drawn within the Catholic Church. For some, the Order of the Beloved is a perfect example of service to God. To others, it is a threat to the very existence of the Church."

"Yes, regarding the ambiguity. But why? Why a threat? These people, and I have always argued this to my superiors, these people are perfectly harmless," said Father Dougherty.

"Harmless to other human beings—not so harmless to social order, to the patriciate," stated Harold.

"I do not understand your point," objected Father Holden. "We were always treated by the ruling class, if not with equality, at least with curiosity, and at worst as anomalies. Popes and princes have found us neither more nor less than a passing interest. Even those who have feigned immortality, like the Comte de Saint-Germain, were little more than court jesters. We have never been considered revolutionaries—because we are not."

"Yet it is true that entire religions, cults, and sciences are many ... please excuse my English. What I mean is that they are all devoted to the discovery, or of the offer—the promise of the secret of immortality," Father Quindilar argued.

"Yes. Excellent point. Alchemy, for example, is more than a two-thousand-year attempt to reproduce, chemically or mystically or otherwise, immortality," said Harold. He turned slowly and studied the crowd of faces that surrounded him. (The air was humid but not hot or stuffy, for Nathan had the engine running, and the air conditioner worked very well.)

"We are straying somewhat from the point," Harold stated. "Either this is a van full of people, many of whom have a very serious mental disease, or this vehicle is carrying people who have what almost every other person on this planet wants: immortality."

"We know from history," he continued, "to what horrendous, brutal, and ridiculous lengths human beings will go to achieve what you claim is something so simple, within someone so unaffected, that almost everyone either ignores it or fails to find it—overlooks it. After speaking with Mr. Tie, I am beginning to understand that the process of looking for immortality may, in fact, be that which prohibits or inhibits the disclosure of immortality."

"That is not incorrect," replied Mr. Tie.

Harold coughed violently, but he fought the cough back. He went on, "Now the critical question comes in two parts: First, do the existing social, religious, and political institutions reveal or conceal immortality from the masses?" There was silence in the van. "Father Holden, would you give us your opinion?" Harold requested.

"I would have to say that they hinder its discovery," answered Father Holden. Those seated around him nodded in agreement.

"Then the second part of the question is: If these institutions believed that this secret could be revealed, but that the process of the revelation of immortality existed *outside* of their spheres of influence and was perhaps even inimical to their prolonged existence, how would such an institution respond?"

"As we say in my field, there is no haploid answer to that question," I objected.

"Clearly not, Judy," Harold replied. "But we have examples. The Mormon Church has buried the issue. It would rather ignore it than deal with it. The Catholic Church, at least part of the Catholic Church, tried to contain the issue, to compartmentalize it, so to speak. But a government—a government is grounded in force, not in faith.

"Let me ask a few more questions," Harold insisted.

I must stop and say that my heart ached for him. For, as you know, he is seriously ill. By this point in the conversation, his face was covered with sweat, and he was nearly exhausted.

"My questions are for you, Miriam. Do you mind?" asked Harold.

"Not at all," she said, though she appeared surprised.

"Are you a citizen of the United States?" Harold asked. I must say that this seemed an outlandish question to all of us.

"No. Not legally. I was born in what is now a part of the country of Egypt. I have lived all over the world. I have no real citizenship."

"How long—since the last time you moved here—how long have you resided in the United States?"

"Well, I come and go. I guess you could say that I have lived here for about eighty years now. Yes. Since the third decade of the last century."

"During that eighty-year period, have you ever filed an income tax return?"

Miriam smiled. "Come to think of it, I have not."

"Do you feel a need to pay income taxes?" Harold asked. "To establish a home?"

"No," Miriam replied.

"Do you need police protection?"

"Not until recently."

"Do you ever require medical attention?"

"No. We are rarely ill. We can heal ourselves."

"Yes. I had surmised that already. You must explain it to me. But let us finish this. Can you think of anything that you need from the state? Anything at all?" asked Harold.

"No. Nothing."

"What could possibly be a greater threat to this government, to any government, than for this gift that you have been given to be shared with the many?" asked Harold.

"I understand," replied Miriam. She had lost her smile.

"It is so," replied Father Dobo.
We were all very frightened.
"Franky, outside," Nathan ordered.
Nathan and Mr. Graylett left the van and spoke again in private.

[Author's note: The conversation was recorded on Johnson's body wire.]

NJ: So what d'you think?
FG: Craziest bunch I've ever come across.
NJ: What'd you think of what the professor said?
FG: He's the worst one! How'd you get stuck with these people?
NJ: Don't lose sight of the fact that some very important people want these folks dead.
FG: Sure, but I ...
NJ: Did you hear about the deputy sheriff who was wasted in Idaho?
FG: Okay. Sorry.
NJ: Franky, these people are going to go back West if they have to crawl. And if we let them do it alone, one by one, maybe all at once, they will all be murdered. Maybe because of the reasons that the professor gave us—maybe they have us fooled. But they are going to be killed, and so is anybody dumb enough to get in the way of the assassins.
FG: Okay. So, I need guidance from you.
NJ: I did something on my own. I might have bought a couple of days for moving these people—it was a political move. It may or may not work. Even if it's successful, my family's still vulnerable. So first I want a unit sent immediately to the truck stop on Highway 318 just outside of Lund, Nevada. It's north of town, maybe three miles. My wife and kids and my cousin will be there in less than six hours. If the delay works, then they are the obvious targets. I need to be able to pull them out of there if there's trouble.
FG: I'll ask Lowry.
NJ: No. Just do it. *It's my family,* Frank.
FG: Okay. Consider it done.
NJ: Second, we need to figure out a staging area in the Southwest, as close as possible to the end destination, and we need to see if Lowry will release you to set it up.
FG: Where is it?
NJ: I don't know yet. In some ways, these people are real smart. I mean tactically. No one in their group knows exactly where they are headed. They all know gen-

erally. They are figuring out their destination by consensus as they move toward it. That way …

FG: Yeah! If there are informants within their groups, then nobody knows the whole story until the last possible moment. Makes lots of sense—for crazy people. [Laughter]

NJ: How close do you need?

FG: Desert—three hundred kilometers—maximum. Try to get us within fifty or closer.

NJ: If it's coming together for them like we think it is, then let's settle for three hundred. I'll try to get you a closer radius when I learn more.

FG: You're the boss.

[Judy's letter continues.]

Mr. Graylett spoke briefly with us again before finally leaving. He asked if one of the members of the party could tell him, within three hundred kilometers, our final destination.

"We have been told that it will be near the Four Corners area," Father Holden replied. "How near, I do not know. I doubt if anyone knows. If you are looking for a central point, I would choose a locale nearby."

Mr. Graylett thanked him and left with his men. They melted back into the forest. I watched them through the windshield of the van. Their disappearance was subtle and spectacular.

Nathan allowed us to use the restroom and to refresh ourselves, but then we were back on the road. I could not tell if we were followed by Nathan's SWAT team. Though I doubt that I would be able to detect them if so.

We stopped only once more that day, near Christiansburg, Virginia. I called the children. Benjamin was home. He was concerned about us. Several others made telephone calls as well. (Nathan will not allow us to use our cell phones—especially when in the van.) We were allowed to visit the restroom and to buy snack food, and then we resumed our journey.

We are spending the night in Wytheville, Virginia, a small town just off the interstate. Our rooms have the same arrangement as in Washington, DC. Except here Nathan is not permitted to nail open the doors. Nathan had Chinese food delivered to our rooms. Nathan has been out of the hotel a good part of the evening. Much to Harold's delight and to my surprise, Miriam and I are becoming fast friends. She is a wonderful woman. Perhaps I will write more about her later.

One more thing: I have tested the recorder that Nathan gave me. He asked me a few days ago if I would wear it, and I told him that I would think about it. I will attempt to use it if I speak alone with one of the immortals.

It is late. I have written much today and will try to do so tomorrow. Harold is insisting that I send you as much detail as possible. I know that Father Dougherty is also keeping a careful journal.

Harold was somewhat feverish tonight. I hope it is only because he worked so hard today. He is such a brilliant man, and I love him dearly. I shall close for tonight and remain

Sincerely yours,

[Signed]

Judy

On the Author's Travels with Sylvia Johnson and Her Children, June 2, Continued

We left Twin Falls in a hurry. Just like southern Idaho weather, the temperature had dropped fifty degrees in the last two days. It was a blustery, snow-squalling, Winnie-the-Pooh kind of spring day. I was glad that the heater in Sylvia's mini-van was working, even gladder that I was not one of the farmers we passed along the highway as we traveled south to Nevada. Bundled against the wind and the dust in polyester parkas, they bounced around on their rubber tractor seats, plowing up and down and back and forth across the barren fields.

Sylvia drove. The kids and I sang. I taught them "Do-wa-ditty-ditty-dum-ditty-do"—the farmer version.

> There he was, just a-plowin' up the ground, singin'
> Do-wa-ditty-ditty-dum-ditty-do
> Wishin' he was in his house where it was nice and warm, singin'
> Do-wa-ditty-ditty-dum-ditty-do
> He looked cold (He looked cold)
> He looked old (He looked old)
> He looked cold, he looked old
> All he did was sneeze and wheeze, singin'
> Do-wa-ditty-ditty-dum-ditty-do
> Do-wa-ditty-ditty-dum-ditty-do.

The kids loved it. Their mother, evidently not much of a connoisseur of sixties music, objected. She said I shouldn't make fun of people like that. Jeremy really grooved on the *do-wa-ditties* and didn't shut up for almost an hour, until we reached the little town of Jackpot at the Idaho-Nevada border. Kaylynn and Sherry were starting to think that I was hip. To be upfront, the idea that I would never have a family of my own ripped at my guts every time I thought about it.

There was another distraction—beside the farmers and the *do-wa-ditties*. I thought, I hoped, that the Idaho state cop who trailed us most of the way to the Nevada border was behind us by coincidence. I told Sylvia that such was the case and not to worry when she kept interrupting our singing with nervous questions about him.

"There are always state cops on this road. They stop the drunks coming back from Jackpot," I assured her.

After we crossed the border into Nevada, it became clear that our police escorts were all too blatant to be coincidence. We pulled into a Chevron convenience store in tiny Jackpot, Nevada, a border town with four casinos, a few service stations—and not much of anything else. A Nevada state trooper pulled right in behind us. He climbed out of the car and approached the blue Dodge Caravan. Sylvia reached for her black diaper bag, but I pulled it from her hands. "No fuckin' way!" I said under my breath. We both smiled at the officer. Sylvia rolled down the window.

"Headed back home?" he asked.

"Vegas," she answered with a smile.

"Just wanted to warn you that your license plate is about to fall off," he said, and pointed to the front of the minivan.

"I'll fix it as soon as we get back," I told him, leaning forward to look past Sylvia at him.

"Okay," he said, and he went inside the store.

"Let's get out of here," Sylvia demanded, and she started up the engine.

"Forget it. Let's take the kids inside. Take them potty and get them something to eat and drink. Look, if they're gonna stop us, it's not gonna be in a gas station. It'll be out along the road someplace."

"You're right. Come on, kids. Let's go potty and get some dinner," said Sylvia.

"Leave the diaper bag," I insisted.

"Okay," she relented.

I went to the pay telephone, which was on the front of the building, and called the senator's private number. He answered immediately.

"Did you get me my three days?" I asked him.

"The Order of ... whatever it is ... and your cousin, the FBI agent Nathan Johnson, will not be approached for three days. That's all they'll give me, and that's all I'm giving you," said the senator. His voice was low and intimidating.

"Good," I did not want to say much because I was certain that the conversation was being taped. In fact, I wished that I were taping it.

"What you are doing is a federal offense," he practically growled.

"What you did is a felony," I replied.

"Let's see who ends up in prison first. Want to make a bet? Tick, tock, tick …"

"Fuck you." I slammed down the receiver. My hands were shaking.

There were no further incidents with the police in Jackpot. We fed the kids, fueled the minivan, and headed south for Ely. I drove. We were running late, so I had to drive fast. A state police car tailed us, usually just out of sight. The kids fell asleep. Miles and miles of sagebrush and rock gullies melted one into the next. Sylvia nodded off. I passed the time checking the rearview mirror for the cop and thinking about how to structure a cohesive plot from the events swirling through our lives. It all seemed pointless to me.

We got to Ely, Nevada, around five thirty. I found another convenience store, this one a Maverick. We stooled the kids, bought some snacks, fueled the minivan, and then found the sheriff's office. I parked right in front of it. It was 5:40 PM. A couple of minutes later, a state police car drove around the block once and then parked about fifty feet behind us.

We handed the snacks back to the kids to steal a glance at the trooper's car. They ripped into the bags of cookies and red licorice. They drank their little plastic mini-bottles of milk.

"Fuck!" I swore as I turned forward and adjusted the rearview mirror to get a better look at the patrolman, who was still sitting in his car. I handed Sylvia her black diaper bag. "If that guy gets out of his car … I guess we are supposed to take him into the station with us."

Sylvia opened the black bag on her lap, ensured that the clip of ammunition in her pistol was full, loaded the weapon, and flipped on the safety. "He better not put up much of a fight," she said.

She pretended to reach over and put her left arm around me. With her right hand, she reached back and beneath my bellyband and removed the tiny pistol I kept strapped there. She bent down, slid a bullet into the chamber of my pistol, and then flipped on the safety. Reaching around me again, she stuck the weapon under the bellyband. The backs of her fingers rubbed against the top of my hips. Her perfume was wearing thin; her skin smelled salty with sweat. I started to get an erection. "You're all set," she said. Sylvia kissed me on the cheek.

Nothing much happened for about ten minutes—except that I battled my erection; I tried, in my mind, to talk it down. It was a long, hard, ten minutes. I covered my crotch with the tail of my flannel shirt. The officer in the police car stared through his windshield at us. I checked him out through the rear view mirror. He kept reaching down below the dashboard. I assumed that he was adjusting his radio, waiting for instructions. I also scrutinized the county building where the sheriff was supposed to be waiting. It was well after five o'clock, so most of the cars in the parking lot had left for the day. The place looked deserted.

Finally, just before six o'clock, the state policeman picked up his microphone and spoke into it, then hesitated as if awaiting a response. He got out of his car. Sylvia hid her pistol between her legs. The officer walked slowly to the minivan. He came around to my side, to the driver's side, and tapped on the window. He was a big man. Tall, slightly overweight, he wore sunglasses and kept the brim of his hat low, nearly covering his eyebrows with it. He was the same state trooper who had stopped us in Jackpot.

"Are you Mrs. Johnson?" he asked across me to Sylvia.

"Yes, officer," she answered.

"Sheriff would like to see you inside," he said.

"Give us a second. We have to change the baby," I told him, and rolled up the window. The patrolman walked back to his car. He leaned against the front left wheel well and waited.

"Why didn't you go in?" Sylvia demanded.

"We're not supposed to go in," I retorted.

"We are if ... "

"Get out the directions," I ordered her. Sylvia opened her purse. She took the notes I had written down when Nathan had spoken to us over the telephone earlier that day. "Give 'em to me," I commanded. "See. If everything is okay, then the sheriff is supposed to come out to us. Nathan didn't say anything about being invited to go inside. One way or another, the sheriff should come out to meet us. Where the fuck is the sheriff?"

"How should I know where he is? Maybe we should just go inside. Maybe we should ... I don't know what ... maybe we ... what should we do? Must you always use the effword?" she whined. Sylvia was starting to lose control.

"I don't know what to do. Shut up and let me think," I barked at her from fear. The senator was apparently right. I would be the first one in jail.

In the side mirror, I watched as the state trooper flipped off the leather strap that held his gun in its holster. He started walking toward the minivan. He thought again. He stopped, walked back, reached inside his patrol car, picked up the mike, and said something into it.

"Sylvia, get the kids down on the floor," I ordered. "Get one of them to throw up. I need a sick kid right now."

"What's wrong ..." she started to ask me, but then she glanced up at the rearview mirror and saw the state trooper throw the microphone into the car and reach down for his weapon.

"Sylvia, get your kids on the floor. Make one of them throw up," I repeated. Our eyes met for a moment. In hers, I saw confusion and trust. I do not know what she saw in mine.

"Kaylynn, Sherry, get on the floor—now. Kaylynn, you stay on top of Jeremy," Sylvia instructed them. The words were perfunctory, for she immediately reached back, unlatched their safety belts, and body-slammed her kids on top of each other on the floor between the front and rear seats. "And don't move a muscle or make a peep until I tell you," she commanded in a voice so severely magisterial that the inside of the minivan was instantly silenced.

"Is it six?" I asked Sylvia.

"Almost—five more minutes."

I opened the door and got out of the car to face the trooper. "Get one of the kids to throw up. It might buy us some time," I said to Sylvia. "I'll stall him for a couple of minutes. If the sheriff doesn't show—one way or another, we're out of here."

Transcripts of Three Conversations, All Three June 2

[Author's note: It is difficult to determine the exact place within the general chronology of this book of the conversations that Nathan Johnson taped over the next two days. I assume that the following conversations occurred around the time that Sylvia, the children, and I arrived in Ely, Nevada—the circumstances of which were portrayed in the preceding section. I can say with certainty that the conversation with Sheriff Duffy preceded the conversation with Hepworth, because they are on the tape in that order. I found the third conversation on a tiny digital recorder. It logically follows the conversation with Duffy and, perhaps, with Hepworth. The reader should understand that Jim Hepworth was a "situation manager" for the FBI. At least, such is my conjecture from listening to the recordings.]

Taped conversation between Nathan Johnson (NJ) and
Sheriff Dewey Duffy (DD)

DD: Sheriff Duffy speaking.
NJ: Dewey. Hi. Is everything still on track?
[Silence]
NJ: Dewey? We have a deal.
DD: You know who called me—just fifteen minutes ago?
NJ: We have a deal.
DD: Yeah, I know, Nathan. But do you know who called me?
NJ: I don't care if Jesus Christ called you. We have a deal.
DD: Congressman Weltham. He called me, personally, himself.
NJ: Who is Congressman … never mind. What did the congressman want?
DD: It isn't bad, Nathan. It was just a little favor. He wanted me to keep your wife and kids, and your cousin in protective custody—just for a couple of days.

NJ: Goddamn it, Dewey. That's my wife and kids. It's like I told you: there are pros working this. Hit men. Professionals like you've never seen. They've already killed a deputy sheriff in Idaho. They're trying to go through my family to get at me. I'm glad that the congressman is concerned, but I'm telling you that the Bureau is gonna handle this. If you hold my family, they'll go right through you to get 'em. Goddamn it, Dewey, if you hold my wife and kids, and anything happens to ...

DD: Hold your horses, Nathan. I didn't tell him I'd do it.

NJ: What did you tell him?

DD: He's my congressman, for hell's sake.

NJ: *What did you tell him?*

DD: I told him that you were a personal friend and have asked me a favor, and I told him that if he needed them held, he'd better get the state boys to do it.

NJ: You told him to get the state police to hold them? Shit, Dewey. I thought I could depend on you. I thought we had a deal.

DD: Take it easy. I also told him that he couldn't do it in my county—seein's how I'd given you my word. I told him that he could pick them up in Tonopah because your wife was takin' a circuitous route back to Vegas so's not to be noticed.

NJ: Okay. That might be even better. Okay. Thanks. Sorry I got upset. But it's my family.

DD: They pulled up front a couple of minutes ago. There's a state trooper followin' 'em. I imagine he's been tailin' 'em since Jackpot. I'm gonna head out there right at six—just like we talked about—and send 'em to Tonopah—just like I promised the congressman. If I know you, that should work just fine 'cause you never trust anybody—including me—and you probably got somethin' else figured out anyway.

NJ: You're a good friend ... and a smart cop.

DD: Well, they're still gonna have to deal with the state boys. But I imagined you've got that all figured out too.

NJ: Thanks, Dewey.

DD: Get your butt up here and see me some time.

NJ: I'll do it.

Taped conversation between Nathan Johnson (NJ) and Jim Hepworth (JH)

NJ: One two one six ALR.
?: For?
NJ: Jim Hepworth.

?: Hold one.
JH: Nathan. What's up?
NJ: Is the transport for Lund …?
JH: On its way.
NJ: I'll need it by seven o'clock, maybe six forty-five.
JH: ETA 8:58 PM local time.
NJ: Can we get it sooner?
JH: Wait one.
[Silence]
JH: New ETA, 8:50 PM local.
NJ: Sooner?
JH: Wait one.
[Silence]
JH: No. That's it.
NJ: Description?
JH: White Ford van. Boyd's Coffee stickers, sides and rear. Driver's door unlocked, keys in pouch behind the front seat.
NJ: Plates?
JH: Nevada attached. Colorado, Utah, New Mexico, and Arizona in the pouch with the keys. Wrapped. The signs on the van are magnetic tape. They just peel off. There is a set marked with the Sherwin Williams logo in a flat brown box in the side storage compartment of the van.
NJ: Driver? Backup?
JH: Negative. Can't clear it. Still hands-off. Just the van.
NJ: Shit.
JH: Yeah. Tell them to be careful with those magnetic stickers. They cost a couple grand apiece, and we can't requisition replacements for them. Everything in this operation is voluntary. The guys delivering the van are paying for the gas.
NJ: I understand.
JH: Where do you want it parked?
NJ: Let me think. Let's park it … behind the motel … at the northwest corner.
JH: Northwest corner of the motel. Roger. We got one more development.
NJ: Shoot.
JH: MOSSAD is moving some of its DC agents around.
NJ: Israel? Shit.
NJ: Yes. Could be bad. Then again, maybe they have word about Khalifah and Mohammed Ali al-Samman. MOSSAD would love to catch them—especially in the U.S.

NJ: I hope. Anything else?
JH: Not sure. There are some North Koreans here on a diplomatic mission. Eight came into the country. Last time we counted, there were only five in the group. Also disappeared around DC. We're looking hard for them.
NJ: Shit.
JH: The Russians and Ukrainians are quiet. Nothing from the British. But you never know about the British.
NJ: Okay. That's good. I was starting to think every government in the whole world was after these poor bastards.
JH: Nah, we're on your side. We're rootin' for you. That it?
NJ: Yeah, thanks. One two one six ALR. I'm gone.

Digitally recorded conversation between Nathan Johnson (NJ) and Sheriff Mark Petersen (MP) of Nye County, Nevada

NJ: Sheriff Petersen?
MP: This is Sheriff Mark Petersen.
NJ: This is Nathan Johnson with the FBI. I don't think we've met. I know Dewey Duffy really well; in fact, I just got off the phone with him. Look, I've a huge favor to ask you.
MP: Let's hear it, Agent Johnson.
NJ: My wife and kids are going to be headed your way in an hour or so. They're in Ely now. My cousin's with them. White male, mid-thirties, about five ten. He's okay. A threat has been made against me, and there is a chance that someone might try to get to me through them. They're heading home to Vegas—but I'm sending them through Tonopah, roundabout, just in case. The state police already know the situation, but if you could have a car meet them at the county border and bring them into Tonopah to spend the night, maybe a couple of nights, until this thing blows over, it would …
MP: Funny you should call. I just got off of the telephone with Congressman Weltham. He asked me if I'd keep them here for a couple of days in protective custody.
NJ: He's a good man. That was a nice thing for him to take some of his time to do.
MP: I'll have a car waiting. We'll get them in here, and nobody on God's green earth is gonna lay a finger on them. You've got my word on it.
NJ: They're in a blue Dodge Caravan. Nevada plates. One hundred and seven KCA. I owe you for this.

MP: Just doing the job I was elected to do. Blue Dodge Caravan, Nevada, one hundred and seven KCA.
NJ: That's it. And I owe you for this. Anyway, gotta get going.
MP: Don't worry about them.
NJ: I'll try not to. Thanks.
MP: Good luck.

On the Author's Travels with Sylvia Johnson and Her Children, June 2, Continued

"So, what's the story?" I asked the state trooper after I had identified myself. We approached each other in front of the Ely, Nevada, sheriff's office. His hand rested on the butt of his revolver. I put my hands on my hips, close to the pistol tucked down the back of my sweatpants. I figured that he would probably be faster on the draw and might get off the first round. But I'd get off the second, and with Sylvia backing me up, this guy was as dead as that buffalo back in Yellowstone if he pulled his weapon. The sun settled over his shoulder. It nearly rested on the mountains to the west. It was going to be a gorgeous sunset. I tried to focus on the mountains and the sun. My heart pounded; my stomach twisted. I settled for not keeping my eyes fixed on his trigger finger.

"I've just been ordered to escort you to Tonopah," the state trooper said. He was a tough old buzzard, heavy and tall, with thick fingers. He had a twenty-year gold service medal pinned above the flap of his shirt pocket.

"We're supposed to talk to the sheriff first, to get our instructions from him. But the baby's been sick. He just threw up all over the back seat. Sylvia's trying to clean it up—keep the kids out of the mess. Stinks like, well, like baby puke. That's why I had to get out." I laughed, motioning over my shoulder at the minivan. Sylvia had crawled onto the back seat. The kids were under her legs, safely pinned to the floor. Though I didn't see it, I had no doubt that she held her 10 mm just out of view. Toying, as I assume she was, with her pistol, she looked as if she were cleaning vomit off the back seat.

"I don't know anything about the sheriff. I just know that I am supposed to take the woman and the children to Tonopah. They are under protective custody." The state trooper moved his hand away from his weapon.

I kept my palms on my hips. "I don't think those kids are goin' anywhere, as sick as they are. Sylvia wants to stop and get a motel. But we're going to speak to the sheriff first."

"Doesn't matter. I have my orders." His hand dropped again. Thick thumb rubbed thick forefinger.

"Well, geez. Can't we just talk to him?"

"Ho, there! Kenny!" the sheriff's grinding voice came from the front of the building. "What the hell are you doin'? Scarin' these poor folks?" The sheriff was a squat, muscular little man. He was about five and a half feet tall; but I'd bet that he weighed nearly two hundred pounds, solid as a bowling ball.

"I'm not scarin' anybody, Sheriff," the trooper retorted.

"Put your loop back over your hammer," the sheriff demanded as he pulled a cigarette out of the pack from his shirt pocket and lit it. "You wanna play Marshall Dillon—you go play him in somebody else's county."

"I'm just being careful," the state trooper countered.

"Try being courteous—for a change. You've got an unarmed man, a woman, and three little babies. Which one do you think is gonna overpower you?" the sheriff badgered the state trooper. "Or were you thinkin' 'bout maybe shootin' all five of 'em?"

The officer flipped the leather loop back on to the hammer of his pistol. "These people are still in my custody," he challenged the sheriff.

"The hell they are. We are doing a favor for this woman's husband, who happens to be an FBI agent, and a damned good one. Congressman Weltham has asked my office, and now Sheriff Petersen's office, to offer them protection for the next couple of days—*if they so desire.*"

Sylvia was out of the car. She held Jeremy under her left arm. I presume she thought that we were safe because she was not brandishing her pistol. There was vomit and spittle all down the front of the confused and crying little guy, who could not understand why his mother had just poked her finger down his throat.

"Sheriff Duffy. Right? It's a pleasure to finally meet you. Nathan's told me so much about you," she said. She offered her hand, dripping with Jeremy's vomit, to Duffy. (Nice touch, I thought.)

The sheriff gave her a speedy two-fingered salute. "Howdy. S'pose he has. So let me tell you about that husband of yours, 'bout Nathan." The sheriff took a deep drag on his smoke as he began his story. "Me and Nathan were chasin' two idiots shootin' wild horses out on BLM land. They were shootin' 'em with machine guns. Crazy bastards. There were these two guys, and they were both carryin' full auto AK-47s. We drove right up on 'em. Nathan had his pistol and got out, kinda hunkered behind the door, and told 'em to throw down their weapons. I was tryin' to get the shotgun out of the rack in my jeep when they started shootin' at us. Nathan ducked down, rolled on the ground under the jeep. They blew out the windshield, and there was bullets zingin' all around me. I thought, sure as shit, I was dead. Then Nathan shot one of them right in the kneecap. The guy fell, screamin' so loud that the other one just plain threw down his rifle. Then the one guy started bawlin' like a baby, like your little boy there. One of them screamin' 'cause he had half his leg blown off; the other one just a-bawlin' 'cause he's scared to death. The one that was leg-shot soiled his pants. Damnedest arrests I ever made."

"Sheriff, I don't mean to interrupt, but my Jeremy is sick. Have you talked to Nathan?" asked Sylvia.

"Just a few minutes ago," Sheriff Duffy answered.

"What does Nathan want us to do now?" she asked him.

"He wants you to drive on down to Tonopah tonight. Circle around that way to get to Vegas. I'll escort you as far as the county line, and Sheriff Petersen will meet you there."

"I'll be following too," added the state trooper.

"Can I wash the baby inside and get some paper towels, and then can we get going soon?" Sylvia asked, pointing at the sheriff's office building, her eyes pleading with both the sheriff and the state trooper.

"Whatever you need," answered the sheriff.

"I'll wipe up the car," I offered. In five minutes, we were back on the road. The sheriff in his car led the way; the state trooper stayed right behind us.

*   *   *   *

"Who wants to be sick next?" I asked the girls, who were buckled into their safety seats. Sylvia was driving. I was studying the map.

We were less than five miles from the turnoff from Highway 6 south onto Highway 318. The road from Ely had twisted its way through a stretch of steep hills on the western edge of the Shell Creek Range. The hills around us were covered with pinyon pines. As we descended onto the Egan Range, the trees became increasingly intermingled with tall, healthy 'big sagebrush' *(Artemesia tridentata)* that grew nearly as high as the bantam trees. Night was falling all around us, over the scrub forest, in a purple and gray haze.

"Gross. Not me," protested Kaylynn.

"Me needer," joined Sherry.

"Listen, girls, Daddy's going to call us at a telephone that is just a few minutes from here. But the police who are following us don't want to stop. If somebody gets sick, then we can stop and talk to Daddy. Mommy needs to talk to Daddy. It is really easy. Just stick your finger way down your throat, and you'll throw up. Be sure and do it on the floor mat," Sylvia advised.

I unbuckled my seat belt and climbed over the seat to explain better. "Okay, here we go, Kaylynn, point your finger." We both pointed fingers at the ceiling. "That's it. Now. Open your mouth. No, wider. You need to stick it way down. It will choke you a little. Okay, ready? Don't close your mouth. Keep it wide open. Wub, tube, cub ob spick it dobwn thereb," I said, and demonstrated with my finger in my throat. I took mine out—for clarity's sake and because Kaylynn was cooperating. "A little farther. Okay. There you go. No. No. Head down. Aim for the floor mat. Head down. Okay. Enough. That's enough. Take your finger out. You'll make yourself sick."

We had vomit. Lots of vomit. We had the stench from the butyric acid of Kaylynn's half-digested milk and cookies wafting through the enclosed cab. We had Kaylynn crying. We had Jeremy screaming in fear—he thought maybe he was about to get poked in the throat a second time. We had Sherry puking, aroused by the smell of her sister's vomit, all over the seat. Some got on my sweatpants. We had our excuse to turn off Highway 6 and pull into the truck stop, where Nathan would soon be calling.

> But all the smells that are somewhat putrid and fetid are bad in all vomitings.
>
> —Hippocrates, *The Book of Prognostics*

On the Author's Travels with Sylvia Johnson and Her Children, June 2, Continued

I told Sylvia to be sure to signal early so that the sheriff, who was now driving in front of us, would know that we were turning off of Highway 6. Sheriff Duffy allowed us to turn without interference, though the state trooper behind us immediately turned on his cruiser's red and blue strobes and pulled us over.

"Don't roll down the window until he's right up on us," I ordered Sylvia, because I wanted the trooper to get a full whiff of our excuse for stopping. We watched him climb from his car and ready his weapon. However, as before, he left it holstered. He sauntered to the driver's side of the minivan. The sheriff did a quick three-sixty and then pulled behind the state trooper's car. He trotted up to see us as well.

"What's the prob ..." the trooper started but gagged on his words as the stench of Kaylynn's and Sherry's vomit rushed through the lowered window in acrid greeting.

"I told you my children are ill. I'm going to drive to this truck stop—it's just a mile or so out of the way—and call my husband. He may want us to spend the night there."

"I'm afraid we can't do that," the state trooper answered.

"Can't do what?" asked the sheriff who had just lumbered up. "Oh, Lord, what a stink." He quickly lit a cigarette. "You gotta do somethin' with those kids."

"That's what we were just talking about," replied Sylvia through the open window. "I want to call Nathan from the truck stop. See if it's okay if we spend the night there."

"Sounds like an all right idea. Good place to eat dinner. Hey, Kenny?" The sheriff said, slapping the state trooper on the back. "That stink make you hungry?"

"Let's get going," grumbled the trooper.

Two rows of fuel pumps sat out front of the truck stop. The truck stop was in the midst of a wide graveled lot where the big diesels could line up side-by-side and park for the night. The restaurant, gift shop, restrooms, and truckers' showers were housed in a brick building just north of the pumps. The small cinder-block motel was a separate two-story building just to the west of the restaurant, store, and restroom facilities. The motel office was in the gift shop. The pay telephones, where Nathan would call, were in the wide walkway between the restaurant and the gift shop and right next to the restrooms and truckers' showers.

The telephone stalls were visible down the hall from the restaurant and, through the windows, from the parking lot in front of the building. As soon as Sylvia parked, I hurried into the building and pretended to make a call to Nathan. The state trooper watched me from his car. Out of the corner of my eye, I surveyed him. He spoke to someone over his police radio again, and then he followed me inside. I hung up the telephone as soon as he entered the building. "He's busy right now. Said he'd call back in a few minutes," I lied to the trooper as he approached me.

Sheriff Duffy helped Sylvia get the kids inside the building. Sylvia rushed them into the women's room to wash them down and to change their clothes.

There were four pay telephones on the wall, separated by thin insulated aluminum panels. None of the telephones were in use at the moment, though a skinny young trucker was hanging around as if expecting a call back. I stood in the middle of the walkway, equidistant from the telephone stalls, and waited—not knowing which one would ring, because I had no idea which number Nathan had.

"Which one's he calling on?" the state trooper asked. I was uncertain if he was testing me to see if I had called Nathan, or perhaps he merely needed to use the telephone.

"I gave him all four numbers, in case the lines got tied up. So go ahead and use any one of them. He'll get through," I answered.

"I'm going off shift soon, I'm already on overtime, and I want to speak with him before I leave."

"He said it would be just a couple of minutes. But with Nathan, that could mean thirty seconds or half an hour."

Sheriff Duffy walked over. "Nathan's gonna call right back," I told him.

"Good. I need to talk to him. I'm gonna go order some supper. You want me to order for you, Kenny?" the sheriff asked the trooper. Duffy snuffed out his cigarette in the metal ashtray built in to a telephone stall.

"No, thanks," said the trooper. "I think I'm gonna split. I just got off the horn with Lemar. He'll be down to relieve me in a few minutes."

"Whatever." the sheriff shrugged his portly shoulders and waddled off to order dinner. "Give me a holler when you get Nathan on the phone," he remembered to say before he entered the restaurant.

At that instant one of the telephones rang—second from the right. I let the young trucker pick it up. It was Nathan.

[Author's note: This call was recorded by Nathan as well. Participants were Nathan Johnson (NJ), the state trooper (ST), Sheriff Dewey Duffy (DD), Sylvia Johnson (SJ), and this author (ME).]

NJ: Hello? Hello?
ME: Yeah, Nathan? That didn't take you too long. Who were you talking to?
NJ: What?
ME: [After a pause] Oh, is everything cool then?
NJ: You got people next to you listening?
ME: Yeah. The kids are doing a little better. Sylvia's in the restroom with them. Sheriff Duffy's just ordering dinner. No, here, he's comin' back. And there's a state trooper here wants to speak to you. He's going off shift, so I'll put him on first.
ST: Officer Haverly speaking.
NJ: Agent Johnson, FBI.
ST: We've been ordered to place your family in protective custody for a few days. We were supposed to accompany them to Tonopah this evening. I'm sorry that your children are ill …
NJ: Ill? My kids are sick? Put my wife on the telephone.
ST: I'm in a bit of a hurry …
NJ: Let me speak to my wife about my children, please. Officer Haverly, if you were in my shoes, wouldn't you want to know about your children first?
ST: [Aside:] He wants to speak to his wife. [To Johnson:] They are going to get her from the restroom. If we could just clarify about tonight …

NJ: Once I find out how my kids are, then we'll talk about what's up. Now, please, where is my wife?
SJ: Hi, sweetie.
NJ: Can anyone hear me but you? Answer that question and then talk about the kids.
SJ: Of course not, sweetie. They'll be okay. But I think they should get some rest. All of this travel in the car is making them sick. All three of them threw up in the last hour.
NJ: Good. Perfect. Go and check into the motel. Take everything out of the Dodge—you'll be leaving it. I'll tell my cousin the details. Go and get the rooms—soon as we're off the phone—out of the way. Far corner, second floor if you can. But first tell me that you think you should spend the night there.
SJ: Yes. I think the kids have had all that they can take for one day. [Hesitates as if listening] I agree. I'll go get the rooms right now.
NJ: Is Sheriff Duffy around?
SJ: Yes, sweetie.
NJ: Put him on.
DD: Hey, Nathan!
NJ: Dewey. My kids are sick, and I want them to spend the night at the motel. Can you talk the state police into lending you a couple of patrolmen so you guys can keep a close eye on the room? Those kids are getting beat to death by all of this travel. All I'd want is for you to keep an eye on the room. Don't let anyone in. Can you do that for me?

[Author's note: Although it was not completely audible on the tape, at this point, Sheriff Duffy and state trooper Haverly argued for a minute or two. The trooper, who wanted to go home, finally gave in and agreed to call for a second trooper in addition to his replacement.]

DD: Okay. We'll get two state boys. I'll wait to leave until my deputy can get here. But it's gonna be around ten, our time, before everybody shows up.
NJ: That's okay. Thanks a million, Dewey. I owe you.
DD: No, you don't. I'm the one who owes you.
NJ: Is my cousin right close?
DD: Yeah.
NJ: Put him on.
ME: Are we having fun yet?
NJ: Just wait 'till I tell you.

ME: I just want to get out of here and get back to work. I knew it. I just knew if I got stuck with your wife and kids that I would end up in a mess like this …
NJ: Don't overdo it, asshole.
ME: Okay. Okay. So what's the plan for tomorrow?
NJ: That's better. There will be a white Ford van with Boyd's Coffee stickers on it parked at the northwest corner of the motel within an hour. You make sure that those cops are in the dining room when it shows up. Maybe you can stage it so that the kids are on their way to the room. Whatever you do, as soon as you're sure you can't be seen, it's right out the back and into that van. The driver's side will be unlocked. You gettin' all of this?
ME: Yeah. But I've got to be in Idaho day after tomorrow at the very latest. I don't give a shit how sick your kids are.
NJ: Good. Get everything and everyone into that van. Keep the kids and Sylvia down and out of sight until you're clear of the police. Keep your face turned from them as you drive out. Keys are in a pouch behind the front seat. Drive right on out of there. Hopefully they won't check the room until morning …
ME: By the way, your car smells like a puke factory, and I'm sure as shit not cleaning it up. I already cleaned it once today.
NJ: Drive right back to Ely in that Boyd's van. They won't expect you to backtrack. From Ely, take Highway 50 to Utah. Take Interstate 70 to Grand Junction, Colorado. South from there to Durango. I think that's the fastest way. Except for Ely, the route isn't terribly important. You look at a map and pick your own.
ME: No. There's no place around here to get the fucking car cleaned out.
NJ: I need you in Durango, Colorado, at the Wagon Wheel Best Western by tomorrow night. Call you there—pay phone in the lobby around seven your time. Durango, Colorado. Wagon Wheel. Seven tomorrow night. Got it?
ME: Fuck you. See if I ever do any more favors for you.
NJ: Love you, Cuz. Oh, and sometime tonight, take off the Nevada plates and put on the Colorado plates. They're behind the front seat, same place that the keys will be. And the stickers on the van are magnetic. In a flat box inside are some extras that say *Sherwin Williams*. Stick those on when you change the plates. Be careful pulling off the Boyd's stickers. You're gonna want to save them. Put them between the sheets that separate the others. Have Sylvia help you. She's got steadier fingers. Now let me talk to the sheriff.
ME: Yeah, same to you. [Aside to Duffy:] The asshole wants to talk to you.
DD: Howdy.

NJ: Don't worry about my cousin. He'll calm down. He didn't expect all this excitement.
DD: He's just tired like the rest of us. I better get on the horn and get things arranged.
NJ: You do that. Thanks again, Sheriff Duffy.
DD: Talk to you some other time, Agent Johnson.
NJ: We'll do it. Night.

Let all accept thy will when thou art born a living god from the dry tree, that they may attain to divinity and reach by the speed of thy movements to possession of the Truth and the Immortality.

—Rig Veda

By faith Enoch was carried away to another life without passing through death; he was not to be found because God had taken him.

—Hebrews 11:5

Excerpts from the Unpublished Notes of Professor Harold Weintraub. Dated June 2

[Author's note: This section was probably written by Professor Weintraub on the evening of June 2, some time after the discussion in the van with Mr. Graylett, Nathan Johnson, Judy Weintraub, Father Dougherty, and the "immortals" that was reported above. Because Professor Weintraub was not a person disposed to self-revelation, there is a slight awkwardness in the prose and in some of the ideas that follow.]

Today was the most unusual day of my life. What was once, and not long ago, a heterodox *divertissement* with a quaint old man who called himself Elijah has become … what precisely has it become? Not a belief—if by *belief* is meant a conviction. I do not *hold* that the people with whom we travel are immortal. I do not hold it as a belief; yet today I acted, I spoke, I behaved as if these people's opinion of themselves was … reality.

I pointed out the obvious political consequences of what would happen to them, should those who run the state also be convinced. It would mean the liquidation of the immortals, especially if they held themselves capable of teaching their achievement of immortality to others. It is all such nonsense. Such insanity. To sit here in this hotel room, when I should be in a hospital being treated for my disease, my wife at my side documenting every word spoken, being pursued by agents of, God knows, agents with orders to murder these defenseless people.

Am I caught up in the insanity of it all? Am I that credulous now—now that I am ill? Is my need so great that I would turn away from what I have spent my life seeking? Where is Truth with her veiled face? Am I strong enough to consider objectively that perhaps that veil has finally been lifted? Yet the very supposition involved in entertaining the notion! My God! Have I lost my mind?

I shall calm myself and begin again. I have presented now and then, over the last twenty-five years, as an intellectual exercise and at my leisure, a unique hypothesis about immortality. It is not immortality as a religious concept but rather immortality as an idea, or a perpetual process, ostensibly achievable in the here and now.

The genesis of this notion within me is confused but accessible. For I believe—no, I am *certain*—that I was approached, as a youth of perhaps eleven or twelve, by a man who told me that his name was Enoch. I was something of a prodigy, having memorized most of the Pentateuch in Hebrew by the age of nine. People came at times to test me, to gawk at me.

It was on a Sabbath. As I recall, it was a lovely spring afternoon in Brooklyn, probably about this time of year. I had stayed because Rabbi Lowenstein wanted to put me on display after temple for some people. (I do not remember who they were.) Such events happened often. I believe that these demonstrations were conducive to the production of generous tithes. I resented the fact, even at that age, that such a beautiful day, God's day, was being wasted. And I resented that I was being employed like a trained monkey to make money for the synagogue. My mother always dressed me in black knickerbockers, a white shirt, and a red bow tie. My hair was very thick and black then, and Mother greased it tight to the sides of my head. It just stuck there like ... [Sentence unfinished.]

In any event, every week it was the same. I hated those knickers. I hated my hair, and I hated the questions. Enoch had been there, at temple. He had been there more than once. I remember that he seemed different. His face, in the crowd, was kind and understanding—rather than benighted and gaping. He did not ask me any insipid questions, while the others asked plenty.

This is why I was walking home alone: My family usually went home right after temple, before my performance, leaving me to make my own way. One day, Enoch followed me on my way home. His presence did not startle me. He stopped me by putting his hand on my shoulder and then on the crown of my head. Thinking back on the occasion, I believe that he was a rather small man, for when I turned and looked up at him, his face was not distant. He was thin, but his face, like his hand, was strong, full of life. I do not remember their color, but his eyes looked tired. I remember that his eyes looked so very tired that I felt sorry for him. He said to me, "I have come to speak with you."

I asked him if he had come a long way because he looked so weary.

"Yes. A long way and a long time. I am the father of Methuselah. Do you know my name?"

"You're Enoch," I answered, with a sigh of disappointment, for I thought that he just wanted another demonstration.

"Yes, I am," he laughed. "But I have not come to test you. I have come to promise you a gift. I have come so that you may test me, if you like. So that you will know that the gift I bring is real. I have come to offer you life eternal. I will speak with you when you are older, when you can understand the gift."

"We are having supper. Are you hungry?" I asked him because, as I said, he was thin, and he looked tired.

"No," he said, and yet he smiled and seemed very pleased with the invitation.

As a child, I naturally concluded that the smile was an acceptance, that his "No" was simply a courtesy. I had performed in the same fashion any number of times when offered sweets that I was not allowed to eat before a meal. The "No" I spoke, with the smile I tendered, in reality meant, "Please make the offer after my dinner." I warranted that it meant the same coming from him, so I said, "My father likes to have guests over after temple. My mother prepares extra food for them. In our house, it is permitted, and you would be welcomed."

"Today I cannot. But may I walk with you a little way?" he queried.

"Yes," I said eagerly, for I did not like to walk home from temple alone.

"Do you remember my name?"

"Enoch," I answered promptly, because by then I considered him my friend. "My name is Harold Benjamin Weintraub."

"I know. You are very special. You are right; I am Enoch. Do you remember what I did after my son was born?"

"You went for a long walk," I answered.

He laughed. Then he asked, "Why do you think my walk was long?"

"Because it took you three hundred years," I said, as a matter of fact.

He laughed louder. Then he put his hand, as he had done before, first on my shoulder and then on the crown of my head. He said, and I am certain that I remember this correctly, "I am still on that walk. This is that same walk."

"But you walked with God," I answered in confusion. "Enoch walked with God for … for three hundred years." I had quoted the scripture in English to define more precisely the issue before us.

He smiled. It was a sad smile this time. I noticed that his smile had the same tiredness as his eyes. "Oh, it is longer than three hundred years. Much longer. Someday you will understand the long walk. Then we will talk another time. We will walk together." He smiled at me, said good-bye, and crossed the street. I never saw the man again.

Of course I kept the incident completely to myself. At times, as a teenager, I tried to convince myself that it had only been a dream. But I knew that it was real. I knew that he was a real man. However, I did not believe that he was Enoch. How could I ever believe that?

The articles I wrote, mostly under pseudonyms, were an outlet for some of the fear and anxiety of that trauma—and of that uncertainty. Yet the idea in them was also enticing. The idea was so idiosyncratic, so outlandish, so lucid, that most people thought it a facile joke. "Do you want to live forever?—then do it!" It was that simple to me. But it was more. It was an SOS—my cry in the wilderness.

Elijah got in touch with me through the articles. This was, of course, many years later. Once he had figured out who I was, he came to the campus at Harvard to find me. He stopped me one day as I was going from Widener back to my office with some books. He placed his hand on my shoulder and then on my head in exactly the same manner that Enoch had more than forty years before. "Life is a long walk. Don't you think, Professor?" he said to me.

Excerpt from the Journal of Nathan Johnson

Late. Wytheville, Virginia, June 2.

I'm going to type out part of what happened today because I know that it was not taped (I forgot to put a fresh one in my Nagra) and because it is important and bizarre. I'm tired, so I'm gonna write this in a hurry. Don't expect Tolstoy.

I'll put it down in chronological order. We stopped at a gas station near Quantico today. I let the members of the group out to relieve themselves and to buy food. While this was going on, I made a telephone call to the hotel we are staying at tonight to double-check on the reservations. I did this on purpose to test the group. Any of the members could have listened in on my call as they loitered about in front of the store, chatting and waiting for instructions from me. As soon as I finished that call, I ordered them all back into the truck. While they waited in the van, I called my wife and cousin and then met up with Frank Graylett. Meeting Franky was the most encouraging part of the day. Most of that is recorded, or Jerome or Judy can write about it.

At our next relief stop, I think it was Christiansburg, several members of the group made telephone calls. I called Duffy and Hepworth and some other sheriff. Nye County. I can't remember his name right now. [Sheriff Petersen. The conversation was transcribed above.] I am fairly certain that we were not being followed, though the van is being tracked electronically by satellite. Anyway, I figured if someone in our group were going to try to set us up, that they would know where we were spending the night and arrange an ambush.

We drove to the outskirts of Wytheville at about 9:30 PM. It was already dark. Even though we didn't get far today, this was our destination for the evening because I was very concerned about my family and had arranged to call my cousin at a truck stop in Nevada at about nine o'clock our time, though I didn't get through until after ten.

I drove around the outskirts of town and parked about two blocks from our hotel. I told the others to wait in the van and that I would be back in about half an hour. (By the way, Father Dougherty has standing orders that if I am killed, or if I leave and don't return at a specified time, he is to go ahead and try to make it to the final destination. Wherever that is.) I went to assess the hotel area for a possible setup.

The hotel is a four-story rectangular brick building with temporary parking under a front entrance canopy and a large paved parking lot in the rear that can be reached by entrance lanes on either side of the building. There are trees alongside the back parking lot. I figured that I would hide among those trees and scope the building for unusual movements, inspect the roof and exits. I searched quietly in the blackness of the trees for what I figured would be the best spot to keep an eye on the back lot. From there, I thought I would eventually sneak in the back entrance, go once through the hotel, and make certain that everything was okay. I should add that there was very little traffic in or out of the hotel the entire evening.

Just as I got to the best spot in the trees, the spot from which one could scope the entire back of the building, I stepped in something slippery. I couldn't see it because the ground was so dark. I thought maybe it was oil or something, but as I bent over to touch it, I could smell it. Fresh blood. I stuck my finger down into the dead leaves and the new grass. It was still warm.

As I said, it was night time by now, and I didn't want to risk exposing myself by turning on my flashlight. So I took a step back into the cover of the brush and trees, unsheathed both of my weapons, and stared into the darkness, waiting for my eyes to adjust.

Soon enough, I could see the path where a body had been recently dragged through the grass, back a little into the trees, but mostly parallel with the edge of the parking lot. I crept forward along the trail, which was barely illuminated by the parking lot lamps. It was quiet except for the distant rumble of the freeway traffic. I operated the slide on my 10 mm and my Uzi and flipped off the safeties.

I had snapped a laser point sight underneath the barrel of my Smith and Wesson when I left the van. But the laser wasn't sighted in, so it was more for show—the red dot of a laser beam placed right between a man's eyes gives the guy holding the pistol enormous credibility. Because the gun wasn't sighted, I kept a full auto Uzi submachine pistol, thirty-round clip, in my left hand. I have a non-projecting pro-point laser on the Uzi that is sighted.

Though the physics are different, these sights both work in low-light conditions. The laser point sight shoots a beam at the target—where anyone looking could see the dot on his chest. With the nonprojecting pro-point, only the shooter can see the dot. It's inside the tube of the scope. In either case, day or night, you just put the red dot on the target and squeeze off the trigger, and *that's all, she wrote.*

I had only gone about ten feet when I heard voices. They were just ahead of me in the trees, a few feet out of sight. They were whispering, probably in a foreign tongue. I wish I could tell you what they were talking about, but I haven't a clue.

To my left from the parking lot, I heard a pop from a weapon with a silencer. It sounded like a firecracker under a pillow. At the same instant, I heard a car window collapse and heard bits of the tinkling glass hit the ground.

I ducked back deeper into the brush and turned my head to the parking lot. A man dressed in black fatigues jumped up from behind a parked car. He was carrying a small rifle with a scope on it. He ran several steps toward a big sedan. As he approached, he rapidly fired three more times into the slouched figure sitting in the driver's seat. Then he knocked in the remainder of the driver's side window with his elbow. He unlocked the door and lifted and shoved a body over into the other seat. He started the dark-colored four-door sedan and slowly drove in reverse to the back of the parking lot, no more than fifty feet from where I was hidden.

"That's all three of them," he spoke in English into the trees. He had a strange-sounding foreign accent.

The man in the car and the two men in the woods exchanged a few more words. They were speaking Hebrew. No doubt about it.

The man in the car backed as far into the brush as he could without hitting a tree. He then got out and opened the trunk. I could hear the grunts of the two men in the woods in front of me as they tugged on what I guessed were corpses. I was sure that they were hauling bodies because I could hear the flesh of the limbs flopping against the ground with each heave.

They made enough noise dragging the bodies to allow me to hide behind a tree, a position that gave me a clear view of the entire car from the driver's side. While the men in the woods were wrestling with their loads, the man in the black fatigues hauled his victim out of the car and heaved the body into the trunk. It took the two others a minute or so to drag the remaining two bodies to the car.

They talked in soft voices while they worked. The only thing said in English was, after a particularly stressful tug, "Fat motherfucker."

When all three of them were at the trunk, two of them hoisting the last body by the legs and shoulders, I pushed the button on my pistol grip that activates the laser sight. I touched each of the men's foreheads with its red dot. "FBI," I said. I kept my body pretty much behind the tree, my arm extended out around it. I held the laser sight on the head of the man not holding a corpse. "Nobody moves, nobody dies," I said. My Uzi was loaded and ready in my left hand.

"Which FBI? Who?" asked the man who had backed up the car. He had slung his rifle over his shoulder. It was a short, stubby piece with a triangle-shaped wire stock and a long banana clip.

"Keep your hands up and away from your weapon," I warned him. "You other two, just hang on to your friend there. Keep your hands on his arms and legs. Hold him up real high," I said to them. I figured they couldn't get at their weapons if they kept the corpse elevated at about five feet. "Higher. Hold him up, damn it. That's good enough. Keep him right there," I told them. I stepped from behind the cover of the tree. "What'd you use on the guy in the car?" I asked the driver, pointing at his weapon. "Looks like a 9mm H&K MP5SD3, silenced, squeezed off the first one, then set it for a three-shot burst. You probably used hydro-shock hollow point titaniums to get you through the glass. Right?"

"Right. Exactly right. Are you Johnson?" asked the man who had driven the car and who, I had postulated, was the leader.

"He must be Johnson," one of the others grumbled from beneath the weight of the corpse.

"First, who are you?" I demanded. "Keep him up there," I cautioned his companions.

"We are your friends. Do you know what we have done for you?" he asked me.

"Who are you?" I repeated.

"These dead men were not your friends. That one my associates are displaying for you is Khalifah. He and his men were sent here; they were waiting for you to arrive; they were waiting to kill you."

"I assume you are the MOSSAD agents we lost track of in DC."

"The Koreans, do you know about the North Koreans?" he asked, ignoring my assumption. "We have yet to locate them. They are not your friends. Watch for them. And the Mafia. And the ... well, as you may know, you have very few friends. In fact," he laughed, "we may be your only friends. It would be unwise for you to kill us."

"Who are you?" I held the red dot steady, right through the darkness, right between the leader's eyes.

"Here. If you will allow us, we will disarm ourselves. Then we will prove to you who these men are, or rather were. Then you may decide if we can finish cleaning up this clutter so that you may spend a safe evening in this hotel and then be on your way."

"All right. You first. Drop your weapon. Then you can disarm your pals. No. *No!* You two keep that body up in the air."

That's about all that was said. The leader disarmed himself and the other two men. Each of them had two pieces. I made the two of them hold the corpse up at shoulder level until I was finished frisking them. They were getting really tired of it. Even though they were all three clean, I kept them at gunpoint the entire time. They wore black fatigues and had charcoaled their faces and, as I said it was night, so there is no point in trying to describe them for you.

I examined the body of the one they said was Khalifah with my flashlight. It sure looked like him, with his fuzzy, splotchy, gray-black beard and squinting dark eyes. The squint—he was famous for his squint—was still there, even in the dark and even though he was dead as a doornail. He looked as if he were trying to spot his recently evicted soul—searching in the night sky for it. He was sprawled on top of the pile of bodies in the trunk. The bullet had pierced his temple; the blood from the back of his head was coagulating, black as the boot on the foot of the corpse beneath him.

"You guys got Khalifah. Congratulations," I told them.

The leader of the team told me that one of the two other dead men was Mohammed Ali al-Samman. I think he was probably right. That would mean that the dead men in the trunk had murdered several hundred people between them, including a bus full of school kids in Israel and an Air Italia 737 planeload of people.

"Now if you will let us be on our way, we have some incriminating evidence to remove—a little misleading evidence to take its place. Then we will drop the bodies off some distance from here, in the opposite direction from where you are heading, which, I understand, is still somewhere west of here?"

"I couldn't tell you that for sure," I answered—because I could not and, obviously, I would not. I threw their weapons in the trunk on top of the corpses, took the keys to the car, and slammed the lid down. I followed them and made them stay together under gunpoint. After working the woods for a few minutes and cleaning up the glass in the parking lot, they said they were ready to leave. I wished them a pleasant evening and handed the car keys to the leader. When they had driven away, I quickly finished exploring the hotel and the area around it. Everything seemed secure, so I went back to the van.

In one of our rooms, we had a group meeting, which just ended. It should all be on tape or in their letters. I didn't mention the incident in the parking lot at the meeting. No one asked. I am tired and want to sleep tonight, because I may get very little sleep in the coming days. I really doubt that I'll take the time to write again. It is just too much trouble. Besides, I have asked Judy and Father Dougherty to write down events as soon they happen. That will just have to do.

Two things seem certain now. First, some person or persons in our party have betrayed us and will, in all likelihood, continue to do so. Second, some other person or persons—maybe in our party, maybe not—are fighting back, counterpunching, so to speak. And those guys I met tonight have one hell of an uppercut.

On the Author's Travels with Sylvia Johnson and Her Children, June 2, Continued

Sylvia was quick to get the kids clean. She dragged them, kicking and screaming, into the restroom near the telephones. In the men's room next door, I scrubbed Sherry's puke—there wasn't much—out of my sweat pants.

After she had finished cleaning up, Sylvia rented two rooms. Then she brought the children to the little store. She bought them some books, and they sat in the restaurant and read. She was killing time. The kids weren't hungry. So, after half an hour of reading, she took them to the motel room.

Trooper Haverly's replacement didn't show up until around 9:00 PM. The sheriff and Haverly's replacement, a cleancut, blond, virile young man named Lemar Atkinson, ordered dinner right after Haverly departed. I had coffee with them. Lemar was the kind of handsome all-American state trooper who probably gets laid a few times during his career, while patrolling a desert highway, in lieu of issuing a speeding ticket. Toward the end of their leisurely dinner, I noticed a white van with Boyd's Coffee emblems on both the side and rear doors as it pulled into the parking lot and drove around to the back of the motel. A few seconds later, a red Nissan sports car followed the path the van had taken.

It was night by now—a black one. We couldn't quite see the door of the motel room Sylvia had rented from our booth in the restaurant. We could see the front stairway going up to the motel landing. The stairs were illuminated by amber lights fixed to tall aluminum poles planted next to the gas pumps, at the graveled entrance, and by a few other light poles scattered around the parking lot. Our rooms were just a few feet beyond the upstairs landing, behind a cinderblock wall, and beyond the lights.

"I should help her with those bags," I told Sheriff Duffy and Trooper Atkinson, when I saw that Sylvia had gotten the kids into their room and had come back down to unload the minivan. Sylvia was lugging two or three of her duffel bags to the stairs. "You guys finish your dinner. I'll be back for some pie," I said.

"Wait a second, and I'll help you," I hollered at Sylvia as soon as I passed through the entrance to the restaurant. "They can see us from the window until we get to the top of the stairs," I softly told her when I reached her side.

"What did Nathan say?" she asked. She handed me one of the duffel bags without looking at my eyes. I grabbed the box full of documents and my own small travel bag from the rear of the minivan. Sylvia had changed into a white T-shirt and a pair of black sweatpants. Her hair was down, draped over and across her shoulders. She walked in front of me up the stairway. She bent her head forward, as if in contemplation, when she was really straining for my response. The incandescent lights at the corners of the building made everything orange or, if hidden in the shadows, black. So Sylvia, the motel and parking lot with its three or four diesel rigs, the restaurant, and the half-dozen cars in front of it were all bathed in a maleficent orange glow. It reminded me of Halloween. There were coyotes howling through the darkness to each other, a single coyote to the west and the pack to the northeast. The night air was still and crisp and clean; only the smell of blossoming sagebrush mixed with the new growth of alfalfa, of life coming, not going, belied my perception that it was All Hallows Eve.

"Is there a stairway around the back of this place?" I asked her as we climbed and clanged up the wrought iron stairs.

"I don't know," she replied. "What did Nathan say?"

"Let's go look, and I'll show you what he wants us to do."

We dropped off the bags in her room. The children were jumping up and down on the twin double beds. Suddenly they *were* hungry. All three started screaming for food, having recently lost theirs by various strategies.

"We'll be right back and get you some dinner," Sylvia promised. She slammed the door on their perturbation.

We walked around, away from the front stairs and out of the view of the sheriff and trooper, on the concrete landing to the back side of the motel. Halfway across the landing, there was a stairway down. The coffee van was parked at the near corner of the building, about eighty feet from the bottom of the rear stairway.

"See that van?" I asked Sylvia, and pointed directly below us.

"What? The white one?" she asked.

"The only one down there." I laughed because, except for two darkened diesel truck-trailers, the back lot was empty. We walked over to the stairs.

"I see it. What does that say on the side of it?" she asked. I guess she could not see the words through the shadows as we walked up to the vehicle and peered through the windshield. The van was empty. I imagine that the driver who had delivered it had fled in the red sports car.

"It says 'Boyd's Coffee.' That van is ours now. The driver's side door is unlocked; the keys are in a pouch behind the seat. I want you to load everything that we have inside it while I go back and visit with the sheriff and the state trooper for a second. As soon as you get the stuff loaded, go back up and get the kids. Get the van running. I'll be back in ten minutes, and we're out of here."

"But the kids are starving."

"Well, that's what Nathan told me to do. And if we don't leave soon, we're gonna have more cops here to deal with, and I doubt that we'll be going anywhere."

"Okay," she said grudgingly. "My kids'll be screaming up a storm."

"They'll live. We'll stop in an hour or so. Just get everything loaded. You've got ten minutes. I'll be at the van in ten minutes, and we'll be out of here."

Even though it was the long way around, I climbed the rear stairway with Sylvia and walked around the landing by our rooms. The kids were going nuts. Sylvia opened the door to Pandemonium. I descended the stairs and returned to the restaurant.

"Where's the sheriff?" I asked when I had sat back down at the booth opposite Trooper Lemar.

Lemar had just polished off his coffee. "Ready for some pie?" he asked me. "The girls make great pie here."

"Sure. Where's Sheriff Duffy?"

"I don't know. I think he said he was going to the john. If they've got any boysenberry left—that's the best." Lemar motioned for the waitress.

She was a muscular woman, young and blithe, with an attractive smile. There were a number of women's league softball trophies above the front counter on a shelf. I guessed that she was a good part of the reason for them being there. "What's for dessert?" she asked us.

"Boysenberry pie. You got two pieces left?" Lemar asked her.

"Yup," she answered. "It's been real slow tonight. It's usually long gone by now."

"Better make it three pieces. One for the sheriff. You play softball?" I asked her, looking down the hallway for the sheriff to come back from the men's room.

"Shortstop," she answered. "How'd you guess—oh, never mind, you saw the trophies. Yup, we took district three years in a row. Never do much at state. We got second two years ago. That's the silver one in the middle. You gentlemen want ice cream?"

"I do," answered Lemar. He was trying to catch her eye. She wasn't playing.

"Not for me. Put some on the side for the sheriff. He can take it or leave it," I said.

"That it?" she asked.

"More coffee," replied Lemar.

"What was your batting average last season?" I wanted to know.

She smiled and looked at me, wondering if I would play. "Four-eighty."

"Wow. Impressive," I replied ingenuously.

"It's slow pitch," she responded with a full, wide smile.

"Well, four-eighty, it's still impressive. Shoot. Damn it. I've left my wallet up in the room. I'll be right back," I said, feeling all my pockets. It was clear that the sheriff had been far too long in the can. Something was wrong.

"I'll be back for my pie. When the sheriff gets out of the can, you tell him that I'm payin' for dessert," I said to the trooper.

"Will do," Lemar answered automatically, because he was watching the waitress's ass as she walked back to the kitchen.

I trotted to the restaurant door and then ran to and up the stairs. I knocked on the door to Sylvia's room. It was dead quiet; the lights were out; the door was locked.

I took the spare key out of my pocket and opened it. The room was empty. The kids and all the luggage were gone. I ran out and around the landing to the back corner of the motel. I looked down through the orange light on to the van.

"Mommy, we's hunry," I heard Sherry cry from inside the van. I wanted to laugh; I wanted to cry; I wanted to scream because I wanted the fuck out of there. Below me stood the sheriff. His short legs and muscular arms were spread-eagled against the front of the van, arms splayed over the hood, legs planted firmly apart in the gravel. Sylvia had disarmed him. I could see the gun that she had thrown out into the parking lot. She had her black ten-millimeter pistol against the back of his head. She was trembling. I could see it from twenty feet above and through the orange glint reflecting off the white hood of the van. Her hand was shaking like a leaf.

"Sylvia," I said, bending over the rail and cupping my hands to my mouth to soften the words, "that's not a buffalo, that's a county sheriff."

Excerpts from the Journal of Father Jerome Dougherty

Late evening, June 2, Wytheville, Virginia.

I am not certain, but I believe that something quite traumatic happened before we checked into the motel. Nathan parked the van several blocks away from the motel and walked there to see if it was secure. Some thirty minutes later, he came running back. He was quite pale and clearly upset. However, Nathan is the type of man who thinks through his fear. So we were greeted with these words rather than with anger or hysteria.

"I believe that this building is now clear for the night. But I want everyone to stay in your rooms and leave the doors open between them. You ... we were very lucky today." He refused to elaborate.

At about ten thirty, Nathan called a meeting in our room (Nathan and I share a room) of everyone in our party. The immortals and the Weintraubs sat in semi-circles on the edge of the two beds. Nathan and I moved two chairs out from under a small table, positioned them at the end of the beds, faced the party, and sat down. Nathan began, "It is clear, after today, that a little maneuver I worked out to buy us time to travel across the country without interference is working. I mean it's kind of working—we weren't followed today by any agency of the US government, and no attempt was made by them to stop us.

"Unfortunately there is a cost, an unforeseen cost, involved," he continued. "My family—I have a wife and three children—is being pursued by people whom we must assume are your enemies. In other words, they are trying to get at me, at us, through my family."

"I pledge to you that we had no idea ..." Mr. Tie began.

Nathan leaned forward in the chair, smacked his fist into the palm of his hand, and forcefully stopped him. "You people, as old and wise as you are supposed to be, don't seem to know too goddamn much about anything."

"Mr. Tie did not say that it was not surprising. He only said that we had no idea," Father Holden defended him. "There is much that you have not shared with us. You cannot possible expect that we can read your mind or consistently guess your expectations. We may be long-lived; we are not gods."

"Perhaps we have all been a bit too furtive," Judy Weintraub placatingly suggested.

Nathan, as he is wont to do, examined each of their faces, if only briefly, before he said, "Well, to put all my cards on the table, even if I bought into the immortality stuff, which I haven't, I don't know with certainty that any of you people are who you claim you are. What kind of church records are there, Father Dougherty?" Nathan inquired of me.

"There are very few," I admitted.

Nathan surveyed the faces again. "I mean, how do you join this immortality club anyway? How do you, Father Dobo, know that Miriam here doesn't work for the CIA?"

Father Dobo looked at Miriam and smiled. When he smiles, the flesh pulls taut around his yellow eyes, to his ears, and he looks very much like a panther. "Unless the CIA was founded in—when was it that we first met?"

"Seventeenth century," Miriam replied. "Paris. You were curious about the new *Academie Royal des Sciences.*"

"Of course." Father Dobo then turned to Nathan and said, "So with Miriam—I know."

"What about the rest?" Nathan asked brusquely.

"Let us make something clear," answered Father Holden. "Immortality is a choice, as is death. One can grow tired of life. One can step away from immortality. I have known people who have made both choices. The later choice, by which I mean death, in as far as I know, is always final. I cannot make either choice for anyone but myself and remain an immortal."

"But don't forget Jesus," Father Hugo said.

"And Socrates," added Miriam.

"Yes, of course. Death is *almost* always final," clarified Father Holden.

"If I might add something here," I voluntarily entered the conversation at this point. "There is a feeling that I have ... a new feeling. I don't know how to describe it, for it is far from clear in my own mind, but today, when I mentioned that I felt like I was finally going home, Father Holden whispered something to me today when we met with Mr. Graylett. Father said, 'Welcome.' I must tell you that for a moment, I felt as if I might ... I might not taste of death."

"I am happy for you, truly I am. Your feeling may be real, even eternal. But it could change tomorrow, Father Jerome," Mr. Tie said, with a sad smile for me. "Of the sixteen priests, of the *Lo-han,* only three of us remain. It is possible to grow weary of life. Almost everyone does."

"Wait a second." Nathan interrupted at a time that displeased me, for I was hoping to learn more about what I have been sensing. "What happens if *someone else* chooses death for you? That Native American I autopsied, the one called Helaman, was dead. And it sure didn't look like he wanted it."

"It is extremely difficult to kill an immortal," answered Father Quindilar.

"Never underestimate the power of the human body to regenerate itself," added Father Dobo, who sat on a corner of the bed in front of me. "The desire, the instinct for life, is so great in the human spirit that, once chosen, it is nearly impossible to extinguish. It is thus extremely difficult to take a life that will not surrender. I know that this is so."

"Since you have brought it up, let us take Helaman as an example," Father Hugo said to Nathan. "Of all of us, he was the most politically active. Even if you don't live a long life, you find out early on that these political issues are messy. Nevertheless, Helaman refused to take the easier path that most of us choose—that it is best to let governments take care of themselves. That was not his style. He was deeply involved in the civil rights movement here in America. About forty-five years ago, in the southern part of this country, he was shot in the chest and left for dead. What is it? 'In the sight of the unwise, they seem to die.' I suppose the injury would have killed a person who had, as Father Holden put it, 'chosen death.' That was not our Helaman. 'For, though he was punished in the sight of men, yet in his hope was he filled with immortality.' Helaman loved life with every fiber of his body. It is possible to regenerate. And regenerate is the correct term, like a starfish. One must simply do it. One must simply will it. I came to the States. It was in 1963 or 1964 ... remember, Jerome? I took care of Helaman for a number of months. There is no other way to put it than that he willed the wound away."

"That is physically impossible," objected Dr. Weintraub.

"Judy, I saw the scar—during the autopsy," Nathan said with amazement. "The bullet went through his heart."

"Yes, I believe that it might have," responded Father Hugo. "It was in the upper middle portion of his chest."

"This would lead us to a question that has haunted me," said Professor Weintraub, who was not feeling well and lay sideways with his head on his wife's lap.

"Why are the murders done in the same fashion? Why are the wounds inflicted ... in the manner they are inflicted?"

No one spoke for a few seconds. Heads turned side to side, each of us looking to the others for answers. "Such massive damage to the brain ... I suppose that the answer is obvious." Father Holden summarized everyone's fear.

"This sounds unbelievable but there was ... there was a portion of Helaman's brain that was still warm—still ... still alive. I ... the local sheriff and I ... we felt it," Nathan stammered, looking to the Weintraubs and myself.

"So, Nathan, do you think there is a specific region of the brain that must be destroyed?" asked Harold. He sat up, intrigued by Agent Johnson's comment.

"I don't know, but I have been working on it," Nathan said, leaning back in his chair. Our attention was immediately drawn to him. "Does anyone have a theory why the blows are directed at the center of the brain? I have reason to believe that the murderers are specifically trying to destroy the *corpus callosum*—or maybe the sphere surrounding it," he stated.

Everyone was silent.

"Okay. Have any of you heard of the sixth chakra?" Nathan continued to search for an answer.

"Above the brow, here, above and between the eyes. The site of the third eye. Why do you ask?" wondered Mr. Tie. He pointed at the location on his own forehead.

Before Nathan could respond, Judy Weintraub said, "Let me add that the *corpus callosum* links the two hemispheres of the brain. If I recall correctly, two sections of the *corpus callosum,* the splenium and the isthmus, link the visual and verbal portions of the hemispheres."

"I think you're right, Doctor," replied Nathan. "But according to a group known as Sedona Watch, those contending with a woman named Plutonion, there is something called an auric light, which goes around or through the *corpus callosum* and into the pineal gland. They claim that this light acts as a detector for internal vision—whatever that means. I'm guessing that our murderers figure that by extinguishing that light, they can eradicate this internal vision and thus kill an immortal. If what you are saying about regeneration is true, then they just might be right. I'll put it this way: it would certainly kill any of us mere mortals. Does anyone know anything about a harmonic convergence or about Sedona Watch or about a woman named Plutonion?" Nathan asked.

"How did you learn about this?" Father Holden firmly demanded. He stood up from the bed, almost as if in a physical challenge. Nathan immediately arose to face him.

"Find out about what?" asked Nathan. But his voice was suddenly serene, even soothing, for the look in Father Holden's eyes was obviously not menace—it was fear.

"The convergence, the gatherings? How do you know?" Father Holden pleaded as he stood eye-to-eye with Agent Johnson.

"Then you are involved in these events?" Nathan asked.

"We ... we have played a part in the creation of the myth," Father Holden carefully answered.

"What do you mean?"

"I will give an answer in full if you will first tell me how you know," Father Holden promised.

"The people who I think murdered Helaman had a flyer, a newsletter, describing the events."

"My God!" said Father Dobo. "We *are* betrayed."

"Explain," commanded Nathan.

There was silence again. Finally Sister Maria, whose English is just adequate, spoke. "Nine, ten years Jesus visit us. He say our time soon be ... at hand. He believe ... he tell to us we would soon to teach ... the world was at most prepare. He say we should prepare for the moment. Please, Father ..." she lowered her head in submission—beseeching Father Holden to continue for her.

Father Holden sat back down upon the bed, thought carefully for a moment, then said, "Some of us, most notably Father Patricelli, foresaw the political dangers of such a gathering, similar to the hazards that Professor Weintraub so eloquently elaborated for us this afternoon. Measures were taken to ensure that we could meet without hindrance. We should have known. Father Dobo, we should have seen this. Father Patricelli was murdered first because he was the one most concerned with our protection."

"What's this got to do with the harmonic convergences?" Nathan asked.

"Misdirection," Father Hugo answered. "There are very few places in the world where our safety could be assured. However, there is one place in the Southwest, a place of refuge that is being prepared for us, a place where we will not be pursued, a place where we will meet and decide."

"Where?" asked Nathan.

Father Quindilar answered him, "We do not know. As Father Hugo said, it is to be prepared for us."

"Look, tomorrow night, by nine o'clock, I need to know. I need a specific location for my wife and children. I need a rendezvous point. Can you get it for me? No. You *must* get it for me," Nathan declared.

The immortals huddled together on the bed in front of Nathan for a few seconds. They stood together to indicate that the meeting was adjourned. Then Father Holden said, "We will give you your point of rendezvous by tomorrow evening. We may have to stop several times to make telephone calls. It cannot be guaranteed—especially now that we know that we have been betrayed—that it will be our *final* destination. We shall do our best to make certain that it is a safe point of assignation for your family. You see, Agent Johnson, any one of us could be the quisling, the impostor, so to speak. Yet it is not ours to judge that person, for tomorrow that person may be one of us. Making such a judgment is tantamount to joining them in death. Can you see, perhaps a little more clearly, why the direction in front of us is always so indeterminate? Immortals have no future."

"Oh, Richard," Miriam objected with a smile. "It sounds like you've been reading Professor Weintraub. We do know some. We do know where it will not be."

"I don't understand," said Nathan.

"Shall I tell him?" Miriam asked, turning to the others, who were moving to the doors to their rooms.

"Most emphatically," laughed Father Hugo, who was then the first to leave the room.

"I am Plutonion," Miriam said. "Good night, all." She followed the others out the door.

After all had made their ways to their respective rooms and Nathan had made one more tour of inspection, he and I knelt together in prayer for his family and his cousin, my student, and for our own safety and well-being, should such be the will of God. Thus ended our day.

Les fugitifs, feu du ciel sus les picques,
Conflict prochain des corbeaux, s'esbatans
De terre on crie, ayde, secours celiques,
Quand pres des murs seront les combatans.

—Nostradamus

On the Author's Travels with Sylvia Johnson and Her Children, June 2—June 3, Continued

I do not know how the dead lamb ended up beneath the light post on the edge of the back parking lot only twenty or thirty feet from the Boyd's Coffee van. Maybe it had been there before, and I had not noticed it. Maybe the wind had shifted a little, because the smell of decaying guts and flesh hit me smack in the face as I hollered down from the motel walkway through the orange light and the shadows, urging Sylvia not to shoot the sheriff. Maybe some rancher had recently tossed it out of his pickup. Maybe the coyotes had dragged it that far and then been scared off by Sylvia.

I say 'maybe' because I don't remember the ravens being there before either. Big, black, bloated desert ravens fat from feasting on the multiple miscarriages of spring, like the remains of the lamb rotting beneath the glowing orange yard light.

"Sylvia," I said, bending over the rail, cupping my hands to my mouth and repeating the words, "that's not a buffalo, that's a county sheriff. Let him up." The ravens flapped and fluttered a foot or two away from the tiny white carcass each time they heard my voice. Then they skipped right back over and took turns stabbing at the eyes and innards with their sharp black beaks.

"Get this woman offa me," the sheriff pleaded. He tried to turn his face upwards, but Sylvia nudged it back down with the barrel of her pistol.

"He tried to sneak up on us," Sylvia answered without turning her head. The ravens pecked away.

"For chrissakes, he's on our side," I replied. The birds flared again. I guess the sound of a human voice, coming from above, was unnatural and startled them.

"I didn't know it was him. He shouldn't be sneaking up on the children …"

"I wasn't sneakin' up on you or the kids. I was just checkin' the back of the motel to make sure that you were gonna be safe," interrupted Sheriff Duffy.

"Goddamn it!" I swore. "Let him up!" I yelled at her. This time the ravens scattered.

"Okay. I'm sorry, Sheriff," Sylvia said with relief. She pulled the gun away from his head and limply held it at her side.

I ran down the stairs. I picked up the sheriff's gun on my way to the van, dusted it off, and handed it to him. The ravens fluttered and hopped back to their dinner.

"I don't know which of you looks more frightened." I laughed, trying to bring some normalcy into our interaction. "I'm really sorry too, Sheriff, but Sylvia's got every reason in the world for being extra cautious. I don't know how much Nathan's told you, but …"

"Mommy. Please. We's hunry!" Sherry screamed as she pounded on the windshield.

"Excuse me, I've got children who need me," Sylvia said. She climbed into the van and tried to settle them down.

"I know all about it," Sheriff Duffy answered me. He slipped his gun back into his holster and brushed the dirt from the van's hood off of his shirt. "I figured that Nathan would be tryin' to slip you out of here. If I was him, I sure wouldn't want you to spend two days under Sheriff Petersen's custody. The only reason he got elected was 'cause his daddy was sheriff for forty years. Hell, most of the people in Nye County could never remember votin' for any sheriff except a Petersen. But Mark isn't half the man his father was. Mark ran the family ranch into the ground; now he's doin' it to the whole county." Sheriff Duffy must have been awfully embarrassed to shovel that much explanation to me.

"Well, Nathan trusted you. Not him," I replied. "That's all I know, and that's all I really need to know. You and I had better get back into the café for dessert. I'll excuse myself early, and then I'll get us out of your hair. We'd certainly appreciate it if you'd give us until morning before 'discovering' that we left sometime during the night."

"I figured that's what he'd probably do. I just wish he'd a just come right out and asked me," complained the sheriff.

"Telephone taps, bugs, you know—all that techno-spy shit. Nathan's paranoid as hell about that stuff, Sheriff," I said, putting my arm around his thick neck and walking him around the back of the motel to the restaurant. "He hasn't told me half as much as he's told you."

As far as I know, Sheriff Duffy did not give away our plan. He and I went into the restaurant and ate our boysenberry pie with Lemar. Duffy's hands shook a little as he ate, but Lemar was too busy coming on to the waitress to notice. I left, ostensibly to go to my room and to sleep. Three minutes later, Sylvia, the kids, and I pulled out of the truck stop in the Boyd's Coffee van and retraced our route back to Ely. We passed a state trooper and another county sheriff's office car on our way. Neither of them gave us a second look.

We entered Utah around eleven that night. I pulled onto a dirt road on the east side of Skull Rock Pass on Highway 6/50. It was cold outside. The kids just couldn't get to sleep. We had work to do, so we just let them cry. While Sylvia converted our Boyd's Coffee truck into a Sherwin Williams paint van—the magnetic logos peeled right off—I slapped on the Colorado license plates.

Sylvia was having a terrible time making the kids comfortable on the cold, hard steel floor of the van. I figured we were in no hurry to get to Durango, so I stopped in Green River, Utah, a small town off of Interstate 70, at two or three in the morning. Sylvia rented two rooms in a small motel on the east edge of town. We all slept soundly. At least I did. There was no noise coming from the children through the wall between our adjacent rooms, so they probably did too.

The next morning we arose early. We took the kids across the street for breakfast at the River Bank Café, a small family-owned establishment. Then, while Sylvia returned to the motel room to bathe and dress, Kaylynn and I went to shop for food for our trip. There was a small IGA grocery store several hundred yards from our motel. The last thing I wanted to do was to strand Sylvia, so Kaylynn and I decided to walk. "I'll be there to pick you up in half an hour," Sylvia promised me from the door to her motel room.

"No hurry. Durango's about six or seven hours away—at most. We don't have to be there until seven," I replied.

It was a very clear and nippy desert morning. The sky was perfectly blue. The desert around us was red and gold, clay and sandstone, with little blobs of green bunch grass here and there. Kaylynn and I trekked along in the gravel and dirt against traffic on the shoulder of the road because there were few sidewalks in Green River.

Kaylynn's attire for the day was blue jeans, jogging shoes, and a red and white Stanford sweatshirt. Earlier that morning her mother had spread mousse through her blonde hair. It made Kaylynn's long, thick hair stick together in even thicker strands. Her hair looked very much like fresh-pressed yellow linguine hanging to dry. I touched her sticky hair, sometimes her soft shoulder, as we walked—she to the outside, me next to the road. She was thin and graceful. She took dainty but deliberate steps and sang to herself, being especially mindful not to sing out of tune and particularly careful not to step on the broken glass or the discarded chewing gum or the road tar. Kaylynn was a very easy child to love.

We had gone perhaps one hundred yards from the motel when we reached the first intersection. Kaylynn stopped at the corner. Then she turned to me and resolutely tugged on my sleeve until I gave her my complete attention. "Are we going to die?" she bluntly asked me.

"You mean—I don't understand—soon?"

"Yes," Kaylynn answered.

I started across the road, but she yanked hard at my sleeve and would not continue. Perhaps my touch bothered her or perhaps, just the opposite, my touch was too infrequent to be sufficient solace. In either case, she took my hand, would not let it go, and would not move until she got an answer.

"Why?" I asked.

"Mommy killed that mean buffalo," she said.

"That buffalo could have hurt you kids. It was awful mean and awful mad," I answered.

"But Mommy almost killed that policeman last night," she said with compunction, as if that incident were something she wished very much had not occurred, and as if there had been something she could have done to prevent it but had not.

"Your mommy wouldn't kill anybody. It was just a mistake. She thought he was somebody else," I reassured Kaylynn.

"That's what Mommy told me," Kaylynn said, with a short whine that indicated that the answer was not satisfactory.

"Well, that's the truth. That was all, just a mistake."

An old farmer in a green rusted pickup truck stopped at the intersection in front of us. Next to the farmer, partially on top of the farmer, with its head poking out of the same window, sat an old Irish Setter. The dog's face, like his master's hair, had turned white. The farmer was thin with tough, thick, desert-worn skin on his face and hands. The dog was heavy, thick-boned, with a long, square snout. "Walkin' into town?" the farmer asked. The dog stuck his black, drippy nose and pink, panting tongue as far out of the driver's window as his neck could reach.

"To the grocery store," I answered.

"Get on, get on back there to yur own side," grumbled the farmer, and he elbowed the old dog in the ribs. "Wanna ride? Just drop the tailgate 'n hop on."

"We'll just ..." I started to decline.

"Can I ride in the back of the truck? Can I? Please can I?" Kaylynn had abandoned daintiness and deliberateness. She jumped and hopped up and down in a permission prance. At the same time, she jerked on the tail of my jacket and impelled me with a fusillade of *Can I? Can I? Can I? Can I? Can I?*

We crossed the road and rode the rest of the way to the grocery store on the tailgate. We thanked the farmer and his dog. I shook the farmer's hand; then I held Kaylynn up, and she patted the nose of the dog.

The ride had but momentarily derailed her train of thought. "Did we do something bad? When Mommy killed the buffalo? Did that make the policeman come to the truck last night?"

"No, of course not. It was not your fault that the buffalo chased you. He was just in a very bad mood. He was just a big old grouchy buffalo."

"Then why are the policemen after us?"

"They aren't after us. They just didn't want any one else to hurt us."

"Okay. But who is anybody else? What's their names?" Kaylynn asked, because my response was far too transparent for even a seven-year-old.

"I don't know," I answered genuinely.

"Then are we going to die?" She still had hold of my hand.

"When you're an old woman, and I'm a really old man, then we'll talk about it."

"I wish Daddy were here," Kaylynn told me as we walked across the parking lot to the front of the grocery store.

"Me too," I told her.

"But I'm glad you're here," she said as she looked up at me. "You're fun, and you're silly." She finally let go of me and raced to stomp on the old rubber pad that opened the automatic door.

There is little else to report about that day. Sylvia picked up Kaylynn and me and the groceries right on schedule. I drove from there. We took the route that I was given by Nathan. We arrived in Durango, Colorado, at 5:30 PM. We rented two rooms at the Wagon Wheel Motel and then fed the kids their supper.

Then, at about 6:40, I sat down and waited in the lobby of the motel for Nathan's telephone call. I had no way of knowing beforehand, but it would be the last telephone call that I would ever receive from him.

> She took the greatest pleasure in handling it, in washing and dressing it, for it seemed to her that all this was a confirmation of her maternity and that she would look at it and feel almost surprised that it was hers, and would say to herself in a low voice as she danced it in her arms: "It is my baby, it's my baby."
>
> —De Maupassant

Transcript of a Digitally Recorded Conversation between Dr. Judy Weintraub and the woman "Miriam"

[Author's note: The ensuing conversation is taken from a digital memory stick that has neither date nor vocal identification anywhere on it. I received this recording in the last batch that, as I mentioned at the beginning of this book, was given to me by Father Dougherty on June 5 outside Taos, New Mexico. By placing the transcript at this point in the manuscript, I realize that I am guessing the time, the place, and the names of the participants in the conversation. However, I am familiar with Dr. Judy Weintraub's voice. (Identified in the transcript below as JW.) Although we have never met or spoken, I assume that the other woman is "Miriam" and have abbreviated her name as simply M.

Because of the state of exigency that occupied these three days, that is June 2 through 4, my best guess is that this conversation took place late on the night of June 2, probably after the group meeting called by Nathan (described above) or, possibly, early the next morning. These are the only two times, as far as I have been able to determine, during which the leisurely and candid discussion that follows could have taken place.

One further comment, although it is impossible to include such detail in the printing of a transcript: I wish I could somehow convey to the reader the sense of loneliness and weariness, yet the childlike hope, the playfulness, and the longing in the voice of "Miriam."]

JW: Oh, this darn thing. Nathan gave it to me. It's a digital recorder. It's tiny, isn't it? I think it's cute. But it's uncomfortable to wear. I just turned it on to record. Nathan asked me to wear this. He told me to ask you first before I recorded. Is it all right?

M: [Pause before answer] I suppose the others would say that at this point in time, a record is probably critical. So, thank you. Yes.

JW: There was something else I wanted to tell you before I turned this on, but I can't remember …

M: You may ask me anything you like—I have nothing to hide.

JW: No. It was personal … oh, yes. Yes. I just wanted to tell you how much I respect you. Last week, when Harold left alone with you, I had … I had misgivings about you. However, since I've had a chance to get to know you, I have very much enjoyed your company. I love the way that you handle the men in the Order and that Mr. Tie. They all tend to be so arcane.

M: [Laughing] Thank you. I appreciate your friendship as well. Elijah told me that you were a great scientist. He truly enjoyed his visits with you. He thought that, in many ways, your work was close to the truth. Because of my relationship with Harold, I wasn't certain if we could be friends. I am very glad that things have worked out.

JW: Elijah thought my work significant?

M: Yes.

JW: Why? I am asking because I am flattered.

M: He said that your notion of … I would call it 'livingness'—what do you call it?

JW: Symbiosis?

M: Yes. That is it. Elijah said that real synthesis, I guess that would mean something like your symbiosis, had to take place first in the individual human being, then in families and in the various communities and religions, then in the world as a whole. We had to learn to live with ourselves through respect and acknowledgment of the necessity of the individual for the good of the whole. After that … he said that anything was possible.

JW: Even the teaching of immortality?

M: Even that—so Elijah believed. I, like Father Hugo, I am unconvinced.

JW: This reminds me that there are so many things I want to ask you. We used to speak with Elijah, of course ...

M: He was very fond of you and your husband.

JW: Yes, but he was a *man*. There are so many things I wanted to ask about immortality, but from a woman's perspective.

M: There are fewer of us. And I think our insight is quite different.

JW: I noticed. Why do you think that's the case? Why are there fewer women?

M: I have thought about it. I think I understand. It is not easy to talk about, and it is not easy to put into words. Those are two different problems.

JW: I will help keep things straight when I can. And I promise to be a good listener.

M: This is very exciting for me. To speak with another woman—with a woman of your intelligence.

JW: Thank you. Now, don't wander off track like the others. Stick to the first question: Why are there fewer women immortals than men?

M: [Voice shaking] I will try. Even though there are fewer women, I think that it may be easier for a woman to understand than for a man. Is that a contradiction?

JW: I don't think so. It's all right.

M: [Voice shaking] I have wanted tell someone this for a long time. Not to a man. To a woman, a woman. That is why I was so hoping that I could speak with you. Because with a man, even with an immortal, there is always tension. Sexual tension. I have been hailed, pursued, and courted by men as a beautiful woman ... for more than three thousand years. It wears so thin. Can you understand? The need just to talk—to be understood.

[Author's note: There is what sounds like sobbing at this point on the tape. Apparently Miriam has broken into tears.]

JW: Please. It's all right. Come sit here beside me. Here. Now, better? [More sobbing] Stop it now. You are making me feel ashamed. I thought you were trying to steal away my husband. What a silly goose I was! [Laughter] Here. Here's another hug. It makes me feel better too. There. Take your time.

M: [Pause] Thank you. Where to begin? We women are connected, to the earth, to life, in a way that men are not.

JW: By our menstrual cycle?

M: Yes. No, that is too trivial. I would rather say by life—by life itself. My body is that of a ... how old would you say that I am?

JW: I can't say. That is always such an awkward question ...

M: Believe me, I will not be offended by your answer.

JW: I would say late thirties.

M: See, you were only off by three dozen hundred years!
[Laughter]
JW: If you are immortal, why does it matter how old you appear?
M: Because my body is exactly how it appears. My body functions like that of any thirty-one-year-old woman. I have not yet passed through menopause.
JW: You mean that you can still have children?
M: Physically, yes. In principle, I can. And I have … it is extremely difficult … it is hurtful to explain.
JW: Your offspring aren't immortal, are they?
M: There, you have guessed it at once. I knew it would be easier to understand than to explain. No. Of course not. Why should they be? Immortality is a choice. A choice rarely understood and even more rarely selected. That is the most difficult part of all.
JW: I hadn't thought of that possibility. Somehow the sexual drive, the procreative process, and childbirth never entered into my reflections. I mean … perhaps I even shut them out. I knew that you and Harold were friends, and it did intimidate me. Perhaps I was jealous. I have passed the childbearing years.
M: There is no reason to be jealous. I do not think that Harold is physically attracted to me. Do you?
JW: With Harold, it is difficult to say. [Laughter] Sometimes, most of the time, he is so cerebral that he seems disconnected from his erotic nature. But Harold is still a man.
M: Let me put it from my perspective. I have never 'pursued' Harold, if that is the right word for it. I was not interested in him sexually. Outside of reasons of morality, my reason for not wanting sexual relations with any man is quite specific and not at all ordinary. Procreation, for an immortal—especially for a female—is the most hurtful of all experiences.
JW: I am beginning to understand …
M: To give birth, to love a child, to watch her grow, to watch her age, and finally to watch her die. The process of life … the ordinary process of life is so foreign to us, so hurtful, because there is nothing we can do to change it.
JW: You mean your children age, but you do not. They are like the demigods.
M: Yes. *Precisely*! Some *are* the demigods. Many of the myths of the mating of mortals and immortals are essentially true. 'The sons of God with the daughters of man.' The nameless daughters of man in the Bible, a book for men, about men. There is, in Genesis, a list of long-lived men. Where is the list of the longer-lived women? I am ashamed to say that my own tradition was perhaps the least tolerant, the most fearful. They feared life and the gift that woman brings,

and so they created a god who hated it. Mr. Tie says that all religions have stood in the way of immortality—but none, I do not mean this to offend you, none so much as ours.

M: [Pauses, then continues] The Greeks were much closer to the truth. I believe that they nearly understood. Remember the story of Thetis and her son Achilles? That story, the basic story, is true. Don't look at me as if I'm insane. Thetis, I knew her. She gave up ... in the twelfth century. Her struggle for the life of Achilles was recorded faithfully. She was an immortal fighting for the life of her mortal son. It was a battle she could not win. It is a battle none of us have ever won. Her story was written plainly and openly—yet no one has understood the meaning—no one has taken it seriously.

M: [Pauses, then continues] This should not be totally alien to you. Your husband often complains of the difficulties of writing on immortality. There is a tension between the preservation of life through love and sharing and the preservation of the ego through work or an art object. Socrates lives on in the flesh, Plato only in his dialogues. One has only to look to Homer to see the impossibility of doing both. This is the lesson of Homer and of Plato. They had a choice, and they made it.

JW: Choice?

M: To write or to be immortal. Or rather, to choose their form of immortality. They understood. I think your husband understands.

JW: You think Harold can choose to be immortal?

M: Yes.

JW: Can't you see that my husband is very ill? He has cancer. The last thing in the world he needs to be told is that he can live forever. He needs treatment—soon.

M: Because he understands—that does not mean he will choose our way. One more example, for I can see that you do not believe me. This one from another part of the world, from another religion. Jabala is still alive. You will meet her in a day or two. Her story is recorded for all in the *Chandogya Upanishad*. How many have read it? Countless millions. How many have understood? Two or three. She had attained immortality. Her son, Satyakama, sought the secret from her. She wanted to teach him, but she could not—because it is unteachable—the fact is so recorded. It was written by her son. His immortality was obtained through writing his mother's secret. Not at all unlike Plato and Socrates. Or Peter and Christ. Do you think?

JW: And what about you? Are you a goddess? Is my Harold your Plato? Your Homer? Or your Peleus?

M: Please. Please listen to the words of my mouth. A moment ago, you were my friend; you held me in your arms when I wept. But I cried because I was afraid you would not understand. Now you are being hard. Now you have moved away. I will be strong. I will not cry. I am not insane, and I am not a goddess, far from it. Neither was Thetis, nor Persephone, nor is Jabala, nor Sariah. Please. Listen to me. In my life I have wanted nothing more than to share my gift with my children. I have even mated with another immortal. I have shared the dream with a man who knows. Yet, for every child I have failed, even the child of that union. I failed. It is not a matter of breeding. It is not a matter of upbringing. It is neither genetic nor environmental, as they say today. I have stood helpless and watched every one of my children die. I have given birth six times. Three died from diseases or illness, one in war, one by accident, and one from old age.

JW: I cannot even imagine it.

M: The most difficult of all was the child who died from old age. I was there at her bedside. She was eighty-seven; I was over two thousand years old. I have not become pregnant since, not in eight hundred years.

JW: Why not?

M: I see them. I watch them watch me. We know our children so well. They know us intimately too. By touch, by taste, by smell, as well as by sight. Do you know what people examine most carefully to see if they have aged?

JW: I hadn't thought of it. Faces, I suppose.

M: No. I mean to gauge one's own aging.

JW: I would still say the face.

M: No, they look at their hands. You all do, you mortals. You look at your own hands for age. Even more than at your faces. Because a face can be so tired in the early morning—look twenty years older than it did the evening before. The face is a liar. That is why we make it up. But you look at your hands.

M: [Pauses, then continues] They did. My children. When they were young, of course, they played with Mommy's hands. Every child does. As they grew older and I held them, their hands had changed, grown so much bigger, while mine had remained the same. Then came their first wrinkles about the knuckles, then below the fingertips. But not Mommy's hands. My hands were eternal. It grounded them, at first. Gave them comfort, a security in one thing in this world that would never change, until they were old enough to know that my hands should be wrinkled and spotted, just like theirs. Then it frightened them. Death became a million times as real, a million times more terrifying for my children, than it will ever be for yours. Because a part of them, not enough to prevent it, but a part of them knew that it did not have to be. They knew there was a secret in their mother's hands.

JW: Failed—you said that for each one you've failed—would you explain that more to me?

M: You are a mother? Yes?

JW: Of two, both teenagers. Well, one just turned twenty. God, sometimes they are such inconsiderate monsters!

M: [Laughing] As were all of mine. They will mature. As mine all did. They will learn to love you in new and beautiful and subtle ways. They will remember to be grateful for the life that you have given them. They will repay you—for I have a feeling that you are a wonderful mother.

JW: I don't know how wonderful. I have spent more time than I probably should have on my career. No, I don't really believe that. Sometimes, even now, Benjamin, the baby, surprises me with his love, though most of the time I'd like to wring his neck! [Laughter]

M: I know those feelings and sympathize and delight in them with you. However, there comes a point in the existence of an immortal where our children slide by us in age and in time. That is how I failed them. I could not give them my secret. It was impossible, no matter how much I wanted it, to save them from themselves—to save them from death.

JW: I see that it is painful. Still, I need to hear more, to understand better. Could you expand on that for me? Especially on the notion of time?

M: Let me think. I believe Father Patricelli had the best explanation for time, for what time feels like to us. I can vaguely remember growing up, adolescence, being a young adult, a new mother; all of that was like a distant journey. I knew those experiences, somewhat, I think, like you know them. I was in time then, just like you are now. Let me see if I can say it another way. I have, a long time ago, *spent* time, so I am aware of the process you are in.

JW: You were not born an immortal?

M: That is correct. None of us are ... Let's leave out Jesus ... At that time, at the age you see me now (I was thirty-one, not 'late-thirties'), at the point of decision, the nature of time changed for me.

JW: I'm embarrassed. I wish I had guessed low. But I was trying to be honest.

M: When I grew up, people aged more rapidly. The life span was much shorter than it is now. We walked everywhere and spent most of our days hiding our faces from the desert sun. If I look only a few years more than my thirty-one, then I am lucky.

JW: You are being kind; you are very beautiful; I was rude and ...

M: Nonsense. You are a scientist. The human body has grown bigger, stronger, and more disease-resistant, and it lives longer. You are well aware ...
JW: Still, please accept my apology. You were speaking about the passage of time.
M: Yes. Your husband has written some on this. He wrote, "We do not care because we are in time; we are in time because we care. To be present is to be concerned." He has come remarkably close to describing it accurately. He is one of the great geniuses in history.

[Author's note: Miriam's quote, and it is exact, is from Harold Weintraub's famous "reversal" of Heidegger in Weintraub's article, "The Present as Care," reproduced in his book, *The Search for the Everlasting*, which was cited above.]

JW: Yes. I believe it too. I would thank you on his behalf—but he already knows. [Laughter] Let's stay on the subject. Tell me about time.
M: I will try. There was no conscious decision on my part to become immortal. No exact thought such as, 'I choose not to die.' For my part, I loved people, which was not difficult to do, being raised around my brother. As I matured, as I reached adulthood (and you will notice that many immortals stop aging, as I did, in their early thirties), I thought less and less of my needs, things like hunger, thirst, even sexual drives, and concentrated more on either thinking, quite abstractly, or in serving other people.
JW: But what does that have to do with time and its passage?
M: I'm almost there. I ate when others ate. I rarely slept. I found great pleasure in sewing, painting, and in creating abstract designs, even if that meant only drawing in the sand with a stick. I became very thin, not because I had no desire for food, but because I did not live for that desire. If food was there at the moment of hunger, then that was fine. If not ... I did not notice it. Is that clear?
JW: Somewhat. Please go on.
M: I discovered, at about the age of thirty-one, that I no longer looked forward to ... to anything. I looked 'forward' to now. My dealings with people were always immediate and sincere. So I was not haunted by any past. I had missed nothing, for everything that I wanted was always now or that which was before me. The closest I came to thinking of the past or the future was in watching my children grow old. It was so perplexing to me, so vexing. Aging made no sense. It was especially difficult to see it happening to those so dear. I think that is why there are fewer women who are immortal. We are closer to life. Maybe too close.
JW: I am somewhat confused, especially in your descriptions of your children. Didn't you mark the time for them to ... to take their first step, for example?

That is looking into the future. Planning their first step. Helping them keep their balance. That is not living in the now. Why are you smiling?

M: I am smiling because you have confused the parent with the child. When my children held my finger, it was they, not I, who wanted to become something other than what they were. I found delight in their need, not in mine. And it was in the moment of that particular need.

JW: I am still lost.

M: With good reason. This is very difficult to describe in words. Most words are made for *before* and *after*. Not many words are made for *now*. Our discussion about a child walking might help you understand. There is a far more profound reward in learning the subtleties of children's desires as they move toward taking a first step. First they must learn simply which foot is hooked to which leg. I took great joy and pleasure in something so small. At that moment, I was not thinking that in six months my child would walk. The child would do that with or without me. I was thinking, "Isn't it a wonderful thing that my child is learning which foot is hooked to which leg?" I watched her carefully figure it out. Moment by moment, movement by movement. Where was time while this was going on? I do not know. I did not care. I was not the least bit concerned with time. Either for my sake or for the sake of my child. That the child would walk in six months was understood ... Father Patricelli would have said that it was a given for me. It was not an objective.

JW: Sometimes, sometimes I think I feel that way too. At home, after work, when I slip into our hot tub and the bubbles pop up all around me. Sometimes I can just feel the bubbles and the warm water take all of my thoughts and worries and regrets and just melt them away.

M: It is not unlike that. Take it a little further. You must imagine it as a constant. As a complete way of life. As an unending process.

JW: But what about earning income, paying taxes, bills, retirement, a mortgage, tuition, insurance?

M: What about them?

JW: Don't you worry ... aren't you concerned?

M: No. I would rather live.

JW: Is it really that simple?

M: Yes, it is. You should think about this. You should discuss it with your husband. He understands. He could help ...

JW: I'm sorry. I think I've finished for now. I must look in on Harold. His health is slipping again. He can't help me a bit if he is dead.

M: Go to him. He loves you. I doubt that he would ever leave you, even if he could. Thank you for speaking with me. I enjoy your friendship. I am happy that you are going with us.

JW: I am very happy to have met you. You are a most delightful woman. Though I must tell you, truthfully, that I believe almost nothing of what you say.

M: I understand that.

JW: Tell me one more thing: between us, where are we going?

M: Have you forgotten that the recording device is still on?

JW: I'm sorry. Here, I'll shut it off.

M: Never mind. Don't bother. Let it run. I can only give you the same answer—whether it is recorded or not. I do not yet know. But soon. We shall soon. Nathan has demanded it for the sake of his family. We all respect that. We all understand, and it will be given to him. I have one other secret to tell you. Something Moses, Elijah, and I knew. Something we have been keeping from your husband.

JW: What is it?

M: Enoch will be meeting with us soon.

JW: Enoch?

M: [Giggling] Yes. He hasn't seen Harold since Harold was a boy. Please don't spoil the surprise for us.

JW: I won't. I must be getting back to the room. I think the shutoff button is this one right here …

I give heat; I withhold and send forth the rain. I am immortality and also death; I am being as well as non-being, 0 Arjuna. The knowers of the three Vedas who drink the soma juice and are cleansed of sin, worshipping me with sacrifices, pray for the way to heaven.

We have drunk soma and become immortal; we have attained the light that the gods discovered.

—*Rig Veda*

A man has only one way of becoming immortal on this earth—he must forget that he is mortal.

—Giraudoux

Excerpts from the Journal of Father Jerome Dougherty

Midnight, June 3, Van Buren, Arkansas.
I have never had such a hectic day; nor have I ever traveled so far in an automobile in one day. It is late now, and we have just checked into this Holiday Inn. I have taken my watch off and left it on the dresser. It may be later than midnight, and so this could be June the fourth. I will write a few notes and then I must sleep—for much is being demanded of me, physically and mentally, on this journey of ours.

    Nathan awakened the party at 5:00 AM this morning. The van was waiting out in front of the hotel. He had purchased small cartons of milk, doughnuts, fresh fruit, and bottled juices for us. Except for the doughnuts, which were so fresh that they were yet warm, he had it all stored in a large plastic cooler that he had purchased at one of our stops yesterday. We were on the road by five fifteen. Nathan drove two hours or so, traveling eighty-five to ninety miles per hour, on the freeway numbered 81.

He then stopped for gasoline at a small town called White Pine, just south of the freeway, in Tennessee. This allowed us to refresh ourselves. Several of us purchased coffee because Nathan had forgotten to include it in the earlier repast. Or perhaps he omitted it on purpose—I sometimes forget that he is a Mormon. Miriam and Fathers Quindilar and Holden made telephone calls in efforts, I am certain, to give Nathan the location he has demanded, so that we may meet with his family. After no more than ten minutes at the service station, we were off again. Though all three reported progress, none of them could give us a precise location.

I drove for the next two hours. Nathan lay on the back seat in the van and tried to catch up on his sleep.

Our prayers being answered, Harold was feeling better, at least this morning. He and Father Quindilar had a rather feisty and zestful conversation about proofs of the existence of God. Unfortunately, even though they sat in the bench directly behind the driver's seat, the van is noisy, and I was concentrating on driving, so I missed some of the detail.

[Author's note: I cannot find this discussion among the recordings made in the van. I assume that Nathan failed to turn on the recorder before he fell asleep. Hence we must make do with the sketchy account of the conversation provided by Father Dougherty, who, one should keep in mind, was neither a logician nor a mathematician.]

To summarize their discussion, Father Quindilar has been working on a proof of the existence of God based upon Georg Cantor's Continuum Hypothesis. Essentially, Father Quindilar asserted that it could be shown by incontrovertible mathematical proof that infinity, I believe he said "absolute infinity," is the equivalent of "everything." He further asserted that the three-valued logic, quantum logic, could be used as an analogy in an argument for the existence of an eternal soul. He said that he had carefully read Professor Weintraub's works and that he believed that he had found support for his theories therein. "Modern mathematics," Father Quindilar stated, "whether it has meant to or not, has created room for both God and an eternal soul."

It was not clear to me whether Harold considered the discussion amusing, annoying, or merely a distraction from the boredom of the daylong drive. He did not, however, at any time agree with Father Quindilar. I found this to be a disappointment at first, until I began to reflect on the tremendous difference between the thought of these two men. If I could summarize the difference, it would be that Father Quindilar is a man of faith, while Professor Weintraub is not.

"You have, I am afraid," Harold said to Father Quindilar in summary, "misunderstood much of what I have said about immortality. First, I have written little or nothing on the proofs of the existence of God. One must go back and wrestle Kant to the ground before that victory is claimed. I know of no one who has accomplished the feat. Certainly it is not I. From your explanation this morning, it seems that you have yet to do it. Second, regarding the immortality of the soul, I have never argued for that. In fact, I have quite specifically argued *against*, the assertion that the soul is a unique *eternal* entity, separate and apart from the body. I do not believe that any mystical hocus-pocus ectoplasm can be derived from mere *potentia*. The quantum logic you speak of is nothing more than a necessary tool for explaining a statistical entanglement that occurs in quantum mechanics. My point is more subtle. What happens when one reaches the position where one is no longer an *observer* of life—thus enmeshed in the uncertainty of Heisenberg—but a *liver* of life? Does one become the quantum object that the theorists attempt to observe and statistically, and statically, describe? At that moment, what influence does the human mind play in the role of the phenomenon? I have suggested that we are no longer observers in the audience—that at such an instant, we would find ourselves in the play itself. If you do not understand my work, then you should start with Palle Yourgrau."

It was at about this point in the conversation that Nathan awoke. "Anybody need a break or need to use the telephone?" he asked. I watched him in the rearview mirror. He looked young and frightened, like a child awakening from a bad dream. He rubbed his eyes and straightened his short brown hair with his fingers as he walked with sleepy uncertainty on the shifting floor of the van to the cab. Several people answered his question in the affirmative.

"Father, let's pull off at the next exit and gas it up," Nathan said. He was so tired that he leaned his head on my shoulder. "Remind me to check the recorder before we start," he whispered in my ear.

I nodded my head in affirmation and patted the side of his unshaven face. "You are fine. Your family will be fine. We will meet them tomorrow, you shall see. The Lord is watching over them," I assured him.

He knelt between the two front seats and guided me off the freeway and to the nearest truck stop on the edge of Cookeville, Tennessee.

It had been foggy when we started. The sun had burned the fog away quickly, and we stepped out of the van into a clear and clean spring morning. All of the members of our group took turns working the three telephones in front of the store. (Most of the immortals also carry cellular telephones—but Nathan has prohibited their use.) Patently, different members stay in touch or know the next location of certain other immortals. This means that telephone calls are made and initial discussions held and preliminary decisions made. Then our members speak to each other in an effort to formalize these tentative agreements. Then they are back on the telephone for more talks.

Nathan allowed this to go on for about twenty minutes. Then he ordered everyone back into the van, and we drove three or more hours before we stopped for another break and another round of telephone negotiations. Nathan drove the remainder of the day. This routine repeated itself four times and continued into the evening. I assume that the immortals coming from other areas are also on the move, also traveling in the general direction of our final destination.

I rode in the back and would report on the conversations of the members, but there were few. Professor Weintraub's health is fading, as it seems to do in the evenings, and Judy was occupied with him. The immortals spoke little. Their faces were almost continually set in consternation—something I have rarely witnessed.

[Author's note: Some of the conversations about to be reported are difficult to understand. Father Dougherty's recollection and reconstruction of these conversations is, in many places, at odds with what appears in the transcript. Even though Dougherty's account makes more sense than what is heard on the recording, I have chosen to include the recorded version, rather than Dougherty's reported version, because I believe that the reader should make up his or her own mind on the substance of these conversations. Thus, almost all of the words in quotation marks in the remainder of this section are taken directly from disk V3.]

At our eight o'clock stop, after the telephone calls had been made, Nathan ordered all into the van, slammed and locked the doors behind us, and then demanded an answer. "Where do I meet up with my family tomorrow?"

There was no initial reply, but Father Holden, seeing that no one else had an answer, falteringly said, "Agent Johnson—may I—may we, Mr. Tie and myself, speak with you? Candidly?" It was getting dark outside, and Nathan had not turned on the overhead lamp in the back of the van. All of the conversation came from the shadows. It was unsettling—in spite of the earnestness of Father Holden's voice and request.

"You mean alone?" Nathan asked.

"No. Heavens, no. We have no secrets—that is part of our hesitation," responded Father Holden.

"Okay," Nathan replied. "But I want an answer, not another evasion. So, what's up, gentlemen? I'm getting tired of this bullshit."

"We know that you are, expressly," replied Mr. Tie.

"Let's have it," demanded Nathan, speaking to those in the rear of the van.

"Agent Johnson, it is not practical or safe to give such information until the last possible moment," came Father Holden's voice from the backseat.

"I've told you that the last possible moment is in one hour," Nathan, who was sitting next to me, responded firmly. His neck was bent forward as he peered into the darkness.

"And we have diligently attempted to meet your request," answered Mr. Tie.

"It's not a request," stated Nathan.

"Agent Johnson," Father Holden spoke again from the dark, "yesterday, your effort to test the ... the trustworthiness of the members should have taught you one le—"

"How do you know?" Nathan stopped Father Holden, practically hissing the words.

"We may be innocents; we are not ignorant," answered Father Dobo, who sat on the middle bench, directly in front of us. I could see the grin from his white teeth against his black face. Judy sat beside Father Dobo. She held her husband, who was, I think, asleep.

Mr. Tie laughed from the shadows, from the same seat as Father Holden. His laughter was high-pitched—musical. Then he said, "I, for one, noticed the blood on the side of your shoe. Today we made our calls. I can tell you that there is no assurance, none whatsoever, that the MOSSAD will assist us tomorrow. They had good reason to kill Khalifah and the others, but that was yesterday. You should have already learned how very fickle governments are about ... about our *ongoing* existence."

"You know ... about everything?" asked Nathan.

"We know enough," replied Father Holden. "Yesterday, between the time that you revealed our resting place for the night and the relocation of the Arab assassins to that very place, was less than four hours. What makes you think that today we can designate, twelve or sixteen hours in advance, a place where your family will be safe?"

Nathan hesitated before he answered. "I see the point. So when will you know?"

Mr. Tie laughed again. This time the resonance of his voice was, at least to me, daunting. "Not 'When will we know?' Rather, when should we tell you—for the safety of the members of your family and of our party?"

Father Holden immediately took up the conversation. "When we tell you, we will tell all the others so that we can minimize the damage that comes when that information is made known to those hostile to us."

"How do I know which of you to trust?" asked Nathan.

"Think it through. Logically, deception would be easy. The shorter the period of time, the less likely the lie," answered Father Holden. "We hide nothing. You may listen to our telephone conversations. If one of us refuses that to you, then you might be suspicious of that person. We have been watching you. We think you will know what is true and what is not. The answer we give will be made before the entire group. Nothing here is secret. If different suggestions or locations are offered—then you must simply decide which of us is telling the truth."

"We know that the *truth* is the *now*. Let us come as close to the now as possible," Father Dobo reassured Nathan as he patted his shoulder.

"Okay. So tonight I just tell my family to hang tight?" Nathan asked.

"No. Tonight, soon, we will announce, to the entire group, our final destination," Mr. Tie replied.

Father Holden quickly followed, "You must then communicate with your family a place where tomorrow you can leave them a message. Let us narrow the gap to an hour or two. We will meet them on our way. For the sake of your family …"

Nathan, seeking clarification, interrupted Father Holden, "You make the announcement of the destination—I assume it may or may not be a lie—and I'll tell my family what?"

"You may not be able to tell them anything. We shall leave a message for them, to be picked up tomorrow evening in a place we leave to your discretion," answered Father Holden. "Direct them there for now. For reasons of timeliness, you must choose a location near the Four Corners area. Tomorrow, at the last possible moment, we will let you know, and you may be able to leave the message for them. They may, it is not yet clear, but they may end up meeting with a man named John. We will probably pick him up. However, if we do not, then they must bring him. Tell them that the message tomorrow may be from John rather than from you. You may code it, if you like, and then you can share the code with John so that he can be identified by your family. Hopefully, both John and your family will join with us. Then we can safely—as safely as possible—proceed to our destination. Is that all clear?"

"Yeah. I got it. Where is John now?" questioned Nathan.

"It is where he will be *tomorrow* that is of concern to your family," replied Father Holden from the darkness.

"How will they know him?" Nathan asked. "I mean apart from the code."

"John is ... they will know. He has recently been seriously injured—burned. It will be manifest," answered Father Holden.

It was starting to get cold in the van. Sister Maria pointed out the fact. Nathan climbed into the cab, started the engine, and turned on the heater.

"Are we agreed?" Mr. Tie shouted from the rear over the noise of the motor and the heater's fan.

Nathan turned on the overhead lamp in the cabin of the van. "Okay," Nathan said as he poked his head through opening. The light was not bright enough to hurt my eyes, and they easily adjusted.

"Then we shall now declare our final destination," stated Father Holden. He sat erect on the bench and, as is his habit, brushed back his silver hair on both sides of his head, just prior to making a declamation, thus focusing one's attention to his face.

"We will?" asked Miriam incredulously before he could finish. She was sitting on the rear bench between Mr. Tie and Father Holden and seemed quite confounded by the announcement.

"Yes," answered Mr. Tie. "It is time."

Father Holden cleared his throat, smoothed his hair a second time, and recaptured our attention. "Our destination, of course, is neither Sedona nor the Valley of the Gods, though we hope those who ... who do not appreciate us are at those locations." Father Holden laughed with a nod of both thanks and, if I am not mistaken, reassurance, to Miriam.

"It is our hope that they are enjoying, and finding further truth and enlightenment, in and through the harmonic convergence," added Father Hugo through the passageway, for he sat in the rider's seat in the cab. The back bench broke out in laughter.

"Tell it to us. Where it is," demanded Sister Maria. "Others need to know." She sat on the bench next to me and seemed quite skittish about the whole matter.

"We want to discuss that briefly first," said Mr. Tie. "There is the serious difficulty of Agent Johnson's family and their safety."

"Yes," Father Holden said. "It seems circumspect to us that we announce the final destination now, so that all those traveling to meet with us can reach the site quickly and safely. Rather than direct his family to that place, we (and I include, do I not? Agent Johnson), deem it prudent to meet them prior to that point in time, at a place to be determined as we proceed to our destination."

"I've already said, 'Okay,'" replied Nathan leaning over the bench between Father Quindilar and myself.

"I agree," said Father Hugo from behind him.

"It should be so," nodded Father Dobo.

"I also agree," Father Quindilar affirmed, speaking from my left. "But where is the site? I am afraid there is little time for those from the West. They need to be soon told."

"Miriam? Sister Maria? Are we unanimous?" asked Father Holden.

"Yes," said Sister Maria.

"I suppose," Miriam said. "But I wish that we could wait even longer before this proclamation. We are two days away."

"If we go all night, we can make it in thirty hours—or less," Nathan responded.

Miriam shrugged her shoulders. Something about the decision clearly upset her. "I will not stand in the way," she said. "Make your announcement."

Father Holden pushed his silver hair back from his thin face, took a deep breath, cleared his throat again, and proclaimed, "We will meet at dawn, the day after tomorrow, in a place where the time for our arrival was secreted long ago in a kiva … in a kiva built for this very day; in a blessed chamber where the sun will break precisely through the stone doorway in greeting; we will meet at Chaco in New Mexico at the *Casa Rinconada.*"

Telephone Conversation, Recorded on the Evening of June 3, between Nathan Johnson (NJ), Sylvia Johnson (SJ), and the Author (ME)

ME: Hello.
NJ: Fith.
ME: Yeah, fire in the hole.
SJ: [In the background] I wish you wouldn't keep saying that. Why don't you make up some other secret word? That one is really annoying, and it's filthy."
NJ: Tell her it's good to hear her voice too.
ME: [Laughing] He says it's good to hear your voice too. Attaboy, Nate. Don't take any shit offa her.
SJ: [In the background to the author:] Give me the phone. [To her husband:] I'm sorry I was gritchy, but ... I wish you wouldn't ... I mean it's ... never mind. I'm sorry. How are you? Is everything okay?
NJ: Pretty good. Things are coming together. Let my cuz listen in while we talk—okay?
SJ: Don't worry. He is.
ME: [In the background] Right here takin' notes. What does 'gritchy' mean?
NJ: Grouchy and bitchy—gritchy. I want both of you to listen carefully. I need you to drive on to Cortez, Colorado, tonight. It's only about forty-five, maybe fifty, miles. It's a straight shot west on Highway 160. Got it?
SJ: Cortez tonight. I guess the kids can handle it.
NJ: Once there, I want you to camp out at a place called 'The Frontier.' It's another Best Western. You can spend the night there. As a matter of fact, check in for two nights. Shouldn't be any trouble. Oh, somewhere along the way to Cortez, put on the New Mexico plates.
SJ: How about the stickers on the side?

NJ: Leave them. Leave it a paint truck. Just change the license plates. Tomorrow, starting at four in the afternoon, I want you to check the front desk for a message. Once you get there, someone will need to stay close to the front desk for the next twelve hours. I may not be able to call you, but you will get a message. If the message says that we are going 'piggyback' then follow it explicitly. Get to the place indicated as fast as you can legally drive and by the shortest route. Hopefully the route will be in the message. If not, just get there quick. Oh, if they want a password, tell them ... "turtleneck." Got all of that?

SJ: Yes. He's writing. What do we do if they don't mention 'piggyback'?

NJ: Head to Las Vegas. Get to my office. I don't think that's going to happen. Now, once you get to the location in the message, hopefully, I'll be there.

SJ: If you're not?

NJ: If I'm not there, the message should also give you the name of somebody who'll be there, or who'll get there shortly after you get there. Or maybe you'll go someplace and meet him. None of that is set for certain. Anyway, watch for that person. You should be able to recognize him. I think he's been burned, so his face may be scarred. If he doesn't tell you first, ask him his name. If he says it's 'John,' then do exactly what he tells you to do. Remember, burned face and John. If he doesn't show in, say, an hour, head to Vegas. Same thing—get to my office. Got all of that?

SJ: Yes.

ME: [In the background] Got it.

NJ: I love you. I'm sorry ... I'm sorry I got you into this mess.

SJ: Oh, I love you too, Nathan. Just take care of yourself. We'll see you tomorrow?

NJ: Maybe tomorrow. We're driving straight through. Probably tomorrow night. Next day for sure.

SJ: I can hardly wait.

ME: [In the background] Me too.

NJ: [Laughing] Good night.

On the Author's Travels with Sylvia Johnson and Her Children, June 3, Continued

It was dark by the time we toted the children out of the motel bed and back into the paint van. They greeted our efforts with screaming reluctance. Not that I blamed them. I was getting tired of chasing around the country myself.

They dropped off to sleep minutes after I drove out of Durango and headed for Cortez, Colorado. They were hypnotized, as usual, by the steady hum and gentle rocking of the van. The night was very dark, and there wasn't much to see along the road. Time after time, as we drove along the edge of the mountains, we passed through black ravines filled with the smell of fresh pine.

Sylvia, too, quickly fell asleep, once again against my shoulder, stretching her lithe body along the front seat. I opened the window to keep myself awake. The scent of the fresh mountain air mingled with the now familiar smell of her nearly spent perfume. I breathed both in deeply. I have read about the bonding that takes place between people who continually share a high-stress or rapidly changing environment. I have read that such stress often finds an outlet in sexual need. I have always imagined myself above that kind of brutish response to a tortuous reality. Yet as I drove along the winding mountain road, from one uncertain day to the next, I must confess that I wanted Sylvia like I have never wanted a woman before.

I put my arm around her and stroked her hair. She snuggled tighter, gripping my arm. I let my hand fall to her shoulder. My fingers nearly touched her breast.

"Mommy! Buffalo! Mommy!" Sherry moaned in her sleep.

Sylvia jerked her head, pushed past my arm, and climbed over the seat to quell the fears of her child.

She did not let me know if she had felt my touch, if she had sensed my need, if she had—or had not—felt her own; if she had been asleep or awake when I touched her. I looked in the rearview mirror, but I could see only the shadow of her face in the darkness of the van and the dim green phosphorescence from the dials from the console.

Half an hour later, we reached Cortez, Colorado. Nothing was said. We checked into our separate rooms, where we waited for tomorrow.

That something besides the sensations actually is immediately given follows (independently from mathematics) from the fact that even our ideas referring to physical objects contain constituents qualitatively different from sensations or mere combinations of sensations, e.g., the idea of the object itself, whereas, on the other hand, by our thinking we cannot create any qualitatively new elements, but only reproduce and combine those that are given.

—Gödel

Mathematics arises when the subject of twoness, which results from the passage of time, is abstracted from all special occurrences.

—Brouwer

Excerpts, continued, from an Unfinished Article by Professor Harold Weintraub, "On Gödel, on Cantor, and on Continuum: A Peek at Immortality?" Started in 2002. [Notes omitted, though some citations are explained by this Author.]

Let us grant the formalist thesis that mathematics is simply the manipulation of specified symbols according to commonly (within the métier) accepted rules. Let us further postulate that the world's leading formalist announces that he or she has consistently completed mathematics. Our hero stands at the lectern ready to deliver the denouement to the world.

There is an ambiguity *overlooked*—or, more accurately, *underlooked*—by all who would grant the possibility of this scenario. It is this: Assume that *knowledge* of a consistent and self-contained (i.e., complete) theory of mathematics is possible. Secondly, assume, as we have, that someone has acquired such knowledge. (Inconsequential here is the means of acquisition. Whether by rote, intuition, laboratory accident, or an act of God—it is of no bearing.) There will always be an unbridgeable difference between discovering a consistent and complete mathematical theory and *teaching others* how to construct the same theory *and proving that the knowledge shared in this second construction is the same as, or equivalent to, the initially discovered knowledge.*

The question here is neither dialectical nor positivist; it is *intuitional*. Cantor's later papers in the *Gesammelte Abhandlungen* are very closely related to the question of the relation of intuition to the conscious awareness of the state of lived life that I have discussed at length elsewhere. Gödel, as well, became interested, and was involved with these questions from the time he first grappled with the limitations of the system of Russell-Whitehead until he died. Both Cantor and Gödel made significant discoveries in the field of mathematics of "dilemmas" that have yet to be overcome or resolved or, frankly, even coherently explained in the context of the progression of mathematics or logic. With the single and partial exception of Paul J. Cohen, they have all but halted such progression. Yet both men were most reflective on the nature or the cause of their own discoveries.

Gödel believed ... well, we shall let him speak for himself on this matter.

Classes and concepts may, however, also be conceived as real objects, namely classes as "pluralities of things" or as structures consisting of pluralities of things and concepts as the properties and relations of the things existing independently of our definitions and constructions.

It seems to me that the assumption of such objects is quite as legitimate as the assumption of physical bodies, and there is quite as much reason to believe in their existence. [Author's note: The quote is taken from the article "Russell's Mathematical Logic," written by Kurt Gödel sometime in the late 1930s or early 1940s.]

Now we are ready to revisit our contest for locating complete human beings. The reader will recall that after initially failing the test, a clever gentleman has returned with his mother and our questionnaire, which reads as follows.

STATEMENT A: A complete person will never say that STATEMENT A is true.
QUESTION: Is STATEMENT A true?

And he has answered our question thus—"My mother will never say that STATEMENT A is true."

Our rules committee is in a panic. But only for a few moments because, thank God, someone has had the foresight to make Professor Hilbert our chairman.

"Young man," Hilbert addresses the gentleman, with a bow to his mother, "section EW, subsection B6, article 555, specifically stipulates that 'to answer for any other person who is, by either mental or physical incapacity, unable to answer for themself, [*sic*] the answerer must have been previously found to be a complete person.' We have evidence, as witnessed by staff members that you, yourself, do not meet these criteria. We are sorry, but since you do not qualify as a complete and consistent human being, neither does your mother qualify under the rules." Nor does anyone, nor can anyone, for, as one can almost hear Quine tell us at this point: "*We see the familiar pattern of transfinite recursion setting in.*"

I believe—more, I am quite convinced that the way to break out of this pattern is a *lived intuition*. It is quite similar to the mathematical intuition, the class or concept Gödel mentioned in his remark above, which has thus far been *overlooked*—or, better, *underlooked*.

I have, at various times and various places, indicated that such knowledge might lead to a form of immortality. Not historical immortality in the sense we think of when we speak of, say, a Christopher Columbus—a discoverer of something already existent and our remembrance of him for his perseverance. Immortality in the sense I am speaking of is a direct intuition of the idea of the living of life. Could such an intuition be "known?" Yes—where knowledge is the equivalence of an internal, eternal process of lived self-recognition.

Could such an intuition be taught—or shared? I openly admit that I cannot answer this question. Like the rest of mankind, I sit waiting for Moses to return from the mountain with it. The nearest I have come to finding an answer in the affirmative is in reading the works of Brouwer. For I find absolutely intriguing, almost mystically so, his assertion that the basis for mathematical intuition and thus all mathematical knowledge is based not upon our intuition of oneness—but of our intuition of *twoness*.

Perhaps it is only the loneliness of this human existence that makes me want, so desperately, to believe that this is true …

[The unfinished article ends at this point.]

> I have traveled here in search of Utnapishtim; for men say he has entered the assembly of the gods, and has found everlasting life. I have a desire to question him concerning the living and the dead.
>
> —Gilgamesh, *The Epic of Gilgamesh*

> There is a plant that grows under the water, it has a prickle like a thorn, like a rose it will wound your hands, but if you succeed in taking it, then your hands will hold that which restores his lost youth to a man.
>
> —Utnapishtim, *The Epic of Gilgamesh*

Excerpts from a letter from Dr. Judy Weintraub to the Author, Dated June 4

So I did make notes about yesterday and might sometime share them with you. However, after asking for permission and then reading Father Dougherty's journal entry for the same period of time, I decided that his was a sufficient, more detailed, probably more accurate description of the day's activities. That is why you have not and will not receive a letter from me written about yesterday's events. This omission allowed me to spend the evening caring for my husband, whose health is failing again.

I am not exaggerating when I tell you, as I suppose I have too often, that he needs immediate and radical medical intervention. I think that even he is beginning to see that. Hopefully this trip will be ended today, and we can fly back to Boston to begin the treatments.

None of this is or should be taken to indicate that he has lost his dogged determination to finish the trek. On the contrary, he believes, a conviction that might be engendered by his fever, that tomorrow may well bring a "resolution" to his illness—or at least to some of the questions concerning immortality that have plagued him for so many years. He seems almost to hold that the answers to the latter may be a cure to the former. This, I think, alarms me more than anything else. For such an idea, I believe, borders on madness. There are only two "resolutions" possible for his illness: remission through treatment ... or death.

Enough of Harold and his state of mind. Oh, except to say that he is still writing—though *scribbling feverishly* is more accurate. I can make little of it, and I told Harold as much. His response to me was that you, that *his student*, would understand; so I will get copies of his work to you in a few days after we are settled at home in Cambridge. Which reminds me that I did speak with the children yesterday by telephone. They are getting along, though they both expressed concern for their father.

Now, on to my recounting of today. We were up again very early and on the road well before six o'clock this morning. Perhaps it was due to Father Dougherty's remonstration, but this time Nathan included coffee in our morning's victuals.

Nathan requested to speak only with Father Dougherty, Harold, and myself at the start of the day, after Nathan had loaded and then locked the others and all of our belongings into the van. The four of us spoke in a deserted section of the hotel lobby; at least it was empty at that hour of the morning. We could see the van through a window behind the couch where we sat.

"It should be clear to everyone by now that one or more of the people in our group are trying to stop us from getting to wherever it is that we are going," Nathan began.

"Chaco Cultural National Historical Park—I borrowed Judy's laptop and looked it up on the Internet last night," said Father Dougherty. "Chaco is something like an American Stonehenge, with various types of solstitial alignments made of rocks, roads, and even kivas—their lodges or sanctuaries or, one might say, their equivalent of our churches or synagogues. Chaco was the center of culture for a people called the Anasazi. *Casa Rinconada* is the largest of the kivas in the monument."

Harold, who does much better in the mornings after he is rested, joined the discussion. "I agree with Agent Johnson. There are traitors among the group. I believe that I can identify one of them. I also doubt, I have great misgivings, that we are really going to Chaco—or, at least, that such a place is our final destination."

"Explain," commanded Nathan.

"Where shall I begin?" asked Harold.

"Begin with the traitor," Nathan replied. "And, please, if either of you disagree with Harold, butt right in. I want an honest discussion," Nathan said to Father Jerome and to me. Nathan's eyes are red and puffy, with dark circles around them. I am afraid he is pushing himself very close to exhaustion.

"Quindilar. Father Quindilar is your impostor," Harold stated, quite bluntly.

"How do you know that?" disputed Father Dougherty.

As I said, we were in an unoccupied portion of the lobby. Harold and I sat side by side on an orange vinyl couch. Father Dougherty and Nathan had pulled two orange cushioned chairs in front of us—so that Nathan could keep an eye on the van behind us. "Simple. Father Quindilar is a theoretician. He is a wonderer. He is a writer, a speculator. He is looking for the answers that the immortals already possess," answered Harold.

"Father Hugo is a writer," objected Father Dougherty. (Father Dougherty, as I may or may not have noted, is very bright and spry, especially for his age. He is weathering the trip better than any of us, excluding our friends, the immortals.)

"A writer of history—we have had this discussion before. There is nothing speculative, at least not in his own mind, in Father Hugo's work, nor in Father Dobo's. Elijah was free to translate and transcribe at the UN because they were not his ideas, not his words, thoughts, or needs. Father Quindilar *needs*. He needs eternity—or the promise of it. Not unlike you or Judy or myself, he expresses that need for his ideas *in writing*. That is the difference," answered Harold.

"You seem to me to be assuming that these people, excepting Quindilar, are what they claim to be. If they are suffering from a mental illness, there might be cycles, say, cycles of delusion. If that were the case, then any one of them could betray the others at any time," speculated Nathan.

"Doubtful," Father Dougherty responded. "We have done several psychological analyses of the group, and such behavior would be entirely inconsistent with our findings."

I was certain that Harold also wished to speak to Nathan's suggestion, for he sat up stiffly. "Here we agree," entered Harold, sliding to the edge of the couch, taking my hand.

(He holds my hands often now. This is something that he has not done since we dated. The gesture is more than one of fear or need. When he touches me now, I feel his gratitude; I feel companionship; I sense his strength there for me; and, most of all, I feel love. I apologize for this personal digression, but it is important, at least to me.)

In any event, Harold is still Harold, and he persisted in his argument, stating, "Their illness, if that is what they have, radically affects the victim's ability to live in either the past or the future. When these people admonish us to live with them in the now, I think they know and mean exactly of what it is they speak. Whether or not that is healthy, I have not yet decided. Whether or not it means immortality, I do not yet know. What I do know, because I see it, is that this Quindilar does not share in the pattern. That much became very clear while listening to him speak yesterday. Hell, he's busy trying to make his mark in the realm of theology. He wants to be—not that he has a prayer, or the brains—but he'd like to be the next Aquinas. He is a defender of the Faith. Immortals, as far as I can tell, have no faith to defend, except that which they have in themselves."

"That is less obvious," objected Father Dougherty.

"Perhaps to you," replied Harold. "I don't mean to be rude to you or to Agent Johnson, but you have your different faiths, and they mean a great deal to you. Faith influences your lives. I certainly do not mean to question the strength that your faiths instill in you or the inherent value of leading a life of devotion to … certain theological perspectives. Whatever else it is that they accomplish with the people they persuade and trust, they bring about a radical examination of the beliefs held by those persons. Elijah did it to me. I cannot imagine that one of the members of your Order has not so challenged you, Father."

"Admittedly, they have," Father Dougherty answered candidly. He sat back in his chair.

"So maybe it's Quindilar. I'll keep the wraps on him today. Anybody else?" asked Nathan.

No one spoke for a moment. Then Father Jerome Dougherty said, not without regret, "Sometimes I wonder about Sister Maria."

"Why?" asked Nathan.

"I don't know. It is only a feeling. It just seems that over the years, she has grown older … more quickly than the others."

"Okay. Judy. Can you watch her? Try to catch any telephone conversations she has today."

"I will do it," I replied.

"They're probably all getting antsy waiting for us in the van, so I have one more question, then we're out of here: What do you think about this Chaco business? Do you really think that's where we're headed?" asked Nathan. "You expressed doubt before, so let's here from you first, Professor Weintraub."

"Yes. As I did mention earlier, I have serious reservations about the immortals choosing Chaco as our terminus. I believe that the harmonic convergences are purely a ruse. Miriam almost admitted as much. Was it yesterday? My illness … sometimes I can't remember. I do apologize. And it is most depressing. In any case, I think these events and their recurrences were created to put their pursuers on the wrong track. I think Chaco falls into the same category. I doubt that any of the Stonehenge type of solstitial alignments, which, as Father Jerome mentioned, were built at this place, have any meaning to the immortals—metaphysical or otherwise."

"How does this fit in with your idea of 'living in the now'?" asked Father Dougherty. "If Miriam is, as she openly claims, Plutonion, then her actions in planning this gimmick, the 'ruse,' as you call it, would not be those of an immortal, for she would clearly be thinking and acting to bring about a future event."

"Good question, and well stated," Harold replied. "I am not certain how to respond to it. Except to tell you that the immortals know the minds of their enemies only as a present moment. Changing the mind of a mortal is a series of steps in changing the present. Thus it appears to us, to mortals, as if the immortals are planning ahead. When in fact, they are just slowly making us look away, from one instant to the next. Miriam, Plutonion, was not concerned about changing her future; she has no belief in the reality of a harmonic convergence. She was, moment by moment, changing the beliefs of others. They were the ones who projected her myth into the future. That is my answer. I know it is insufficient."

"So why not Chaco?" Nathan repeated his question.

"Because," I joined the conversation, following my husband's lead, "if these people really are at peace within, immortal or not, at this point in time they are looking for safety, for a harbor, so that their peace can continue. Unlike most of the rest of us, they do not need a quick fix for the problems in their lives: an alignment of the planets, a harmonic convergence, a visitation by celestial beings, a chance to spot Elvis Presley at a shopping mall. They don't need it. They believe that they are already whole. Also, unlike the rest of us, they are, so it seems, being stalked and killed. What they need is a place to be left alone, a refuge. I don't know if Chaco offers that or not."

"Okay. We gotta get going. I think there is enough agreement here so that we can figure out a plan of action for today. I want each of you, me included, to try to catch the drift of their telephone conversations. I noticed yesterday that when I walked by them, as they were speaking on the phone, they seemed oblivious to my presence. I'll need you to pay close attention to what is said today, and by whom. Let's meet again early this evening, just the four of us, and try to figure out whether these speculations of ours have any truth to them at. Agreed?"

We all said yes.

My hand is tired and unsteady, for I am typing this as we travel along this afternoon. I know that Father Dougherty is keeping track as well. So I will close for now and remain
Sincerely your friend,
[Signed]
Judy

P.S.
I remembered one more thing I needed to say, a personal note about Harold. I don't think I have told you this. His face is becoming quite thin. This is most worrisome to me. He has always been strong and stout. His weakened condition is most distressing to me. I know I have said this before, but I will say it again: he requires medical attention *soon*.

J.W.

> But these immortal atmans are subject to beginningless karma, and are, for this reason, created conjointly with bodies that are determined by their various karmas. By means of these bodies the atmans perform acts that are prescribed by the sastras to each station and stage of life, not for the sake of the results of their acts but to be released from their bondage to these bodies.
>
> —Ramanuja, *Commentary on the Bhagavad-Gita*

Excerpts from the Journal of Father Jerome Dougherty

En route from Albuquerque, New Mexico, to Shiprock, New Mexico. Late evening, June 4. As noted, we had been forewarned in our morning meeting with Nathan to keep our eyes and ears on the members of our party as they made their telephone calls throughout this day. Nevertheless, our pattern of travel was much the same as yesterday. The only exception was that Nathan allowed the members of the group less time for their telephone calls. Judy, Harold, Nathan, and I attempted to monitor all of the conversations. We drove almost nonstop, pushing very hard (and *very* fast) to cover as much distance as possible in this day. We passed through a bit of western Oklahoma and all of northern Texas during the day. The earth, even the desert, was fresh and alive with the new growth of spring—sparse though the vegetation often was through the vast stretches of flat rock and sand. The air was pleasantly warm and rich with the smell of earth and life. It was truly a magnificent day; at times we drove with the windows down.

At every stop, Nathan, when he was not making telephone calls of his own, stuck very close to Father Quindilar. For the record, I was not certain that this was necessary. Even after the events of this evening, I am still confused. Professor Weintraub's speculations on who is or is not a faithful member of the Order seem flimsy to me. I must admit that my own suspicion of Sister Maria is almost as groundless. Though I did not mention it this morning, I often suspect that Mr. Tie is not all that he appears to be. Though I do not know her well, I also wonder about Miriam. In fact, unless one assumes that these people are, in reality, immortal, many of their claims seem, at one time or another, ludicrous.

There was, however, a noticeable difference in the telephone presentations made by the various immortals to their compatriots. Late this afternoon, about two or three hours east of Albuquerque, we stopped in a small desert town called Tucumcari. After loading the immortals back into the van, Judy, Harold, Nathan, and I met outside to discuss our findings—our meddlings.

"What's the scoop?" Nathan asked. "Judy, my recorder's dead. I gotta put in some new batteries. Can you make sure yours is running? Let's get this conversation on tape if we can." His tired eyes turned to each of us for answers and, if I am not mistaken, for strength. He had driven through most of the night, spelled occasionally by me and once, for about an hour, by Judy.

We stood in front of the glass garage doors of a service station on the main street of Tucumcari. There was little traffic, and we were the only customers at the station. A thin young man with long greasy hair and oil-stained coveralls filled the tank with gasoline while we spoke unhindered. Loud music, "trash music"—or perhaps it is called "thrash music"—blasted from a boom box the lad had playing in the office. As I indicated, the immortals had already had their turns at the telephone and in the restroom. Nathan had promised them that we would stop in Albuquerque for dinner.

"I think it's already going," Judy answered, discreetly lifting her white blouse to inspect the tiny recording device. "I've been listening to Mr. Tie and to Miriam. Yes. It's still running." She lowered her blouse and tucked it back into her dark blue pants. "They are not directing their associates to go directly to Chaco—although they are telling them that Chaco is the final destination. Rather, they are having them meet first in Mexican Water, Arizona. They promise more explicit instructions once they have made it there."

"Fascinating," responded her husband. "Father Dobo keeps mentioning to his associates, whoever they may be, that they must first see John, then they are to proceed to Chaco as instructed by John." (I should probably add that Harold has weathered this day rather well—though his skin is very jaundiced, at times taking on an almost green hue. He even offered to drive once, early this morning, but, of course, we would not even consider it.)

"That is not making sense to me," Nathan said. "Quindilar is pushing his people to move directly to Chaco. He wants them there as soon as possible. Who is this John?"

"I can answer—partially," I replied. "Father Holden is giving his telephone confidants the same instructions as is Father Dobo. Apparently, there really is a man named John who is scheduling the movements of at least some of the other immortals."

"You think it's the same John that my family is supposed to meet?"

"That is the logical conclusion," answered Professor Weintraub. Judy and I agreed.

"So, in effect, we have some groups traveling a roundabout route and some heading directly to Chaco?" asked Nathan.

"That is correct. Sister Maria spent some time trying to convince Father Holden to divulge the location of this man John to her. I think she was unsuccessful," stated Harold. "But she is telling those with whom she speaks to maintain their pace—but to be ready to leave for Chaco."

"Where are her people now?" Nathan asked.

"They are in Utah, in the Valley of the Gods. Sister Maria had placed her money on Plutonion," said the Professor.

"Where is John?" asked Nathan.

"I don't know," Harold answered.

"Neither do I," said Judy.

I sneezed, excused myself, and then answered, "I am not certain. Though I do know that Father Holden directed someone he was speaking with to go to Mexican Hat, Utah, until further instructions from John."

"It's almost like a code, then? One group to Mexican Water in Arizona, another to Mexican Hat in Utah. Look at the map," Nathan told us. He held his atlas against the dirty glass of the garage door for us to view. "The two people who are at least somewhat suspect are ordering their parties here, directly to Chaco, or holding them in place but ready for Chaco. All of the others are keeping their parties moving north and west of Chaco. Within easy reach of either here, Sedona, or, here, the Valley of the Gods, or Chaco, or some other destination. Whoever is running this show is keeping everyone guessing until the very end."

Harold coughed but held up his hand to reserve the next comment for himself. When he was able, he said, "If it is the case that those who threaten the safety of the group are being directed to Chaco, then the other members of the party are buying time—perhaps for a final dash to a refuge undisclosed to anyone."

"Perhaps to a destination yet unknown," added his wife.

"Okay. Good work, you guys, excuse me—you too, Judy. Let's get back on the road and see how this plays out," Nathan concluded.

We ate dinner at a buffet-type restaurant in Albuquerque. After our meal, several members of the party made another rash of telephone calls.

None of them appear secretive in their conversations. Except this time it was clear that at least Father Holden and Father Dobo were speaking in some type of code, for they were telling their contacts to meet John at the "revival house" for final instructions before proceeding to the destination.

Let me preface what happened next with a description of our places in the van. (This event transpired after we had finished our dinner and our telephone calls.) Judy and Harold were on the back bench, Harold's head on Judy's lap. In the middle bench sat Father Dobo, Sister Maria, and Father Quindilar, who sat to the inside or on the driver's side—that is, away from the sliding side door. In the front bench, squeezed together, were Father Holden, Miriam, Mr. Tie, and Father Hugo. I was in the rider's seat in the cab. Nathan was kneeling in the doorway between the cab and the "box," as we are beginning to call it, or the rear of the van, and facing the benches. I was listening to the conversation and looking over Nathan's shoulder at the others. The round plastic lamp on the top of the middle of the "box" was on. The unremitting travel is wearing everyone down. The faces I saw were all weary.

After scanning the faces of our party for a moment, Nathan fixed his eyes on Father Holden and asked, "Okay, when do I call my family? They've been waiting all day. We're running out of time."

"I thought that you understood? You cannot call them. However, if you agree to one condition," stated Father Holden, "then the message can be given soon, and we should be able to meet with them in less than three hours."

The next event happened with such speed and ferocity that only then did I realize exactly how powerful, how deadly, how desperate—and, I hesitate to say it, but perhaps how unsteady a man Agent Johnson is—or has become. He moved with such swiftness that I did not even see him remove the gun from his shoulder holster. He grabbed poor Father Holden and slammed him against the inside of the sliding door on the side of the van. Nathan held a very large silvery pistol against Father Holden's chin; the barrel of which forced his head upward in a dreadfully frightening and, physically speaking, uncomfortable manner.

"We're talking about the lives of my wife and kids. You're not setting one more fucking condition. Because, I tell you what—I'll tell you all what," Nathan pulled the gun away from Father Holden's chin and waved it at the others in the rear of the van. "If anything, anything at all, happens to any one of my family, I'll throw you all to the wolves out there tracking us."

"Agent Johnson, please," Father Hugo pleaded from the front bench, "I think you're forgetting the agreement we made earlier today. As I recall, Father Holden quite specifically stated that you might not be able to contact them. It is for their safety, not ours, that we asked you to give us this leeway. We've tried, we have diligently tried to arrange all the various schedules to allow you to make this call to your family, but it hasn't worked out. I can explain. Please release my friend. Please."

"All right, get back on the bench," Nathan ordered a disheveled Father Holden. "Tell me what's going on. Tell me why I can't call my family." Nathan squatted on his haunches in the doorway, his gun resting on his thigh.

Father Holden took his place on the bench, straightened his clothing, and answered, "I will put it concisely for you. Not even you can know the next part of our journey—for you would be tempted to pass the information along to your SWAT team. To tell you the truth, no one can guarantee that they are any longer on our side. They may have explicit orders to kill us."

"They would never do it, not in a million years," Nathan flatly stated.

"Perhaps not. Even then, your message could be intercepted or relayed. Certainly not every member of the FBI is your friend. Clearly your government, as a whole, is positioned against us. That is all that is meant." Father Holden had caught both his breath and his composure with amazing quickness.

"Okay. Let's assume that you're correct …" Nathan began, but was interrupted by Father Quindilar.

"I have another offer … I mean a suggestion," Father Quindilar began. "I believe that we should notify everyone concerned to travel, with all speed, to the place called Chaco, to the destination announced by Father Holden. Right now. Let us make the telephone calls. We are within an hour of this place. Your family cannot be much greater, much farther away. I am sorry, my English is poor when I speak quickly. We could meet them there much more soon than the three hours Father Holden speaks of. We have too many of these secrets. We move quickly to the last place. Then all will be together. Then they be safe."

"Father Quindilar, that is totally out of the question," Father Hugo said, turning around to look at him over the top of the bench. When Father Hugo turned back to Nathan, his face was red. It is hard to believe this, harder to say it, but I believe that his face was red with anger.

"Wait. I want to consider all options. Why do you think that would be safer?" Nathan asked Father Quindilar.

"It is simple for me to tell you why. Your family would be already traveled then. It would be our last communication with them until we reached our destination with everyone. There would be no more ... there would be less chance of someone finding them," Father Quindilar replied.

"Who in the Vatican sent you?" Father Dobo asked Father Quindilar. Like Father Hugo, Father Dobo was visibly upset.

"Padre Dobo, por favor!" Sister Maria pleaded.

"No one. Never. How dare you challenge my integrity," Father Quindilar exclaimed in anger.

"Peace. Please. Let us have peace," Mr. Tie joined. "It may be that Father Quindilar has a point. We know that we are being followed. We know that the dangers are many. There must come a time when we simply push forward to the destination. Father Quindilar believes that the time is now. Father Holden, what say you in response?"

"We cannot go without John. He is depending upon us. Father Quindilar seems to be suggesting that we leave one of our own behind," answered Father Holden.

"Nonsense," replied Father Quindilar. "Others coming on their own. We can notify him—and the others. We can tell all to go their way with very fast speed. Which would be more safe for your family? To move again and travel on the word of a stranger—or to meet with us in only an hour?" he asked Nathan.

"Maybe Father Quindilar has a point worth considering," Nathan carefully answered—drawing out his words.

"Let us make the calls now," Father Quindilar stood.

"This is absurd," Miriam said entering the argument for the first time. "Father Quindilar asserts, *mutatis mutandis*, what he must know is not so, not yet. Look at the now. There are several who need to learn through John—who can only find out through John where we are going. John cannot leave. We who are familiar with him know that he *will not* leave until his task is finished. Each has a role to play. Father Quindilar, I want to know why you have suddenly stopped playing yours."

"I am not worried for me, myself—only for Nathan's family," replied Father Quindilar.

"Qui s'excuse, s'accuse," Father Dobo said vehemently.

"I am sending those whom I have told directly to Chaco," Father Quindilar stated. "It is all of you who drag this out."

"Those you call, I have called as well. They are specifically admonished to ignore everything you tell them," said Father Holden. "No one, no immortal, has yet been sent to Chaco. They have gone to John, who has told them the destination."

"Father Dougherty, it's getting chilly. Will you start the motor and turn on the heater? Then stick your head back here. I want to ask you and the Weintraubs a question," Nathan requested.

I did as asked. Then I inquired of Nathan, "What is it?"

"Which of these alternatives do you think is reliable? Which do you trust?"

"Perhaps we should discuss this privately," I suggested, but Nathan shook his head.

"Let's do this like the immortals do it. Right now. Right here. It's time to decide."

"May I make a suggestion?" asked Professor Weintraub, who had sat up. His face was very pale—even under the dim lights of the van.

"Shoot," said Nathan.

"First, find out what the condition is that Father Holden mentioned at the beginning of this turgid conversation," Harold said. His voice was weak, and it was difficult to make out the words over the engine noise.

"Say again," Nathan asked, because he too found Harold's voice difficult to hear. Judy repeated Harold's proposition.

"Father Holden? Will you tell us?" Nathan followed up Harold's suggestion.

"Gladly. The condition is elementary," Father Holden said placidly, pushing back his hair. "At the appointed time and place—which, if all else is going well, I assure you is quite near—I will discuss it with John and then will be able to announce the location where we are to meet him and your family. Do you understand? I will make the call to John. John will tell us after he has advised your family of his next location. *At that time*, we will share the information with everyone in the group. That way nothing is hidden from the members of this party, which is how it has always been. On the other hand, once we are on the road, we shall travel directly to meet with John and your family. Even if someone chooses to share the location with our enemies—we will be in such close proximity to your family that it should not matter."

"I have one more question for Father Holden," said Professor Weintraub.

"Speak up, if you can," requested Nathan.

"One more question for Father Holden," repeated Judy.

"I will answer it truthfully," Father Holden replied.

"Which route will we follow—if we choose your alternative?" asked Harold.

"I would like next to stop in Shiprock, New Mexico. A town that is northwest of here," Father Holden answered.

"I'm sorry, Father Quindilar," Nathan began, "but the fact is that any number of people could be waiting for us at Chaco. Many of them unfriendly. Northwest takes me towards my family—not away from them."

"But ..." Father Quindilar began to object.

"I think you have your answer," Professor Weintraub said firmly.

"I must agree," I stated.

Judy Weintraub added her concurrence.

"When will you make the call?" Nathan asked Father Holden.

"In two and a half hours, if you hurry. I'll make the telephone call from Shiprock—we will all make our calls from Shiprock—then, my friends, the race shall be on."

On the Author's Travels with Sylvia Johnson and Her Children, June 4 to June 5, Continued

The kids were up early. I had told Sylvia, the night before, to send them to my room for breakfast so that she could sleep in. But, my God, the fidgety, somehow completely rested miniature monsters were up at 6:00—that's AM—and pounding on my door by 6:02.

Kaylynn had given me a new name, *Uncle Vomit*. I didn't think it was all that amusing. Nor did it enhance the dining pleasure of those sitting around us at the greasy little café, across the street from our motel, where we ate breakfast fifteen minutes later. "Please pass the syrup, Uncle Vomit," Kaylynn hollered. The other two kids burst out laughing. "Pass the butter, Uncle Vomit," giggled Sherry. Jeremy turned it into a little breakfast sing-along. *"Do-ditty.* Dumb Unco Vomit!"

The customers sitting in the booths and at the counter near us looked either a little scared—or a lot queasy. Some stared at me in horror, as if I were a dormant volcano rearing to regurgitate. Given the fact that I had gotten maybe three hours of sleep that night, was pale as a ghost, hadn't shaved, and hadn't changed clothes for a couple of days, those sitting around us and trying to eat had plenty of reasons to be on edge. Since many of the customers at this particular time of the day were burly, burned-out truck drivers, I had reasons to be apprehensive.

"Shut up! Shut up! Don't call me that anymore, or I'll drag you out of here by your hair!" I said emphatically—but under my breath.

"Do-ditty, dumb Unco Vomit!"

"Shut up, goddamn it! That's it, we're leaving right now!" I grabbed Sherry by the arm—she was closest.

Apparently these kids did not get grabbed by the arm very often. There was instant silence at our table, broken only by Sherry's sniffling. The twist of an arm, combined with the threat of ending a breakfast that had only just arrived, subdued them for a while. It would, however, be mid-morning before they ceased using the appellation and "Uncle Vomit" was eliminated (once Sylvia put her foot down) from their list of nicknames for me.

We took the long way back to the motel after breakfast. I figured it would give Sylvia a little more time to rest—and maybe burn off some of the quantum amounts of energy in the bodies of the little beasts.

I should not call them either beasts or monsters. Sylvia's children were generally well-behaved and courteous. My problem was that I was seeing them at their worst. It is not easy for an adult to live out of a car and motels night after night. I am certain that is was much tougher on the kids. I bought them some cheap toys at a convenience store that was open at eight in the morning. We walked around some more, and by quarter to nine we were back at the motel.

I let them stay in my room, play with their toys, and watch cartoons until they started to get hungry again, which was at about eleven. That is when I left the room, walked outside, and knocked on the door to Sylvia's room.

"Just a sec," she shouted from far inside. I could hear the shower running. "One sec. Is that you?"

"It's me," I answered.

"One sec. How are the kids?" she shouted.

"Still alive. Starting to get hungry again," I yelled back.

"Be right there," she laughed.

The door opened. Sylvia was soaking wet, wrapped in two white towels. She had wrapped one towel around her lower body like a skirt and was holding another over her chest. She held the latter in place with her right hand and locked the towel beneath her left armpit. Her hair was black when wet. Black and straight, it stuck to the side of her neck and to her back, though I only imagined the latter. Her face was more defined because there was no distraction by the outline of fluffed hair. She was beautiful. Her face was well-proportioned, balanced well enough that my eyes took it in as a whole. High cheekbones, small straight nose, and high arched brows, plucked thin. Her chin was slightly too pointed. Other than that, though, she was simply beautiful. I stared.

"Thanks for taking care of them," she said softly—as if not to interrupt my concentration on her face.

"Sure."

"Thanks for everything," she said.

I dropped my eyes to her shoulders. It was an intrusion she would not allow. She immediately pulled the towel further up and tighter, all the way to her neck. "You can send them back over," she said.

"Yeah," I raised my eyes. She was smiling. It was one of those condescending smiles that women give to men when we are being driven hormonally. "I'll kick them out. When do you want lunch?" I asked her—eye to eye.

"Half an hour? I want to be back here soon to wait for Nathan's message."

"I'll hurry up and shower and change," I told her.

"Tell the children to just come on in. I'll leave the door cracked."

"Okay," I said. I left for my room and did as discussed.

Starting at about three, Sylvia and I took turns waiting in the motel lobby for the message and taking care of the kids. She did offer me an hour and a half for a nap at about six, right after dinner. I took it. We were both disconcerted because Nathan had left us not knowing exactly how the message would arrive or who would deliver it. As the evening drew on, this disquietude became more and more unsettling.

By ten o'clock that evening, I sent Sylvia back to her room and told her to try to get some sleep. I had bedded her children down at nine. "Look, if this message comes in real late, you may have to drive, at least part of the way. You'd better sleep while you can." She grudgingly obeyed and left for her children and her motel room.

I waited alone in the small lobby that also served as the registration and reception area. The clerk, a Vietnamese immigrant who smiled all the time and had not understood a thing we had told him all evening, hung up the 'Ring Bell' sign in the window of the door at 11:00 PM. I had tried to explain to him that I was waiting for a message. He smiled and nodded and attempted to remove me from the lobby.

"I must wait here for a message," I told him. The little man tried to push me out of the door.

"Yes, yes, you wrait fol mressage, now good night."

"The message is coming here," I pointed at the telephone on his desk.

"Terephlone not fol guest. Terephlone at Cilcrl Kray," he said, and pointed at the telephone booth on the front of the Circle K kitty-corner from the motel.

"I'll wait here for the telephone to ring, ring, ring," I said slowly, pointing first at one of only two chairs outside the registration counter and then at the telephone on the small desk behind it. I sat down and put my hand to my ear, pointed at the telephone with the other, to make my point clear.

"Oh, you wrait for ling, ling?"

"Yes. I'm waiting for *that* telephone." I was still pointing.

"Okay. I go to bed. You be sul rock the dool when you reave?"

"Yes. I promise," I said, and demonstrated my door-locking ability for him.

"Okay. You be shul and rock the dool and good night."

"Thanks. Thanks a lot. Good night."

The call came at about 1:00 AM, so the date was now June 5. I had been reading *Wired* magazine, trying to stay awake. I had bought the magazine the previous morning while walking around with the kids. The first ring brought me straight up in the chair. I got to the phone, reaching over the counter to the desk, just as the second ring started.

"Frontier Motel," I said into the telephone.

"That car for you?" yawned the manager from behind the curtain that hid his small apartment.

"Frontier Motel. Can I help you?" I asked again.

"I need to speak with Sylvia Johnson," said a stranger's voice.

"Yeah. It's for me," I quickly answered the motel manager, cupping the transmitter with my free hand.

"She is unable to come to the telephone right now. Can I take a message for her?" I tried to keep my voice unruffled.

"Hello, my name is John. I am calling for Sylvia Johnson. I have a message for her. Are you certain she cannot come to the telephone?"

"Yes. She's asleep. But I'm wearing a turtleneck. I'll get the message to her," I said, using the code word Nathan had mentioned.

"Oh, yes, the turtleneck. Fine. Tell her that John called. Tell her to proceed immediately to Aneth, Utah. From there, she is to turn south on Highway 262. About five miles southwest of town, on the west side of the road, is a retreat. There will be a sign that says, 'First Fundamentalist Baptist Retreat and Revival Center.' I will meet her at the first cottage unit at the north end. If I am not there, wait one half hour, then you are to do whatever it is that you would have done had we not spoken. Do you have the message?" The voice spoke excellent English—though, if pressed, I would have guessed that the speaker was not an American. He was too expansive and precise in all of his vocalizations. He sounded like a Greek nobleman schooled in America. His voice was extremely kind and soothing; yet it was neither quiet nor passive. He seemed to speak with inner strength and peace.

"Is that everything?" I asked him.

"Yes. Except tell her to get here quickly. Everything seems to be happening with much rapidity. I am also told that her husband is most eager to see her."

"You're sure that you've said everything?" I asked him. "I mean that's the whole message?"

"Yes. Quite certain. The details are consequential. Please be so kind as to repeat it back to me."

I had already written it down, so I repeated it back. He made a couple of clarifications in the process. "You sure you've told me everything I need to know? Last chance," I said.

"Yes. That is everything. Now, can you get her the message ... wait. I almost forgot. Thank you. Yes. Yes. You are, of course, instructed to come 'piggyback'—whatever that may mean," the voice said with relief. "I almost forgot."

"Okay, John. Sounds like you're the man. How long does it take to get to you from here in Cortez?" I asked.

"As I explained, take the road that goes west, by the airport, just a few miles south of town. It is gravel most of the way, but it is the shortest and quickest route. You should be here in less than two hours."

"How will I know you?"

"You will know. I ... my face has been scarred by fire."

"Sorry to hear that," I said.

"It is healing."

"Is Nathan headed there?"

"I am not at liberty to say any more. In any event, I am not certain. Drive carefully. I will see you soon," the voice said. He hung up the phone.

I replaced the handset and started for the exit. "Be sul rock dool when reave," the manager said sleepily from behind the curtain.

We drove again through the night, through the high desert plain. The air was sweeter than it had been the night before. The children slept soundly on the makeshift pads on the metal floor of the van, even though the gravel road west from Cortez was coarse and bumpy. The major difference tonight was that both Sylvia and I were wide-awake—and that we were both anxious about finally meeting Nathan.

There was only one event of consequence that occurred between Cortez, Colorado, and the Native American village of Aneth, Utah, which we reached at about three fifteen in the morning. About halfway between the two towns, the van I was driving hit and killed a jackrabbit. It stood frozen by the beam of our headlight in the middle of the road as we sped along through the gravel, the dust, and the night. Its body thumped and banged the bottom of the van several times as it was pounded back and forth between the road and the underside of the vehicle.

"What was that?" Kaylynn asked, suddenly awakened by the blows from the flailing carcass.

"Nothing," her mother assured her, "only a bump. Go back to sleep, honey, just a little while, and Daddy will be there."

Intoxicating the ale of Inis Fail; more intoxicating by far that of Tir Mar.

A wonderful land that I describe: Youth does not precede age.

Warm sweet streams throughout the land, your choice of mead and wine.

A distinguished people without blemish, conceived without sin or crime.

We see everyone everywhere, and no one sees us: The darkness of Adam's sin prevents our being discerned.
> —The Wooing of Ètaìn (an Irish myth)

A man's enemies are the men of his own house.
> —Micah 7:6

Author's Note. Followed by Excerpts from a Letter from Dr. Judy Weintraub to the Author. (This letter is dated August 2, but describes the events of June 5.) Followed by Excerpts from the Journal of Father Jerome Dougherty

The developments that took place during the last twelve hours of the existence of the Order of the Beloved, the events that make up the remainder of this manuscript, are arduous and troublesome for me to relate. I mean this from both professional and personal perspectives.

First, I must say that it is difficult for me even to admit this weakness, this sense that I have of my inability to present an unbiased and accurate conclusion of these events. To put it bluntly, I despise writers who apologize in their work for becoming too involved with an issue or a situation to be impartial and then go on to give a personal or an "emotionally insightful" account—and call it 'art' instead. That isn't truth; it isn't art. My response to such immaturity is to advise them, as Professor Weintraub once told me, to "Get a grip." A good writer should know when to leap into the fray of feelings—and when to keep a safe distance between himself or herself and the incident under objective examination. I want to be able to aver that in this particular case, over those twelve hours, it was impossible for me to follow my own advice. But I know and here admit that such an assertion is a lie or, at the very least, partially untrue.

I wanted to say all that and not sound like a bad translation of Serenus Zeitblom—who, page after page, in his most famous work, vouches for his capacity (within the same pages that he apologizes for his incapacity) to sustain his veracity under enormous personal, political, and psychological pressures, until credibility fades into unbelievability. I do not think that I succeeded.

What is true, unfortunately, necessarily, historically, hence *eternally* true, is that the records kept by the others of their own participation in the calamity, if a calamity is what occurred, and even that is uncertain, were reduced by circumstances to almost nothing. To state it succinctly, Father Dougherty, Nathan, and the Weintraubs were too occupied during these critical hours with the business of staying alive to jot down their daily data and their recurrent routines and any odd or casual happenstance.

Thus I must rely heavily on extrinsic sources in delineating these final hours. Nathan and Judy did continue to make recordings, using both of their body wires as well as the digital recording machine in the van. I have in my possession six full or partially recorded tapes, plus conversations in digital format, that Nathan and Judy captured during this time.

Involved as she was with the care of her husband at several crucial moments, Dr. Weintraub's testimony is of only limited value in reconstructing many of the material events of the last hours. She realizes this and has shared her justifications and apologies with me. Most graciously, about two months after these final hours, she sent me a detailed letter describing her account of the events. Her letter has proven most useful. and portions of it are reproduced, as noted, in several sections below.

For reasons that will soon become apparent, Father Dougherty changed his style of writing for the last entry of his journal. I believe that he did this because, consciously or not, he had made a decision to alter his life radically. These entries are, however, of special importance, and certain portions will be included in the account that follows.

There are also a few, very few, rough notes made by Nathan—all of them voice recordings. It appears to me that he attempted on two occasions to record information to aid in the composition of future reports to his superiors in the FBI. Unfortunately, those reports were never completed.

Finally, there is my own participation in and my own observations of this episode. Much of it was after the fact; some of it was tainted; some of it was ... regrettable. Nevertheless, my role in these events is also as agent and cause, no matter how insignificant. As painful and disparaging as my part turned out to be, I have diligently attempted to make it a ground for truth in writing and in editing the account of the final hours of the Order of the Beloved that follows.

* * * *

Excerpts from a letter from Dr. Judy Weintraub

With these things in mind, I have provided you with the following details of our last few hours together—to be specific, the morning of June 5:

After our stop at a service station in Shiprock, New Mexico (it was brief), it became clear to everyone, if it was not already, what was going on. The situation had been exactly what it had appeared to be—a simple game of cat and mouse. The announcement by Father Holden that we would meet Nathan's family in a "revival center" just outside Aneth, Utah, sent everyone scrambling for the two telephones. Nathan made certain that Father Holden got his call off first. He allowed Miriam to go second, Father Hugo third, Father Dobo next, Sister Maria fifth, Mr. Tie (spelled, if I remember correctly, T'i) sixth, and Quindilar last. I assume, looking back on the matter, that this is the order of trust he placed in these people.

Holden spoke with the man John, who was coordinating the movement of Nathan's family and perhaps of many of the immortals we had not yet met, for several minutes. Each of the other members of our party was then given two minutes to make their call. These conversations were simple. All of them consisted of the caller telling their affiliate that our next destination would be south of Aneth, Utah—that and nothing more.

Were those affiliates friend or foe? I had no way of knowing, either then or now. I did finally understand how the immortals were able to move about in relative safety; they had always kept everyone guessing about their next destination; that time and that ability had now come to an end.

During a part of these conversations, Nathan left Father Dougherty in charge of monitoring the group. Then Nathan pulled me around to the side of the building.

"I need to ask you a favor." Nathan spoke quickly to me, glancing to his left and right to make certain that we were alone. I asked him what it was. "I need someone to back me up, to carry a weapon. Father Dougherty won't, and your husband can't. I need someone—someone they would not suspect. Will you do it?"

"I've practiced with my son at the range in Brookline."

"Pistol?"

"I keep a .38 special in my nightstand. Harold despises the thing."

"Amazing. Great. That's just what I have for you. A little Colt, snub-nose, five shot, .38 special revolver. Stick it in your purse."

"I must tell you that I don't think I could ever shoot a human being," I forewarned him.

"Just fire it over their heads. That'll freeze 'em. I might need some control if one of these people turns on us. It would serve notice. It might give me a chance to react. Oh, but don't fire it inside the van—unless you do intend to shoot someone. The bullet would go bouncing around the armor plating like a little pinball from hell."

He handed me the weapon. It was small and heavy. I shifted it in my hands. I flipped open and examined the revolver's magazine. The pistol was loaded. "It's just like the one at my house," I told him. I flipped shut the magazine and put the pistol in my purse. Nathan smiled at me. I forgot to give the pistol back to him, so I have it with me. To this day, it is a grim little memento.

To continue with the story, Nathan and I hurried back to the front of the service station. Nathan quickly loaded us into the refueled van, and we set off traveling west on Highway 504. I remember checking my watch. The time was approximately 1:15 AM.

As soon as we were in the van and moving, Father Holden made his way to the front of the van and presented us with another announcement. As always, he straightened his hair as a prelude to his address. "I now know how we will be told our *actual* destination," he said with a smile.

"Not Chaco, is it?" Nathan yelled from the driver's seat. "Everybody talk real loud so I can hear," he commanded. Though I did not get to the cab to view the speedometer, I would guess that we were going at least ninety miles per hour.

"Not Chaco," Father Holden replied to Nathan; then he turned to face those of us sitting in the box.

Harold and I occupied the rear seat again. He was half asleep on my lap, struggling to stay awake, to play a part. His forehead was feverish, his skin a pale, unnatural yellowish green. But I would have to say that, by this time, his overall health had improved slightly.

"I would wager that half of the FBI's most-wanted list is huddled out in the Chaco desert right now," laughed Father Hugo from the seat directly in front of us.

"Louder," shouted Nathan.

"I said, the bad guys are two hours behind us," Father Hugo loudly proclaimed.

"Yeah, at least most of them," Nathan yelled back. "So where are we going?"

"John knows. John is directing everyone; from now on we shall follow his order. The people are moving, as directed, to the destination. He will tell us as soon as we arrive," answered Father Holden. He was having trouble keeping his balance around some of the corners that Nathan was taking, so he braced his arms in the doorway to the cab to keep from falling.

Father Dobo, who sat in the front row, spoke next. "John is the axis through which all must pass to reach their objective. Someone had to be it. John has always been so loving in his service. Thus it has been for a long time."

"Yeah, well, then that means the bad guys are gonna try to pass through that axis too," said Nathan.

"Yeah, the bad guys too." Father Hugo imitated Nathan. "Fortunately, the bad guys are hours away. We will be … home long before they arrive."

"I sure hope you're right. Because you've had us all fooled—the good guys are a hell of a long way off too," Nathan said.

"The reason we did it our way is because, in reality, there is no good or bad," said Mr. Tie. "There only *is*. So drive quickly, Agent Johnson, and no blood will be shed. Oh, my friends! What joy and what relief! I think we have done it! I sincerely think we have! Think about what we are about to accomplish. There are only a handful of us, twenty-five that we know of. There are almost no similarities between us. We are different races, creeds, classes, and, most important, we were born at vastly different intervals. We have all thought about this: There is no pattern to immortality. Yet now, finally, we shall all be together. To learn. To teach." Mr. Tie was also sitting in front of us on the middle bench. Mr. Tie hugged Father Hugo. He hugged Sister Maria. He turned around and hugged me. Mr. Tie was so happy that he wept.

* * * *

Excerpts from the Journal of Father Jerome Dougherty

En route to Taos, New Mexico. Early morning, June 5.

[Father Dougherty was, before this point in the journal, addressing this author.]

So it is for you, my love for you, that I will finish what I can. I will relate this early morning's tragedy, and the decision I made later this morning, and then I must put this journal away—forever. Understand that I am nearly finished, nearly home. Within minutes, I will come face-to-face with my Lord and Savior. There is no more need, no more desire, to preserve myself in this journal. I am whole. I am home. It is nearly finished.

As for the events of last evening and very early this morning, Nathan drove at breakneck speeds to the location where we were to meet John. We drove east on Highway 160 through Four Corners, then turned north on Highway 41 and drove a few miles through Colorado until we entered Utah on Highway 262. The road, especially in Utah, went up and down many small hills and curved through ravines. The night was particularly dark, with only a sliver of a moon. I sat in the cab with Nathan, my seat belt strapped tight around my waist. At times we were traveling at speeds in excess of a hundred miles an hour, and it was frightening—to say the least. Everyone in the box sat in their seats and held on tight to the armrests to keep from being tossed out of them. We went from Shiprock to the so-called Revival Center in just over an hour, arriving at about 2:15 AM.

The "First Fundamentalist Baptist Retreat and Revival Center" is merely a series of eight connected white cinderblock cottages, with a trailer house at the north end of the row. These buildings sit perhaps two hundred feet off the highway. The cottages are right in the middle of the desert, on a small bluff that runs between two small hills. This much I could tell just from the headlights as we topped the butte that overlooks the "Retreat." There is a curved gravel semicircle driveway that enters the retreat from two points on the highway. On the north side of the retreat is a rather steep ravine that runs right behind the trailer house. At night, this ravine appeared to be a huge black chasm.

Nathan slowed the van down to a crawl as soon as he saw the sign for the retreat. We drove slowly along the highway until we reached the first of the graveled entrances. Nathan turned off the headlights and stopped the van.

"What's the matter?" I asked him. "This is the place." The sign next to the graveled entrance read: *First Fundamentalist Baptist Retreat and Revival Center. Eight Air Conditioned Cottage Units for Rent.*

"I know. Just checking ... shit. We've got a mess," Nathan suddenly declared as he stared into the night at the string of rooms and at the trailer house.

I followed the direction of his gaze. There was a single car parked in front of one of the cottages, the unit nearest the trailer. Lights were on in that cottage. The rest of the windows, including those in the trailer, were dark.

"What is the problem?" Father Holden asked from the bench behind us.

"I don't think we got here first," Nathan said. He stayed on the highway and drove past the retreat. He continued over the top of the next hill. He stopped the van when we were out of the line of vision of anyone in the buildings. "The light in that room—did you see it?"

"I'm sorry. I could see very little from my seat," answered Father Holden.

"I saw it. There was a light in that one room, the one in front of the car. Why does that mean that something is wrong?" I asked Nathan.

"The light was shining up, coming from the floor. A lamp probably got knocked over. Maybe there's nothing wrong, but I'm getting out here. Father Dougherty, turn the van around and pull into the driveway. Get out and see if you can find John. If you get in trouble, just hang tight. I'll be around. Judy, Judy, can you hear me?" Nathan spoke into the back of the van.

"Yes," she answered. Her voice came out of the dark.

Nathan flipped on the overhead light so that he could see her. "Judy, come up here. Bring your purse."

"Can you sit up by yourself?" Judy asked her husband.

"I'll be fine. Go. Get up there," Harold told her.

When she had made her way to the doorway to the cab, Nathan stopped her. "Take out your gun," he said. I had no idea that Dr. Weintraub carried a weapon, but she did pull a small revolver from her purse. "Now, if any of these people, I mean any one of them, attempt to leave this van—shoot them. Understood?"

"I understand," she answered.

"Harold, don't try anything stupid—you'll give your wife the excuse she's been waiting for," Nathan joked. Father Hugo, Harold, and Miriam thought it was humorous. The rest of us were silent.

"Okay, Father Jerome, drive on back. Drive right up to the building. Park *behind* the car. Got it?" Nathan asked me.

"You mean behind it so that it cannot be moved?"

"Exactly. Right on its bumper. Get out just like nothing has happened—like you're looking for this John," Nathan told me. "Give Judy the keys to the van. Judy, lock it up. Don't worry. I'll be there. We gotta move fast. I'm guessing there's just a couple of bad guys that have beaten us here. If that's true, there could be a lot more bad guys on the way. Oh, Father, turn the headlights back on and drive slowly. That'll give me time to get there before you do—they'll know you're coming." Nathan climbed out of the cab and ran into the desert, disappearing into the ravine that led to the back of the trailer house. I took my new position in the driver's seat, turned the van around, and drove slowly back to the retreat as ordered.

> By The Guide, the highest intellects ought most certainly be liberated [from death] ... If one recognizes one's own thought-forms, by one important art and by one word, Buddhahood is obtained ... if thou recognize not ... [then] all the Wrathful Deities will shine forth in the form of Dharma-Raja, the Lord of Death.
>
> —*Book of the Dead* (Tibetan)

> I shall have my being, I shall live, I shall germinate, I shall wake up in peace ... my body shall be established and it shall neither fall into ruin nor be destroyed of this earth.
>
> —*Book of the Dead* (Egyptian)

Excerpts from a letter from Dr. Judy Weintraub to the Author. (This letter is dated August 2, but describes the events of June 5.) Interspersed with Excerpts from the Journal of Father Jerome Dougherty

So I stood in the passageway to the back of the van with the pistol in my hand. I doubt very much that I was an intimidating presence, though I gripped the pistol with a finger on the trigger and my thumb on the hammer—to illustrate that, at least, I knew how it operated.

Father Dougherty drove up the driveway and parked behind the sole car at the retreat. It looked like a rental car: new, plain, simple, and square. There was no one on the cement walkway in front of the rooms. There was no one in the car. After shutting off the engine, Father Dougherty handed me the keys. "Lock the door behind me," he said. After he climbed down and shut the door, I did lock it.

Harold had hobbled to the front of the van and sat in the passenger's seat. Father Holden asked to be allowed to enter the front cab, but I refused. I kept the gun on all of the members of the party and made them remain in their seats.

Father Dougherty walked a few steps down the sidewalk to the room with the light on and knocked on the door. It was opened from inside. I could not see by whom. I vividly recall that Father Dougherty looked desperately back at the van but then turned and entered the room. It appeared to me that he entered under duress.

* * * *

The door was opened, much to my surprise, by Davide Palucia, whom I had not seen since Italy, since the investigation of the death of Father Patricelli. He hid behind the door and held a square black gun that looked almost like a plastic toy. "We've been waiting for you. Come in, Father Dougherty," he said in English. He was dressed in one of his gaudy black satin suits. His long greasy hair was pulled back in a ponytail. He looked like the common gangster that he was.

I glanced back at the van, hoping to apprise them of the situation. "Ah, no, no, no. Come right into the room, or I will put a bullet in your brain," Palucia threatened as he pointed the gun at my face. I stepped inside.

Not surprisingly, Monsignor Leonardo Greco of the Curia Romana was present as well. "Hello, Father Jerome," came his greeting. He seemed to have put on a few more pounds since I had last seen him in Italy. Monsignor Greco also carried a plastic pistol. He stood at the window and slightly pulled back the curtain to keep his eye on the van. "Agent Johnson?" he asked.

"He is waiting in that vehicle. He told me to get John and that then we would leave," I lied. Under the circumstances, I deemed it appropriate behavior.

Palucia closed the door behind me. Only now was I free to look about the room. There were two other people present. One was a well-built man in a blue suit. He was sitting in a chair next to the bed and smoking a cigar. He had gray hair and tired, irritated eyes that he rubbed with the hand not holding the cigar. I could smell the cigar—but I could also smell burning flesh.

For in the bed, hands and feet tied together behind his back, was another man, or, rather, the scarred remains of a man. The flesh on his face and hands had been recently burned away. I could see the white of the cheekbones through the thin membrane of pink scar tissue pulled tight on his face. His hair on the front half of his head was completely gone, as were his eyelashes and eyebrows. His lips had been melted away, as had some of the cartilage in his nose. He must have squeezed his eyes tightly closed when the blast hit his face, for his eyelids were merely charred. His fingers were pink, fleshy stubs. Blood was still oozing from where the scabs had been worn off the tips of his fingers as he clutched at the bedding. He was dressed in white cotton pants and shirt. The shirt had been ripped open, revealing a chest that was covered with white and red burn blisters.

"How rude of me," said Greco. "This is Winston Shields of the Central Intelligence Agency. And this man," Greco pointed with his weapon to the person on the bed, "claims to be John—the Beloved of Jesus Christ."

Shields nodded, took a deep breath on the cigar, and then shoved the bright, burning tip against John's chest. "We're not getting anywhere," he complained.

"Stop it! In the name of God!" I commanded, but Palucia hit me hard in the ribs with his pistol. The blow knocked me to the floor.

"Father Dougherty." The voice came from the bed, from John. It was calm and consoling. "Please do not place yourself in jeopardy for me. I have known far greater pain then this."

I pulled myself back up to my feet. Palucia walked around to the other side of the bed and stood next to the CIA agent to get, I believe, a closer view of the torture. Perhaps he wanted to assist.

"You'll think pain, goddamn you," shouted Shields. He stood up and smashed his fist into the poor man's face. I watched in horror. I heard the cheekbone crack.

John closed his eyes. He took a deep breath and parted his lips slightly as if to focus all the energy of his soul on his injured mouth. Blood ran from his lip, but only for a moment, before it stopped. "Gentlemen, I do not understand why you treat me thus; you cannot kill me unless I choose to die." He said the words clearly, forgivingly—even though I am certain that a facial bone had just been broken.

"I'm getting really tired of this shit," Shields said, crushing his cigar on the floor with the toe of his shoe. "Let's kill this one now. He is one tough bastard. Looks like we'll have to do that brain-chopping you fellas told me about. Let's get it over with. Then we can take the van. We'll take the van to the rendezvous and finish the rest of them there."

"What about Father Dougherty?" asked Palucia.

"What about Agent Johnson?" asked Greco. "There is also Sister Maria to consider. If not for her, we would never have waited near the Valley of the Gods. We would be in New Mexico with the rest of the team. Does she come with us— or do we leave her here to wait for her daughter?"

"We are agreed that none of those assisting are to be harmed," replied Shields, "only the diseased. You caused enough trouble when you killed that deputy. There simply will not be any more. We'll leave Johnson, Dougherty, and those two others traveling with them. You can do what you like with Sanchez and Quindilar—they're your people."

"The FBI agent?" asked Greco. "If he is in the van, how will you deal with him?"

"Take Dougherty outside at gunpoint, and make a trade. The agreement is to eliminate only the sick ones. You boys know that. The Vatican was specific, my government was specific—all of the parties have agreed to that point. We'll take the van and the diseased and leave the rest of them here."

I noticed that Palucia glanced at Greco and shook his head. *"Io ti ho detto di ucciderli tutti,"* Palucia said.

"Anche quello vestito di blu?" Greco asked.

"Hey, keep it in English. You guys know that I'm in charge here. You're gonna do exactly as I fucking tell you."

"Uccidiamoli tutti," Greco agreed. Palucia smiled at Mr. Shields, raised his gun, and pointed it right between the CIA agent's eyes.

*   *   *   *

We could, of course, only wait and watch through the windshield of the van. In a matter of seconds, I caught a glimpse of Nathan. He came from behind the trailer house, hunched over, running quickly. He worked his way behind the cinderblock building, where I lost track of him. I assume that he was quickly searching each apartment, rapidly working his way to the door that Father Jerome had just entered.

Within a minute, I saw him again. His body was crouched low, knees bent nearly to the ground, so that he could not be seen from the window. He held his ear to the door. In his right hand, he held his large stainless steel pistol. It was pointed up. As he listened at the door, he pressed the pistol against the side of his face again and again. I would guess that the reality of the cold metal was emotionally supportive. He patted the weapon against his face as if touching a trusted friend.

Without warning or, as far as I could tell, without cause, Nathan suddenly stood, took a quick step away from the door, and kicked it in.

To live only as a self of body or be only by the body is to be an ephemeral creature, subject to death and desire ... to hold the body only as an instrument, a minor outward formation of the self, is a first condition of divine living.

—Sri Aurobindo, *The Life Divine*

For believe me: the secret of harvesting from existence the greatest fruitfulness and the greatest enjoyment is—to live dangerously!

—Nietzsche, *Die Fröhliche Wissenshaft*

Excerpts from a Tape (a Report?) Made by Nathan Johnson, Augmented by the Author. Followed by Excerpts from the Journal of Father Jerome Dougherty

A search revealed that the trailer house and all the units, except the one with the light on, were probably vacant.

There was a rear entrance to the cottage. It was a storm door with cardboard stapled over the bottom pane. Someone had locked it, however, with a simple metal hook and loop. There was a small window to the left of the rear entrance, but I could only see a portion of the main room from either there or the back door. I could see most of a bed. There was a man bound and lying on it. I could hear voices coming from other areas of the front room, just beyond the rear entry. I did not want to risk making any noise trying to sneak in the back way. I decided that the best approach, given the possible number and location of hostiles, would be to go directly through the front door and into the main room, where I assumed they would all be situated.

After moving to the front of the occupied unit and crawling beneath the single front window, I knelt at the left side of the unit's front door. In this position, I could not be seen from that window. I listened there. I could distinguish five voices. Three of them sounded hostile. One was Dougherty. Although one voice insisted that only "the sick" should be killed, that same voice apprised me that the killers of Deputy Billy Budge were in the room. Not being able to view the situation, I had to assume that there were three targets—minimum.

I studied the hinges. The door would swing in from right to left. That was good. There should be no one behind the door, and I would have a clear shot at the man at the window.

I listened carefully, trying to calculate the approximate position of the hostiles by their voices. I have often practiced similar hostage circumstances—but we almost always drill as a team—and we always use dummies when firing live ammo. I had never worked a situation in which there were this many potential hostiles by myself, either in practice or in actual conditions. I reviewed in my mind all that I knew about entrance in this type of situation. I knew that the three most important things to remember were to stay calm, to scan prior to shooting, and to squeeze off every round, making each shot count. I tugged my bulletproof vest into place, checked my gun, held its cold metal against my face, and waited.

Though it was in a foreign tongue, I soon heard what I thought was a command to kill. At this point, I quickly stood and kicked in the door. Fortunately the door kicked in easily and swung far to the left, giving me an instant view of everyone in the room. "FBI," I identified myself in a loud voice. "Drop all weapons."

There was a young man in a black silk jacket [Palucia], pointing what appeared to be, and what turned out to be, a 9 mm Glock at the head of an unknown [Shields]. The unknown [Shields] was standing behind the bed to my left. There was a man in the bed. He looked as if he were wearing a hideous mask. I had no time to take notice. He had been bound, with his hands and feet tied together behind his back. He was obviously not an immediate threat.

The young man [Palucia] was behind and slightly to the left of the unknown [Shields]—who was just to my left as well, nearly straight ahead, both on the far side of the bed. They both faced the bed and, thus, me. Father Jerome Dougherty was standing almost in front of the door, to my immediate right. About five feet from Father Dougherty, in the front right corner, stood a heavy man [Greco], also armed, also with a 9 mm Glock. He was wearing the robes of a Catholic priest. I assume that this was the person who had been keeping watch at the window.

The young man [Palucia] started to swing his pistol away from the head of the unknown [Shields] and toward me even before I had finished my warning. I fired two rounds at his head at approximately the same instant that I hollered the command to drop all weapons. The range was less than fifteen feet. At least one of the bullets hit its mark. I perceived, though only peripherally, brain matter spewing from the exit wound. I assume that he died instantly.

I leveled my weapon and pulled quickly to my right, for the priest at the window [Greco] had refused to follow my command and had raised his pistol into firing position. My first shot, a quick one, was into his chest—to kill if he was not wearing a bulletproof vest and to disrupt his timing if he was. He fired one round from his weapon at almost the same time that my first shot hit him. His bullet struck me in the lower left quadrant of my abdomen. My vest absorbed the impact, but the shock knocked me off balance. It spun me in a half circle, in the direction of a chair at the foot of the bed. At this point, as I staggered toward the chair, I hollered for Father Dougherty to get down.

The unknown [Shields] had, by this time, unholstered his weapon, a snub-nosed revolver, and appeared to lower it on me. He fired twice and missed—both times, I think, shooting above me as I fell. I twisted in the air and returned a quick three-shot spread at his upper chest because I was off balance and falling into a chair.

I had no choice but to hit the chair and roll to the floor. This was fortunate for me because the priest at the window [Greco] had been wearing a vest, and my first shot had merely knocked him against the far wall. He fired at least five rounds wildly, rapidly, the bullets hitting the chair and the wall behind me. Dougherty had not yet changed positions. It was a miracle that he was not hit by any of the bullets fired by either of the two men at me. Some of their shots must have come within inches of him.

I fired once more from the prone position. It was an interesting shot because I had rolled into position between Father Dougherty's legs; he was still standing about three feet inside the doorway. My gun was right beneath his crotch when I discharged it. I aimed this last round at the large man's [Greco's] head. It struck just below his left eye. I definitely saw his blood and brain matter splatter against the wall behind him. I assumed, correctly, that the hit was fatal.

Still lying on the ground, I rolled over twice, pistol extended in front of me, to find the unknown [Shields]. I had no idea if any of my shots had hit him. On the second roll, I came face-to-face with him at the end of the bed. He had dropped his pistol and fallen to the floor. One of the rounds had penetrated the neck. He was clutching at the wound with both hands. The bullet must have hit the external jugular vein because blood was gushing from between his fingers. There was a second wound in his lower left shoulder that might have done some damage to his heart or lungs. I did not discover that wound until later.

I crouched at the end of the bed. "Father, any more in here?" I asked Father Dougherty who had finally flattened himself against the floor. "Father?" I shouted.

"No more. Please, no more," he cried from beneath his arms.

I threw the unknown's [Shields's] weapon out of his reach. He grabbed at my leg with blood-soaked hands. "Help me," he gurgled. He tried to pull himself up my left leg. Because I was not certain that the unit had been cleared of hostiles, I was forced to kick him off, putting my right boot hard to his face.

I quickly surveyed the bathroom and the back exit. There were no other people in the unit. I went back and knelt beside the unknown [Shields]. He was dead.

*   *   *   *

The door behind me flew open. I heard Nathan start to shout something. He only got as far as "FBI" before the shooting started. Shots were being fired all around me. The multiple discharges in the small room were deafening. Palucia fell first, with a ghastly wound to his head. Greco gave a huge grunt and fell back against the wall. Then he began firing his pistol rapidly. Some of the shots, I am certain, came very near to hitting me.

From the corner of my eye I saw Nathan stumble. I think he said something to me as he fell toward the bed—though I could not hear him over the explosions of the weaponry.

Mr. Shields, from the CIA, also discharged his weapon at Nathan. Nathan fired back, and I saw Mr. Shields grab his throat, fall first against the side of the bed, and then tumble to the floor. The last shot came from directly beneath me, from between my legs. I could feel the vibrations, or perhaps in ballistics they are called reverberations, against my thighs and testicles. A moment later, I fell to the floor and covered my head with one hand, my privates with the other.

No more weapons were fired. Nathan asked me something. I could not make out his question because my ears were ringing. "No more, please. No more!" I hollered—meaning no more shooting.

I kept my head covered, with both hands now, for I could hear someone moving about the cottage. I prayed that it was Nathan—and I prayed that he was not injured. I peeked out between my fingers. Nathan was gathering the weapons of the dead men from the floor.

"What will you do with those?" I asked.

"Well, I'm betting that one of these Glocks was the weapon used to kill a young deputy sheriff up in Idaho. I'm going to ship them back to DC and find out for sure. One of them had better be the murder weapon—or I'm up Shit Creek without a paddle. Oh, I wanted to ask you something. Father, what does *Uccidiamoli tutti*—it's Italian, isn't it? Is that how you say it? *Uccidiamoli tutti*—what does it mean?"

I uncovered my head and looked up at him. One of his pant legs was smeared down both sides with blood. He was reloading the clip from his stainless steel pistol slowly and deliberately, shoving one cartridge at a time into the top of it.

"It means, 'Let's kill them all,'" I answered.

"That's what I thought," Nathan replied.

> At times the truth shines so brilliantly that we perceive it as clear as day. Our nature and habit then draw a veil over our perception, and we return to a darkness almost as dense as before. We are like those who, though beholding frequent flashes of lightning, still find themselves in the thickest darkness of night. On some the lightning flashes in rapid succession, and they seem to be in continuous light, and their night is as clear as day.
>
> —Maimonides, *The Guide for the Perplexed*

Excerpts from the Journal of Father Jerome Dougherty

While I untied John, Nathan returned to the van to escort our party to one of the other cottages. I had to assist John out of the bed and to the meeting. He had a difficult time walking, at first even moving his legs, because they had been bent backwards and tightly tied to his arms.

John, as I have already mentioned to some extent, has recently had his face and hands severely burned. He apologized to me for any displeasure or uneasiness that I might experience due to the disfigurement of his extremities. Last March in Pittsford, Michigan, he had been living on a small farm. Someone had tried to kill him with some type of incendiary device. He was just coming in from feeding the animals. He told me that he was wearing a heavy coat but had just taken off his hat and gloves when the explosion transpired. He was able to get out the door and throw his body into a snowbank. Although the burns covered over half of his body, only his face and hands were badly burned. As I described them above, they were literally burned to the bone. John briefly told me how he was working on rebuilding the flesh but explained that it would take months for him to be able to heal the burns completely. "The skin is a complex organ—the cheekbone is not so much," he stated.

I told him not to worry about it, that I had ministered to a number of burn victims in my life, and that his appearance did not cause me any concern. I asked him about his cheekbone. I said that it sounded to me as if it had been broken by the blow from the CIA agent.

"It was," John answered me. Then he took his blunted fingers and wiggled his jaw and his cheeks back and forth. "Not now. Bone is much easier to heal than is skin. See, I've healed it already." By this time we had reached the cottage and the meeting, so I could ask him no more about such a miraculous recovery.

"They're dead. All three of them," I heard Nathan say as John and I entered the door to the third cottage from the end.

"Mia bambina! Hai ucciso la mia bambina!" Sister Maria screamed. She suddenly attacked Nathan, arms flailing wildly at his face.

I ran into the room and held her back. "Sister Maria!"

"What's she saying?" Nathan petulantly demanded. His patience had vanished.

"She said that you killed her baby girl," replied Father Holden.

"There were only men in that room. Who's her baby girl?"

"I haven't the foggiest …" Father Holden started his response.

"Lei ha una figlia?" I asked her.

"Keep it in English, or I'm gonna get awfully pissed," commanded Nathan. To make the point clear, he unsheathed his gun.

"I asked her if she has a daughter," I translated for him.

The immortals, except John, who had remained outside, were seated around the edge of the bed. The Weintraubs occupied the room's only two chairs. Nathan stood between the foot of the bed and the bathroom, blocking the way to the rear exit. I stood in the front doorway.

Sister Maria prowled back and forth like a cat caught in a cage between us. "I have daughter. Born of Asmodeus. She is Naamah. She get immortality of Lilith. She steal it from you. She steal it from you," Sister Maria said, pointing at Nathan, then laughing hysterically as an outlet for her relief. "Now you know. They want to make you and your wife the first—but already she begin. She has the Nigredo. She steal the white stone from you. Once more. You die. Your wife die. This time there be no Adam. There be no Eve."

"This woman is insane," said Miriam with denigration. "I have always known it."

"Now, Miriam, don't be so harsh. We are all quite insane—according to several leading authorities," said Father Hugo.

"Please excuse my appearance," John began. He pushed by me as he entered the room, speaking to Nathan and nodding to the Weintraubs. "My name is John. I have been waiting here for you. I was recently burned, and my countenance can be repulsive. I think I can explain the source of this woman's anger. First I want to thank you for all your help. Without you, coming last, we would not have been able to send the others ahead. I do need to explain to you, Agent Johnson, that a young woman—I assume now that it was this woman's daughter—came with the others. She left with another man, just before you arrived, to contact the main group at Chaco and send them to Taos. I had cut down the telephone lines here. The nearest telephone now is twenty miles away."

"Was she in her early twenties, with long black hair?" asked Nathan.

"Yes, that is an appropriate description," replied John.

"And the man—mid-forties, also Hispanic, scar here?" Nathan asked as he drew a finger across his lip.

"That is the man. They are probably on their way to Taos at this moment," John answered.

"Taos? Why Taos?" Nathan asked.

"Because that is *Ch'ool'ii*—our destination," John said. "Sariah awaits us near there. I have sent the others along. You and your family are the last. We must hurry if we are to reach there before those ... who would stop us. We must go soon."

"You die," Sister Maria screamed in Nathan's face again.

Nathan became very angry. He slapped her soundly across the face with his bare hand. A gesture I would not deem proper, perhaps, however appropriate. Then he shoved her against the wall and roughly searched her body through her black habit. Sister Maria had a small pistol tucked in her bra. Nathan emptied the weapon and then handed it to Judy. "Now you sit on that bed and shut the fuck up, or next time it will be my fist.

"Judy," Nathan continued, again turning to Dr. Weintraub, "will you check all her belongings for any other weapons, information, drugs. Anything that you think looks suspicious—I want to see it."

"I'll do it," Dr. Weintraub answered, and she left for the van.

"Thanks," Nathan said after her. "I want one thing made clear: I'm not leaving here without my family," he flatly stated to the rest of us.

"But it is imperative ..." John began.

"Not moving another inch," declared Nathan.

"I understand your feelings about your family. However, waiting here is in no one's best interest. If we wait here, they will be back for us. They will not be two or three. They will be many. They will not be unprepared," explained Father Holden.

"You called my family. Right?"

"Of course I did. They are on their way," replied John.

"Then we'll wait. They should be here in minutes."

"It is only 3:00 AM. It could be as much as an hour before they arrive. I called them last, just before I cut the lines. It was for their safety, I wanted them to arrive only when it **was** certain that everyone else had started for Taos. I will remain here, go with them, and give them instructions. That is what we discussed. We will simply follow you," John stated. His legs were still wobbly, so he sat in the chair that Judy had occupied.

Harold Weintraub gathered his strength, stood, and faced Nathan. Then he spoke. "You must understand by now. We are in a race, an adroitly planned and brilliantly executed race. A race in which, in theory, as many of the immortals as possible could survive and meet and find safety. John, if this was your idea, you are to be congratulated."

"You still do not understand," said Father Hugo. "This was no one's idea. It just happened. We all saw the end, probably all about the same time. What we were not certain of was Taos. For that, we have Sariah to thank."

"Why Taos? Do you understand Taos?" Nathan asked Professor Weintraub.

Harold coughed and then smiled knowingly at Nathan. "I've been doing a little research in this *Book of Mormon* of yours. I would guess that Sariah is a Native American, one of your 'three Mormonites.' So is Lemual."

"Sariah is considered the greatest magic woman in the world by her tribe. Though they mistakenly put her age at a mere 137 years," interjected Father Dobo. "All of the various Pueblo peoples consider Lemual a god."

"I would suggest that the safety we are speaking of is that of an Indian reservation, which is nearly a country unto itself," continued Professor Weintraub. "No government can follow the immortals there."

"Professor Weintraub," Father Hugo commented, "it is little wonder that you are known as one of the world's most intelligent men."

"I still don't feel right about this, about leaving my family behind," Nathan said. "What if someone else … someone against us shows up? Then what?"

"I sincerely doubt that it will happen," I answered. "In the room, just a few minutes ago before the shooting, the discussion among the three men was clearly focused on the death of the immortals. It is the immortals that they are after.

They called them 'diseased.' Your family may once have been an important bargaining chit, had our enemies been able to capture them. But they didn't. Thus, I also believe, Nathan, that it is no longer the case that your family is in immediate danger. Now that the finish line is known, everyone has reason to move with all haste to it. That is where we must confront the adversary."

"I concur. Still, if you are worried, I have a suggestion," stated Professor Weintraub. "It could be arranged so that this place looked as if the government had succeeded ..."

"Of course," interrupted Nathan. "I could make it look as if Father Dougherty and I had been killed. John could stay hidden here somewhere. If anyone comes before my family, then they simply follow the trail to Taos. As you said, Father Dougherty, we'll pick that fight on our own terms. If my family arrives first, John steps out of hiding and he, my cousin, my wife, and my children will all be on their way to meet us. Father Dougherty, let's load everyone back into the van. I want you to help me throw the body of the priest into the car. Then I want you to drive that car to the north entrance to this place. Park it so that it blocks the entrance—got it?"

"I understand," I responded.

"Let's all hurry. We have some work to do."

Oscula autem sunt adhesio Spiritus cum spiritu.

—*Garden of Pomegranates*

On the Author's Travels with Sylvia Johnson and Her Children, June 5, Continued

Sylvia and I both knew there was going to be trouble. As we neared the Revival Center from the north, we could see that a car was blocking the first entrance. There were bullet holes through the windshield. There was a second car, a much older car, parked in front of the northernmost cottage—the cottage where John had told us to meet him. The only light coming from the compound was from that unit.

I immediately turned off the lights and the engine of the paint van and coasted to a stop on the outside of the car that blocked the entrance, keeping it between our vehicle and the lighted room of the compound.

There was just enough ambient light to silhouette a body hunched over the steering wheel of the car. "Oh, great," I said. "Now what?"

"We check the body. See who it is … was. You … you check the body. I'll keep the van running in case we need to get out of here," Sylvia replied through the darkness. "Get your gun out. Go on. Get it ready. Go see who that is."

"What fucking insanity," I swore. I pulled the tiny Walther pistol from behind my back, pulled back the slide, and flipped off the safety. "Hand me a flashlight, would ya?" I asked Sylvia. "And roll down that window so I can talk to you without screaming. We sure as shit don't want to wake up the kids."

She opened up one of the bags and handed me a small black metal tube. Then she rolled down the right side window of the van. "Keep the light pointed down. Don't give us away," she exhorted.

"Yeah, yeah," I said. I climbed from the white van and gently closed the door. Sylvia slid into the driver's seat.

The desert air was cold. I shivered as I walked around the front of the van to the driver's side of the car, gun in one hand, flashlight in the other. It was a new sedan. It was a rental. There was a Budget Rental Car sticker in the window.

I turned on the flashlight. I aimed the beam at the head of the corpse. "Oh, Christ, it's a priest!" I said to Sylvia, for I could see part of his white collar. Only the back of the collar remained white. The entire front of the collar, the face, the shirt, and the jacket were all drenched in blood. The face had been relentlessly mutilated, slashed twenty or thirty times with a knife. There was really no face left at all, only shreds of flesh hanging from bone. Somebody had made damn sure that there would be no quick identification of this corpse. It had not been done long ago. Steam was rising from the warm evaporating blood—sucked up into a thirsty, black desert sky.

The window of the rental car was down. I reached in the coat pocket and pulled out the blood-soaked wallet. I held the flashlight between my teeth and opened the wallet. The flashlight tumbled from my lips. "Oh, God. No. Jesus. No!" I started to cry. I was holding the driver's license of Jerome Dougherty.

"What? Who is it?' What? *Tell me!*" Sylvia demanded through the cold night air.

"It's Father Dougherty. They must have just killed him. His body's still warm. Jesus, Sylvia, we gotta get to the police," I half cried, half mumbled.

"The hell we do," she responded. "If that's Dougherty, then Nathan's got to be inside over there. We're going in. I'll lock the doors to the van. We'll leave it. I'll try to keep an eye on it and the kids. You go around to the back. Secure the back exit. I'll take the front," Sylvia said. As she spoke, she rummaged through her black diaper bag. "Here's an extra clip for the PPK. Get over here," she ordered me, looking up. I stumbled from the car to the passenger window of the van. She handed the extra clip of ammunition to me. It came with instructions: "Don't touch the casings, you'll leave fingerprints. And don't be afraid to use your weapon. If you do use it, you might need these," she said.

"What are we doin', Sylvia? Let's stop and think about this. What the fuck are we doin'?" I asked her. My mind was hopping and spinning, like a dragster burning out its tires before a race, to give it better traction. Smoke, noise, and show—but not any *go*.

Sylvia pulled another long black tube out of her diaper bag. She snapped her flashlight on and ascertained that it worked. She immediately shut it off. "We're going to find my husband. We are going to save him." She was already rolling up the windows to the van and locking the doors. She jumped out and shoved back the slide of her 10 mm Sig Sauer while on the run.

I trotted next to her. We neared a row of black doors spaced equally apart in a long straight wall of white cinderblock. I breathed the cold air in deeply; I held tightly to my slipping sanity. We looked at each other in the dark—I think for strength, or maybe for the solace we would need for what we feared was ahead. I could not see her eyes in the dark. To be honest, I did not want to see them. Thank God I could not see them.

I split off to the south and ran around to the back of the row of units. The last I saw of Sylvia, she was creeping toward the front door of the lighted cottage. Looking north at the far end of the row, I saw a splash of light on the ground coming from a back door or window. I ran until I was thirty feet from the light. I tiptoed the remaining steps.

The back exit was an old storm door. The bottom pane had been broken out, and someone had wired and stapled a cardboard square in its place. This made it easy for me to look over the top of the cardboard into the room and to remain, for the most part, concealed.

I could not take in the entire room, but I could make out the bed, and I could see the front door and window. The lock on the front door looked as if it had been broken, as if it had been kicked in. The current occupants had secured the room by wedging a chair beneath the doorknob. I could see the top of Sylvia's head. Her eyes were peering over the edge of the window, looking through the gap in the curtains, fixed in a cold, unbelieving stare on something to my left and out of my view.

That she could have seen anything more horrific, that there could exist anything more perverse than what I witnessed taking place on the bed is beyond my devising.

"Give it up," a man's voice, a deep voice, came suddenly from behind the bathroom door that was just to the left in front of me. He was yelling at the woman on the bed. He was yelling in Spanish. The sudden, loud, foreign voice, one so near, frightened me, terrified me, but I did not move. I was transfixed by the naked woman, by the ritual, by the corpse.

The dead man's body had been stripped naked and laid on its back. Pillows had been tucked beneath the head; arms placed at its side; legs straightened, toes pointed. The face on the corpse on the bed had been slashed, just like the body in the car. The shredded facial muscles hung in dripping pieces from the exposed white skull and jawbones. An eyeball dangled by the optic nerve over the cavity where once had been the nose. The eyeball bounced in syncopated rhythm as the young naked woman yanked up and down on the lifeless penis.

"There is a drop—come and see for yourself—there is a drop of sperm here," she answered, turning to the door so that the man in the bathroom could hear her. I could see her face now. Thin, sharp nose, black eyes, yellow teeth bared in anger. I could see her chest. With one hand, she massaged one of her enormous dark nipples, while the other hand worked the dead man's cock. There was blood, fresh blood, splattered over her arms and face and chest. Her black eyes flashed with fury and frustration. "Goddamn it. Why don't you believe me? Come and help me. Get ready to rewind the tape. It is almost finished. It must happen at the same moment. Enrique, I am telling you, there is sperm here."

She returned to the business at hand. Her long black hair hung down her deeply tanned back. She carefully licked the blood from the prepuce of the corpse's penis. Then she tugged on the organ over and over, like a milkmaid working a cow's stubborn tit.

"Here, see, there is sperm." She turned again and grabbed a remote control from the end of the bed. She pointed it behind her, into the portion of the room that I could not see, and jabbed at the buttons. "Enrique. Rewind. There is sperm," she wailed. She dropped the remote control and then immediately crouched over the dead man's torso and squeezed his organ as she wiped it against her vulva. Her black vaginal hair was wet with the dead man's blood and with her come. She whimpered as she worked her clitoris with the fingers of her free hand. She tried to shove the penis inside her vagina with the other. Not only was it limp, it was lifeless.

"Hear, Hagith. Witness, Pipi. Asmodeus, my head is bare. Mother Lilith, I am Naamah," she said through tears of frustration. "I brought you the Nigredo. Give me the new name. Yield up the stone to me!" Then she slid back through the blood-drenched sheets and began to lick and yank on the penis again.

"You are crazy," the voice came again as the door to the bathroom opened. A squat man's square back blocked my view as he stepped out of the bathroom, zipping up his pants. He wore only blue jeans and a T-shirt, so his shoulder harness was visible. "It's over. He's dead. He's ... Quick! There is someone out front," he shouted. He yanked his pistol from the leather holster beneath his left arm. He must have seen Sylvia at the window.

"Sylvia!" I screamed. It was too late. The gunshots had already exploded, drowning out my warning in a fusillade.

Excerpts from a Letter from Dr. Judy Weintraub to the Author; Letter Dated August 2 but Describes the Events of June 5

I found nothing more in her belongings that would suggest that Sanchez posed a danger to us. Before we boarded the van, Nathan searched all the other immortals and all their belongings for weapons but found none.

Sister Maria persisted in her vociferous and sometimes depraved denunciations. Nathan was in no mood to put up with it. Over the protestations of the members of the group—not, however, including Harold and myself—Nathan secured Sister Maria's hands, feet, and mouth with duct tape. The tape was tightly wrapped several times around her head. This looked quite painful, and I am certain that her hair had to be cut when it was time to remove the tape from her head.

We followed the same route from the so-called "Revival Center" that we had taken there. The return trip, however, was much smoother; Nathan was driving the speed limit or slower. I presume that he was waiting for his family to catch up with us. We refueled at Shiprock, New Mexico. Nathan allowed us to use the restrooms and to buy some refreshments, but only he used the telephone. Father Quindilar was the sole person to object to this limitation. Nathan's response was quick and crude. He said, "I trust you about as far as I can throw you. So you shut the fuck up and sit in your seat, or you'll join Sister Maria back there in my version of *One Hundred and One Uses for Duct Tape.*"

When we were on our way again, Father Holden made his way to the front of the box and said loudly, for all to hear, "We want everyone in this vehicle to know that you are all free to join us when we reach Taos."

"Sister Maria's not free to do anything," Nathan quickly replied. "She's under arrest for conspiracy in the murder of a law enforcement officer."

"You too are welcome," Father Holden said to Nathan, ignoring his comment about Sister Maria. "Your family is welcome."

"Father Holden, you're not getting the point. I am going to drop off anybody who wants off in Taos—with the exception of Sister Maria. Then I'm heading to the closest Bureau office, and I'm going to try to clarify this whole affair before things get out of hand."

"Right here," said Father Hugo, who was sitting in the front row with Harold and me, eating a bag of potato chips, "right here, things are already quite out of hand."

"Not entirely. I have the murder weapon, I hope. I'm betting on it. I have a witness to the shooting at the retreat, Father Dougherty. I gave the command for them to drop their weapons. I fired in self-defense. It'll withstand an investigation. I think I'm going to be okay."

Harold, who had been leaning against my shoulder, sat up at this point. "Think again, young man. I would assume that all three of the men in that room had specific instructions from their governments to be there and to stop the movement of this group of people. My guess would be that deadly force had been authorized."

"Only against the immortals," Father Dougherty spoke from the front right seat. "The CIA man, Shields, said that only the 'diseased' were to be killed. He said that was the order given. That is what the argument was about. The Italians disagreed."

"That is somewhat reassuring," Harold said.

"Not for me!" Father Hugo objected. Most of us laughed.

"We do not know what difficulties await us at Taos," Father Holden forewarned. "We do not know what degree of force has been authorized to stop us from attaining our goal. I would only suggest to Nathan that he keep an open mind. And I will repeat my invitation. All are welcome, including Sister Maria. That which she has so diligently sought, she may soon find. If she can but empty her soul of bitterness."

Sister Maria kicked and knocked herself about and attempted to scream in response. However, I learned from her effort that four or five layers of duct tape make quite an effective acoustic insulator.

"And what about the Weintraubs?" Father Holden asked, glancing down. "Will you be joining us?"

Harold looked at me. There were beads of sweat on his forehead. His hand, cold and damp, shook in mine. "Can you heal him?" I asked Father Holden, keeping my eyes on my husband. "If we come—if we believe—can you heal him?"

I distinctly remember what happened then. Father Holden smiled sadly and touched both Harold and me on our foreheads. "There are secrets that, perhaps, now we can teach. There are other truths that we will never be able to convey. Your husband is a wise man. Your husband understands this. Your husband knows the answer to your question. Why don't you ask him?"

"Harold?" I asked. We looked deeply into each other's eyes, into eyes so familiar—yet, in the past, eyes that had always been distant. At that moment, finally, our eyes were so very near. There were tears running down his face, against his jaundiced skin. I must tell you that I had never seen my husband weep before. I gripped his cold hands tightly together on my lap. "Tell me, my darling. Tell me."

"I can only heal myself," Harold said.

Thou shall not allow a witch to live.

—Exodus 22:18

On the Author's Travels with Sylvia Johnson and Her Children, June 5, Continued

I do not know how powerful the squat man's gun was, or how fast he was pulling the trigger, or how good his aim was. I do know that Sylvia's gun was more powerful and that she was faster and better. His back was turned to me when the shooting started. He was wearing a white T-shirt. At the exact moment that the explosions of the weapons filled the air, the back of his white T-shirt started to burst. Instant, giant, red, water balloon splotches. A blood tie-die. One, two, three ragged holes, the size of my fist, erupted through the shirt as his body arched back toward me and the screen door.

I ducked and fell out of the way of the body and the bullets as he crashed through the storm door, bringing most of it with him. He landed on his back amid the door's screen, on the sidewalk. He smacked to the ground with the thud of muscle against concrete and the short huff of his last breath.

I stood there, gun in hand, staring down at the body, pointing the pistol at the dead man. The three holes in the front of his T-shirt were neat, tiny, and round—each about the size of ... a bullet.

Swift movement, low and to my left, from the doorway, caught the corner of my eye. Instinctively, I lifted the gun. It was the young woman, who was bending down to pick up the dead man's large black pistol. She grabbed it with bloody fingers. She was naked; her face and body were smeared with blood.

"Don't pick it up," I told her, pointing my pistol at her head. She started to stand. She was turning to face me, perhaps eight feet away. She had the black pistol. I took a deep breath to try to calm myself. I could smell fresh, warm blood in the cold desert air. Human blood. My ability to reason shut down. My desire to live kicked in.

"Drop the gun!" I screamed. I could feel my finger on the trigger. My eyes jumped with terror from her hand, clutching the weapon, to her feral, empty, animal-crazed, black eyes. Eyes beyond hope, eyes beyond reason, eyes that probably, at that moment, looked much like mine.

"Drop the gun!" I screamed again. In the distance, I could hear Sylvia pounding against the front door, trying to break through the bracing. "Shoot them!" Sylvia yelled.

My eyes skipped again. The naked woman was lifting the pistol as she stood. She was swinging it toward me. While my eyes were doing a dance of fear, ignoring the inevitable, her eyes were locked with one purpose on my chest.

"Drop it!" I screamed as I jerked the trigger. The pistol cracked in my hand. How could something so small snap so hard—report so sudden and so loud? The percussion left my ears ringing. I pushed the pistol down, pointing it at her torso. Her gun was still moving up at me. I did not stop to look in her eyes.

"Drop it! Drop it! Drop it!" I screamed in rage, each time pulling the trigger, after each time forcing the bouncing barrel of the gun back down to her bare chest. Every time I screamed, a neat, tiny hole appeared on her chest—every hole about the size of ... a bullet.

She fell back. Her head hit the side of the building. The force of the fall careened her body. She flopped to the sidewalk and landed, twitching, on her side. My hands were shaking, but my mind was in pure self-preservation mode. I popped out the partially used clip, slipped it into my pocket, dug out a full clip, and shoved the fresh clip into the handle of the pistol.

"Is she dead?" Sylvia asked, running up behind me from around the north side of the building.

"Jesus Christ," I swore, spinning round with the pistol aimed at her, ready to fire. "Don't sneak up on me."

"Is she dead?" Sylvia asked again, ignoring my remark. She kicked both bodies with her tennis shoe, keeping her gun fixed on them all the while.

"I think so," I said.

"I emptied my pistol on him. How many hits did I get?" she asked me.

"Three. Maybe ... I don't know. He's dead, Sylvia. Who gives a fuck about how many times you shot him? *He's dead.*"

As she poked at the corpses, I stepped over the broken door and into the apartment. I first checked the bathroom. It was empty. I walked into the main room.

Glancing over at the dresser against the far wall, I saw what Sylvia had been staring at. It was a portable television with a VCR built into the bottom. A tape was playing. It was a tape of the woman I had just killed. I stared too.

She was naked on the videotape. Her breasts, with the same saucer-sized black nipples, bounced up and down as she straddled the man beneath her. The light had been dim. The quality of the video was poor. I looked closely. The man between her legs was Nathan. She was fucking my cousin. *She was fucking Nathan!* She was chanting the same kind of black magic bullshit she had used when she was trying to fuck the corpse. But she *was* fucking Nathan. He seemed a little confused, maybe a little sleepy—but he was definitely enjoying it.

I shut off the TV. I threw the bedspread over the corpse. I searched the sports coat on the chair. I pulled out the wallet. It was, as I had feared, Nathan's.

"It's Nathan—isn't it?" Sylvia asked as she walked up behind me.

"Let's get out of here. Check the kids," I suggested. I tucked the wallet back into the sports coat.

"That's Nathan's jacket," Sylvia flatly stated as she walked over to the bed. She put her hand on the cover.

"For God's sake, Sylvia, don't lift it off. They've cut up his face. You won't be able to tell. Please. Leave it alone. Nathan's gone."

She turned to me. Her eyes were terrified, confused, and angry. "I saw it from the window. I saw what she did with him. I saw everything." She pointed at the television.

"Come on, Sylvia. I don't understand this. You don't understand it either. We've got to keep it together. Let's get back to the kids."

She took a step toward me. "I need you," she said.

"I know. I'll stick with you. We'll find the police."

She stepped again. She was against me. She pressed herself against me. "I need you now."

"Jesus. Come on, Sylvia. This is nuts ..."

She pulled my face down to hers and kissed me. She thrust her tongue into my mouth with urgency, with a need—*with a will*—I had never felt before. Her hands pulled down my sweatpants. My penis swelled in her hands.

We were insane. We were sad. We were scared. We were grasping at life. We were trying to create hope from nothingness. I lifted up her dress. I attempted to pull down her underwear. "Here. Wait," she said. Her Mormon garment was one piece. She yanked all her clothing down from the shoulders. In a moment she stood naked before me. She was thin and muscular, with fair, flawless skin. Her breasts were small, but the nipples were pink, healthy, perfectly round.

She knelt down. She reached up and pulled me down to her. "I'm pregnant," she said. It was a confused apology that sounded more like a promise.

"I know," I answered, kneeling beside her. She stripped me of my jacket and my T-shirt. Now I was naked too.

She put my hand on her still-flat stomach. The muscles were tight. Her skin was smooth. "I need you," she said.

"I know." I kissed her breast. I licked her perfect pink nipple. I kissed her neck. She led my hand down down to her vagina. My fingers quickly found the warmth, found the smooth silky wetness.

She lay on her back and spread her long muscular legs. "Get inside me. I need you to come inside me."

I moved over her. She took my penis and slid it into her. She rocked her pelvis gently. Inside her was so warm, so strong, so alive—so real and *alive*.

I ejaculated almost at once. "I'm sorry. I'm sorry," I whimpered as I thrust again and again. Then, holding her abruptly, holding her tightly in my arms, I shoved myself as deeply inside her as I could. My sperm rushed into her warmth, her need, her life. "I'm so sorry."

"Shush. It's okay. Shush, baby. It's okay." She rocked me in her arms. I could feel the walls of her vagina rippling against my penis, pulling me in deeper, needing it all. She rocked me. "Shh. It's okay. Shh." She rocked me while we both cried.

Moments later, as we lay there in each other's arms weeping, someone banged on the door. "Mrs. Johnson. Are you all right? Mrs. Johnson. Are you in there?"

I pulled out of Sylvia and fumbled around on the floor, feeling for the pistol. Both naked, we scrambled to the far side of the bed. Sylvia had her Sig Sauer pointed at the door. The window was broken out. But the curtains, except for the bullet holes, were still in place. Now I knew why Sylvia wondered how many times she had hit the man. Sylvia had shot him three times in the chest—only guessing his location, *without being able to see him*. I reached out and gathered up our clothes.

"This is Mrs. Johnson. Who are you?" she asked in answer. She turned to me, motioned toward the highway, and whispered, "My kids."

"Thank God. My name is John. I have been waiting for you. I heard the shooting, so I waited with your vehicle to protect the children. I was uncertain. I am to take you and your family to your husband," came the voice from outside.

"My husband?" Sylvia asked. *"My husband?"* she screamed, tightening her grip on the pistol. "My husband is dead."

"No. No. Perhaps I should have alerted you sooner—but everything is fine now. I thought that the man and woman would not be here long. I thought it best to stay with the children. They are fine, and your husband is alive. The bodies are a ruse, a stratagem—Agent Johnson set this up to protect you. You can trust me. We are turtleneck and piggyback. It is a long story. Believe me, Mrs. Johnson, your husband is alive."

"One second," I replied to the stranger's voice. "I'll get the door. It's jammed."

Sylvia and I squirmed and danced and hopped back into our clothes with joy, sorrow, guilt, relief, exhaustion—with a hysterical embarrassment and confusion the likes of which I have never known. As soon as we were dressed, I walked to the door. I was giggling like a three-year-old.

"Wait," Sylvia said. "Don't open it yet." She stood at the foot of the bed, 10 mm still gripped in her right hand. With her left hand, she straightened out her cotton dress. She ran her fingers through her hair. Then she flipped the bedspread, uncovering the corpse from its feet up to its bloody chest. She leaned over and viewed the dead man's penis. "This isn't Nathan," she said, looking over to me—laughing and crying. "This isn't Nathan." She lowered her pistol. "Let him in."

Jesus means something to our world because a mighty spiritual force streams forth from Him and flows through our time also. This fact can neither be shaken nor confirmed by an historical discovery.

—Schweitzer, *The Quest for the Historical Jesus*

How shall we bury you? asked Crito.

Any way you please, answered Socrates. Assuming that you can catch me and that I don't slip through your fingers.

—Plato, *Phaedo*

Conclusion of the Journal of Father Jerome Dougherty

Having already spoken with Nathan and the Weintraubs, Father Holden turned to me. "Jerome, will you come with us?" he asked me.

"I don't know," I replied. "I have so many questions."

"It may be premature, but I will try to answer," Father Holden promised me.

I was sitting, as I have most of the trip, in the front passenger's seat. I have done this because, at times, I have relieved Nathan from driving. Also, I have sat here so that I could keep this journal as current as possible—so that I could finish this journal.

Father Holden was standing in the doorway between the cab and what we now refer to, almost lovingly, as the "box."

"Is this to be a private conversation?" Harold asked, leaning forward on his elbows from the bench directly behind me.

"Oh, no. Please join us," I replied.

"Yes. The answers will be the same, regardless of the source of the questions," smiled Father Holden. He knelt on the floor so that he was exactly eye-to-eye between the two of us.

"I wonder first, and most important, about my Savior. I have devoted my life to him, and now I am told that he is but one of several ..." I began.

"Who told you that?" asked Father Holden.

"Well, I assumed that ..."

"You assumed!" he laughed. "You assumed that one immortal was the same as another. That we are rather like ... what are they called? Clones?"

"Well, no ... then explain it to me," I requested.

"What would you like me to explain?"

"His death and resurrection. Were they real?"

"First, you should not forget that I am a priest and servant in His Holy Church. I love him as my Savior too, in nearly the same manner that you do."

"May I listen in here?" asked Father Hugo. "I have been anyway."

"Please join us," laughed Father Holden. "And Dr. Weintraub, Judy, please feel free."

"As long as I'm listening, I'll want to add at least one thing," said Father Hugo. "There is a great variety and difference of opinion about Jesus among us. Sariah, whom you will soon meet, is also a follower. She met Jesus here, in America. Her feelings about him are no different than yours. But Mr. Tie once saved Jesus's life when Jesus was a baby. So, in some sense of the word, Mr. Tie is Jesus' savior! He considers Jesus neither more nor less important than any of us. At 455 years, I am one of the younger ones. So I am not certain how much my opinion is worth, but I tend to think that as immortals, we generally share that same feeling of equality through difference."

"All that is true," continued Father Holden. "But to answer Father Dougherty's question specifically, I can only tell you what I know. Jesus claims that he died. That he brought himself back from death. He has the scars to prove it. In which case, Jesus is different from all of us—except, perhaps, Socrates; but he is totally evasive on the issue. Strictly speaking, however, now that I think about it, now that I am attempting to convey it to a mortal—this is new for me, you understand—perhaps there is a change, a death you might call it, that we all go through."

"Explain," Harold urged him.

"The only point, the only moment in time that I can remember that was, perhaps, a focal point—the point where I went from mortal to immortal—was, perhaps, a deathlike experience," said Father Holden, turning his attention from me to the members sitting on the bench between us.

I should add that I think the other members were asleep on the back two benches. Father Quindilar has taken to hovering around Sister Maria, like a whipped puppy, ever since he was threatened by Nathan. Father Dobo and Mr. Tie sat in the middle bench, leaning on each other's shoulders. One of them was snoring. Miriam was beside them with her head resting on her jacket, which she had rolled and placed against the wall of the van.

"How do you know it was like death?" objected Father Hugo. "Everyone that I have ever known has had that particular experience just once—and none have ever reported back to me."

"I don't *know* if it was deathlike. It will be interesting to speak with Jesus about this. Brad, instead of being so skeptical, tell me if something like this ever happened to you," Father Holden continued. "I once had recurring dreams. They started when I was still a child. They were more like visions, but I will call them dreams. In the dream, there was a column of light. It had neither a top nor a bottom—no beginning or end. White and hot and bright beyond belief, it rotated with such scintillating intensity that I was afraid to touch it."

"I have had that very dream!" I exclaimed.

"Fichte speaks of an idea like this in, I believe, his later versions of the *Wissencshaftslehre,*" added Harold.

"Were there voices? And sparks flying from it?" I asked excitedly.

"Yes. Even so. The voices of many people. Some speaking in my tongue, many others speaking in languages I did not know—not at the time," Father Holden stated.

"Yes! Yes!" I proclaimed ecstatically. "Not so long ago, I had that very dream!"

"The light frightened me. Yet the voices called me to it. I was afraid that if I stepped into the light, I would be consumed, I would die. Did you ever have such a dream?" Father Holden asked Father Hugo.

"I think we are discussing such matters prematurely. I know that I am expected to always be the lighthearted one, but this is a very serious matter. One we need to consider as a whole," Father Hugo replied.

"Why?" I asked.

"Why?" Father Hugo repeated, as if asking himself. "Because I have a feeling that Father Holden is about to tell you that one day he stepped into that light. He is going to tell you what happened when he entered it, how he survived the process, and how it changed him. I think that it is premature."

"Why?" I asked again.

"I think I understand and agree," answered Father Holden. "There are those, like Sister Maria, who take such talk in the wrong manner. Who try to synthesize or reproduce or steal and corrupt such a vision, such knowledge, when it has not yet come to them."

"What about someone like me?" asked Professor Weintraub. "I have never had such a dream. However—like Fichte, and perhaps, Maimonides—I have thought about such an idea. I have postulated that the Truth is similar to that which you have described."

"It is another reason for us to be careful. Everyone comes to it in a different way," stated Father Hugo. "Much of what Father Holden said rang true to me—but not all of it. I too was much less visionary, much more idea-oriented. I saw truth as a process in history and myth, more like Hegel—whom I knew, by the way. Anyway, that process did lead me to the light, and I did step into it."

"So what happens then? After you step into the light?" I asked.

"Father Dougherty," Father Holden said to me with such kindness that it did not feel condescending, though it may sound that way when written, "you will only know that when you are ready to take the step."

Miriam, who apparently was only resting in the middle seat, spoke up. "Brad and Richard, shame on you. Shame on you both. I think that you see, Father Dougherty, how difficult a task it will be for us. All of this speech about 'columns of light' makes me very nervous. My experience, while I suppose I could describe it that way, could also be expressed in a way that did not mention stepping into a column. There are so many other feelings and sensations involved. We should not take lightly, and I do not mean this as a pun, Barbêlo. As usual, the men are trying to make it far simpler than it is. It is obvious why alchemy and those silly secret societies are practiced and run by men," Miriam said with playful condescension as she scanned the faces of the men in the box.

"I do not understand the reference to Barbêlo. Has … has the name something to do with the tetragrammaton?" I asked Miriam. I admit that, at that moment, I was guessing.

"It is Sethian, from *The Apokryphon of* …" Professor Weintraub started to answer for her, but she stopped him.

"Not now, Professor," Miriam quickly responded. "There will be time," she said to me and smiled.

"As you wish. Well, for myself, I must know if you can teach me how to see it again. How to look into the light and not be afraid." I said to Father Holden.

Father Holden smiled at me and ran his fingers through his long gray hair. "In that matter, we may be of some service," he replied.

"You should put a little more emphasis on the 'may,'" counseled Miriam.

Father Hugo nodded in agreement with her, then added, "I think the truth is that we don't know with certainty. Jesus thinks that we must. Mr. Tie thinks that we can. I myself don't know."

"The questions you have for Jesus, you may soon ask him yourself. Each one of us has a different story; each one of us a different, yet not so very different, way. You will, of course, be free to leave us anytime that you wish. We would love to have you. You have been such a dear friend and compatriot over the years. Father Patricelli told me that he could see it in your eyes—that you were one of us. I am not so wise or so in touch with the human soul as he was to make such a statement. However, I believe that he spoke the truth. Come with us. Find out," offered Father Holden.

"There is one other thing that has troubled me," I said to Fathers Holden and Hugo and to Miriam.

"It is?" asked Father Holden.

"It may be nothing. It may be silly," I wavered.

Father Hugo offered me some potato chips from his bag. I declined. "Nothing that troubles you is so silly that it is not worth discussion," he assured me.

"It is about my writing. I have felt less and less of a need to write in the last few days. My journal, which has always given me great pleasure, is suddenly a burden. Is there something wrong?"

Father Holden's smile had never been more comforting. I love the man deeply. He said to me, "Jerome, you understand that when you join us, the desire will leave you completely. You will live through—how did Patricelli put it?—'through acts of loving kindness.'"

"Let me put it this way," added Father Hugo. "You won't need to leave something to be remembered by because you won't be going anywhere. At least you won't be going anyplace from which you cannot return. Sure you won't have a chip?"

"No, thank you. But thank you for your many kindnesses to me, for understanding me, for loving me," I said to them.

"Come with us," Father Holden asked me again.

"I will."

Thus it is my decision to go with these people, my friends, to wherever it may be that they are going. I will live with them and learn from them.

We are less than an hour away from our destination. The sun is just rising over the San Juan Mountains that loom before us. The sky is striped with layers of clouds that change in color, moving toward the horizon, from purple to brown to red to orange to the yellow light of the first rays of the newly risen sun. I had not thought of it before, but it is obvious where the patterns for the blankets of the Navajo came from. They simply took the time to watch the sunrise. That, I discover, is now my calling as well.

For I am beginning to understand the meaning of the words of the *Wisdom of Solomon:* "For righteousness is immortal ... The souls of the righteous are in the hands of God, and there shall no torment touch them. In the sight of the unwise they seemed to die ... for though they be punished in the sight of men, yet is their hope full of immortality. And in the time of their visitation they shall shine.

"The beginning of wisdom is the most sincere desire for instruction, and concern for instruction is love of her *[Sophia]* and love of her is the keeping of her laws and giving heed to her laws is the assurance of immortality, and immortality brings one near to God."

I have finished this journal for you, my son and my love. Do with it what you will. My only desire regarding it is this: May God be with all who, perchance, read the words herein. May you understand that, to the best of my ability, I always wrote with an honest heart. In due time, I pray that you, as well as I, shall find the courage to step into the light.

In Christ's holy name,

Amen.

The Queen remarked ... "Now I'll give you something to believe. I'm just one hundred and one, five months and a day."

"I can't believe that!" said Alice.

"Can't you?" the Queen said in a pitying tone. "Try again: draw a long breath and shut your eyes."

—Carroll, *Through the Looking Glass*

On the Author's Travels with Sylvia Johnson and Her Children, June 5, Continued

"I must alert you," the voice behind the door said, as I removed the chair that was blocking the front entrance, "that my face and hands have been badly scarred. I do this to prepare you in advance and to apologize for any displeasure or uneasiness that my countenance might produce in you."

"That's quite a disclaimer," I responded as I opened the door. I immediately knew why he made it. In a severe flash burn, the exposed areas of flesh and fat are literally melted away. The scar tissue that grows from the little flesh that remains tightens over the bone. The face of John, which has already been described by Father Dougherty in a previous section, resembled that of a well-preserved mummy, one in which the facial bones are covered by a single layer of tight skin. There was a difference: though his skin was taut and consisted primarily of scar tissue, it had somehow taken on a healthy salmon color—usually such tissue is a deep, crusted brown.

John looked like he was wearing the scariest Halloween mask that I had ever seen. "Wha! Whoa! John! That's ... uh ... that's one helluva sunburn!" I stammered.

"Someone tried to roast me with propane. I was wearing my winter coat at the time. It saved most of me from looking this grotesque. I am working on the healing process. It will take a few months," John said with a very toothy and lipless smile. He gently shook my hand. His fingers had also been badly burned, as previously described by Dougherty.

"Are they starting skin grafts?" I asked John. Sylvia had not yet said anything. I think she was still staring at him from behind me.

"Self-healing. I have the dermis in place. I'm building up from there. That's why there's color in my face. I will grow the epidermis when I've finished with the muscle and the subcutaneous cellular tissue and—well, it is rather boring. And it is emotionally difficult for me to look this repulsive. The skin is a complex organ, and not many people understand that; healing takes much time and concentration."

"Yeah. Right. Well, so, uh, John, are you one of these immortal types, or are you one of their disciples?"

"I am, in reality, both."

"No riddles, okay, John? We've got a lot of dead bodies and confusion here. I'm a little edgy, understandably, I think; and Sylvia's uptight. You'll notice she's holding a very nasty-looking pistol there. No offense, but I'd kind of like to know exactly who you are before we offer you a lift. I personally think Nathan's driving around with a van full of fruitcakes. But I'm trying to be open-minded. So just give us the straight shit."

"You are the writer," John said, catching me off guard. "We appreciate the fact that you have chosen to record this event. It is one of momentous historical significance, and it should be recorded fully and fairly."

"How do you know about me? And who told you I was going to write about ... about all this mess?"

"I'm going out to check on the children," Sylvia interjected at this point. She had gathered up Nathan's clothes and wallet to take with us. She handed me my pistol and bellyband; then she waited behind me while I armed myself.

"We should go with her," John urged. "We must leave here as soon as possible. Nathan specifically instructed me to tell you to drive 'like a bat out of hell.' You can trust me. Remember, you are 'turtleneck,' and I am 'piggyback.' The only other person who knows this is Nathan."

"He's right," Sylvia said to me. However, she kept her distance from him, standing behind me and to my left. "Nathan's ahead of us. This is the man he told us to trust. I think we should leave right now."

"All right. But I'm gonna be watching you every second," I cautioned him. He smiled. The man with no lips smiled.

Sylvia climbed into the back of the paint van with her children. Obeying her command, I parked in front of the first rental unit, the southern one—the one without the bodies. Sylvia took the children to the bathroom, stole a couple more blankets from a bed, and then quickly loaded the blankets and the kids into the van. John, who sat in the front seat next to the right side window, kept his head covered. The children were still tired. They did not notice him and quickly fell back to sleep. Their mother soon joined them on the floor of the van.

"So, tell me who you are, and I'll try not to laugh," I said as I drove the van south, away from the Retreat. It was still dark, but the sky was graying in the east. The sun would be rising soon. I drove about eighty miles an hour when the road was straight. I did not push any of the curves.

"I am John. I am known historically as 'John the Beloved.' Which does, in fact, make me both an immortal and—did you say *apostle* or *disciple?*"

"Disciple."

"A disciple. I am both. In fact, I am all three. I once was a writer. So I know a little about what you do and how you feel. I know your cynicism, skepticism, and bitterness. I realize that they are somewhat of an occupational hazard, especially for someone who has not quite reached the pinnacle of his art or career, as I suspect you have not. As for me, recently I have been trying to give some order and direction to our attempt to gather about twenty-five individuals. These people are, whether you believe it or not, immortal—in the sense that all of them will live at least a thousand years before dying."

"That's a whole lot to swallow," I countered. "But the writing part was a good guess. You're pretty observant and have either good instincts or good inside information."

"Thank you. I have lived a long time, and people are my life's work. I'm not going to ask you to 'swallow' anything. I only hope that when you write this story, you will allow it to unfold in its truthfulness and in the fullness of time."

"What the hell does that mean?"

"I think, I am *certain,* that you will know what I mean once you have read and heard it all. I know that the Weintraubs and Father Dougherty have been either making notes, or keeping journals, describing their travels with my friends. I have been told that your cousin, Agent Johnson, has recorded their conversations during the last few days. There will be enough material. You will understand."

"Understand what? They've been chasing around America with a truck full of loonies?"

"That you simply will not find to be true. Look, young man, my friends and I are, whether you like it or not, as articulate and *at least* as shrewd and as sane as you are. We are certainly more mature."

"Golly gee whiz. You must think that, somehow, pissing me off is gonna make me write a really nice story about you."

"I think that you have the fire, the intelligence, the *hybris* necessary to do a wonderful job. All that you lack is a little faith."

"You ought to take up writing again, John. I think you'll find it wreaks havoc with faith nowadays."

"Think of it as faith in the material—most of which is being prepared, as I understand it, by people whom you greatly respect."

"How do you know so much about my friends and me?"

"I have been speaking for the last several days with their traveling companions. I was already familiar with the works of both of the Weintraubs, and Father Dougherty has been a friend of the immortals for years. Understand that we have allowed you access to this material because of your respect for the people involved. That alone says a great deal about your character and your potential as a writer."

Traveling on Highway 41, we had reached the southwestern tip of Colorado. The terrain had flattened out some. I pushed the paint van up to ninety. "You know, John, I'm gonna speak frankly here. You haven't allowed me access to jack-shit. Nathan called me and sent his wife down with a box full of documents long before you knew that I existed."

"You are wrong again, young man," John smiled at me. I was glad that it was still dark in the cab. Even if he really was Christ's best friend, his smile was hideous. "You have been thinking about us, studying us for several years. You met Elijah. You were younger then, and he thought you were pretentious about your intellect. Nevertheless, he thought that you had potential. He often inquired of Professor Weintraub about you. We have followed your career. It has been a rough start for you—has it not?"

"Elijah refused to speak with me. I was impressionable ..." I said, tactlessly avoiding a response to his all too painful question.

"Yes. We would not speak with you *then*. It was too soon. We were not yet convinced that we could teach our truths to the many."

"Starting up a new church? Satellite ministry? DVD subscriber series? Weekly fundraiser newsletters? Orphanage in Oradea? The works?"

"You are humorous, after a fashion, a ludicrous fashion. Have you read my book?"

"Which one? *The Gospel According to the Wimpy Platonic One?* Or the other book—*Revelations*—where you were obviously hallucinating?" It was growing lighter. The sun would soon be up. His face was a hundred times more repugnant in the light.

John laughed. His countenance became disconcertingly ugly when he did. Rather than repulsion, or at least along with it, I felt sympathy because laughter appeared to be an agonizing exercise for him. The flesh on his face stretched beyond a limit it seemed to have already exceeded. I could almost feel it starting to rip. A tear trickled down his cheek. "There was one more. The one hidden for so long. The one recently recovered."

I thought for a second, wondering if he were playing a trick. "What? Oh. Yeah. You mean the *Nag Hammadi* stuff?"

"You are so very bright. Read it. Of all my books, only in that one did I write the truth as I knew it was becoming—inside here," he said as he pointed at his forehead. His skull protruded through the thin layer of pink tissue that covered the bone.

"So what were you up to in the others? Propaganda, lies, and deceit?"

"Hiding, pretending … precautions, preparing myself for that one book. One can only write … what one is able to write, politically able to write, to survive to write again. Until one is free to write … as you are fortunate enough to be. Read it."

"If you insist," I laughed.

"I do. It will teach you humility and respect … for your elders."

"John, I think you and I are going to be great friends. Who knows, maybe centuries from now we'll look back on this moment …"

"Unfortunately, we will not have time for that depth of nurturing. We are only a few hours away from our point of mutual departure," John interrupted me. "So you must ridicule me as much as possible in the short time remaining."

"Okay, I'll back off—if you will. Tell me how you think I ought to write this book."

"That is very, very simple. Tell the truth. We think that you can do it. We trust that you will. You may find, as I did, that, though *simple*, it is not as *easy* as it may seem to tell the truth."

The children were up as soon as it was fully light, which was not too long after the conversation I have just related. They were frightened by John at first. But his voice was kind, and he had immeasurable patience. We stopped in Farmington, where we fueled the van. Sylvia bought snacks to feed us for breakfast so that we could stay on the road. John made a telephone call. Within an hour, the children were clambering over the seat and climbing on John as he played simple games with them in a fond and forgiving fashion. He paid attention to them as little individuals. They quickly loved him for it.

Rather then be frightened by his face, they felt sorry for him. "Does it hurt when I touch it?" Sherry asked him.

"My little dear, it feels wonderful when you touch my face," John replied. He allowed her to poke around his ravaged skin with her curious little fingers.

"You don't have whiskers like Daddy," she noted.

"It will be quite a while before I can grow a beard again," he answered.

John tended the children. Sylvia tried to sleep. I drove as fast as I deemed prudent, which was between sixty and ninety, depending on the road conditions and on my hunches about speed traps.

At about eight that morning, at John's request, we stopped in a little nothing of a town called Tres Piedras on the east side of the San Juan Mountains. We stopped so that the children could go to the restroom and so John could use the telephone. The air was cool and clean and smelled of the pine forest that surrounded us. It is going to be a lovely day, I thought. Then John returned with the news from Taos.

It would not be such a lovely day after all.

> I am First Man and I head for [the mountain] *Ch'ool'ii* in pursuit of long life and happiness, he sang ... *Altse hastiin* is who I am, sang he. And here I am climbing *Ch'ool'ii* in pursuit of long life and happiness for me and my people. Here I am arriving at the place where the lightning strikes, in pursuit of long life and happiness for my people.
>
> —*Dine Bahane* (Navajo)

Excerpts from a Letter from Dr. Judy Weintraub to the Author. (This letter is Dated August 2, but Describes the Events of June 5.) Interspersed with Excerpts from Conversations Recorded by Nathan Johnson

The sunrise that morning, over the San Juan Mountains, was truly spectacular. Those of us who were still awake, which included Fathers Holden, Hugo, and Dougherty and Miriam and myself—and Nathan, of course, who was driving—all remarked on its majesty and vast array of colors. Father Dougherty had spent a good portion of that early morning writing in his journal. He spent some of it, he told me, describing the sunrise.

"Four hundred and fifty-five years of sunrises, and this may be the most beautiful yet," remarked Father Hugo.

"It is amazing, always to me simply amazing, how moved I am by this earth, by its beauty," stated Father Holden. "To be an essential part of it, as you have suggested, Dr. Weintraub, is a great honor."

"Do you give credence, then, to my theory of the symbiotic relationships of life on this planet?" I asked him.

"Elijah said that he had discussed this with you. To answer you truthfully, I think that it is much larger and far more complex than you have suggested," he replied after pondering my inquiry for a moment. "For I have come to believe that the earth is not a oneness within itself. Look out at the newly risen sun, whose coming we have enjoyed with such wonder this morning. Without the sun, the earth is nothing but a cold rock floating in empty space. And the sun is sustained by a chain reaction that is part of the sum of the totality of creation. So if your question is 'Do I take from and share my life with this planet?' then my answer is 'Yes.' However, if you ask me, 'Is the earth a single existing entity, whole within itself, and am I simply a part of it?' then I must answer 'No'—for you have underestimated creation, the sun, the earth, and me."

"Then you really do believe in God?" I asked him.

"I don't know. It is perhaps a strange comment, coming from an immortal, but I do not know if there is a God."

Miriam joined in. "It is not strange. I too wonder about the exact nature of deity. I am almost certain that there is a God. But whether it is an old *man*, even older than my brother, with long flowing robes, white beard and whiter hair—*that* part I don't know about."

"Doesn't Christ teach that he is the son of the Father?" asked Father Dougherty. "And who else could the Father be but God Himself?"

"That is a question that you'll need to ask Jesus," answered Father Hugo. "Let me put it this way. When I first discovered that I was immortal, I mean when it first dawned on me with a certainty, with the same certainty that you have now of your temporal existence, I thought, initially, that surely my extra-long life must be a gift from God. Since I assumed that it was a gift from God, I also assumed that God was a humanlike gift giver—the Santa Claus of immortality. As I have watched the brutality of nature, the indiscriminate cruelty of disease, the wantonness of men and their wars, the command that death has over most of this world, I've come to lose that faith. There is no grace. If you ask me why I think I am immortal, I will no longer tell you that God chose me, because that would mean that God is cruel and arbitrary—and that I am merely lucky that he was looking my way. No. Now I will tell you that I do not understand."

"Then what makes you think that you can teach your secret?"

"I've never said that we could. You'll have to wake up Mr. Tie, or wait for Jesus or Enoch. I don't know," Father Hugo replied. "Nathan, are we getting close? I think it's about time for another stop at a restroom."

"The junction with Highway 522 and Highway 150 is just ahead. Taos is only a few miles south of there. We can stop in Taos."

"No. We are not going all the way into Taos," stated Father Holden, his voice rising in excitement. "We might ... even be able ... to see them from ..."

"There they are!" Father Hugo shouted. "Look! There they are! Everyone *wake up!*"

The junction that Nathan had mentioned is like a trident with its three prongs. Each prong is a road. Highway 64, on which we had traveled, points to the northwest. Highway 522 heads almost due north. Highway 150 runs to the north and then turns northeast. It forms the western border of the *Pueblo de Taos* Native American Reservation and terminates at Taos Ski Valley resort at Carson, New Mexico. A service station with a large paved lot sits on the southwest side of this three-way junction. There, in the parking lot waiting for us, were about a dozen people of different ages, races, sexes, and nationalities. The youngest was a Hispanic male, perhaps in his late twenties; and the oldest was an Asian woman who might have been ninety years old or more. They were gathered around five or six new mid-sized cars, all of which appeared to be rental vehicles. They all wore ordinary travel clothing. Even the women were dressed in slacks or blue jeans and wore either tennis shoes or hiking boots.

Nathan pulled into the parking lot. The group of people waiting for us there clapped and waved and surrounded the van as it rolled to a stop.

The immortals were the first to step from the van. They were greeted with hugs, kisses, and salutations in at least a dozen languages. As Father Dougherty, Nathan, Harold, and I climbed down from the van into the parking lot, we were nearly assaulted with handshakes, hugs, thanks, and congratulations from an odd variety of strangers.

Because I know it will be important to your book, I will list their names, some spelled phonetically when necessary, and tell you a little, for that is all that I know, about each one:

1. Moses. Short, muscular man, about thirty-five years old. Tanned complexion. Even though he was fairly young, he had white, not gray, hair, and a short white beard. Brown eyes. Nervous. Wanted to move everyone along.

2. Enoch. Short and thin with receding gray hair. Very normal-appearing, middle-aged male. Yet Harold, who had just woken up, looked at him as if he'd seen a ghost. "It's Enoch! My, my God! *It's, it's him!*" Harold faltered when he first saw the man. (As you know, Harold never falters.) Enoch approached Harold and said, "It has been many years. Are you ready yet to make the long journey? For

now, I believe, we are ready for you." Harold did not reply. Instead he excused himself and went into the restroom at the service station.

3. Jesus. Mid-thirties, as expected. Short auburn hair. No beard. Perhaps five feet eleven, also thin. His complexion was the typical light olive Middle Eastern hue. Clearly, along with Moses, Enoch, Mr. Tie, and Father Holden, he was one of the leaders.

4. Gustav. A young, dignified European gentleman. Also very thin.

5. Jabala. A fairly young and beautiful (East) Indian woman. Dark, dark eyes. Very excited to see Miriam.

6. Ka¡klu (?) A very short black man. A ¡Kung bushman. Knew both Father Hugo and Father Dobo well. He spoke to them, with great enthusiasm, as they got out of the van.

7. Lowlynn (?) Chinese. Male. Small. Mid-thirties? A Buddhist monk. Friends with Miriam and Mr. Tie.

8. Key (?) A tiny and frail Asian woman. She was the oldest of the group in appearance. She was very shy. Father Hugo knew her. She stayed close to Jesus.

9. Gunta (?) A dark-skinned young man. Looked rather like an Egyptian or native of some other northern African country. Friends with Moses, Father Holden.

10. Youngtoo (?) Buddhist monk. Again, mid-thirties. Spoke with Mr. Tie and Father Hugo.

11. Fernando. Handsome, young Spanish man. Tall and thin. Seemed to be closely acquainted with Father Holden.

12. Socrates. I did not see Socrates at first because he was using the restroom. You can imagine Harold's surprise when he entered the restroom, already shocked at seeing a man he believed was Enoch, whom he had met sixty-some years ago—and then waiting in line at the urinal behind Socrates! He is an old, short, squat, and ugly man. If he truly was Socrates, then Plato's descriptions of him, as I recall reading them in college, or hearing Harold recite them around the house, are quite accurate.

There was little time for chitchat. Even before all the introductions were made, Father Holden demanded to know where Lemual and Sariah were. Enoch said that Sariah was waiting for John to call and that Lemual was taking care of some last-minute details with the leaders of the reservation. Moses insisted that we leave the service station as soon as everyone had taken the chance to buy food and drink and to use the restroom. Nathan agreed, and that settled the matter. We gathered quickly into our respective vehicles for the short, very short, remainder of our trip.

The rendezvous point was only a kilometer north on Highway 150, along the border of the reservation. There were vast stretches of sagebrush, broken by small farms and pastures on both sides of the road. To the east, perhaps ten kilometers across the sage-covered plain, towered the *Sangre de Cristo* mountain range. Banks of soft white clouds sheltered the mountain peaks.

There was a welcoming committee awaiting us at the meeting place, which turned out to be merely a wide spot in the road. It was, to be more precise, the turnoff to a primitive dirt road that cut an eastern swath through the sagebrush to the base of the mountains. Further down the highway and on the left or west side of the highway, on private property, was a resort called Quail Ridge Inn. We could see the entrance sign from where we stopped.

A number of four-wheel drive vehicles had parked along the highway at the entrance to the dirt road. Some were those pickups with giant tires. Others were more comfortable-looking four-wheel drive passenger vehicles, or SUVs, such as Chevrolet Blazers. All of them were driven by Native Americans. Some of the Native Americans were in full ceremonial dress. They had arrived in their finest raiment to greet their new guests. Six or seven of the same type of vehicle were lined up on the dirt road, one behind the other, facing east. I assume that these were the vehicles that were to carry the immortals to the mountains.

Lemual drove up right behind us in another four-wheel drive with, we soon learned, several members of the tribal council. Lemual was a thin but muscular Native American. He was probably about thirty-five years old. Nathan quickly climbed from the van and met with Father Holden, Lemual, Enoch, and the Native American leaders for a few minutes. I do not know what information was exchanged between them.

*   *   *   *

[Nathan recorded the conversation on his body wire. I have identified the following participants: Nathan Johnson (NJ), Father Holden (FH), Enoch (E), Lemual (L), and an unidentified tribal leader (TL).]

L: Richard! You made it! Let me introduce William Red Sky, John Chevez, and Chief Little Waters. Father Richard Holden. Enoch. Agent Nathan Johnson of the FBI—correct?

NJ: Pleased to meet you, gentlemen.

L: Hello. I can say that I think that nearly everything is in order. How far behind is John?

FH: I'm not certain.

E: He is going to call Sariah from Tres Piedras. It could be any minute. It could be yet an hour.

TL: An hour will be too late. There could be bloodshed. My suggestion stands—that you should leave now. We will follow with Sariah and John.

FH: I doubt that the others will leave without them.

E: I, for one, will not go until they both arrive.

TL: This is no time to be stubborn.

L: I told you that we would not leave for the mountain except as one.

TL: The mountain will be there whether you come together or one at a time.

E: Our promise to each other was to gather at the foot of the mountain.

NJ: What about my family? I'm thinking about turning around and going back for them.

E: There is no need. John called from Farmington; everything is fine. They will arrive with John.

NJ: Great. I'm glad they're okay. But you're not listening to me. What I mean is that I've done my job. I want to take my family and this Sister Maria and head to Santa Fe.

FH: We thought that you might join us.

NJ: No, no. Oh, no. I got you safely here. I've taken care of the men who killed a law enforcement official. My job's over. I just want to get to our office in Santa Fe to clear up the affair. Then I want to get back to my life—to my family.

L: The 'affair,' as you call it, Agent Johnson, is out of control. I am afraid that extensive efforts are being made to stop you.

TL: About an hour ago, a warrant was issued in Utah for your arrest for the murder of a certain Winston Shields. It would be much wiser for you to let your family come to you.

NJ: I have a witness. I have evidence ...

L: Your wife and your cousin have killed two more.

NJ: *What?*

L: I think that they killed the two who murdered Helaman.

NJ: A Spanish man and a young woman?

L: Yes, so John told us.

NJ: But those two killed Helaman. They were murderers. I'm sure Sylvia only fired in self-defense.

FH: Nathan, of course your wife and cousin would only fire in self-defense. However, they do not have a witness, and your witness has decided to come with us. And think again about the evidence you have for the murder of Helaman. I ... I

think that there is still something that you do not comprehend about the political nature of what is transpiring here. Those who want to destroy us have tried with great, albeit covert, effort to do it even before we reached the mountain. How much greater do you think their effort will be—how much less covert—if they were to learn that we were *coming down?*
NJ: This is America. This nation was founded on law and order ...
E: When we come down, we will come with a new law and a new order.
NJ: This is insane. I'm taking my family as soon as they get here and leaving. *Is that understood?*
L: Agent Johnson, I have gone to great lengths to convince the leaders of the Taos Pueblo Peoples to offer you and your family sanctuary. They have also agreed to take your evidence and your wife's evidence and to present it to the proper authorities when the time comes. Isn't that correct?
TL: We have agreed.
L: Right now your government is not your friend. It is your enemy.
FH: Think about it. It is, obviously, your choice. Our offer stands. Our debt of gratitude to you could not be deeper or more profound. Please think about it.
NJ: No thanks. Discussion's over. Are the trucks on the dirt road for transporting these people?
TL: Yes.
NJ: And you are certain that my family is safe and on their way here?
L: Yes.
NJ: Are these your tribal law enforcement people?
TL: All here but the radio operator in the station at the pueblo.
NJ: How many?
TL: Five, including the captain.
NJ: Have they got an extra walkie-talkie? With police channels on it?
TL: I will see that you are given one immediately.
NJ: Let's go get these people loaded. Tell your men to be ready to roll.

*   *   *   *

While Nathan spoke with the tribal leaders, Moses was busy attempting to load the immortals into the transportation contributed by the Native Americans. He had his hands full. It was such a happy reunion amongst, I'll say it, old friends, that Moses found his task impossible. The immortals stood along the side of the road in little groups and chatted and laughed. Moses, all the while, was exhorting them to hurry and pick a vehicle. Father Dougherty excused himself from our presence, grabbed his belongings, and joined in the festivity.

Harold and I sat together on the first row seat in the rear of the van. Nathan had decided, at our last stop, to restrain Father Quindilar as well as Sister Maria. They remained, to proffer a pun of sorts, tightly wrapped in the back of the box.

"We made it," Harold said to me. He was only slightly feverish, having slept some portions of the early morning hours.

"Yes," I answered him. "What will you do now?"

"Isn't it obvious?" he asked.

I must tell you that my heart sank. I knew that he had decided to go with them. I knew that I could not. I knew that he would die up there in the mountain, in the clouds.

Harold took my hand, as he had so often those last few days, and said, "I will go with you."

My heart beat wildly with joy, with love, and, I admit, with relief. "Darling, I think that we should leave as soon as possible. The quicker we get you to the hospital, the better."

"As you wish. Help me say good-bye. Then we will go," he said. I assisted him through the side door of the van and down to the pavement. He leaned on my shoulder for support. His skin was not so jaundiced as it had been the day before. At least it appeared not to be. Perhaps the bright morning sun made it look healthier.

At just that moment, Nathan and the others who had been meeting together at the south end of the row of cars parked along the highway came rushing toward us. Nathan was barking orders for all those who were planning to go up the mountain to get immediately into the designated vehicles. People started to move. Someone handed Nathan a radio. He spoke into it as he walked toward us. I could not hear what he said.

[Nathan's tapes contain the following brief conversation, which I believe took place at this point in time—RR stands here for Radio Response.]

NJ: Caracara, this is Jackrabbit. Do you read? Over. Caracara, this is Jackrabbit. Do you read? Over.
RR: Jackrabbit, this is Caracara. Over.
NJ: Caracara, what is your ETA? Over.
RR: Jackrabbit, are you with the vehicle?
NJ: Roger.

RR: Time from liftoff to vehicle location is twenty-four minutes. Over.
NJ: Caracara, recommend that you get airborne and proceed. Over.
RR: Roger, Jackrabbit. We're on our way.

"Have you decided which way you're headed?" Nathan asked us kindly, after he had gotten the group in motion and tucked the radio inside his jacket, on the side opposite from that huge pistol.

"Home ... to Cambridge," Harold said.

"Glad to hear it. You'd better get out of here soon. Chief Waters," Nathan said to the Native American who seemed to be in charge.

"Yes, Agent Johnson," responded Chief Waters. He was an elderly man with long, braided, gray hair. He had high cheekbones and a solid, regal physique. His skin was deeply tanned and deeply wrinkled.

"These are the Weintraubs, Harold and Judy. They have been of invaluable assistance in bringing our group to you and your people. Professor Weintraub is ill and now needs to return to Boston as soon as possible," Nathan stated.

"Chancy," Chief Waters called out to one of the young men. "Are you and your rig free for a few hours?"

A tall, spindly youth with long, black hair and a fuzzy mustache came running up to us. "I didn't hear you, Chief."

"Can you take these two people and their luggage to Santa Fe and get them on the next plane for the East Coast?"

"Sure." Chancy smiled at us. "Where's your bags?" I pointed them out to him in the back of the van under the rear bench. Under Nathan's orders, Sister Maria and Father Quindilar were still sitting on the back bench. Chancy helped them stand so that he could remove our two suitcases. Much to my consternation, he loaded our luggage in one of the pickups with the giant wheels.

"You must leave now," Chief Waters warned us.

Another car pulled right up next to us. A very old Native American woman stepped from the right side. Chief Waters trotted to the car to help her out. "Welcome, Mother Sariah," he said.

"They are coming. Just behind us. Is everyone ready to leave?" she asked, her voice and gait very strong for a woman her age.

"Everyone is being loaded," he assured her. She walked briskly toward the line of vehicles forming on the dirt road.

As we passed the front of the transport van, I took off the digital recorder I had been wearing. I shut it off and tossed it through the open window onto the driver's seat.

Chancy had to help both Harold and me climb the four or five feet up into the seat of his "monster" truck. (Benjamin told me the name of the vehicle when I related this story to him.) Miriam ran over to Chancy's truck just as we got in. I rolled down the window. I reached down to grab her hand.

"Thank you both for sharing each other with me. Please, please, as soon as Harold is feeling better, come back and stay with us. We have so much more to talk about," Miriam said to me. Her beautiful dark eyes, so sincere, filled with tears.

"We will try," I promised.

At that instant, one of the Native American men, who had been standing on the roof of his pickup with a pair of binoculars and looking up and down the highway, shouted out a warning for everyone to get into their vehicles.

"We gotta leave now," Chancy said. With a mighty roar from the engine, and with such a bounce that I thought his pickup would flip over, we spun round in the dirt and screeched on to the pavement. We went south through Taos to Santa Fe.

A few minutes later, on our way to Taos, we passed a line of seven or eight trucks and Humbees [*sic*] turning north on to Highway 150. Some of the vehicles had *Property of the US Government* written on their sides. We were riding up so high in the pickup that we could see down into the cabs of the vehicles. Harold and I both noted that many of the men riding in this convoy were carrying weapons. I am not certain exactly which types, but there were all different kinds of weapons.

I think I have now said all that I know that might be of assistance to you. I have read the varying accounts in the newspapers and the magazines of what happened that morning. I know that you are probably the only person in the world alive and available and capable of telling the truth. I am counting on you. Harold, I think in his own way, is counting on you as well.

Thank you for sending me the first few sections of your manuscript. It reads well. Keep it up. I look forward to working with you on the project and stand ready to be of any assistance that you require. I hope this letter has filled in some of the missing pieces that we discussed over the telephone. I am sorry that it took me so long to write it all down. As you know, life has not been easy for me the last several weeks. And I wanted to be certain that this information was as accurate and honest as I could convey. Talk to you soon.

With love and warmest regards,
[Signed]
Judy

P.S.
I have enclosed a copy of Harold's latest writing. His psychiatrist suggests that he may need to be institutionalized. I strongly disagree. I would like your further input. If you could visit, I am certain that it would help. He needs someone strong enough to challenge the absurdity of it all. Please reconsider.
J.W.

> I sorrowed then, and sorrow now again when I direct my memory to what I saw.
>
> —Dante, *Inferno*

On the Author's Travels with Sylvia Johnson and Her Children, June 5, Conclusion

"All I want to know is if my husband is okay," Sylvia demanded of John.

As badly scarred as his face was, it was hard to tell exactly what sort of look he gave her in response. I would guess, from his eyes, that it was sullen, not quite defeated. He stared east, down the mountain and over the pine trees, from Tres Piedras toward Taos. "At this moment your husband is fine. We must proceed with all haste to our destination. I will explain on the way," John said as he started loading the kids through the side door into the van. "Jump up!" he said to them, grabbing each of them under the arms to give them a boost. They giggled because he tickled each one of them on their way up.

"So tell me," Sylvia ordered him again when we were on the road.

"The group from Chaco is ahead of us. Only a few minutes. They are just outside Taos. I suggest that you drive even faster," he told me.

"What group? Who are you talking about?" I asked. I stepped on the gas. "Sylvia, have the kids hold on back there. There are lots of corners, and I'm going to go fast."

"Who are they?—as individuals—I cannot tell you. I do not know," he replied.

"John, cut out the nonsense. Just tell me, generally speaking, who we're talking about," I insisted.

"We are talking about those whom Nathan would describe as 'the bad guys.'"

"Why are they bad?" Sylvia asked. She was standing behind us, clinging to the top of the front seat. She had forced the kids to sit on the blankets on the floor and to hold onto the shelving over the wheel wells. This prevented them from being splayed against the sides of the van as I negotiated the curves in the road.

"I made no such judgment. I would rather say that they are confused," John said—too piously for me.

"Goddamn it, John. I feel like I'm talking to an autistic fucking born-again teenager. *What threat is there to us from them?*" I demanded, saying each word loudly and slowly for him.

"I will be more specific. Right now there is no threat to you. At this point, I would postulate that they are trying to kill us all at once."

"*All of us?*" Sylvia asked in dread.

"No. The immortals—they call us 'the diseased.' You … you are in danger only if you stand in their way of killing us," he attempted to assure Sylvia.

"Like dropping you off in Taos?" I asked him.

"Do not fret. As I said, at this point they are waiting to kill us all at once. They are waiting down there," he said, and he pointed toward the wide, flat floor of the desert valley in front of us. "Drive faster."

* * * *

"Turn here," John told me when we reached the pitchfork-shaped junction that Judy Weintraub described above, "onto Highway 150. Nathan and all my friends are waiting just ahead."

"Where are the bad guys?" I asked.

"There as well," he honestly replied.

Fortunately we ran into the good guys first. There were about ten cars and trucks parked on the east side of the road. Seven other vehicles, all four-wheel drives, were in single file on a dirt road that led to the east—to the foot of the *Sangre de Cristo* Mountains. These SUVs, wagons, and crew cab pickup trucks were all filled with people. Each one appeared to have a Native American driver. The riders in each were, I assumed, the "immortals."

On the north side of the dirt road, just north of the line of four-wheel drive vehicles, two white and blue Jeeps were parked in the sagebrush. They were new Jeep Cherokees. They belonged to the police force of the Taos Pueblo Tribe and were so labeled on their sides. Their blue and red strobes barely blinked in the bright morning sun. A third police Jeep was parked right in the turnoff to the dirt road; its patrol lights were faintly flashing too.

Nathan came running out from behind that third police vehicle. He waved us off the highway. I parked along the right side of the police Jeep. The white armored van that Nathan had just driven cross-country was parked on the other side of the police vehicle.

"Write a good book," John told me. He gently squeezed my hand good-bye. He climbed out of the paint van and was quickly ushered into the last of the line of the four-wheel drives, which happened to be an older Ford Bronco, two-tone, burnt sienna and white.

Nathan slid open the side door of our paint van. Sylvia jumped into his arms. His children hopped all around him.

"Kids, you can hug Daddy in a minute," Nathan said to his children. "Sylvia, get them in that white van, right now. There could be shooting any second. It's armored. They'll be safe in there. Walk around behind it and then stay in there with them. Keep the doors locked until I knock. I'll be back in just a few minutes, and we'll get out of here and go home."

"I missed you, Nathan," Sylvia said, trying to catch her husband's eyes. "We thought you were dead …"

"Not now. I'll be right back," Nathan promised.

"But we thought …" she tried again.

"I'll be right back," he interrupted her again.

In the meantime, Father Dougherty had climbed out of a blue Chevy Tahoe, one of the four-wheel drives parked on the dirt road. He ran toward me, carrying a small cardboard box under one arm. He came trotting back to greet me. When his shoes hit the road, the powdery clay puffed up in little tan clouds around them.

Father Dougherty dropped the cardboard box next to the van and opened up the driver's side door. I descended into his arms. He gave me a big hug and kissed both of my cheeks. "I am so thrilled to see you," he said. "I've gathered up all the disks and tapes and journals and notes. Everything you'll need is in there." He pointed to the cardboard box. "And you know what?" Father Dougherty asked me with a playful, nearly impish smile that I had never seen before. It was a smile, I would guess, that he had lost sometime during his childhood. I think he had just found it again.

"What?"

"It's all true!" He smiled and then laughed.

"Come on, Father."

"It is. All true. Know what else?" he asked me, giggling with delight.

"What?"

"I'm going with them, up into the mountains, to learn … to learn what I think I already know."

"Congratulations. You sound like one of them already. Has everybody in the world gone nuts?"

At that moment Nathan appeared around the front of the van I had been driving. "Come on, Cuz, come and watch the end of this. Father Dougherty, is that the box?" Nathan asked him.

"Yes."

"Did you get everything?" Nathan wanted to be certain. We walked to the front of the paint van.

"Yes."

"All the tapes out of the cubbyhole? The memory sticks? The hard drive under the dash?"

"Yes!" Father Dougherty declared with a smile. "I got them all."

"Great. Throw it in there." Nathan pointed to the open sliding door of the paint van behind me. "You're not gonna believe it," Nathan said to me. Father Dougherty set the cardboard box inside the van. "Oh, Father, wait, this tape has stuff on it." Nathan shut off the tiny tape recorder he had strapped around his waist and handed the last of the tapes to me. I gave the tape to Father Dougherty, who put it in the box.

"Come on," Nathan urged again. "Come watch the end of this with me."

Father Dougherty, Nathan, and I trotted up the dirt road to the line of four-wheel drives. "Get back in that Bronco," Nathan ordered Father Dougherty as he pointed to the last of the rigs in the line. Father Jerome hugged me a final time and whispered in my ear, "I love you. Come with us."

"Sorry, Father, it seems I've got a book to write," I replied.

"Let's move it," Nathan said to me.

Nathan and I walked a few feet to the two police Jeeps that were parked in the sagebrush. It was not until this time that, looking north beyond the police vehicles, I noticed the bad guys.

The bad guys had seven rigs too, all of them either four-wheel drive quad cab pickup trucks or Humvees, parked side by side in the barrow pit. Each vehicle had its front bumper right up against the rusted barbed wire fence that demarcated federal BLM property from tribal lands.

"Pretty exciting, huh?" Nathan asked me. As we approached the head of the tribal police, Nathan pulled out a handheld radio. "Caracara, this is Jackrabbit. Over," he said, holding down the transmit button.

"Go ahead, Jackrabbit," the voice crackled back as soon as he released it.

"Caracara, ETA? Over." Nathan asked.
"Twelve minutes to your vehicle. Over."
"Roger. Jackrabbit out."
"Who's Caracara?" I asked Nathan.
"Couple of my buddies. Two years ago, I saved both their lives. They were running to get into their … never mind, no time now. Drug wars story. I'll tell it to you later," he promised.

Nathan interrupted the tribal police leader, who was giving instructions to his deputies. "Sheriff, can I make a recommendation?"

The leader, whose long black hair fell in two ponytails from under his white Stetson cowboy hat, was scared shitless. His brown hands were shaking. His black eyes darted aimlessly. He seemed incapable of holding them on any single object for longer than a split second.

He was surrounded by four of his men. They were scared too. They fidgeted with their combat shotguns or their semi-automatic pistols. The twenty or so men, two hundred feet away on the other side of the fence, appeared to have much bigger weapons—and a lot more of them.

The leader wiped his brow with the pearl-buttoned cuff of his dark blue cowboy shirt and said, "It's *Captain* Gray Wolf. Who are you?"

"Nathan Johnson, FB—"

"Yeah? You're Ja-Johnson?" the captain stuttered, failing, at first, even to maintain control of his voice. "Why don't you trot your federal ass on over there and tell your fellow feds to stay the fuck off of our land? Who do those men think they are? They cross that fence, and we've got a war on our hands. They cross that fence, and I'm going to give my men the order to fire."

"Captain, listen. That's exactly what those assholes want you to do. Look, either those men already have orders to cross that fence, or they don't. If I were you, I would send one man over to negotiate with them. I'd have the rest of your men accompany the convoy to the mountain. Drive alongside, stay between the feds and the convoy. If they do cross, you can fire on the run. You can protect these people."

"Goddamn feds. They *can't* have orders to cross that line. It's against treaty law; it's against the *goddamn federal law* for them to be comin' across that fence. Who the fuck do those men think they are?"

"They're carrying automatic weapons." One of the deputies explained, with a simple muttered phrase, who the fuck those men thought they were. He was terrified; he had gone a whiter shade of pale.

"Shut up, Pete. Shut up. I don't even want you thinking about it," the captain commanded. "They're not gonna shoot anybody. They can't shoot anybody. So what do you say, Johnson? You gonna talk to those bastards or not?"

"Sheriff, I mean Captain, those bastards have been chasing me clear across the goddamn country. If I walk over there, on tribal land, they'll shoot me in the head and send you a memo telling you my corpse is your problem. We're on your turf. You're the one who needs to do the negotiating. If you'd listen to me for just a second, your best bet for getting these people safely up that mountain is to send one man over and have the rest of …"

"I've already heard your advice, Agent Johnson. I already told you—those men have no right to trespass on our land." The captain once again examined the row of government vehicles nosed up against the fence. "Goddamn feds have been pushing us around too goddamn long. It's our land. Everyone in the Jeeps," he ordered his men. "We are going to park right in front of them. We're gonna stop them before they even get started. They're not moving one inch on our soil."

"Captain …" Nathan pleaded.

"*Not one inch!*" he screamed at Nathan. "Move it!" Captain Gray Wolf ordered his men. They started to climb into their Jeeps.

"Come on, Cuz! We gotta get out of here," Nathan snapped. He turned and ran to the lead car in the caravan. "Get moving! *Get moving!*" he shouted at the driver of the first vehicle transporting the immortals, waving his right hand toward the mountains and the clouds. The engines of the four-wheel drives in the caravan started to race. Behind us, the two Jeeps carrying the captain and his men pulled to within fifty feet of the line of government trucks waiting at the reservation boundary. The police Jeeps stopped in a cloud of dust. The bad guys were not inside their rigs. They were standing behind their vehicles; they were armed to the teeth.

"Come on, back to the highway," Nathan ordered me. I had to sprint to stay at his side. As we raced by the line of vehicles, several of the people rolled down their windows and offered thanks to Nathan.

We hustled breathlessly to the armored van. We stood between it and the third police Jeep, the empty one. Its lights were still flashing, but I could barely see them through the brilliant light of the morning sun.

Sylvia leaned her head out of the right side window. "Who are these people tied up in the back?"

"Don't worry about them," Nathan said. "We got a much bigger problem. Honey, roll up that window and keep the kids down on the floor."

The captain of the tribal police started to speak through a gray battery-powered bullhorn—a cheap plastic loudhailer—the kind one would see at a RadioShack. "This is the territory of the people of the Taos Pueblo ..." His voice reverberated off the metal of the trucks that surrounded us. It sounded tinny, artificial, and hollow. I could smell the dust and the powdered pollen of the sage that the tires had kicked into the air. I could smell the engine exhaust.

"If those trucks cross that line, we go up the mountain," Nathan told Sylvia and me over the voice of the captain.

"What?" Sylvia demanded. She turned her attention to somewhere in the armored transport van. "Stay on the floor," she commanded. But she immediately poked her head out of the window again.

"No way. Not me. No fuckin' way," I flatly refused.

"Any unauthorized entry at this point ..." the captain's metallic voice trembled through the bullhorn from north of us.

"We don't have any choice. If they'll cross the line, they've been ordered to break the law to kill those people. If they break the law to kill them—they'll break the law to get at us because we'll be the witnesses, because we'll be the ones who know what they've done. Our best chance is to head up."

"Not me. No way," I objected. "I'm not going camping with a bunch of loony tunes. I've got my writing. I'm going back. And that's all there is to it."

From the corner of my eye, I caught the last of the line of vehicles carrying the immortals as it started to roll east. The sunbeams cut through the billowing dust around the Bronco. I could see Father Dougherty. He was trying to talk to John. I could see John's disfigured face hopelessly, or so it seemed, staring at us through the back window. John and Father Dougherty and the Bronco disappeared in a sun-streaked cloud of powdered dirt.

"... will be met with deadly force," the captain droned on. The gray plastic bullhorn was in his left hand; a black pistol was in his right.

"Give me your gun," Nathan demanded.

"What?" I was trying to pay attention to both Nathan and the words coming from the captain's little bullhorn.

"The Walther. Give it to me. I don't want you walking out of here carrying a murder weapon."

"Okay." I handed Nathan the pistol.

"Take this," he ordered as he pulled a bulging envelope from his jacket. "There's about seventeen grand in cash in here. It's an advance. You're right. You should stay. We need you to tell the story. Sylvia, I said roll up that window and get the kids down on the floor."

The captain droned on, "Any attempt, I repeat any attempt ..."
"Attempt" was the last word ever spoken by Captain Gray Wolf.

* * * *

"Stay here, stay with the Indians until it's over," Nathan shouted to me over the gunfire as he sprinted toward the driver's door of the armored van. "Thanks," he yelled. I did not see Sylvia or the kids.

I ducked down on the north side of the lone police Jeep to watch the battle. I had spotted a pair of binoculars sitting on the front seat, so I opened the door and grabbed those. The police radio was on. I could hear one of the captain's men screaming for backup, even though there wasn't any.

"Jackrabbit to Caracara. Over," Nathan's voice calmly popped from the speaker as soon as the policeman's voice fell silent.

"Jackrabbit, this is Caracara. Over."

"Caracara, what is your ETA? Over."

"ETA to your vehicle ... seven minutes. Over."

"We'll be dead by then."

"Roger. We copy. Wait one. (I don't care. She'll hold. Redline the motherfucker.) ... Jackrabbit, ETA five minutes. Hang on, Jackrabbit. Over."

"Hurry," Nathan replied—that was all he said. The white armored van he was driving sped across the sagebrush toward the line of vehicles carrying the immortals.

The Native American police officers put up fierce but brief, resistance. The men on the other side of the fence were much better practiced, much more heavily armed. The gunfire came in heavy bursts for ten or fifteen seconds. Then there would be silence for about the same length of time, and then the rapid multiple pops would sound again. In less than two minutes, there was no return fire from the two Jeeps. I scoped them through the binoculars. The blue and white Jeeps were riddled with bullet holes. From where I stood, I could see three of the five bodies.

The captain's body was hanging sideways in a giant sagebrush bush. There were at least a dozen bullets in him. His white cowboy hat was stuck in the bush too. Although he had lost his weapon, the dead fingers of his left hand still clutched the bullhorn's trigger. The bullhorn was pointed at the ground. A little stream of blood trickled from the captain's wrist, down the gray plastic horn, and drip, drip, dripped to the dry earth. The bullhorn was feeding back—screaming a single, high-pitched "*Eeeee!*"

The seven government vehicles broached the rusted barbed wire fence as if it were made of starter ribbon. They roared across the sagebrush plain toward the caravan in a huge cloud of powdered clay.

They did not advance unimpeded. Several of the Indians, who were watching roadside with me, had hunting rifles mounted in racks in their trucks. As soon as the gun battle with the captain and his men erupted, they rushed for their weapons. They provided an unanticipated assault on the government's thugs from their right flank. One of them had even managed, with a lucky shot, to halt one of the government trucks by shooting the driver in the head. The truck veered sharply, then it flipped over and rolled two or three times. Some of the men around me were systematically picking off the occupants as they climbed from the smoking Humvee. Others were firing into the six remaining government vehicles that raced over the mesa toward the caravan.

The government's lead truck suddenly stopped. A man jumped out of the door with a rocket launcher. It was a long, dark green pipe with some kind of sight on the top. Balancing the pipe on his shoulders, he fired the rocket at Nathan's van. The warhead exploded into the ground a few feet shy of Nathan's vehicle, but the concussion from the blast flipped the van over. It rolled one and three quarter times, coming to a stop with its right side passenger doors facing up. The truck, from which the rocket was fired, started up again beneath a hail of bullets fired by the Indians around me.

The fight was moving away from me, across the plain and toward the mountains. There was so much dirt being stirred up by all the vehicles that I could no longer tell what was going on. I climbed onto the roof of the police Jeep to gain a better vantage.

The caravan was starting to turn back to assist Nathan. It now appeared that at least some of the Native American drivers were armed. Most had switched seats with an immortal and, when their vehicles were turned around, the Indians began returning fire from the passenger side windows.

Nathan must have opened the window to the passenger door, a door that was now facing up since the van was lying on its side. His head popped out of the opening. I could see glints of sun reflected off of his stainless steel 10 mm. He methodically opened fire at the oncoming government vehicles, which were, by this time, less than two hundred yards away from him. Two rigs skidded to a halt in the sagebrush. Nathan reached inside and pulled out another gun. It was Sylvia's Sig Sauer. He emptied it. Another of the attack vehicles was halted. Nathan dropped Sylvia's gun and emerged with his Uzi.

His attackers stopped the remaining three rigs about 150 feet from the overturned van. The men inside all six government rigs began climbing from their vehicles and firing back at Nathan. At first they shot directly at the roof of the van, probably thinking that it would be easy work to finish off its occupants. The armor held, and the bullets ricocheted off—each with a spark and some with a reverberating *"Pa-ping!"*

Nathan sprayed the bullets from the Uzi at the three closest vehicles, then ducked down and popped right back up with his Smith and Wesson.

This simple fact that his guns were being reloaded and handed back to him made shivers run up and down my spine. Sylvia was alive. Because she was aiding her husband, I guessed that the kids were probably okay too.

Though the government's vehicles were over a quarter of a mile away from us by now, the Indians around me continued their relentless sniping. Even at that range, they would sometimes hit one of the thugs as he climbed from a government vehicle or tried to maneuver into a better attacking position. With every enemy that they downed, the Indians would let out a scream—a war cry. I started screaming with them.

Through the binoculars, I spotted another rocket launcher. Two men were unloading it from the back of the first wagon that Nathan had stopped. "There, shoot there!" I shouted at the two Indians standing in the back of the next pickup down from me. They had rested their hunting rifles on the roof of the cab to steady their weapons as they fired long range.

"What?" one of them shouted back.

"Rocket launcher. That last Hummer, the green one. Look, *look! Christ!* They've got another rocket launcher!"

"There!" Looking through his rifle scope, one of the Indians had spotted it too. He pointed it out to his companion. They both opened fire on the vehicle; this kept the two men with the rocket launcher pinned down for precious seconds.

I jumped off the roof. I reached through the open door of the police Jeep and grabbed the mike. "Nathan, Nathan. If you can hear me, they've got another launcher. The big green Hummer. They've got another of those rocket things. Get the fuck out of there. Nathan? *Nathan!"* I screamed into the mike. The firing around me had slowed considerably; some of the Indians had run out of ammunition. The screaming feedback from the captain's megaphone was fading with the batteries.

"We've only got a few more rounds," the Indian in the back of the pickup yelled at me.

"Nathan, get out of there—*now!*"

The radio crackled in response. It was Sylvia's voice. "Okay," was all she said.

"Caracara to Jackrabbit," the radio clicked again. "ETA two minutes, twenty seconds."

"Caracara, they need help soon," I pleaded into the mike. "They are under heavy fire. Caracara—can you hear me? I said, '*They are under heavy fire!*'"

"Caracara to Jackrabbit. Hang in there, Jackrabbit. ETA Two minutes, five seconds—out."

By this time, three of the rigs from the caravan had pulled behind the van—trying to keep the armored vehicle between themselves and the line of fire from their enemy. Even so, the outside one of the three vehicles, the old Ford Bronco, took many hits. The Bronco started to smoke, then caught on fire. Its passengers scampered out and sprinted toward the next vehicle. Some fell and were assisted by the others; some appeared to have been wounded in the fusillade during the race to the next rig. The fuel tank on the Bronco finally exploded, knocking several people to the ground. Father Dougherty and John had been riding in that vehicle. I do not know if they got out in time. I do not know if they were among the wounded.

It was difficult for me to tell much from the ground, so I climbed back to the roof of the Jeep. Nathan had disappeared inside the overturned van. The doors to two of the vehicles from the immortals' caravan swung open almost in unison. Two or three of the "immortals" jumped out from each rig; they ran to, and then ducked behind, the underside of Nathan's armored van. One of the government's trucks drove east to take position for crossfire.

Someone, I assume Nathan, kicked open the rear door to the van. Bullets sprayed around the opening like giant raindrops plopping in the dust, or like tiny bolts of lightning striking the metal roof of the van. One of the young men, the young immortals, probably Fernando from Judy's description, dove through the bullets and crawled through the open door into the back of the overturned van. A second immortal popped inside; I would guess that it was Enoch; then a third, probably Lemual.

Almost as quickly, they emerged. Each held something tightly to his chest as he raced back to the caravan, each one keeping his body between the bullets and his load. I stared hard into the binoculars. They were carrying the children.

Nathan's head popped up and out of the passenger window again. He fired his 10 mm with one hand, Sylvia's Sig Sauer with the other. For a few seconds, he laid down a deadly accurate cover for his children—until both pistols were empty.

"My God!" I screamed. "They're trying to move the kids. *Fire! Fire now!*"

My Native American friends discharged a last desperate volley at the enemy. It slowed but did not stop the hail of bullets aimed at the immortals. One of them dropped to a knee; I think it was Lemual. I thought I could see the bloodstains on his back from the entry wounds. He stood, gripped the child even tighter, and stumbled toward the waiting caravan, out of the line of fire.

Sylvia ducked through the door. Another of the immortals, hidden behind the backside of the van, jumped behind her and shielded her as she ran for her children. This man was black—perhaps Gunta, maybe Father Dobo. Nathan came next. Another immortal, the one who called himself Jesus, offered himself as my cousin's living shield.

I was so focused on the scene at the rear of the van that I only heard the *whoosh* of the rocket launcher. The missile it fired struck the top of the van two or three seconds later. There was a bright yellow explosion. The concussion from the warhead rattled the windows of the Jeep I was standing on. If Sister Maria Sanchez and Father Quindilar were still in the vehicle, I am certain they were killed by the rocket. Nathan and the person guarding him were smashed to the ground, just a few yards from the van, by the blast. Bullets ripped the earth around them as they fell. Nathan's protector was able to lift himself to his right knee. He threw his body over my cousin. The bullets kept falling like rain on the earth all around the two of them.

A moment after the missile rocked the armored van, there was a gigantic roar directly over my head. I ducked down and looked up. A giant black object sliced through the air about fifty feet above me. It whipped the wind from behind and beneath with an instant and incredible fury. It shook the ground under the Jeep; I could feel the vibrations from my feet to my loins. Caracara had finally arrived.

A few seconds later, the long, sleek, black AH-64A Apache helicopter, whose cockpit was shaped like the head of a snake, hovered above the burning van. The helicopter rotated in the air until its flat black nose was pointed at the three enemy vehicles that had stopped together. The chopper's blades, spinning so fast that my eyes were fooled into believing that they could see them, whipped the smoke from the wreckage into a curling black back draft from hell.

Below the chopper, Nathan's protector had somehow managed to find his feet. He stood in the swirling dust and smoke and raised his arms above his head. He rocked back and forth as he tried to maintain his balance in the windy vortex. I could see that his clothing had been ripped to shreds in the blast.

Short, stubby wings protruded from each side of the helicopter. Each hard point on this chopper's wings was equipped with round honeycombed canisters,

Hughes M260 rocket pods, two per wing, four pods in all. Each pod held nineteen 69.85 mm rockets. The gunner, who sat below and in front of the pilot, aimed the outside right canister at the three government rigs nearest the burning van. He punched a button. That punch launched nineteen rockets from the pod. The three vehicles and the men around them, who fired frantically at the black metal bird in the last seconds of their lives, were obliterated by the rockets' spray—in nineteen nearly simultaneous high explosive detonations.

On the ground, directly below the gunner, I watched Nathan's protector lift my cousin's body until he cradled Nathan in his arms.

The helicopter twisted in the air again. The gunner leveled the 30 mm cannon on the bottom of the chopper's nose at the government truck that had pulled to the east to set up the crossfire. The cannon chattered. The truck disappeared for an instant in the dust from the salvo; then it exploded.

Nathan's protector lugged Nathan's body as he staggered away from the burning wreckage toward one of the caravan's SUVs.

The chopper rotated a third time. By now, the two remaining government vehicles were moving, full speed, back across the sagebrush—out of the reservation. The gunner triggered part of a second M260 pod. The rockets vaporized a dark green military Humvee, ripping it into a giant cloud of smoke and metal and ash and flesh.

I turned the binoculars to find Nathan and his protector—but they had both vanished in the battlefield's haze.

The helicopter pivoted slightly to finish the one truck that remained. By this time, the government vehicle was so close to the road that we were directly in the line of fire. I jumped off the Jeep and rolled underneath, just to be safe. The men in the trucks around me also scrambled for cover.

The helicopter did not fire again. It turned and vanished into the western sky—faster, but not by much, than the only remaining government vehicle that disappeared to the south down the highway.

Though I searched thoroughly through the binoculars, I could find neither Nathan and his protector nor Sylvia and the children. I assume that Sylvia and the kids were in one of the caravan's vehicles. I did not, and do not, know if any of them were injured.

The caravan headed east again, this time with six crowded rigs. I watched through the binoculars for at least two hours. When the cortege reached the foot of the mountain, the vehicles turned south. They drove parallel with the range for a couple of miles. Then they turned up a distant ravine and started to climb the mountain. A few minutes later, the last in the line of vehicles disappeared from my view.

I checked the clock on the dash of the police Jeep. I tossed the binoculars back onto the seat. It was noon. The sun was almost directly overhead. The only clouds in the pure blue sky were those that hugged the peaks of the *Sangre de Cristo* Mountains.

Logistic has to be made over, and one is none too sure of what can be saved.

—Poincaré

But even your best love is merely an overjoyed parable and a painful zeal. It is a torch that should illuminate higher paths for you. Over and beyond yourselves you shall one day love.

—Nietzsche, *Also Sprach Zarathustra*

Author's Epilogue

Where to begin the end? I suppose that the reader is familiar with the government's explanation of that day. If you read *The New York Times*, in particular, you got the "inside story from a high-ranking administration official who must remain anonymous"—and some gruesome photos of the aftermath to boot. What horseshit.

The "inside story" was that the Native Americans at Taos had gotten involved with organized crime. They were protecting some notorious Mafia hit men from a government raid that had spilled over onto the reservation. The government had the evidence to prove it. After they had taken care of their own dead, the Indians had gathered the bodies of the government's hired assassins and literally, tossed them back over the fence and onto the highway. I know. I helped them do it. About two hours later, some military trucks came by and gathered up the corpses. I know. I watched them do it. The government had its evidence. It had the corpses of the criminals it had bribed.

The tribe came up with some seeming nonsense about "the movement of the Holy Ones to the Sacred Blue Lake." All the news reports dripped with sarcastic acrimony when describing their side of the story. I'm not sure I should blame the reporters for that—but I do, because I know; I was there.

That is, however, about the extent of my knowledge. It has been over three months, now, since they went into the mountains. The summer is almost gone. It has been hot and miserable here most of the time. However, I imagine they have had wonderful weather up there on the mountain.

I moved my trailer here, away from Idaho. I guess you could say that I am *persona non grata* there. The election is not until November. I'm hanging on to the DVD of the senator.

The senator is a friend of Fred Simson, the owner of all three hundred or so Simson's Grocery outlets. Even before I had made it back to Idaho from New Mexico, Mr. Simson had personally fired Candice. I made a telephone call to DC—I've got nothing to lose—and, by God, Mr. Simson hired her right back, with a raise and a bonus.

She's the daytime manager now, with better hours and better pay. So it all worked out okay for her.

(Who am I kidding? Candice, you know who you are, and I apologize. When you read this, maybe you'll finally understand why I asked you to suffer what you have suffered. I'm so sorry that it cost you so much and that it costs us so much. Try to understand that this book *is* my apology.)

Anyway, as I said, I moved my trailer here, within a week of the incident, to New Mexico. I have been living on the reservation, at the foot of the mountains. The people of the Taos Pueblo have been kind and generous. I guess they want this book finished as much as anyone. They have a lot at stake in the truth.

∗   ∗   ∗   ∗

I have put off writing about Professor Weintraub until now. These words will be forced. They may not be as "literary" as I usually demand of myself. That is the second of two blatant excuses to my readers in one book. I realize that's two too many.

So I will get it over with. To put it bluntly, with all respect, apologies, and condolences to his dear wife, Professor Harold Weintraub has gone mad. Judy has been sending me his manuscript, hoping that I will be able to give her some insight into the new direction her husband's thinking has taken. I cannot—except to say that he is insane. I have not been able to bring myself to tell her. Now, obviously, I must do so sometime before this manuscript is published, sometime before she reads these words. Perhaps I will do the right thing, for once, and go and tell her face-to-face.

Professor Weintraub's cancer went into sudden and, Judy claims, complete remission shortly after they returned to Massachusetts from their trip to New Mexico with Nathan and Father Dougherty. The doctors are calling it nothing short of a miracle; such a remission almost never happens with untreated pancreatic cancer. Judy told me that at least two of the consulting physicians believe that Harold's illness had to have been misdiagnosed, that it was medically impossible for him to have overcome the illness as diagnosed.

According to Harold, however, he has healed himself. (Perhaps this section may not be so lacking in erudition—that's the longest alliteration in the book.)

If I am flippant, it is because I am fearful. The first sentence of Harold's new manuscript begins: "I am the God who writes ..." And this first line is written in Latin, of course. Coming from anyone else, that would be slightly humorous or, if actually intended, outrageously egocentric. It comes from Harold Weintraub. It comes as the introduction to an arcane, abstruse and literally awesome manuscript that has already, in three short months, filled over a thousand pages. It is neither funny nor outrageous. It is frightening and oppressive.

Thus far his manuscript is, by all scholarly standards, monumental. The arguments are subtly structured. The movement is, for those with the capacity to read it, magnificent. He is creating a powerful dialectical engine—not unlike, rather similar to Hegel's *Wissenschaft der Logik*. A few of Harold's arguments are so like Hegel's that they border on plagiarism. For example, about twenty pages into Weintraub's introduction, he states, "Life is thus the process of pure livingness in the realm of the now. This realm is truth as it is without the veil or threat of death, and it is truth as life's own absolute nature as love. It can therefore be said that the exposition of the content of this nature, the exposition that follows, is the portrayal of the mind of God as He is, or as he presents Himself, through the eternity of the moment, to the still temporal and finite mind of man." There is a passage in "The General Notion of Logic" in Hegel's *Vorstellung* to the *Wissenschaft* that is nearly identical.

Read those three sentences a couple of times, and you will understand that Weintraub has just declared himself not only to be immortal; he has also proclaimed himself to be *God*. Weintraub is God because

A) He is immortal;

B) He can articulate why He is immortal; and

C) because He loves us mere mortals enough to let us in on his secret.

Hegel, for those who understand him, made a vaguely similar claim. Hegel died, however, believing that he would live forever in his *perfectly* completed *Logik,* which reflected the mind of God.

Weintraub is the first man to claim to have it both ways, to live forever—and to be able to explain why and how.

It terrifies me to read his words. I am, I will openly admit this, I am afraid—not that I will understand them, for I do understand them. I am afraid that I may accept them as *the truth*.

In any event, Harold has been proclaiming his newfound immortality and divinity to his colleagues at Harvard. He has announced that, come autumn, he will begin a series of lectures on the subject. Many of his fellow professors probably think that the old guy is finally coming out of the closet, showing everyone the real Harold Weintraub. Some of them, Judy told me, are highly derisive. Some are flat out afraid of the man.

It is apparent to all, except his wife, that he must be removed from the faculty before the fall session starts. Because he poses no physical harm to others, his psychiatrist has not yet ordered that Harold be institutionalized, though he has recommended such action to Judy.

She is dragging her feet. I cannot say that she is wrong in doing so. She has asked me repeatedly for my advice on the matter, probably because I know Harold, I understand the manuscript, and I am the most sympathetic person she knows who falls into both categories. I do not know what to tell her. I do not know how to speak about the issue without my own fears getting in the way.

Ecce homo.

* * * *

I have finished this book here at the foot of the mountain, not far from where the battle took place, not far from where I last saw my cousin and … my friends. I have not been invited up the mountain. The members of the tribe, whether under specific orders or not, have prohibited me from going up to the Blue Lake. This is not unusual, for it is a rare occasion, indeed, when a non-tribal member is allowed to visit the sacred Blue Lake.

I assume this is the area where, if they are all still alive, Nathan, his family, Father Dougherty, and the "immortals" have retired. The local Indians have kept a close eye on me. There is no need for them to waste their time; I have no desire to sneak up there.

The way I see it, they will be down before winter. Whatever else they are, they are human beings and, thus, creatures of comfort. There are children amongst them now. The cold and the snow will bring them down.

Or maybe, when it appears that they are ready to descend, an air force jet, out on a training mission, will *accidentally* drop a small, precisely guided nuclear warhead on their encampment. There is no doubt, at least in my mind, that the government has a satellite fixed on their location. I have only a shadow of a doubt that the government would go to such an extreme act to kill them.

Or maybe it takes a long time to figure out how to teach someone the secret of immortality. Maybe it takes decades, maybe centuries; maybe it takes more than one lifetime.

Maybe Harold's finishing it up at this moment.

My bet is that they'll be down come winter.

*   *   *   *

Not much has happened this summer except the writing of this book. I installed a swamp cooler on top of my trailer during the last week of June, when the heat became unbearable. I should add, though I do not know how it all ties in, that Herman Lowry has resigned from his position as director of the Federal Bureau of Investigation. It is rumored that he will run for a soon-to-be-vacated US Senate seat in his home state of Illinois. And, irony of ironies, he will run as a Republican.

I will relate one more incident, and then I will end this. I brought my four cats to the reservation with me. Two of them, Alex and Cleo, the two tabbies, became infected with distemper shortly after I arrived. I waited as long as I could bear it—until they would rub themselves in their own excrement, run face first into the tires of my car, and whirl about, screeching and clawing the air, attacking invisible hosts of vicious dogs. I waited as long as I could—and then I shot each of them in the head with the 357 magnum revolver I now carry at all times.

I dug the three-foot-deep hole behind my trailer, out in the sagebrush, and threw them in while they were still alive. They were so infected, so far gone, that they did not protest or try to jump out. They stood and stared at the wall of fresh dirt as if viewing, for the first time, the face of God. I had to put them in their grave before I killed them because that caliber of bullet makes quite a splatter of a cat's head. And, damn right, my gun is loaded with hollow points.

The size of the bullet did not seem to make much difference in how quickly they died. Their diseased little bodies flopped around anyway. I buried them as soon as they stopped moving.

*   *   *   *

I took John's advice. (A thousand years from now, they will say that this is an interpolation—but it's not. It is part of the package.) The book he indicated that he had written, and that I should read, is called *The Apokryphon of John*. It is one of several ancient texts found, beginning in late 1945, at Nag Hammadi, hidden for nearly two thousand years in a cliff named *Jabal al-Tarif* near the Nile River. I have since read three versions of the original Coptic (which were translated into German by Krause and Labib). What I have found is that *The Apokryphon of John* is a book for the few and for the many. I will end with my translation of a few excerpts from the ancient book and then with a final remark.

"Now hold your head up so that you shall comprehend that which I tell you today, that you shall share these things with your friends in the spirit, those of the unwavering race of completed human beings ...

"Our sister Sophia [Wisdom] did come down virtuously to give back what they did not have. Because of this she [Sophia] is called Life or the Mother of all Living. Through Him that Knew Before [Pronoia] and her [Sophia], the Living have tasted perfect knowledge ...

"I [John] asked Christ, 'Will every soul be taken into the pure light?'

"He answered me, saying, 'These are great problems that you have discerned. Only those of the unwavering race of completed human beings understand the explanation ... They understand the eternal things; they are aware because they are without hatred, or jealousy, neither covetous nor any other sin. They are merely aware of their mortal existence; they know the moment when they shall meet with those who shall greet them. These are worthy of immortality ...'

"They concealed themselves in a secret place, did ... many of the unwavering race of completed human beings.

"[Christ said,] 'I have told you everything. I have instructed you on that which you should write and that which you should share with your friends in the spirit, those of the unwavering race of completed human beings.'"

Lest John be given the last *logos,* because I am neither a Gabarian nor a Zoroastrian, and because there are children with them, I still believe that they will come down before winter.

978-0-595-43539-5
0-595-43539-4

Printed in the United States
138707LV00001B/143/A